Bamford, Susannah
Blind trust

BLIND TRUST

An Evans Novel of Romance

BLIND TRUST

SUSANNAH BAMFORD

M. EVANS & COMPANY, INC. NEW YORK

Library of Congress Cataloging-in-Publication Data

Bamford, Susannah.

Blind trust / Susannah Bamford.
p.   cm.—(An Evans novel of romance)
ISBN 0-87131-606-4
I. Title.   II. Series.
PS3552.A4733B57   1990   90-2700
813'.54—dc20

M. Evans and Company, Inc.
216 East 49 Street
New York, New York 10017

Manufactured in the United States of America

2 4 6 8 9 7 5 3 1

For Kathi Lynne
The Beacon

One

DARCY

January 1888

IT WAS EITHER leave him or kill him.

It had come down to that, at last.

Darcy Statton sat alone in her bedroom on the edge of the gilt armchair that had belonged to the dauphin of Louis XIV. It was after midnight, and the house was filled with a huge silence. Rigid, unable to bend because of the corset underneath her elaborate white satin gown, she tracked the silence through the house, imagining it as a force that moved. It clung to the high corners of the rooms, it scampered down long marble halls, it meandered around the elaborate curls of boiserie, it slid against limestone walls. It pressed against her breastbone, and it whispered of madness in her ear.

Her feet hurt, but she did not remove her shoes. Her husband was to come to her later. That meant that she must send away her maid and sit in her room, with her hair still done and her diamonds on and her Worth gown billowing uncomfortably around her waist and her corset pressing red welts into her flesh and her feet aching, and wait. She had disobeyed him once, she had slipped into a dressing gown and uncoiled her hair, and she would never do it again. Sometimes he didn't come at all, and she would fall asleep in her chair, waking with a start at four or five. Even the difficulty of undressing herself properly and getting herself to bed was nothing next to the relief.

Tonight had been such an ordinary evening. One evening in a long trail of evenings, glittering and dull, the same words said to the same people, the same silent carriage ride home through the snow. There was always snow. Sometimes she felt that summer took place in the time it took her to blink. One day she changed from merino to muslin, and the next day it was time to change back again.

Now she heard the snow hit her windows like the skittering pats of tiny fingertips. Darcy turned her head. She stared out at the cold black night and tried to think of summer; she pictured the lush greens of Central Park, the lawns of Newport, her many floating white dresses, her elaborate hats. She tried to remove any trace of the here and now from her mind. But she was drawn back to tonight. To the snow that fell around them and melted on their wraps as they stepped inside the house, Darcy shivering, for the marble vestibule never provided any warmth. Even in the dead heat of summer, she shivered when she entered this house. She had begun to glide away toward the staircase when Claude had touched her arm. He had said that after he looked over some papers, he would come to her. It was late; she was tired; he knew it. She could not refuse. And while she had nodded the acquiescence it was her duty to give, she had felt a frightening rage. It had filled her blood and her limbs with an awesome strength, and for the first time in her life, she knew how one could do murder and receive pleasure from it.

Closing her eyes, she pictured it. When Claude came later tonight, she would be sitting just as she was now, still dressed in her diamonds and her heavy white satin gown with the gold sash. His yellow eyes would glitter with unusual lights as he entered, nervously drawing his dressing gown tighter around him. First, he would begin his private ritual of examining her, a ritual that she dreaded almost as much as what followed it. She hated the touch of his cold hands, she hated the way his thin fingers trembled, the dead intent look in his eyes. He would run his hands along the material of her dress, fondle the diamonds,

2

examine her lace. He would exult in the exquisite perfection of the Parisian stitches in her underclothes. Sometimes he ran his skeletal fingers along the veins of her wrist, and Darcy knew he was thinking of the impeccable blood that ran beneath her skin, the blood of the Snows and the Graces. That would excite him more than his gropings between his own legs, thin as twigs underneath his dressing gown. He would close his eyes, and his odd, full red lips would purse, his breath coming heavily, as he squeezed and kneaded himself damply. And at last, he would push her down on the bed of carved ebony inlaid with gold that had been dismantled and removed from the master bedroom of a French chateau. Not once would he touch her breasts, her legs, her belly. Not once would his too-red lips touch hers. He would begin.

But this time, this time, something within her would break, would snap. She would reach under her pillow and her fingers would close on the heavy marble bookend. She would raise it above his head, that long head with its lank streaks of blond hair trailing down the scalp. His eyes would be shut, he would be sweating with his efforts. She would feel him, inert against her belly, his hands trying to stiffen himself enough to gain entry. And she would crash it down on his bony skull, and she would feel the ecstasy of his slight body going slack, the exhilaration of pushing his spindly legs, his dank, flaccid torso, off her. And she would leap from the bed triumphant.

No scandal, no calumny, no prison term could defeat the glory of that moment.

Lord, forgive me. Darcy bent over, her elbows pressed into her stomach, and forced herself to breathe deeply. He was her husband. He gave her everything. He was scrupulously polite. Didn't he offer her a shawl when she was cold, a glass of wine when she was agitated, a cold cloth if she was overheated? He rang for her maid if she was the slightest bit upset; he soothed her if she was irritable or tired. Years ago, he had told everyone that her nerves were poor. If she raised her voice even slightly, if she laughed too often or danced too much, he would remonstrate.

Don't overexcite yourself, my dear. You remember what happened the other day.

But I'm fine. I'm fine, Claude! Please let me keep dancing.

Now, my dear. Come, come, my pet. You excite yourself, can't you see that? Let me help you to a chair.

What could she do? Where could she go? Who could she run to? There was no one she could speak to of such things. Conversations in her circle revolved around the weather and upcoming social events. Even her bubbly widowed cousin Adelle, a woman who occasionally spoke with surprising frankness, was not a person Darcy could go to with her marital trouble. She would have to hint, to convey her desperation with eye and hand. And Adelle would laugh, pass it off, uncomfortable and wondering why Darcy didn't keep it to herself.

Abruptly, Darcy stood and went to the window to stare outside at the drifting snow. If Claude could see her, he would remonstrate, for like Mrs. Astor he would not stand by a window at any time for fear the rabble on the street would glimpse him. The carriages from the Fifth Avenue mansions around her would be returning soon, the high-stepping horses clouding the air with their breath, the passersby calling aloud the distinctive liveries, the light blue of the Astors, the maroon of the Vanderbilts. The maids and valets would be waiting up, yawning and cold, to put them all decently to bed.

In that world, women did not leave their husbands. But for the first time Darcy wondered if perhaps more of them would if there was anywhere they could go.

The thought roared through her brain with such fury she had to grip the velvet curtains to keep herself upright.

She could leave tonight.

"No," Darcy said aloud, shaking her head. One had to plan such things. Everyone knew that.

Why?

She had no need of concealment, of train tickets, of the ship to France her mother had taken at dawn. No need to take trunks of dresses and jewels, no need to transfer monies to Europe to support herself and her lover. Darcy had no money of her own. And she certainly had no lover.

She could leave right now, if she dared.

If she dared. Daring, and courage, had fled so long ago, years ago, when she put the bit between her teeth and stopped trying to buck her way through her marriage. Courage. She would have to remember what it was like, when she was seventeen and had taken over the running of her family. How frightened she'd been, how she'd had to force herself to rise in the mornings sometimes, how she'd had to steel herself not to shriek at her father, his eyes rolling at her helplessly, how she'd had to reverse years of training and learn how to *act*. To learn how to do, instead of to simply be.

Deliberately, Darcy pushed open the leaded glass pane and stuck out her hand. She scooped a mound of snow that lay on the sill and buried her face in it.

The shock of the wet and the cold cleared her mind. She forced herself to think, to analyze and plan. Her maid had been sent away to bed with the rest of the servants. Although Claude employed a legion of them, he disliked seeing the help. His standing order was that they pause and stand with their face to the wall if he happened to walk by. He was upstairs now, locked away in his third-floor private office. No one would be about. The snow wasn't too deep. If she could get out of the house, she could get a hack or a horsecar to her father's house easily. He was only a few steps off Fifth, at Twenty-eighth street. She would have to leave so much, personal items she held dear. But there was a price for everything, Darcy told herself. She could do it, and the only way to do it was to leave with just the clothes on her back.

She moved quickly. There wasn't time to change. Without hesitation, driven by fear now that Claude would retire earlier than his custom, she collected her outer garments, her stout walking boots. But she kept on her evening slippers. The soft kid whispered against the Persian carpet runner all the way down the fourteenth-century carved staircase Claude had stripped from a castle in Italy. She paused on the landing and listened. She could hear nothing, and there were no lights lit downstairs.

Darcy started down the last flight of stairs. She hit the bottom and stopped again, listening. Was that a noise coming from the south hall? Impossible. Nevertheless she moved quickly in the opposite direction down the hall, her footsteps barely making a noise on the cold marble floor. She passed the small, exquisite salon, her favorite room, and the room where Claude kept his precious medieval reliquaries, past the long reception hall with its ravishing Bouchers.

And then she heard it. Footsteps coming down the hall behind her. Rapid footsteps, anxious footsteps. Claude.

In a panic, Darcy opened the first door on her left. It was a sitting room with doors opening out to an interior courtyard, and they used it only in summer. Directly to the right of the door was a massive Riesener commode. She bundled up her cloak and boots and hurled them underneath it, then quietly shut the door. Her heart thundering, she darted back down the hall toward the salon.

A moment later, Claude materialized out of the shadows. "Darcy!" His voice was sharp. Then it recovered quickly, becoming the thick, honeyed croon that made her skin crawl. "What are you doing, dearest?"

"I thought I left my book in the salon," she said. "I thought I'd read while I waited for you."

"Why didn't you ask Solange to fetch it for you?"

"I sent her to bed. You know that," Darcy said with downcast eyes. Let Claude think she was embarrassed at this allusion to what would happen later.

"It was lucky I was downstairs in the library, then." His cold fingers skittered down her bare forearm and grabbed her wrist. "Come. I'll help you find it."

"That's not necessary, Claude, I—"

"Come." He almost dragged her into the salon. She heard the pop of the gas lighting. He turned it up high, too high. Harsh shadows loomed toward her. "We'll look together."

She glanced around the room quickly. "I don't see it. Perhaps it's in my room, after all."

"But how can you be sure?" Claude asked smoothly, insistently. "Let's look together, my dear." He took her hand and squeezed her bones together. "I don't like your being up this late, alone. You know how I worry that you'll catch a chill. So if we look carefully and find it together, perhaps you'll learn your lesson, my dear. We'll start here, in the salon. But perhaps you left it in the reception hall, or the library, or the drawing room, or even the conservatory."

"I don't think so—"

"But how can you be sure? We'll have to search carefully. Never fear, we'll find it before we go upstairs."

He yanked her wrist again and brought her over to the sofa covered in Aubusson tapestry. "Not here. A pity." He moved a pillow, then clucked his tongue and dragged her over to the writing table. "No, nor here, either," he said musingly, already pulling her to the other corner of the room. He peeked behind the damask curtains. "Perhaps it slipped—no, not here."

And so he went on. For the next hour, Darcy allowed herself to be pulled to each piece of furniture, each shadowy corner. She was soon cold, with her bare shoulders and thin-soled dancing slippers. But as they moved from room to room her only fear was that they would return to the summer sitting room and find her cloak. It would be just like Claude to bring her through every room downstairs and then end his search there. Her wrist burning while her flesh grew increasingly cold, she dumbly followed her husband down the long halls, from conservatory to library to gallery, as they searched for the book they both knew they would never find. And then at last, with her stumbling behind him, he led her to her bedroom and locked the door behind them.

TAVISH

San Francisco was the damned muddiest city he'd ever seen. Some of the streets he'd been on today had been knee-deep in the stuff, a mixture of dirt and manure and garbage and sweet Jesus only knew what else. It didn't help that it had rained steadily for a week. Tavish was not a fastidious man, but he was disgusted at the look and smell of his trousers.

He didn't think his looks would go over very well at the home of Artemis P. Hinkle. He'd have to look like a gentlemen if he wanted to get through the front door. Well, there was nothing for it but to tramp all the way back to his hotel and change. He'd get a ribbing from Jamie, but he was used to Jamie's ribbings.

7

Even the trouble that brought them to San Francisco couldn't stop the twinkle from appearing in Jamie's eye now and then.

Tavish turned his steps toward his hotel, thinking contentedly of the whiskey he would have with Jamie while he changed his pants and they compared notes of their progress that day. He was bone-tired, and the lack of a decent meal in a week didn't help his disposition. Tonight they would have a good meal, an excellent meal, no matter what. The trouble with adventure, Tavish had often reflected, was that it so often involved bad food. He had given up his roaming life and had sunk gratefully into the simple pleasures of Solace, California, including the succulent meals at Grace Tooney's boarding house. The memory of her wild turkey could bring tears to his eyes. Only Jamie could have convinced him to leave the retiring life in Solace he loved and the pretty widow Tooney he had his eye on in order to ferret out a mystery. Tavish had sent up many a silent prayer that they would be back in Solace by next week.

Jamie would have returned by now from the meeting he'd been so mysterious about. Somebody who might have useful information, he'd said. Well, if it was like any of the other trails they'd followed, it would more likely be someone sniffing a reward for information who didn't have any to give. Jamie, amiable as always, would stand the bloke a drink and send him on his way. Actually, he'd spent most of his time in San Francisco in brothels, where he claimed most of the useful information was floating around in the sitting rooms while the men relaxed with their cigars and whiskeys. He was "following a scent," Jamie said, though Tavish often wondered aloud just what that scent was and got a smirk for his answer.

Tavish was frowning as he went up the stairs of the small hotel on Pine Street. Jamie was enjoying this whole mess just a bit too much, he thought. All he wanted was to go home.

The lobby was deserted at this time of day, except for a well-dressed gentleman who was heading out the back door. The sight of an elegant back was unusual in this hotel, but Tavish was too disgruntled to give the man more than a glance. He got his key from the desk, made his usual futile request for messages, and started up the stairs to their room. He was already grinning as he put his key in the lock, expecting the jibe from Jamie as soon as he opened the door.

What he wasn't expecting were the feathers. Confused, he watched as the draft from the open door partnered them lightly across the floorboards in a delicate dance. He stared dumbly at them for a moment before he smelled it. Blood in his nostrils, and that other too-familiar smell of a recently discharged gun, the combination of smells he'd never wanted to experience again.

Tavish shut the door. His eyes followed the trail of feathers to a scorched pillow at the floor at the foot of the bed. A bullet fired through it would muffle the noise. On the other side, Jamie's stockinged feet protruded out into the room.

Tavish was moving before he could think, grabbing a towel from a chair as he crossed the room. When he rounded the bed, he saw Jamie's eyes flicker open, then close. He was alive, then. Thank Jesus.

With a quick, practiced eye, Tavish located Jamie's wound. There was a bullet in his chest, near the heart. Too near. Tavish pressed the towel to it. He was alternately praying and cursing under his breath when he noticed that he was kneeling in a pool of blood. But the blood wasn't coming from the chest wound.

Tavish looked down. Jamie had pulled the blanket halfway off the bed to cover himself, and it was lying across his lower body. Tavish pulled off the blanket and gagged. The gun had blown off Jamie's manhood. He knew with a certainty that made him sick that it had been the first wound. The warning. Bile rose again in his throat.

When his fingers felt for the fluttering pulse and he touched cold skin, Jamie opened his eyes. There was a film on his normally bright blue gaze. Tavish had seen enough men die to know that Jamie was moments away from it.

"It's not so bad," Jamie said. "It's just that I'm so damn cold."

Gently, Tavish pulled the blanket back over him. Jamie stared at him. Despite the stubble on his face, he looked very young. Incredibly, mischief flickered in his eyes. "Matter of fact, I froze my balls off," he said.

The idiot. What a time to joke. "So that's what happened,"

Tavish said, forcing a grin. "You're going to make it, boyo."

"No, I'm not," Jamie said. "You blathering Mick."

Beneath his anguish, Tavish knew that rage was simmering. "Who?" he said.

"He thought I knew something," Jamie said, his voice a whisper now. "Shot off my friend below there to find out what. At first I was thinking it was just a threat. But then I saw his eyes. I've seen warmer gazes on salmon I caught. I wish I knew what he thinks I know."

"Who?" Tavish repeated. His voice was calm, as though they had a long afternoon to discuss the problem.

A ghost of a smile flitted across Jamie's boyish, stubbled face. "Damn me, if it wasn't our man. Not his agent, the man himself. Mr. Dargent. He's quite a toff. So slick I could have snowshoed down his ass." He coughed, and blood sprayed onto Tavish's shirt. "I know you're going to hate hearing this," he said, his voice a ghost-image of his usual bantering tone.

"What, Jamie?"

"You have to go to New York. That's where Hinkle is. He ran away from us."

"You said he didn't know anything."

"Then why did he run? The trail ends there." Jamie's eyes closed, then opened again. "Watch your back, my friend," he said. His eyes still open, they unfocused, and he died.

"Ah, Jamie," Tavish said, his voice breaking. He reached over and gently closed the eyes of the only man he'd ever loved. He held him in his arms and rocked him, and his eyes watered, damn his half-Irish soul. How he had loved Jamie. But this was no time for weeping.

Two

EDWARD SNOW WAS a timid man who was successful at camouflaging his weakness only when he felt himself perfectly dressed. When he had lost his wife, he had ordered new shirts. When he had lost his fortune, he had had no remedy available to him; even his tailor, usually so accommodating, had refused him more credit. So he had taken to his bed. Misfortune had never strengthened him; it was inexplicable to him how it could do so for others.

It had taken Darcy's marriage to Claude Statton and the reversal in Edward's own fortunes for him to regain his veneer of strength. But at the first sign of trouble, Edward remembered the quaking self that lay in ambush, how close he always was to losing his nerve.

Now his daughter had burst into his home in the middle of his dinner, on an inclement February night, with an icy rain beating against the windows. Her face was streaming rain and tears. And Claude was here, in his house! They were dining with a new business contact from California. They never told Darcy when they dined together, of course. Thank heaven Jorgan hadn't announced her name, just discreetly told Edward he had a guest in the upstairs library. Edward had arranged the dinner so carefully; if he flattered Claude by asking his opinion on this Mr. Finn, perhaps Edward would be able to take his money out of Claude's pool without repercussions. But it was a delicate thing, and if Claude knew Darcy was here in this state, everything could be ruined.

He looked at his daughter, damp and helpless in his armchair, and he almost hated her, for he hated the danger her presence put him in.

He didn't sit. He turned his face toward the fire. "This is very inconvenient, my dear," he said, hoping to stall her. "I have guests for dinner."

"Oh, I *am* sorry, Father," Darcy said. "Of course I should have arranged my marital crisis to suit your social schedule."

"Darcy! Now calm yourself. Your nerves—"

A strange look, electric and frightening, passed over her face. She looked almost savage, and very strong. "Please, whatever you do, don't say that again, Father."

"All right. Drink your brandy."

"It was very difficult for me to leave the house unseen. I've been waiting for three weeks for my chance," Darcy continued in a rapid voice that broke and rushed forward tremulously. "Claude was dining out, and I had a tray in my room. I managed to slip out. I've left him. I've left him for good and I am not going back!"

This would not do, Edward thought restlessly. This would not do at all. He could imagine Claude below them, dyspeptically picking at his dinner, annoyed at Edward's absence, and planning ever more devilish schemes to make him regret his rudeness.

"I don't understand," he said. "You are being hasty, I'm sure. A marriage is a long road, and of course there will be periods of trouble."

Darcy looked down at her clasped hands. She had been brought close to the fire, a rug tucked around her legs, a small brandy placed in her shaking hands. But it was as though she were encased in ice too solid to thaw. Her blood had frozen at the instant she had been ushered into the study and seen the look in her father's faded blue eyes. She had already known, as he'd led her to the fire and chafed her hands, that she would find no refuge here.

"Father, please, I am talking about something greater than the troubles a man and a wife can have. Claude Statton is . . . he is not an ordinary man."

"Of course he is not! He is the most astute businessman in this city! And the most feared, I might add, perhaps even more than Jay Gould, these days."

"What are you saying to me, Father?" she asked quietly. "That I should return to Claude Statton because he is the most feared man in New York?"

"I am saying, daughter, that your duty is to your husband. As you know." Edward could not bear to look at her when he spoke, and he was grateful for the diversion of the fire. He knew very well what kind of man Claude Statton was. But Darcy was Claude's wife, after all! The house she lived in, her clothes, her carriages, the Newport cottage, the famous mansion on Fifth—it was all as right as it could be. Could she not settle for what she had? Was she yearning now for the romance she'd been denied, like an innocent, silly girl?

He heard her words rise from the armchair with a deadly, tired resignation that chilled his blood. "I expected certain . . . realities in marriage, Father. I thought I married Claude Statton with open eyes. But I didn't realize . . . It is as though he married me, hating me, and then deliberately set out to destroy me. I am ground under his heel, and he enjoys seeing me there. How am I to continue to live with him, to sit at his table, to run his house? To live through the days of that hell? And," she said, choking on the word, "the *nights*?"

"Darcy, we must not talk of such things," he muttered.

"I'm sorry, Father. But you must understand. There is something lacking in him, something essential, decency, or honor. I have no choice. I must leave him, I have already been corrupted—" Darcy choked with her emotion, then looked down in her lap to compose herself. "I'm afraid of what will happen to me if I stay."

Edward used his last piece of ammunition. He did it deliberately; he feared no man like he feared Claude Statton. "And so you disgrace us. Just as your mother did."

Tears spurted to her eyes. "Please," she begged. "Please don't. I cannot bear it." He only looked away at the fire, frowning. Darcy continued to cry silently. She knew her father disapproved, he had always hated her tears, but now that she'd started she could not stop. "I've given him what he wanted. He is accepted in society, even Mrs. Astor leaves her card at our house. Why can't I leave him?"

"Because Mrs. Astor will no longer leave her card." Edward stared stonily at the fire. He gave a quick glance over his shoulder, and what he saw on her face made him snap his head forward to the fire again. How he hated her tears, how he had always hated them, even while loving her, relying on her. Her gray eyes turned dark, her lashes spiky and wet, and even as she cried her chin would be set at a stubborn angle, hating her weakness as much as he. She looked so much like Amelia he had to turn away. Edward thought of Amelia, of her leaving, of how Darcy had been the one to save them all. And now he was standing with his back to his little girl as she cried her heart out.

Blindly, he reached behind him and sank into an armchair. "Oh, Darcy," he said softly. "We have been through so much, you and I."

Darcy stirred. It was the only apology he could give, but it was something. Something was there, something that she could use to move him. Guilt or love, did it matter? Pushing away the rug impatiently, almost tripping on it, she left her chair and crossed to him. Before him, she sank to her knees. She bowed her head and rested it against him.

He put his hand on top of her head. She felt his fingers trembling. "You did not have a mother to advise you before your marriage. Perhaps if you talked to Aunt Catherine, or even Adelle—"

She gripped his soft wool coat with her hands. She shook her head. She knew her father did not wish to hear, but she choked the words out. "I cannot speak of such things to anyone. Not even Adelle. He is not a gentleman, sir."

He'd known, Edward thought desperately, he'd always known

and he'd pushed it away. He'd seen the look in Claude's eyes in the beginning, how he'd watched Darcy with a possessiveness that was mixed with scorn. It was as though he needed the scorn, fed the scorn, which in turn fed the desire. And Edward had given his daughter to that man.

His fingers curled and uncurled spasmodically, and he forced himself to stroke her soft, dark hair gently. "Oh, my darling child," he whispered. He bent over her. "My Darcy. What I have wrought?"

She raised her head. "No, Father. I married him." She sought his gaze. She spoke firmly. "Now you must help me leave him."

She gazed at his mouth, desperate to see the words form, the words that would accept her flight and free her from her husband. "I cannot help you," he said.

Darcy pushed herself up from the floor. She looked down at him. Her extraordinary gray eyes were pale now, chips of winter ice. "You refuse to take me in?"

Edward spread his hands. "No. I do not refuse. I cannot."

She turned, her skirts swirling, and ran for the door. "Where is my cloak? I'll go to Aunt Catherine—"

"She cannot protect you!"

"I *must* go!" Darcy screamed, whirling around again to face him. "I cannot return to that house. I cannot return to that man! I'll go to the streets, if I must. Where is my cloak?" she asked frantically.

Edward crossed the room swiftly. He reached for her hands, but she tore them away. "Listen to me!" he commanded softly. "Listen!"

Darcy twisted wildly back and forth. "I must go," she repeated. "I must go. There is no help for me here. Oh, God, there is no help for me anywhere."

Edward fought to calm her, desperate now that Claude would overhear. "I will help you! Listen to me. I will help you!"

Darcy quieted. She turned halfway, but she wouldn't look at his face. She waited.

"You're my daughter," he said gently. "Of course I will help you. But it's too soon," he went on rapidly when she looked up, hope in her face at last. "My finances are so entwined with Claude Statton's that—"

Disgusted, she tore away from him. She stood with her back to him.

"My finances," he went on quietly, "have been entwined with your husband's from the year you were married."

She half turned. "What do you mean?"

"Come, Darcy. Surely that can't surprise you. He delivered me from bankruptcy. He restored our family name and our family pride."

"Ah, yes," Darcy said mockingly. "Our family pride. Do you imagine that having made my bargain with the devil I would forget its terms?"

"And do you imagine that, having made my terrible bargain, all our business together would cease? How do you think I saved this house, how do you think Aunt Catherine and Adelle continue to live as they do?" Edward spoke desperately, almost angrily.

"There's no hope for me, then." Darcy's voice was dead.

"Yes, there is hope. *But not today.* Or tomorrow, or next week. But next month, perhaps. Most likely a bit longer. I am trying to disentangle myself from the web. I have enough now, I think, in my own right, to do so. I have, slowly, over a period of years, protected my interests. I have withdrawn my money from his companies, from stocks he suggested, bit by bit. I've put money in real estate, which he cannot touch. I don't think he can ruin me. But I do not underestimate him, not for a moment. There is one deal I must do. I must! You must trust me on this. A man called Tavish Finn—"

She shook her head. "Another deal, another man! No, Father. Not again."

"No, no, this is certain, this is sure. He has a scheme, a business scheme, he will let me in on. And when this one last deal is completed I shall be done with Claude. And so, Darcy will you."

Darcy took Edward's arm and pressed it to her side. "Father," she said softly, "I have lived with riches beyond my imagining for five years. I could send it all to hell with a flick of my finger without a single regret. We've lived in poverty before. I managed our household well, did I not?"

"You don't understand, Darcy. There would be nothing. Disgrace and ruin for me, no house for you to come to—"

"We could live in Europe." She had to say it, knowing the pain it would cause him. "There are many places we could go," she said softly. "We don't have to live in Paris, Father. Uncle Lemuel has business interests in London. Perhaps he could help us. He is back and forth so often, surely he—"

"Amelia's brother help me? I hardly think so."

"But he would help me, Father."

He squeezed her hand. "And what of Aunt Catherine and Adelle?" he asked. "Without me, they would be vulnerable. And Claude would make them suffer if we left. It would please him to do so, I think."

Darcy fell silent. Edward was right. Her great-aunt and cousin were totally dependent on her father. They had lost their small fortunes due to his bad management, and her marriage to Claude had allowed him to rescue them from the genteel poverty he'd forced them into.

"If you could wait a month or two. No more," he added quickly when she stirred uneasily. "I promise you. Then we can arrange it. We can *plan*. You can come to me, and we can leave immediately for Europe. We can stay away as long as you like. But we will leave ourselves and our family protected when we go. The spring, Darcy. Can you wait until the spring?"

No! her spirit cried. *Not for one more second can I endure it!*

But she looked into his eyes, the faded blue-gray she loved, and she sighed. She saw how much he wanted her to trust him, how afraid he was that she would not, because he did not deserve it. This business scheme could be like so many others and fail. But how could she crush his spirit now, when he needed her faith? No one knew better than she how fragile her father really was. And they had no one but each other.

She leaned against his shoulder and smelled the comforting scent of the cologne in his beard. "I'll wait," she said.

He held her to him. "May God forgive me for sending you back there," he whispered.

"May God forgive us both," Darcy replied softly.

"Now you must go," Edward said. "Quickly. *He must not suspect, Darcy.* Remember that."

Darcy drew her cloak around her. She pulled up the hood lined in sable and thrust her hands in her muff.

"I'll find a cab for you," Edward said.

"No. It's not necessary. It's not too late."

She followed him downstairs. He seemed impatient now, wanting to have her gone. Just the fact that he agreed to let her go alone told her that. When they reached the downstairs hall, he kissed her quietly, and she went out.

It wasn't until she reached the bottom of the stairs that she realized she'd forgotten her gloves. It was bitter cold, and she had far to go. Darcy turned and ran quickly up the stairs. She decided not to ring.

When she entered the front hall, she heard footsteps heading from the dining room to the front parlor. Instinctively, she melted back into the small sitting room that had been her mother's.

"Edward, you are deep. So you have a secret in your life—a mystery caller."

Darcy pressed a hand to her mouth. Claude! Why didn't her father tell her he was downstairs? Her heart pounding, she retreated farther into the sitting room.

"Hardly a mystery," Edward said uneasily. "But a man must be circumspect."

Claude gave the strangled chortle that was his version of a laugh.

"I'm sorry to have to leave you, gentlemen." It was the voice of a stranger, an odd accent Darcy couldn't place. It seemed British, but the tone was softer. There was the hint of lilt to it. "But I have that engagement, as I told you."

"Of course, Mr. Finn," Claude said silkily. "We quite understand."

"Good night, Finn," Edward said jovially. "So good of you to join us at such short notice."

Darcy heard the sounds of the stranger leaving, the front door closing, and then Claude and Edward passing into the front parlor, the room adjoining the one in which she stood. She wondered frantically what to do. She couldn't leave now; Edward's guest might see her. And then she heard the muffled sound of Claude's voice. Darcy drifted closer to the heavy hangings on one wall of the sitting room.

Her mother had created the sitting room by dividing the long front parlor into two rooms. She'd simply closed the French doors and had them nailed shut, then hung heavy curtains in both rooms, disguising the fact that the doors were there. Her father had grumbled that his front parlor had been cut in half, but Amelia hadn't cared. She'd needed a small room to sit for her portrait by Fitzchurch, she said, and Edward rarely interfered with her domestic arrangements. Of course, they should have known that she had done it in order to receive James Fitzchurch in privacy. But they had been blind about so many things then.

Now, standing in the middle of the room Amelia had created to receive her lover, Darcy felt the same impulse to intrigue. She knew that if she moved the heavy curtain very quietly and put her ear against the crack, she would be able to hear her father's discussion with Claude. Especially if they sat in the armchairs by the fire. They would be drinking their second brandy and enjoying their second cigar; they would be relaxed. Temptation battled with her better instincts, and temptation won. Why had they concealed from her the fact that they were dining together?

She heard Claude's voice, muffled to be sure, but recognizable. Darcy moved swiftly to the heavy velvet hangings. Gently, she pushed it aside and leaned forward to the door.

"So you don't wish to reinvest in the pool," Claude said. "You'll take all the dividend for your own purposes. Your tailor's bill must be particularly high, Edward."

"As I told you, Claude, it's just something I want to invest in with this fellow Finn. The trouble with a blind pool is that you don't have the fun of knowing what your money is invested in."

There was a long pause. Darcy smiled sourly as she pictured her husband's expression at the notion of investments being "fun." "I've heard of Finn," Claude said, "from other quarters. I must say I feel I should warn you not to do business with him."

"Really, Claude? I thought him a delightful fellow."

"Edward, there are few men in New York you do not think of as delightful fellows."

"Well, perhaps that's true. But Mr. Finn seems so businesslike, as well."

"Seems so? Edward, I suggest you follow our original plan. The company will be showing great profits this spring, I promise you. I'm in the process of adding some sizable new properties."

Darcy rotated one foot, which was beginning to sting with pins and needles. Perhaps she should go. The conversation was not very enlightening. So her father was in business with Claude. Although the knowledge had shocked her initially, it made sense to her now. Why shouldn't her father take advantage of her husband's expertise?

Then Claude spoke, and with a beating heart she leaned closer to the door. It was a tone she recognized, and she was shocked to hear him speak to her father with such murderous, icy contempt, the contempt that never failed to chill her blood. "Edward, need I tell you the reasons you should follow my advice?"

"Of course not," Edward said carefully. "You are one of the richest men in New York, and you've gained your fortune yourself, without benefit of blood contacts—"

"No. That's not what I was referring to, dear father." Darcy imagined how Edward would disguise his distaste for the affectionate term. But Claude had used it deliberately; he hated any reference to his low birth, even one so gentle as Edward's. She heard the clink of glass, and knew Edward had poured himself another brandy.

"I was referring to a Monsieur Andre Maubert," Claude said.

The glass hit the table with a clatter. "Who?" Edward asked, his voice desperately trying to convey a naturalness Darcy knew he did not feel.

"Ah, you don't remember. He was the French footman in your house. Your wife was still living with you then. A handsome fellow. He left before she ran away with James Fitzchurch."

"He found another position, a better one, in Europe—" Edward blubbered.

"And I've always wondered," Claude continued, his voice silky now, "whose departure you were mourning when they both left so close to each other. And who you were thinking of when you took to your bed. Servants talk, Edward. It's sad, isn't it? And servants often see things they shouldn't. Like a parlormaid by the name of Annie O'Day. She was fired from this house, of course. She took certain papers with her, letters . . ."

Edward's voice was a whisper. "Claude—"

"So tell me, Edward. Do you truly think this investment with Mr. Finn, this continuing association, is good for us?"

"Claude, I beg you . . ."

"Or will you entrust yourself to my hands? The way we always worked together, Edward. From the very day I entered your drawing room and saw your daughter. And you sold her to me."

A mournful moan, torn from an anguished throat, shuddered through the door. It took several long seconds for Darcy to realize the animal sound had come from her father.

"You are my property, Edward," Claude said over the sound of brandy slurping into a glass. "Don't forget that."

The room was so quiet Darcy was certain she heard the brandy being gulped down Edward's throat.

"But come, come, man, don't be distressed," Claude said in that jovial tone she hated. "We'll be rich, far richer than you ever were, ever dreamed you'd be. And perhaps one day soon I will tell you what you continue to invest in when you invest with me. Yes, I believe I should. Oh, perhaps we should call for more brandy, Edward? You spilled quite a bit."

Darcy heard the chairs move, someone try to rise. She heard someone stumble: her father. Then she ran on quick and silent feet to the front door. Gasping, almost blinded with the enormity of what she'd heard, she managed to slip out and run down the stairs.

The snow ahead of her was unmarked, gleaming white, sparkling like diamonds all the way to the end of Twenty-eighth Street to Fifth Avenue, all the way to the famous Statton mansion. She shuddered as she looked back at the sickly yellow light from her father's parlor window. She turned her back on it again, swaying with what she'd heard; she couldn't begin to make sense of it. Lies, of course. But that Claude would black-mail Edward with such lies!

"Mrs. Statton?" A form took shape out of the darkness. A hand rested on her arm, a strong hand that held her up with ease. "Forgive me. Your father pointed you out to me at the Academy of Music the other night. I was dining with him this evening. You seem poorly. Let me help you back up the stairs to him—"

"No!" Darcy tried to take a step backward. The stranger kept his hand on her arm to support her.

"Surely you need to rest a moment—" He paused and looked at her more closely. She could see in the dull glow of the streetlamp that his light-colored eyes were concerned. Then the expression cleared as he understood. What else could he think, seeing her in this wild condition at her father's house, afraid to see her husband. He knew. She felt his fingers tighten on her arm, but because she was too afraid now of what he knew, she did not withdraw it. He bowed, slightly. "Then allow me to escort you home, Mrs. Statton."

"That's not necessary."

"Oh, but I believe it is. If you will not allow me to deliver you to your father, at least let me deliver you to your door. Please," he said in a warm tone. "You can barely stand, Mrs. Statton."

Darcy could not make sense of her rushing thoughts. Better to let this man, she could not recall his name, see her home than to risk offending him. She was panting, thanks to her corset and her agitation, and she struggled to control her breathing. If the man chose to talk, she could find herself the topic of the town tomorrow morning. What choice did she have? She must appear normal, she must go with him.

"Thank you, sir." She took his arm; actually, she was grateful for it, as her legs felt weak. His arm felt like iron underneath her gloved hand as they began to walk toward Fifth Avenue.

"I realize this is not the regular thing to do," the man said. "But I would like to introduce myself if I am to accompany you." Darcy inclined her head, and he continued easily. "Tavish Finn, at your service, Mrs. Statton. We are a bit more informal out West, which is why I find I blunder a bit when I return East. I

22

try not to return very often. Then when I do, I wonder how I could stay away. On a fine night such as this, for example. The snow . . . it softens things, doesn't it? New York then reminds me of London, the city becomes so gray and stately. And New York has this vitality—some would say brutality—that's bracing. Though I'm partial to a calm life, Mrs. Statton, New York does make the blood run quicker, and that can be invigorating. Though, of course, the wildest place I've been is the Central Park. Excepting Wall Street, of course." He smiled.

She opened her mouth to murmur a reply, one of the conventional responses she'd been murmuring since she'd been in long dresses, *Yes, Mr. Finn* or *Do you say so, Mr. Finn*, but he kept on his running commentary, in his slow, strangely accented voice, with its crisp, upper crust British consonants, the soft hint of the slurred vowels of the West, and that odd Irish lilt she was more accustomed to hearing from the maids who did the heavy work in the house. He hailed a cab immediately and helped her inside. He began to talk of the snow, and then the food in New York, and then the fishing prowess of his friend Jamie Alden, and it wasn't boring in the least, it wasn't the endless repetitions of the correct chatter she was used to, and it wasn't as though he was talking to himself, with her only as a captive female audience. It was an oddly personal monologue, as though he had rummaged through his experience like a suitcase and selected with great care the things that would amuse her. And he kept on talking, and the snow fell, and the cab felt snug, and by the time they passed Alva and William K. Vanderbilt's chateau on Fifty-second, she had realized his object. He was sparing her embarrassment and the need for awkward explanations. And somehow, in the long line of gentlemen who had sat next to her at dinner or called in her parlor, all saying the correct things, she thought that he was more of a gentleman than she'd ever met.

But that didn't mean she could trust him, of course. When they stood finally at her front door, their eyes met for the second time. His were pale green, she saw now. They blazed at her with a keenness that made her want to ask him boldly what were the thoughts behind them.

She held out her hand. "I am in your debt, Mr. Finn."

"You don't have to be. After tonight, I think that we will have never met, Mrs. Statton."

Startled, she withdrew her hand. His suggestion revolted against years of training. Share a secret meeting? Everything she'd been taught told her that it was wrong, that it would give him an ungentlemanlike hold on her. If they were to meet again in society, he would have knowledge in his eyes, knowledge of her that no one else was privy to: that she was afraid of her husband; that she'd tried to run away. She did not think for one moment that this man had not guessed that. His suggestion told her so.

Darcy stood thinking, staring at her boot tops. He bent his head slightly so his lips were by her ear.

"I can see I am more used to small deceptions than you, Mrs. Statton. That speaks ill of me, I know. But at least you can be secure that your partner in deceit is practiced. And is honorable, as well." She looked up and caught a twinkle in his eyes. "In his own way."

This time when she looked at him, she met his gaze squarely, letting him know that she had taken his suggestion. There was no need to let him know that she was afraid of him. "Thank you again, Mr. Finn. Good night."

"Good night, Mrs. Statton."

She slipped inside without ringing. Closing the door against the black form on her doorstep, she ran quickly through the dark empty halls to the privacy of her room. She threw off her cloak and sat shaking on the bed. She hoped with all her heart that she would never see Tavish Finn again.

After a moment, she began to methodically strip off her wet garments. She thought of the gleam in Tavish Finn's green eyes, the way he had appraised her. It was strange to think that after a life spent cosseted and secure, surrounded by her own, she was forced to trust a stranger. Her world had once been so circumscribed, so safe. She had stayed married because it was what unhappy wives did, it was something she owed to her family and her tradition, her world of old New York. But that world had changed; Claude Statton had taken it over, just as he had taken over her family, and nothing was the same. It was a world in which her husband could accuse her father of crimes she knew he never could have committed, and her father would bow before him. And now it was a world that fear had entered, and danger. Shivering, Darcy rubbed cold fingers against her skin.

Three

MONEY. HAD THERE ever been so much of it before, and had it ever been so conspicuously displayed? Certainly not in America. Perhaps only a decadent, luxurious court of Louis XV or the indulgences of Marie Antoinette approached it. And didn't they know it, those millionaires steadily pushing up Fifth Avenue until it was fashionable to live even as far north as Central Park. The style of the day decreed that the more elaborate, the more conspicuous, the better, and so they built bigger and bigger mansions and filled them with the best of plundered Europe. They skipped from the fourteenth to the eighteenth centuries, loading their rooms with Sèvres porcelain, with Louis-of-whatever-numeral furniture, with Fragonard paintings and Michelangelo drawings and Gobelin tapestries. With commodes and console tables, with bronzes and bergères.

There was so much money now, and so much more to be had. And so easily! Railroads and steel and coal and lumber; monopolies and pools and trusts. The Steel Trust. The Cotton Trust. The Whiskey Trust. The Sugar Trust and the Cottonseed Trust and the Linseed Oil Trust. Monopolies meant money; and money meant more money again.

And so the money poured from the hands of the many to the few. No longer did a rich man own a factory, or a business, or a store. Now, rich men owned *industries*. No longer did a rich man see the faces of his workers. He saw only the faces of the rich.

And so the money moved. From the plains of the Midwest, from the small cities, from the towns. And as it moved it changed, shrinking down from acres of wheat or blocks of factories to bits of paper that passed from one hand to another. The money moved to New York, to the big-fisted men on Wall Street.

And New York responded with theaters and hotels and balls lavish beyond anything that had ever been seen before. There were more than enough ways to spend money, loads of it. Oh, it was fine! A fine time to be a businessman with nerve. A fine time to be rich.

And at Delmonico's, on a cold, starry evening in February, the social season in full swing, money spilled onto the sidewalks, streaming from carriages like the warm golden light of Delmonico's itself. Satin and lace and fur, white waistcoats, and everywhere diamonds reflecting gaslight and the flickering reflection of thousands of candles and the light of other diamonds around other fair necks. The world had begun to glitter, as hard and brilliant as the new electric light looked next to soft gaslight, and nowhere did it glitter more brightly than at Delmonico's.

The Van Cormandts were giving a ball, and everyone was there. The fastidious exclusion that Mrs. Astor had practiced was disappearing, almost entirely gone now. Once not long ago her friend Mr. Ward McAllister had decreed that four hundred names were what constituted society, simply because it was the absolute limit of people who would fit into Mrs. Astor's ballroom. But now those New York families rubbed elbows with the newly rich and fashionable who had managed in a few short years to follow the shining example of the Vanderbilts and claw their way to a position in society, simply by spending more money than the old families ever could. It had begun in 1883, when Mrs. Astor had left her card at the residence of Mrs. William K. Vanderbilt, who she had formerly failed to recognize, in order to get the Astors invited to Mrs. Vanderbilt's fancy dress ball. No matter that Mrs. Astor did it for the sake of her daughter Carrie. The Queen had paid her call, after years of snubbing those parvenu Vanderbilts, and the limestone and marble walls came tumbling down.

So, in this fine February of 1888, the Vanderbilts and the

Whitneys certainly thought themselves the equals of the Astors. Or if they didn't, if any vestiges of the embarrassment due to old Cornelius Van der Bilt beginning his fortunes as a ferryman crossing the river to Staten Island, they kept it to themselves. Mrs. Astor even rubbed elbows with the charming Mrs. Paran Stevens, the daughter of a tradesman. Even the notorious Columbine Nash was present this evening, resplendent in a gown of gold, her honey-blond hair piled high. If there were those who whispered about Ned Van Cormandt's visits to her little house on Twenty-third Street and the too-exposed bosom of her dress, Columbine Nash didn't seem to care. She appeared to be having a marvelous time. As were the Livingstons, the Jays, the Van Rensselaers, the Kings, the Gallatins, the Goelets, and the Rhinelanders. Everyone was having a marvelous time. Except Mrs. Claude Statton, who appeared pale and hardly left her husband's side. And an elegant, mysterious stranger whose odd, too-Irish name soon made the rounds: Tavish Finn.

Adelle Snow Archer rustled over to Darcy. Her dress, light blue satin brocade trimmed with pink ribbons, elaborate lace, and looped up with royal-blue velvet roses, seemed to precede her. There were women who seemed to inhabit a gown by divine right, and then there were those who seemed to be temporary squatters. Adelle was of the latter variety. As the young widow's fortunes improved, Adelle had begun to abandon the conservatism of her upbringing and dress like the newly rich she'd once shunned. But Adelle was having a wonderful time in her new dress, and even the disapproving look on the face of Claude Statton didn't dim her smile.

Darcy returned the smile, ignoring the slight pang of jealousy that always pricked her when she saw Adelle. It was pure meanness, Darcy knew, and she hated herself for it. It was just that Adelle was so full of life. Next to her, Darcy felt so dry, so desiccated, so envious of Adelle's freshness, Adelle who was ten years her senior, thirty-seven, and like a blooming young girl next to Darcy, a dried-up old maid who happened to be married.

Adelle smiled her public smile, gracious, with a tilted head and wide eyes. Her tiny light brown curls quivered as she shook her head at Darcy. "What an evening! I declare I haven't stopped dancing since I arrived. If only I had a glass of champagne, my life would be complete."

Claude took the hint. He bowed. "If you'll allow me."

Adelle dimpled at him, then watched him go with narrowed eyes. "He hasn't left your side all evening, Darcy. Don't you want to dance?"

"Not at the moment," Darcy said. "I'm enjoying the spectacle." She didn't want to discuss Claude's insistence on hovering near her tonight. How could she begin to explain in a crowded ballroom everything that was wrong? She felt ready to scream at his constant presence by her side. She despised him now, for at last she felt fully justified in doing so.

Her house had become a prison ever since he'd caught her downstairs weeks ago. Although she had slipped down the next day to retrieve her cloak and boots, they had disappeared. They hadn't reappeared in her closet, and she only hoped that some servant had found them and, thinking them forgotten and worth risking dismissal for, had carried them off to her room.

She had spent a long night and a day going over the conversation she'd overheard, and she longed to ask her father about it. But she knew somehow that Edward would not want her to know such things, no matter how untrue. It would embarrass him merely to have to contradict them; to defend himself against such calumny was demeaning. But how could she live with Claude until the spring? Over and over the questions revolved. She felt exhausted with the force of her hatred and the weight of Claude's newly heavy attention to her every move, her every diversion.

"Remember the days when we knew everyone at a ball?" Adelle asked, her small bright eyes roaming over the room. "Why, there wouldn't be more than a face or two you didn't know—indeed, you were lucky if there were. And Aunt Catherine is still disapproving of me for wearing my Paris gowns the same season I get them. Times are changing, and I do welcome it. I find it exciting to wear new clothes, to see new faces." She leaned closer to Darcy. "And prominent among them is Mrs.

Columbine Nash," she said behind her fan.

"Yes, Father introduced me to her."

"No!" Adelle's round eyes grew even rounder. "Uncle Edward goes too far. Why, Mrs. Nash is divorced, though that's not the only source of her notoriety. Would that it was. What did she say?"

Darcy put her lips to Adelle's ear. "How do you do," she whispered, then laughed at Adelle's expression. "It was as brief as that, I promise," she said. "I think Father regretted his audacity immediately. He swept me away very quickly."

"They say Mr. Van Cormandt himself issued the invitation to Mrs. Nash, even though Cora Van Cormandt threatened to shut herself up in her room if he did."

"Well, I suppose someone must have opened the door and let her out," Darcy observed. "And I suspect it was Mrs. Van Cormandt herself. She could hardly resist being hostess tonight. The practice of hypocrisy does keep the New York society world turning—we know that so well."

"Darcy!" Adelle shook her head. "You don't seem . . . yourself. Are you quite all right?"

"Perhaps it's the champagne. But only one glass—nothing scandalous, I assure you."

Adelle immediately accepted her flippancy, for it meant she would not have to press her concern. Her eyes continued to rove around the room. "I must say the most interesting figure here is that tall dark man with the pale skin—do you see him? Over there, under the musician's balcony."

Darcy searched over the heads. Just as she found the man, he turned, and their eyes met. Mr. Finn. His eyes didn't drop, she noted as she quickly looked away.

"I see him," she said behind her fan.

"His name is Tavish Finn."

Darcy peeked back at him and saw that he was still watching her. It was just as she'd been afraid of; he would hold the previous night over her head. "An Irishman?" she asked, to cover her confusion.

"Yes, but they say he is well-born. Look at the way he stands; of course you can see that he must be. But they also say that Mrs.

Columbine Nash is the one who procured his invitation."

"And did Mr. Van Cormandt threaten to stay in his room if she did so?" Darcy asked dryly.

Adelle's laugh was a short explosion, a laugh Darcy seldom heard outside the privacy of Adelle's own drawing room—and then only after a glass or two of sherry.

"I wouldn't want that Mr. Finn around if I were Mr. Van Cormandt," Adelle agreed. "He's much handsomer. And there's something about him . . . But you know all they say about Mrs. Nash."

"Actually, I don't," Darcy said. "I've heard of her work for woman's suffrage, of course."

"Oh, that's the least of it. Her lecture tours were ten years ago now, I believe. Oh, you were too young, perhaps. It's very odd. She's the daughter of an English duke or a lord, or something. Scandalous." Adelle leaned closer in order to whisper. "She advocated free love."

Darcy turned and regarded the angelic Mrs. Nash, who was now moving across the ballroom. She was heading for Tavish Finn, and he was smiling at her approach. It was the smile of a man who enjoyed seeing a woman walk across a ballroom alone and do it well. So few could. Why, a woman at a ball would hardly take a step without the protection of a man's arm. Darcy certainly never had. Suddenly, she had a fierce and utterly irrational wish: she wanted to walk alone across a ballroom straight to a man like Tavish Finn.

"And other things I couldn't mention," Adelle went on, her eyes on Columbine Nash as well.

"Ah, but I think you will, Adelle," Darcy said.

Adelle gave her a quick, assessing look. "This is not talk for a ballroom, Darcy. We are having the most extraordinary conversation."

"Perhaps I am weary of ordinary conversation at last," Darcy said. Columbine Nash was smiling flirtatiously up at Tavish and accepting a glass of champagne. "Tell me what else Columbine Nash has spoken out for."

"Oh, the usual things. Anarchy and labor and the rights of married women. How the entire male sex is corrupt and horrid.

And how the solution of every ill is for women to stop having babies . . ." Adelle's face flushed, and Darcy knew she thought she'd blundered. Every Snow and Grace, everyone in New York, Darcy imagined, was convinced Darcy was in a near state of collapse over the fact that she'd been married five years with no child. No heir to the Statton fortune. No young Claude looking up at her with those strange, triangular yellow eyes.

Adelle fanned herself. "Oh, dear. I see your husband heading this way. And here is that delightful Mr. Travers coming over. I do hope he doesn't say something witty. I never know quite how to respond."

As Adelle turned to greet Mr. William Travers, Darcy quickly melted back into the curtained alcove behind them, out of Claude's view. From the shadows she saw him scowl slightly and scan the ballroom.

She had a moment or two, no more. Darcy sat on a red brocade couch where she would be hidden by a large palm. What a long trial the ball had turned out to be. At least her marriage had taught her well in the art of dissimulation. Of patience.

"You've dropped your petals," a voice said.

Darcy looked up. Tavish Finn was smiling, holding out a handful of rose petals. They were white, and must have come from the small bouquet she carried.

"Thank you. But I don't think they're of much use to me now," Darcy answered. She felt an unladylike urge to be rude. If Tavish Finn was a gentleman, he would not approach her at all this evening. What if Claude saw them together?

"I saw your husband heading to the refreshment room," he said easily. "So I thought I would come to your rescue. As for the petals, I don't think they're of much use, either. When I think of the colors that roses come in, I must confess I wonder how anyone could choose white—so pale, so insubstantial."

"It's their delicacy that makes them beautiful," Darcy said, slightly affronted. White roses were her trademark. Claude had a standing order at the florist, and they were delivered every day. "Why should they shout their allure?"

"But just look at them," Tavish said, indicating the small bouquet in Darcy's lap. He spoke as though they were old friends, with none of the formality required by their circumstances. It was infuriating. "Anemic, tightly furled—you know these buds will never bloom like a good wild rose would, in colors of carmine or crimson lake. Of vermilion, of incarnadine, of butter yellow, of deep claret, of scarlet, of Venetian red . . ." The colors rolled off his tongue easily, and he leaned over to fleetingly touch a flower in her bouquet.

Darcy disguised her involuntary jump by leaning back. She tilted her head to look up at him. "And what of moonlight, and lace, and ivory, and pearl?"

He bowed slightly, and when he looked at her again an odd feeling pierced her. The eyes were so green, so cool. His expression hinted at intimate knowledge—of what, Darcy didn't know. Women? Her own discomfort? Roses?

"Of course," Tavish said. "They have their beauty, too, no doubt. You point out to me, madam, what I should have known. Here I am in New York, in a ballroom full of white rosebuds. What would I do," he said, his eyes never leaving hers, "with a wild crimson rose?"

Darcy's hand tightened around the bouquet in her lap. She tried not to stare at him, but in the seconds it took for her to look and cast her eyes down again, she seemed to note everything. She realized for the first time that he was handsome. Unlike every other man in the ballroom, he was clean-shaven. There was something so naked about his upper lip, the cleft above it, the smoothness of it all. And that upper lip was so odd in itself, so beautifully shaped, too sensual a curve altogether for a man, Darcy decided. She felt dizzy from following it.

"Are you all right, Mrs. Statton?" He bent over her slightly.

"I'm quite well," Darcy said firmly, lifting her head again. Tavish stepped back. "I'm just a bit shocked to find myself having two extraordinary conversations in one evening. I don't know," she added dryly, "if my delicate nerves can stand it."

He looked surprised. And then the most wonderful grin flashed across his face. He stood, smiling down at her.

"Darcy?" Her uncle, Lemuel Grace, loomed behind Tavish. "May I escort you to supper?"

Darcy rose gratefully. "Yes, Uncle Lemuel. Thank you." She

quickly passed Tavish with only a slight nod and felt his eyes on her back as she walked away.

"I didn't know you'd be back from Florida in time for tonight," she said, desperately trying to sound normal while the blood pounded in her ears in a distracting way. "Did you enjoy your trip?"

"I've only just arrived," her uncle explained as he took her arm. "Well, a trip to Florida is hardly a trip to Paris. But my business on the St. John's River went well. The weather was glorious."

Darcy tried to listen. The back of her neck felt hot. She felt herself under observation but didn't dare turn and make sure. She wondered what kind of man would speak to her in such a fashion. An adventurer, she thought scornfully, for all his fine manners. A man who could ruin her father again and send him back to that black hell he had sunk into years ago. And what of that way he looked at her, as if to say, *I know you, Darcy Statton.* He was worse than an adventurer. He preyed on dried-up women such as herself. She was no better than her father if she allowed herself to be seduced by such easy charm.

But her heart, her heart that only beat in anger or disgust, her heart was beating so. And a man had done it. A man who thought of her as a wild crimson rose. Darcy let her arm fall and her fingers open. The bouquet of tiny, furled white rosebuds with its trailing gold ribbons dropped to the floor.

Tavish lounged against the wall and watched her go. A devil had been in him or he wouldn't have approached her. He should have left her secret safe, he shouldn't have risked it, but he couldn't resist it. He could use her, he should use her, for she was a link to Claude Statton. Better than her father, even. Why then, did he merely want to talk to her? To natter on about nonsense, to talk moonshine to her about wild roses, just to see her serious gray eyes flash, her delicate skin flush, just to hear her voice?

He liked her. That was dangerous. And he knew she was afraid of her husband; he was sure she'd been trying to leave him last night. She probably had been surprised as hell that her husband was at her father's house. Fear clearly had been in her face the night before; he had felt her trembling almost all the way home. Here was a double danger. A beautiful woman crying out for rescue. Oh, once it would have made him rub his hands together with glee. Now, he just felt tired.

But he couldn't stop looking.

She walked across the room with her uncle, and she was smiling. Whatever the man said, it had transported her out of that strange, abstracted, *mocking* way she had stood and carried herself and inclined her head with that gleaming hair, so dark it made him think of ebony, of sable. How could a woman convey such proper posture and yet such recklessness at the same time?

Tavish drew back farther into the shadows of his corner and watched her. Yes, he had seen fear last night in her eyes. But tonight in the glittering ballroom he saw more: her unhappiness fueled the recklessness, and he could also see that she did not know of the recklessness at all. She imagined, he decided, that she *was* the proper lady she appeared. She had not yet glimpsed her courage. She did not know that her true self was revealed in her eyes.

Damn it to hell, Tavish swore silently, and resolutely turned his back. He wasn't here to save Darcy Statton. She had married that weasel, hadn't she? What kind of woman would do such a thing? These overbred, oversilly society women deserved what they got, he thought fiercely.

Columbine stood a little away, talking animatedly to a group of men. Of course few of the women here tonight would talk to Columbine, but she didn't care. It was in other circles that she was hailed and feted, one of the most influential women of her generation. He caught her eye, and in a moment she excused herself and came toward him.

"What is it, Tavish?" she murmured. "Have you had your fill already?"

"Tell me about Darcy Snow Statton," he said. "There she is, in the black gown, on the arm of the gray-haired man. And who is he, by the way?"

Columbine looked over her fan. "Oh, my. Mrs. Claude Statton and Lemuel Grace. He's stuffy Old Guard, will hardly talk to her husband, I hear. She's a Grace on her mother's side and a Snow on her father's—you've met her father, Edward Snow. Didn't you dine there last night? He's charming. And she married Claude Statton, imagine. Don't ask me for an introduction, for as soon as I was introduced to her she must have passed some silent signal to her father, for he immediately dragged her away before she was corrupted. Mr. Van Cormandt can get me here, but he can't get me a smile from someone like Mrs. Statton. Oh, you know the kind of woman. She gives balls and goes to them. She wears diamonds. She goes to the Academy of Music on Wednesdays and the Metropolitan Opera on Mondays. She has a box in the Diamond Horseshoe right next to Mrs. Astor. She doesn't talk of anything but the weather. I've never spoken with her, but I know her."

"Hmmmm," Tavish said. He knew her, too. But he knew her in a way that Columbine, with all her insight into her own sex, did not.

"Claude Statton is the wickedest man in New York," Columbine said, smoothing her dress. She grinned. "More wicked than Mr. Van Cormandt. And I have more secrets about his wife's family, should you be interested. But that is a subject for my little sitting room, not a ball at Delmonico's."

"Let's go, then," Tavish said brusquely.

"But I haven't had my supper," Columbine said serenely. Her warm brown eyes chided him good-naturedly.

"Of course," Tavish said automatically. Then he turned and smiled at her. "Forgive me."

Columbine pouted. "Perhaps." She had a very pretty pout, did Columbine, and suffragist or not, she used it.

"Perhaps," Tavish said, smiling, "you'll let me take you in to supper."

"Perhaps," she answered, taking his arm.

As they went to the downstairs supper room and Tavish went through the fussy masculine ritual of seating Columbine, making sure there were no drafts by her chair, finding company for her while he filled a plate and found champagne, his eyes searched the gathering for Claude Statton. He finally spotted him in a corner. Unlike most unprepossessing men, Claude Statton did not gain even a modicum of elegance in his evening clothes. Though beautifully tailored, they could not disguise his sloping posture, his birdlike chest and his paunch. His thin blond hair was damp with perspiration, his scalp showing through like a white moon. He was alone. It took only a moment for Tavish to see that Claude was staring fixedly at something. Tavish turned to follow Claude's gaze.

He was staring at his wife. A cold shiver moved through Tavish like a rolling wave on a winter sea. What must it be like, he thought, to belong to that man? He looked at Darcy again, her back straight, her hands composed, her beautiful dark head inclined toward her neighbor. A perfect, sleek prize. Mrs. Claude Statton.

No, he thought, fingering the rose petals in his pocket, impossibly soft, the softness of the back of a woman's neck. No. Darcy, she was. Darcy.

Darcy slipped off her evening cloak and handed it to the maid. She felt wide awake, but she couldn't bear another moment with Claude. She wanted that long delicious time before sleep to think about the tall man she'd tried not to think about all evening, as he looked at her and she looked away. "If you'll excuse me, Claude, I think I'll retire," she murmured.

"Of course, dear." He waited until the three servants who had come to receive them had moved away. "I'll join you within the hour," he said softly.

She was too shocked to be able to hide it. "Tonight?"

"You seem surprised, my darling. Surprised that your husband would care to visit you?"

"It's just that I'm so tired . . ." Darcy bit off the rest of the sentence. She was breaking so many rules tonight, and now she'd broken the worst one of all: she'd suggested that his attentions were unwelcome, and she'd made the mistake of alluding to their relations in the first place. Tomorrow, she would bear the marks of that mistake, tiny blue-green finger smudges on her flesh.

"Ah." He took her arm and drew her down the hall toward the

staircase. "Perhaps this is the time to speak to you about something. I've been talking to a doctor about your condition—"

Darcy stopped. "My condition, Claude?"

"Your nerves, my dear. You've been especially high strung lately. I'd thought marriage would settle you down, as your family did, but," Claude said, sighing, "it doesn't appear to have done so. So I talked to a Dr. Arbuthnot, a very famous specialist in female conditions, and he agreed to see you. Isn't that marvelous?"

Darcy's blood ran cold. "A doctor," she repeated. "But I'm fine."

"Just a precaution. I've seen how your inability to bear a child has weakened your nerves, my dear. I understand, of course, how the denial of your natural function would place such a strain on you. We won't speak of my private disappointment—I am only concerned with your health."

He had touched on the topic that Darcy often wondered about. Was she really unable to bear a child? Or was it Claude's . . . deficiencies that made it impossible? Certainly the rarity of their successful relations meant her chances were reduced. Still, a doctor might be able to tell her . . .

"What about Dr. Temple? He's been taking care of our family for years. He's known me since I was a child—he delivered me."

"That's precisely it, dearest. How could he really see the case with an open mind?"

"The *case?*"

Claude patted her arm. "Now, there's nothing here to distress you. Just an examination. Perhaps there is some treatment Dr. Arbuthnot can devise. He's had such success with neurasthenic women."

She stumbled backward a step. "Neurasthenic women?"

He nodded. "I've discussed the symptoms with him. It's a type of neurosis of the brain, you see. Fatigue, weakness of the limbs, irritability . . . with no *physical* cause."

An icy finger touched her, a foreboding she couldn't name. She shook her head angrily. "Claude, I don't want to see him. I won't!"

"You see, that's one of the problems, Darcy," Claude said as he took her arm again and led her toward the stairs. "Dr. Arbuthnot quite agrees with me. Obedience, docility . . . lately, they seem to have deserted you. These strange midnight walks, for example. Any husband would be concerned. Solange told me that you even went out walking last night."

"I was restless . . ."

"You see what I mean, then."

Darcy felt sick. She clung to the banister as Claude walked her up the stairs, his voice low and insistent by her ear.

"Yes, I think a doctor would know best what to do. I've spoken to your father, and he agrees. That's right, dearest, he is concerned as well. You mustn't blame yourself, my darling. It's just a matter of nerves, you know. Oh, you stumbled. Here, take my arm. Perhaps I'll take my brandy in your room instead of the library from now on. I should sit with you more in the evenings. I've been remiss; I haven't devoted enough time to you. Here, watch the carpet, I'll have that seen to tomorrow. Let me get the door, dear. You must let me comfort you. No, leave on your diamonds, my darling. And send Solange to bed."

Four

DARCY PUSHED ASIDE her untouched morning chocolate. She was alone in her private sitting room adjoining her bedroom. It was exquisitely furnished with the most delicate French furniture of that classical period of Louis XVI. Claude had told her proudly several times that every item in the room had Royal provenance. The window hangings had been made for Marie Antoinette's apartments, and the elaborate silver chocolate service had been hers as well. Or so Claude thought. Darcy had always loathed the room. She had to watch her skirts every moment, afraid some priceless piece of Sèvres that cluttered every available space would crash to the floor. Today, the elegance and lightness of the pieces nauseated her. She felt a sickness deep in her belly, and she would cheerfully smash every priceless piece in the room if she could.

Why had she done it? What had possessed her, why couldn't she have controlled the impulse that swept her so fiercely last night? Couldn't she have continued to distance her mind from her body, lie rigid until it was over? She never should have aroused Claude's ire at this time. It was an error she could not afford to make.

But she had. This time her revulsion had been too strong. Everything had changed that night at Edward's house as she crouched behind the velvet hangings. She had left that last vestige of belief in her marriage vows at her father's house. The knowledge of what her husband was had hardened her uneasy hysteria to leave into a cool-headed rebellion. No longer did she think it her duty to submit. Perhaps it was her duty to resist.

Enraged by his attempts to push himself inside her, sickened by his breath, and cringing from the dank feel of his skin, a thought had floated across her mind. She remembered with sudden acuteness a simple thing: the way Tavish Finn had talked to her. Yes, he had teased—flirted, she supposed—but he had always spoken to her as one adult to another. The anger at him she'd felt at the ball disappeared in a flash as though it had never existed. There was another way for a man and a woman to be, she had thought wildly. It was not necessary to be patronized, to live with contempt. This was not right. This was not right.

She had done it. She had pushed Claude off with sudden strength, surprising him. With a thud, he had fallen to the Savonnerie carpet.

It might have been funny, to look back on it, if she hadn't seen his expression so vividly. For the first time in their marriage, she had seen a true emotion on his face. He had lost control. His face beet red, he had pointed his finger at her, gasping.

You will pay for that, madam.

But something in the fierce expression on her face must have halted him as he started back toward the bed. He had smiled; remembering that smile, Darcy's stomach tightened with fear. Gathering his dressing gown around his thin legs, he had walked out, the crimson sash trailing behind him like the flag of a cowardly recruit abandoning the field. Darcy shuddered; she was not amused at the memory.

She had remained here all morning, for truth to tell, she was terrified. She had had to hide her hands in her dressing gown to disguise their shaking from Solange. Claude was postponing his revenge. She had known that her husband could be brutal, God knew. But she was beginning to fully understand now how much he *enjoyed* his cruelty. That smile spoke of a perverse satisfaction from what she had done, for now he could retaliate. And he would make her wait for it.

Who could possibly help her? Who would not turn away? Who would not condone her husband and condemn her? Who could possibly understand how a husband could beat a wife down, day after day after day? How he could patronize in public and humiliate in private? How that humiliation only excited him the more? Who could understand such things?

Agitation and despair propelled her into movement. Darcy rose and went to the French windows overlooking Fifth Avenue. She laid her cheek against the cool pane. Columbine Nash, she thought suddenly. She would understand.

"I'm sorry, sir, Mr. Hinkle is not at home." The butler was already closing the door as he spoke in his refined British accent. He didn't like the looks of the tall man. An Irishman he'd bet, by that mad look in his green eyes. Probably drunk. No matter that he claimed to be a business associate of Mr. Hinkle's, he was not getting through the door. "If you'll leave your card," he tried for the third time.

Tavish put his foot on the door. "Here's my card."

"If you'll try his office, sir."

"You don't have the accent right. If you ever run into a real Englishman, you'll be in trouble. This is how you say it: *If you'll try his office, sir.*" Tavish's accent was a perfect imitation of an English butler's; he'd known quite a few of them. "But I'm not going to try his office," he continued mildly. "Because he's home."

Hinkle's English butler, who was from Chicago, pushed the door against Tavish's obstinate foot.

Tavish put his shoulder on the door. He pushed. With only a little effort, the door opened wide enough for him to enter. He did.

"Tell him it concerns Mr. Dargent and the Pacific Improvement Company," Tavish said easily. "Here's my hat. I'll wait."

The butler ignored the hat. With a last glance at Tavish, just to let him know he hadn't been intimidated, not nearly, the butler left.

Tavish wasn't about to wait there like a supplicant. He ambled down the hall and opened the first door on the right. A young woman was reading a book. She looked up, and he saw that she was plain and there was a sulky set to her mouth. She was too plump for Tavish's taste, but she was beautifully dressed. Her one good feature was a head of shining auburn hair.

"Sorry to intrude, ma'am. I'm waiting for Mr. Hinkle."

The girl nodded almost imperceptibly. It was obvious that Tavish was decidedly in her way. She rose without a word, gathered her green silk skirts around her, and rustled to another door in the Italian-paneled room.

"I didn't mean to chase you away," Tavish said.

She stared at him, then raised an eyebrow which said eloquently that she knew very well he didn't care a bit for her comfort.

Tavish grinned. Oh, you had to admire a woman with an eyebrow like that. To his surprise she hesitated, then grinned back, a genuine grin, and he decided she was rather lovely, after all. She turned, there was the shimmer of the beautiful green, and the door closed.

"My daughter," a voice said behind him.

Tavish turned. The man was stocky, whiskered, and obviously having difficulty concealing his anger under a veneer of gentlemanly conduct. "I didn't mean to intrude," Tavish said.

"Business visitors usually wait in my study," Artemis Hinkle said. He kept his distance, but his shrewd small eyes moved over Tavish, missing nothing. "If you'll follow me, please. I like to leave this room for my daughter's use at this time of day."

Tavish bowed. "Of course." How civilized we all are, he thought, following Hinkle's broad back across the hall. My friend has been murdered and perhaps this man is involved. Most likely, in fact. And I am talking to him and bowing to him and admiring the beauty of his daughter instead of wrapping my fingers around his beefy neck and choking the information I want out of him. Not before exacting a little revenge in the nether regions of course. Just in case he was thinking of having more eloquently eyebrowed daughters.

Hinkle closed the door of the study and went immediately to the middle of the room. He did not sit down and did not invite Tavish to do so. "State your business," he said.

Tavish strolled to the rose marble fireplace. "This is a lovely

43

room, Mr. Hinkle." His voice was low, unhurried, and if Jamie had been there he would have recognized the tone and tried to hide a grin.

"State your business, sir."

Tavish turned, surprised. There was genuine loathing in the man's tone.

"What is it that you want, Mr. Dargent?" Hinkle spit out. "You may think you and your friends have me under your thumb, by God, but I am losing my patience, sir. I am tempted to expose your dirty little scheme, and damn the consequences!"

Tavish raised his eyebrows. Hinkle's face grew mottled.

"Do not toy with me, sir. I warn you!"

This was too good to be true. So Hinkle hated Dargent. Interesting. Tavish held up a hand. "I am not toying with you, Mr. Hinkle. But you seem to be under a misapprehension as to my visit. I'm not Mr. Dargent. As a matter of fact, I'm looking for him. That's why I'm here."

"And who are you then, damn you?" he sputtered.

"Ah, I assume that is a request for an introduction. Tavish Finn, at your service, sir, from Solace, California. You've met my partner, Jamie Alden, in San Francisco. My late partner."

Hinkle blanched but only said, "You have my interest, Mr. Finn."

"Good. Mr. Alden asked you a number of questions about the Pacific Improvement Company, which you refused to answer."

"Perhaps, Mr. Finn," Hinkle said, his face still slightly pale, "you will tell me now why you want this information."

"Of course. This company," Tavish said easily, walking over to a box that promised to contain cigars, and did, "had perpetuated a number of outrages against my town, familiar enough in these times, I suppose. But still—"

He lit the cigar, and took his time about it. Hinkle stirred restlessly. "We thought they went too far. There's the bribe, first of all. Very common, we weren't surprised. Pay us this money or our railroad will not pass through your town. We raised it. We're not a rich town, though a nice one. Northern California—a little lumber, a little fishing. Both industries, you'll note, dependent on the railroad to survive. So we paid the bribe, and the company took it, and then the company pocketed the money and built the depot ten miles up the coast, which is now a burgeoning little company town. Of course, we might have let it rest there—who could fight such a company? But then the company went after our industries. They raised the rates on the railroad for our lumber, trying to drive the local companies out of business and considerately offering to buy them out. We like to own our own industries in Solace. So we thought that we should find out a bit about this company, which seemed to have only one representative, who promptly fell off the face of the earth. So," Tavish said, puffing on his cigar, "Jamie Alden and I ended up in San Francisco, searching for Mr. Dargent, the man who we discovered was the company's agent. And we found ourselves chasing a phantom."

"A phantom," Hinkle repeated.

"There's a real man and a real company, I suppose, but it's not the Pacific Improvement Company, which is a dummy company with a board made up of clerks and accountants and flunkies—excuse me, sir, I know you're the chairman. But you seem to be the only respectable businessman on it. Now, isn't that strange? Strange, too, that you run to your house in New York right around the time Jamie Alden is murdered."

Hinkle stared at him, and Tavish didn't drop his gaze. "Is that an accusation, sir?" Hinkle asked softly.

"To a house you haven't visited in two years' time," Tavish continued, avoiding the challenge in Hinkle's voice. "Or is it that, like Mr. Huntington, you believe that if you move in, you'll die in the grand house you took years to build?"

For a moment, he thought Hinkle would throw him out. But the man wanted something, he could see it. Tavish squinted through the miasma of cigar smoke, trying to find the key in Artemis Hinkle's eyes. And then he found it. Fear.

A thrill shot through him. Tavish concealed it by studying the glowing end of his cigar. He kept running into it; it seemed to be the common thread that might lead him somewhere. Edward Snow, Darcy, Ned Van Cormandt. They were all afraid. Whatever, whoever, was frightening Hinkle, it meant that things would move somewhere.

"Mr. Hinkle." Tavish kept his gaze as steady as his words. "Solace is already on the way to becoming just another ghost town the railroad created. It's a lost cause, I think—and I'm not fond of lost causes. I've fought too many of them. And I'm tired, and I don't like the East, and I want to go home. But know this: I *will* find the man who murdered my friend. This Mr. Dargent, whoever he is. I advise you to think about this. Because, Mr. Hinkle, right now you are looking at a man with nothing to lose."

They stared at each other. Then Hinkle sat down heavily across from Tavish. "And you, Mr. Finn, are looking at a man who has everything to lose."

"I am assuming that," Tavish answered. "But I can help the odds, Mr. Hinkle."

Tavish waited while Hinkle looked at him. He didn't drop his eyes. He had been in this situation a few times in his life, over a poker table or a barrel of a gun, often enough to recognize it: Hinkle was taking his measure. He was deciding whether to trust, and the decision was crucial. Sometimes it could be life or death. Should Hinkle decide to trust, just on the basis of a measured look and a short conversation, the two men would be bound in a bond more lasting than marriage.

It took awhile. But then, Tavish saw it, the slight relaxation in the shrewd hazel eyes. He had passed the test. He was inside the gate. Tavish felt his stomach muscles uncoil with relief.

Hinkle was a good businessman, Tavish would bet. Once the decision was made, he didn't hesitate. He crossed the room and reached for a cigar with the air of a man who was ready to get to work.

"I came to New York because I was told to," Hinkle said, lighting his cigar. "And I am in a position to obey such orders, I'm afraid. I receive them by telegram. From the real board. From Mr. Dargent."

Tavish eased himself into a chair. "And Mr. Dargent has threatened you in some way?"

"Why do you say that?"

"Because it is true."

The older man grimaced. He passed a thick-fingered hand over his brow. "I've never seen Mr. Dargent, obviously—surely you

46

know that, since I thought you were him today. I very much doubt that there is such a person. Or, at least, someone with that name." He entwined his fingers and looked down. "I'm here in New York with my daughter from my first marriage. I built this house for my second wife, but she's never set foot in it. She never will. She stays in San Francisco. After this trip, I will as well."

"I see," Tavish said, though he didn't. But he thought it time to be polite.

Hinkle nodded, but Tavish didn't think he was listening anyway. "I first became acquainted with the Pacific Improvement Company when they placed an order for railroad ties with my lumber company. They asked for the cheapest wood—white pine."

Tavish nodded. "And you said—"

"I said the pine would rot in a matter of years—maybe less, in the damp Pacific Northwest. But they placed the order, and I filled it, and more. And I also made some investments they suggested, and I grew richer. Then I was approached by a man who offered me a business opportunity to sit on a board of directors of this company, and I would not have to do anything but sign a paper now and then and watch the stocks rise and do what I was told. So I did it."

Hinkle's cigar had gone out. He sat erect in his chair, not moving. "And one day I came down to my morning newspaper and saw that a bridge had collapsed over the Coyote River. And it was because the ties had rotted, you see. Forty-one people were killed, including seventeen women and eight children."

"I remember," Tavish said quietly.

"But I told myself it wasn't my responsibility and I went on. They control much of the lumber business now in the north, some railroads that haven't been gobbled up by Huntington and his cohorts. And now they're moving into shipping. But you know that. I have no proof, but I believe that there is large capital behind 'Mr. Dargent,' perhaps a blind pool—that's a guess."

Tavish nodded. "I have guessed the same."

"But I've had enough, Mr. Finn, for many reasons, not the least being that I am a pawn in a game too dangerous for me. I resigned a month ago. The next day I got a message."

"Blackmail?" Tavish asked easily.

He nodded. "My second wife is from the East," he said. "She was orphaned at fifteen. There was no family at all. She led a very hard life, Mr. Finn. I hardly need tell you what happens to young women with no one to go to for protection."

Tavish nodded. Hinkle looked away at the fire. He relit his cigar, then stared at it without taking another puff. It went out.

"She was fired from her job and found herself on the streets. She found a protector, a woman who took her in. The woman was good, and kind, and she was a madam. My wife is very lovely, Mr. Finn, but she has a head for business. She did what she could to survive, and she saved her earnings. She came West to make a new life. My first wife died ten years ago. I met Anne, and when she agreed to marry me I thought I was the luckiest man on the earth. When they came and told me what she'd been I did not believe them, not until she confirmed it and offered to go away. She did not, however. I asked her to stay. For," he said very quietly, with no defensiveness, no apology offered, only a quiet pride, "I am still the luckiest man on the earth, sir. No matter what she has been. I fought my way up through the gold fields, you see, and I have no right to cast stones."

Tavish waited. He found himself liking Artemis Hinkle.

Hinkle shifted in his chair. "I don't know how they found out. None of the agents from the company has ever seen my wife, and she changed her last name. Nevertheless," he said, clearing his throat, "they know. My wife has said she will leave me, let them do their worst, rather than allow me to be blackmailed, for us to live under this shadow. But how could I send her away? Even if she were to go, she knows it would only hurt someone else. My daughter, sir. My daughter is everything to me, and to my wife as well, though she did not bear her. And she is engaged to be married. To a man she loves, a man I like and respect, who happens to be from a socially prominent family here in New York. The scandal of my wife's departure might jeopardize that alliance—and my daughter's happiness. I withdrew my resignation."

Tavish nodded. "I see." He pictured the daughter; the intelligent face, the luxuriant hair, the creamy complexion. He'd like to know the girl was able to marry a man she loved. With that sardonic intelligent look in her eye, he'd bet she would have a hellish marriage any other way.

Hinkle clasped his hands tightly. His eyes went flat and angry. "If I could find a way to crush them I would, by God. I have been a scoundrel, in my way. What millionaire has not? But they have threatened the happiness of my family. And they have done it with such contempt, such . . ." He shook his head. Then his eyes blazed at Tavish. "That I do not forgive!" he shouted. He lowered his voice. "But I am trapped like an animal in the snare they have laid, and I blame myself for that. I had nothing to do with the bribe exorted from your town, Mr. Finn, nor with the death of your friend. You have my word."

Tavish nodded.

Hinkle looked down and noticed his cigar was out. With a grunt, he began to relight it.

Tavish puffed on his own cigar. "Perhaps I can ask you some questions," he said.

Hinkle nodded. He looked suddenly exhausted, his face white and pinched. "I am ready, Mr. Finn," he said.

"Of course you should have come," Columbine Nash said to Darcy. She was even more beautiful by daylight. Her complexion was fresh and clear as a young girl's, though Darcy was aware she must be in her mid-thirties. Her light brown eyes were enormous, almost green in the bright early afternoon sun slanting through her parlor curtains. "I must confess I saw you at the window, and I told Bell to admit you. I did so want to see more of you at the ball. We'll have tea, won't we, even though it's a morning call. I've always thought it so silly to refer to a 'morning' call when you can't properly arrive until after lunch, don't you? And you mustn't think of staying only fifteen minutes. I won't stand for it. How do you like my little sitting room? All of the furnishings are rented, with the house. They're hideous, I know. This flowered horror underneath our feet—isn't it a disgrace?"

While Darcy wondered if she should answer, and how, in fact, she could do so gracefully without complimenting the truly atrocious carpet, Columbine fussily adjusted curtains that must have been a rich ruby at one time. Now they were a dull maroon. Beige tassels that must have once been gold hung drearily down, appearing to have been worried at by a too-eager puppy. But the room was welcoming somehow, strangely free of clutter, the bibelots and whatnots Darcy had come to expect from sitting rooms. There was only the shabby furniture, a few odd treasures—a bowl in robin's-egg blue, a round crystal, a paper knife with a handle of ivory— and books piled on every table and shelf, and even on the floor by the windows. There was a copy of what must have been every daily newspaper in New York by Columbine's chair, a pair of spectacles lying askew on top of them. In the corner, a secretary was piled with correspondence. A lone letter lay on the floor by the chair.

As Columbine fiddled with the curtain, Darcy felt the cool shadow touch her face with relief.

"Tea, then, Mrs. Statton?" Columbine asked.

"I would love some tea."

"And cakes," Columbine said, ringing for the maid. "What would tea be without cakes? Americans have to learn about tea, I think. They've barely caught on to us. Oh, dear. Bell was already making tea, she said, and it isn't coming. Bell tends to disappear at the oddest times. I suspect she is conducting a flirtation with the newspaperman two doors down."

Columbine wondered how long she would need to chatter before her visitor felt at all at ease. She had barely been successful at concealing her surprise when Mrs. Claude Statton had shown up at her door. "Did you have trouble finding my house? The willow tree weeps over the door, I know."

"I asked my cousin for the address. I haven't been to this part of Twenty-third Street before," Darcy said. Then she blushed furiously. "It's charming," she said confusedly.

Columbine laughed. "How charming of *you* to say so. My friend Mr. Van Cormandt thinks it appalling. But it suits me. It is near my work. And I have such interesting neighbors. Oh, Bell, here you are, tea at last. Thank you. Please tell Mrs. Hudson that I am again not at home for callers. Now you can go back to Mr. Fresham, who is hanging over the garden gate waiting for you, I'm sure."

The pretty maid grinned, curtsied, and left. Darcy tried to conceal her surprise at Columbine's tone. It wasn't ignorance that made her speak to her servant in such a strange—such a *personal*—manner. As a daughter of an English peer—was her father a duke, had Adelle told her that?—Columbine must be used to servants.

"Bell has been with me forever. She's followed me over hill and dale . . . oh, dear, I *do* manage to spill so often. Thank heavens my mother isn't here. Perhaps you should pour, such heresy—no, how terrible of me, *there* we are. Wasn't it a wonderful ball at Delmonico's? So much to see and to say, wasn't there?"

"I—I don't know," Darcy admitted. "The season has barely begun, and I find I've had all the conversations I'm going to have already. I seem to have the same ones over and over again."

"Well, you must say the same things yourself, over and over," Columbine said practically. She took any possible sting out of her words as she handed Darcy her cup. "I know just what you mean, of course. Back in England, after I came out, and then when I was married to Mr. Nash, of course we went to the same places, saw the same faces, day after day after day . . . Of course things are a *bit* better in England. They don't treat women quite so much like dolls. New York society, of course, hasn't learned to take women seriously. Or perhaps it did once, and now it's forgotten. I've been flirted with and complimented and flattered delightfully—yes, I'm not immune to it; I rather enjoy it, I must say—but I've never been *conversed* with. Now in England, there's the grand tradition of the brilliant London hostess, you know, who stimulates her guests and encourages talk. And we're allowed to talk of politics and art at the dinner table, which is so much nicer. And of course we allow writers and actors in our drawing rooms. So things are a bit more interesting. But just a bit." Columbine sipped her tea. "Oh," she burst out, "try as I might, I cannot decipher this New York society! I fumble along—"

Darcy put down her teacup. "No, Mrs. Nash, I don't believe you do."

"I beg your pardon?"

Darcy smiled thinly. "You don't fumble, I think, except when nervous ladies intrude on your drawing room and perch on the edge of their chairs. You've never spilled a drop of tea in your life. And you don't natter on like this normally, do you?"

A slow smile spread over Columbine's face. "Oh, my," she said.

"I appreciate your kindness. You're trying to put me at ease. But I don't think it's possible to put me at my ease today, Mrs. Nash. I'm afraid I . . . I'm not supposed to be here, you know." To cover the admission, Darcy reached over and picked up a book lying on the small table by her chair. "*Leaves of Grass*," she said.

"It's marvelous. Have you read it?"

"No. Mr. Statton won't allow it."

"I was under the impression that Mr. Statton was very interested in culture."

Darcy smiled. "Of course. Like any man of his stature. We have no armchairs in our house. Only *fauteuils*."

It took a long moment for Columbine to realize Darcy had made a joke. Then, a startled laugh broke from Columbine that petered out into a delighted smile.

"Oh, my," she said again, shooting a look at Darcy.

They exchanged the most conspiratorial of smiles. Darcy caressed the leather binding of the book. How she would love to take it home! It would not be the first forbidden book she'd smuggled into the house. Books kept her alive. "Is Mr. Whitman very shocking?"

"Extremely, wonderfully so. Take it with you."

"Mr. Statton—"

"I'll wrap it for you," Columbine said promptly.

Darcy leaned forward. "Will you tell me about your beliefs, Mrs. Nash?"

"Bless you. No one seems to want to hear about it among your friends."

"My friends . . . you mean the people I dine with?"

Columbine gave her an odd look. "Yes, I suppose that's what I mean. There are times—this might sound peculiar to you, Mrs.

Statton, since I know how New Yorkers are—but I miss the Midwest. Those audiences in Kansas were so progressive. Less afraid of new ideas than New York. But things are changing. Why, Ned Van Cormandt gave me a contribution to the New Women Society. He doesn't want it generally known, of course. But he did give it."

"I shan't breathe a word. The New Women Society? Is that the name of your . . . organization?"

"Yes. Well, I wouldn't call it *my* organization, but I helped found it. I'm trying again, Mrs. Statton. I took two long years off from public speaking. I collapsed, I'm afraid, from overwork. I went home to England and simply sat. It was very difficult for me, more difficult," Columbine said, laughing, "than speaking in a drafty hall and going back to some poor soul's boarding house for some gray meat in a sauce of grease for my dinner. As for my work now, I'm shifting emphasis. Free love is not very popular these days, not with Mr. Comstock on the loose. What a disgrace that man is! Throwing people in jail just for trying to help women prevent conception. I do believe we are slipping backward, with all the steps forward we made in the seventies. So I concentrate on the basic issues. I think some of these new leaders of the movement are making a grave mistake by concentrating on suffrage to the exclusion of other rights that women *must* have."

"Such as, Mrs. Nash?"

"Women are property, Mrs. Statton, in the eyes of the law." Columbine rose and went to the secretary. While she spoke, she searched through the papers and finally emerged with a piece of brown paper and some string. "We need to change that. Women should have their own money, and if they divorce, they should be protected." Columbine returned to the chair and began to wrap *Leaves of Grass*. Her fingers were deft and quick, and not once did her words falter. "But if they *are* married, they should also be free—constricting minds only leads to physical and mental distress, you know. Sexual fulfillment in marriage is *so* important, and no one dares to speak of it anymore . . . well, not nearly enough." Columbine handed Darcy the book. "More tea?"

"Thank you," Darcy murmured. This was the kind of talk she'd come to hear, but she felt overcome with embarrassment. How could Mrs. Nash talk of such things so freely? "I'm sorry to say that I never heard you speak, Mrs. Nash. I've heard how stirring your addresses were."

"'When you look at the history of the repression of the human race, the phallus as an instrument of torture and death is mightier than the rack and the sword.' Oh, I am sorry, I didn't mean to shock you, I was quoting myself, actually. Did you hear Victoria Woodhull speak? No? A pity. I shall never forget it. At one meeting this awful boor asked if she was a free lover herself. Do you know what she said? 'If I want sexual intercourse with one or one hundred men I shall have it!' Oh, she was wicked! Wicked and gifted. I shall miss her. She believed, you know, that the more one discussed the sexual organs freely the less embarrassed one would become. How do you feel about that, Mrs. Statton? Do have a cake."

Columbine held the plate out to her with a friendly gesture. Darcy took it mechanically. She knew she could never force it down her dry throat. "What exactly do you mean, Mrs. Nash, when you speak of constricting minds leading to . . . oh . . ."

"So many things! I'm sure you see as much needless suffering as I do. Women, shut up in their houses, unable to use their minds or bodies freely . . . Why, it's no wonder they have imaginary ailments, and nerves, and all that other upper-class claptrap."

"Claptrap?"

"Oh, I don't mean that women don't suffer genuinely. Of course, they do. But so much of these 'nervous conditions' I hear about—why, you take a healthy, vibrant, intelligent man, bind his torso in whalebone and steel, force him to ride back and forth in a carriage all day or receive the same callers again and again for fifteen minutes, never let him pick up a book or a new thought—what do you expect?" Columbine leaned forward. "Now I am going to shock you, Mrs. Statton."

Darcy waited, wondering how far Columbine Nash needed to go before she considered herself shocking.

"I work with prostitutes, you know. And they have their own

dilemmas, to be sure. But they are free of corsets and their minds are free, and who can say they are worse off than those women from Fifth Avenue you call on?"

"Who, indeed," Darcy murmured.

Columbine picked up a cake and nibbled on it; it was her only method of stopping her mouth. She knew she talked too much. And her guest did look a bit overwhelmed. She watched Darcy covertly. She had the air of a woman who had come to discuss a problem. Why else had she defied her husband and her class and sought Columbine out?

Columbine leaned forward, her eyes intent. She spoke gently now. "Mrs. Statton, I realize we aren't friends, not yet, but perhaps we can be. I feel that we can be. I would like . . . I would like to have a friend like you. I do not for a moment depreciate the courage it took for you to knock at my door. You must need fresh ideas very badly. Or perhaps friendship. And I am here to give it."

Friendship. Darcy felt herself yearning toward this forthright woman with the loud delightful laugh, who had put her finger on a need she hadn't known was there. It was as though she'd been walking on a dusty road on a hot, hot day, and all the while a clear, cold spring ran beneath her feet. If she could only dig deep and find it. Darcy raised her eyes to find that warm friendliness had replaced the shrewd impatience in Columbine's eyes. She felt herself drawn to the woman, no matter how outrageous her talk. Why, she was *kind*.

"I have so few friends," Darcy mused, staring down at her teacup. "My cousin Adelle, I suppose, but there are things I cannot speak of to Adelle."

"You can speak of anything to me," Columbine said. She put her hand on Darcy's arm. "I believe you know that, Mrs. Statton."

Darcy met her gaze steadily. "I believe I do, Mrs. Nash."

And then the door of the sitting room opened with a crash and banged against a small chair. Tavish Finn walked in with his hat in his hand and a scowl on his face.

"For God's sake, Columbine, where the devil is Bell? And what do you mean, you're not in?" Tavish's green galloping gaze swept the room impatiently and was reined in when it got to Darcy. He swallowed painfully. "Forgive me. I didn't realize you had company, Columbine."

Columbine's voice was cool. "I suspected that from the manner of your entrance, Mr. Finn. Though why you feel you may enter my sitting room in such a fashion when I'm alone troubles me. May I present Mrs. Statton. Mr. Finn."

"We've met," Tavish said. He realized he was being brusque as soon as the words left his mouth, but he couldn't help it; he was too busy staring. Mrs. Claude Statton looked pale and unhappy and very damn beautiful. It made his head ache. What a bother that woman was. He'd almost forgotten her today.

Darcy rose. "I should be going. I've stayed much too long. Thank you for the tea, Mrs. Nash."

Columbine looked from Darcy to Tavish and back again. "Nonsense, you can't go, I—"

Tavish broke in. "Mrs. Statton, please do not leave on my account."

Darcy was already gathering her things distractedly. She had removed her hat without thinking; she never removed her hat for a morning call. She felt as though she was waking from a dream. The intimacy she was beginning to feel in Columbine's presence had vanished in an instant, and she desperately felt the need to leave. The very air was disturbed by Tavish Finn's masculinity. His eyes ticked over her. No gentleman looked at a lady in such fashion, Darcy told herself furiously. And why was he so casual with Columbine?

They are lovers, you fool. Why else would he enter with such assurance, such informality? It was easy to see that the coolness with which Columbine had greeted him masked an irritation that was familiar and well-tried. They were lovers, of course, everyone knew that Columbine Nash took lovers.

"Mr. Finn, you said you were leaving?" Columbine asked meaningfully.

Darcy broke in. "No, I must insist," she said smoothly. "I really must go." At least he had interrupted just at the point where Darcy might have been indiscreet. How could she have dreamed a woman like Columbine Nash could keep a secret? Look what her favorite, Victoria Woodhull, had done to that distinguished Henry Beecher. Accused him of adultery in her weekly! Darcy shuddered, thinking of what Mrs. Nash could do with the information that Mrs. Claude Statton was forced to submit to her husband in ways she could not bear. "Good-bye. Good-bye, Mr. Finn."

She hated him, with his assurance and his height and his scowl. She hated the way he bawled Columbine's name. She hated his clean-shaven upper lip, and she hated his hat. Not looking at him, Darcy extended her fingertips for an instant, no more, then fled from the room. In the hallway, there was no Bell or Mrs. Hudson to be found, but her coat was hanging on a hook. Darcy bundled herself into it even as she heard Columbine rising and heading across the sitting room with rapid steps.

Darcy fumbled with the door. It finally opened with a groan, and she tumbled through. Gulping down drafts of fresh air, she fled down disheveled Twenty-third Street, past the tiny, shabby homes and the strange people who turned to look at her furs and her clothes, heading for dear familiar Fifth.

"Tavish, really. I am very put out. Very put out indeed. If I leave a message that I'm not at home, then I'm *not at home*. If you could master the most elementary social rules—"

"I've mastered them, as you well know, dear Columbine. I just don't happen to like *following* them."

Columbine stopped in the middle of her energetic pacing, her deep purple skirt whirling around her ankles. "You interrupted, Tavish, a most important visit. You frightened her away, poor soul, didn't you see that?"

Tavish dropped into an armchair. "I apologize. I *do!*" he repeated to Columbine's raised eyebrows. "I didn't see her at first when I arrived. And then I didn't get a chance to excuse myself and leave. I was about to. Honest. Whatever did you say to her to make her bolt like that, Columbine?"

With a sigh, Columbine sat down in the chair opposite him. "I don't think it was my talk, outrageous as it was. I was trying to put her at ease. You know I can't chatter about dresses and parties and the weather. Perhaps I went too far."

"'The Sacred Cows of Sexual Freedom'?" Tavish asked, his eyes twinkling merrily. "'Our communities are hot little hells'!"

"That was Victoria Woodhull who said that, not me, darling," Columbine said. She raised her arms above her head and stretched, yawning, then eyed him through the arch of her slender arms. "How you do condescend, Mr. Finn."

"No, never. I only tease. You know I am proud of you. Why do you think she came?"

Columbine let her arms drop. She frowned. "She's in trouble, Tavish, that I know. Perhaps she came to me for some kind of help. That's why your interruption was so unfortunate."

"Then I am truly sorry, Columbine. Though why such a woman as Mrs. Statton could need help, I can't imagine. She has everything she desires, doesn't she? That famous mausoleum she lives in, the Worth gowns—why, she most likely has consultations with Mr. Worth himself on her wardrobe!"

"It isn't like you to be unkind, Tavish. Women such as Mrs. Statton can have great sadness in their lives. As I well know," she said quietly. "And you should not have forgotten."

Tavish shifted uneasily. "I'm sorry, Columbine."

"Good. Now why did you barge into my sitting room today? You knew if I'd left that message with Mrs. Hudson that I didn't want to be disturbed. And you were to come at five, if I remember correctly, and I always do."

"I have a question for you and a favor to ask. Which would you like first?"

"The question, please. It sounds more harmless."

"Do you know a Mrs. Usenko?"

She looked at him warily. "That is not a harmless question. Yes, I've heard of her, though I don't know her. Why do you ask?"

"I bribed Claude Statton's messenger boy this morning and had the privilege of reading his city correspondence. Not very enlightening, unfortunately. But there was a message from this lady having to do with some kind of payment."

"Why Claude Statton? You suspect him as part of this group you're investigating?"

"Perhaps. Are you going to tell me about Mrs. Usenko?"

Columbine sat up straighter. "Mrs. Usenko is an abortionist. Like Madame Restell used to be, a high-priced abortionist with society folk among her clientele. She was an assistant to Madame Restell and took over after Madame cut her own throat. She has the accoutrements—a mansion on Madison Avenue, a carriage—she even has ermine-trimmed robes, like Madame Restell did. I hope she does not suffer the same fate. Anthony Comstock has thundered about her, too. Let's hope he doesn't drive her to suicide. Do you think Claude Statton used her for a mistress in distress?"

Tavish drummed his fingers on the arm of his chair. "It wasn't clear in the note. It just mentioned some figures. Odd . . . Now for the favor. I want you to get me invited to the Van Cormandt house party at their place in the Hudson Valley."

"Tavish! I can't do that."

"Yes, you can. Ned Van Cormandt will do anything you want him to."

"But I can't ask him—"

"You can do it."

"You are a pest, Tavish Finn, and I hate you. All right, I'll see what I can do. This wouldn't have anything to do with Mr. Statton would it?"

"Will he be there?"

Columbine nodded. "Along with his wife."

Tavish stood up and began to move around restlessly. "I didn't realize that." That was all he needed, the distraction of those frank, unsettling gray eyes. No lady would look at a gentleman in such a fashion.

But perhaps he could use her, after all. Perhaps Darcy Statton would talk in the peaceful setting of Greenbriars. If he could get her alone.

"I wish you'd tell me what you're doing, Tavish. You suddenly appear in my life again, and all you tell me is oblique and deliberately vague." Columbine tugged on the tail of his coat as he walked by so that he would look at her. "I worry."

"Columbine, I don't know what I'm looking for yet. And don't worry, I'm not in any danger, except for the danger of never receiving my tea in this establishment."

Columbine rang for Bell. "I don't believe you."

"You should. Now, tell me about Mrs. Statton," he said, dropping negligently into a chair. "You said that when she married Claude, rumors were that the Snows were ruined. What happened?"

"I'm not sure. It was after that scandal about her mother."

Tavish sat up. "Scandal?"

Columbine laughed. "I thought that might get your attention. Her mother ran away with James Fitzchurch—the painter. Do you know him? He's quite good. It must have been more than ten years ago. He painted her portrait, and she ran away with him to Paris. They still live there, oh, in separate houses, but together. I hear they're still very happy, and they travel in that circle, you know, that overlooks the fact that she's not divorced. Amelia Grace Snow was a great beauty, the most famous beauty of her generation. Edward Snow never got over it, they say. Sad, really. So Darcy married money, and Claude Statton married a name. It goes on all the time, doesn't it?"

"Can't anyone get tea in this house of yours?" Tavish asked irritably.

Columbine rose majestically and rang again. "You are extremely disagreeable today, I must say. You can drink your tea, and then you must go. You barge in speaking of other women, begging favors I can't imagine how I'll grant, asking questions of a very dubious nature, and you don't even notice my new dress, which is quite pretty. You still won't tell me what you're involved in, and you worry me half to death. I have problems of my own, you know. My girls are doing worse than usual—they are being charged more for board and linens, exorbitant rates. There are stories every day about girls getting sick or in trouble who are no longer helped. They are simply thrown out in the street and replaced. It's quite dreadful for them."

"I presume you're speaking of your, uh, soiled doves."

"Yes, of course," Columbine said crossly. "Does that make them less worthy of the help of their sisters? And they aren't *mine*, Tavish. How I do detest that patronizing tone of yours. I'll be well rid of you this week, if in fact I am able to prevail with

Ned and get you invited, which I doubt. Now I won't talk to you anymore."

Tavish grinned. He bent over her chair and kissed the top of her shining golden head. "It is for your amiable good nature that I love you so dearly, Columbine. And I appreciate the rebuke. You're right, and again, I'm sorry."

"Oh, foot. Just be careful, will you? And don't get mixed up with that Mrs. Statton. I'm guessing she has enough problems without a mad Irishman on her trail. And her husband, I hear, is dangerous. It would be the worst kind of folly to tangle with either of them."

"Mmmmm," said Tavish. "But you forget that I'm half-Irish, dear Columbine, and folly has its own attractions. Now, where the devil is my tea?"

Five

It was to be an active house party, Cora Van Cormandt had decreed, and she allowed no shirkers. There would be skating and walks and tobogganing and midnight sleigh rides. She would not except even Mr. Statton from the merriment, she had declared the day the Stattons had arrived. Yes, even Mr. Statton must strap skates on and take a turn around the lake.

Claude had bowed and said nothing. Of course he would not skate. He would remain closeted with one of the men and smoke cigars. Darcy would be safe for the duration of their stay, for Claude usually left her alone at house parties. The constant attention of a husband would be too marked in such an atmosphere. And Darcy had discovered that there were surprising opportunities for solitude at house parties, if they were large enough. One group always assumed she was with another.

But perhaps it would not be easy here. Cora Van Cormandt was an annoyingly imperious woman who laid down rules for fun for her guests and herded them like a martinet into whatever activities she'd planned. Guests attempted ruses, concocted excuses for one another to escape her, and laughed at her behind her back. But still, the food and wine were excellent, the guests always a mix of "those we know" with a dashing scintillating newcomer or two for spice. Cora had the reputation for being the most lavish hostess in New York, and her house parties were famous. Everyone wanted to be invited to Greenbriars, in any season, at any time.

Darcy had been dreading her visit, but she'd found, unexpectedly, that it was just what she needed. For two days now, fresh air and activity had exercised her body while her mind attempted to push out the thoughts that tormented her.

Over and over, she had examined Claude's odious accusations. She knew her father had not conducted an unnatural relationship with a French footman. That was absurd. Darcy pushed away the thoughts of her father's breakdown and what Claude had implied about its cause. She'd been there, she'd nursed him through it, and the reasons were plain. His whole world had been wrapped up in Amelia, and then when the depletion of his fortune had followed so swiftly on the heels of her departure, the combination had sent him spiraling down into a frightening depression. He'd barely left his room for months, months that Darcy labored to keep the household going and conceal Edward's true condition as much as possible from the New York bankers who could ruin them completely.

Edward had perhaps taken a proprietary interest in the handsome Andre Maubert, but such an interest could be misconstrued by a nosy parlormaid. She remembered Annie clearly, for Darcy had liked her and was surprised when she'd been dismissed. Her father had hinted that Annie had been pregnant, and if that was the case, what better reason than for Annie to lie to get back at the employer who had fired her? What was important was that Claude was fully prepared to blackmail her father, hold it over his head for as long as it suited his purpose to do so.

That meant to get free of her husband, she had to clear her father. For Darcy realized that if she left Claude now or in two months' time, Claude would methodically destroy her father's reputation. Claude had said that he had letters. If it were true, they could only be in one place: Claude's third-floor private office. It took up a large portion of that floor, and it could only be reached by a private staircase that Claude kept locked. But there had to be a way. She would find it.

It was that dull ten minutes before luncheon, when guests slowly trickled into the drawing room and waited to be called. There had been chatter and laughter, but when the ten minutes had stretched to twenty, conversation sputtered and died.

Claude had retreated and sat by the window, smoking. Edith Taft played with the black Brussels lace on her sleeve, then started in on her Etruscan bracelets. Her husband, Newland Taft, and the handsome bachelor Ambrose Hartley stood by the French doors, their laughter occasionally making the restless Maud Valentine shake her skirts and scowl noticeably. It was common knowledge that Maud's friend Cora Van Cormandt had invited her to felicitate her capture of Ambrose Hartley. Cora was said to be anxious for her friend, since Mr. Hartley was inexplicably taking a long time to commit himself. And Maud was no longer young, twenty-four on her next birthday. But Cora had been making her pretty concern too obvious, and tongues were wagging—were the rumors about Cora and young Ambrose a few years ago true? Could she be playing a double game? By the look on Maud Valentine's face, it was a distinct possibility.

If Adelle were there she would certainly know every detail and would have slipped into Darcy's bedroom after her breakfast tray had arrived to discuss it in thrilling whispers. Thank heaven Adelle was not here. Darcy had absolutely no interest in sulky Maud Valentine's marital hopes. Oh, if Ambrose Hartley didn't commit himself, someone else would, someone interchangeable with him. Maude would hardly notice the difference.

Cora rustled into the room, resplendent in rose-colored satin trimmed with white velvet and Valenciennes lace. "Lunch will be delayed just a few more minutes," she said. "Ned should be arriving in a moment with another guest from town. He went to get him at the station."

"Ah, a newcomer. Who?" Edith Taft demanded.

"Yes, Mrs. Van Cormandt, who is keeping me from your excellent hock?" Ambrose Hartley asked jovially.

Cora wasn't listening; she'd turned away, her head cocked

toward the hall. "Oh, here they are, I heard Ned's voice in the hall. I must tell Jackson that we're ready."

She scurried out through one door and Ned Van Cormandt came through the other. By his side strode Tavish Finn.

Confusion shot through Darcy with an alarming charge that almost lifted her from her chair. She felt her face grow warm. She stood and quickly walked to the opposite end of the room from the two men. Behind her, she heard Ned present Mr. Finn to several of the company. She heard Claude's cold how-do-you-do.

It was impossible. Couldn't she escape the man? Darcy looked out at the famous Van Cormandt gardens, now frozen and bleak, and prayed that Tavish Finn would have sense enough not to remark on their meeting under Columbine Nash's roof. She'd never told Claude she'd called, of course. If he should catch her in a lie . . .

She turned. Tavish Finn caught her eye. She didn't bow. From the corner of her eye, she saw Claude watching them as he moved across the room toward her. Fervently she hoped that Tavish would know that the absence of a bow meant that she did not wish to recognize the fact that they'd been introduced. Would this rangy stranger from the West know that fine nuance of etiquette?

His pale green eyes showed no emotion as they recognized her intent. Then his gaze moved past her and he bowed to Mr. Taft.

Claude reached her side. "You look flushed, my dear," he murmured. "We've had to wait so long for luncheon, I fear you have become ill."

"I'm fine, Claude." What was he doing here, how could he be here, what was she to do? Why was her heart beating so? Why were her hands shaking this way?

"That silly Cora Van Cormandt, holding us up for this Mr. Finn of hers."

"Yes, I wish we would go in."

Darcy turned slightly away from Claude, and was face to face with Ned and Tavish Finn. Ned introduced her.

Determined not to show her agitation, Darcy looked at Tavish squarely as she acknowledged the introduction. "And did you have a pleasant trip up, Mr. Finn?"

"Oh, yes," Tavish answered. "It's beautiful country up here. I had my nose pressed to the window during the entire journey."

"You've never been to the Hudson Valley?" Darcy asked, and while they traded the usual observances on the river and the landscape she felt Claude beside her, not saying a word, but watching. Was he seeing her confusion? There was something in the air suddenly, some charge between her and Tavish Finn. Was it merely from the fact that they shared a secret? Try as she might she could not seem to act normally. Surely Claude would see it.

Tavish Finn was a danger to her; he could ruin her father once more with this business scheme. Edward had told her it involved buying up a bankrupt shipping line and refitting it in order to compete with Jay Gould and Collis Huntington's Pacific Mail Steamship Company, which held California transport in a stranglehold. But was there such a company, and was the scheme feasible? She didn't know, and she feared another collapse for her father. It sounded like another of the many schemes he'd invested in and then lost his money.

She had so many reasons to dislike the man, and even more to fear him. And yet her heart had lifted at the sight of him! *What is happening to me?* Darcy wondered crazily.

Tavish began to talk to Claude, who answered grudgingly, his full, wet lips pursed with distaste. Tavish continued to chat amiably. Occasionally, his eyes flickered over to her. Each time, Darcy would steel herself not to drop her own gaze.

Cora called them to lunch. Darcy knew she should eat, she knew Claude would notice her full plate, her untouched glass of wine, but she could not choke anything down her constricted throat. She spoke, she nodded and laughed, and she could have wept with joy when lunch was over and, pleading a headache, she had an excuse to escape to the privacy of her room.

She followed the chattering and laughing women from the table. They stopped as Maud Valentine paused to throw a last gay remark at Ambrose Hartley. Her heart beating, Darcy felt Tavish behind her, close, closer than he should be. A wrapped package was pressed into her hand. She had to take it, or run the risk of dropping it and having the others see. Her fingers curled around it, and she hid it among the folds of her dress.

When she reached her room, she unwrapped it eagerly. *Leaves of Grass*. Smiling, she ran her fingers over the leather. The forbidden, enticing book seemed to burn against her skin, reminding her of the danger of her rebellious heart.

Tavish waited until Ned and Claude had entered the carriage. Then he hesitated, his hand on the door.

"Gentlemen, I hope you don't mind. But I had a sudden vision of Miss Valentine shrieking her way down a toboggan slide, and I believe I've made the wrong choice for the afternoon after all."

"Maud Valentine, eh?" Ned Van Cormandt laughed. "Don't blame you a bit, Mr. Finn. It's a much more delightful prospect than Mr. Statton, myself, and a consultation about a piece of property near the river."

Tavish grinned and touched his hat to hide the foreboding he felt as he waved them off. He'd expected Claude Statton to scowl, or perhaps to urge him to accompany them anyway. But those yellow cat eyes had merely sent him the briefest of messages: *I am watching you, Mr. Finn.*

Tavish knew the man had seen his interest in his wife. That was unfortunate. Not only did he not want to arouse Claude's suspicions for any reason, he didn't want to make things difficult for Darcy.

He had maybe twenty minutes or so to nose around Ned Van Cormandt's papers before there was a chance he would be discovered. Darcy was in her room with a headache and Columbine's copy of Whitman. The rest of the party, with much protesting laughter at being forced to move directly after lunch, had been bundled into carriages and driven off to a toboggan slope with an assortment of servants and maids and hampers full of small delicacies that Tavish knew would be devoured despite the ingestion of a full meal but an hour or so before.

So he had twenty, possibly thirty, minutes. It would take him another twenty to walk to the toboggan slope in time to take a run or two and flirt with Maud Valentine while Ambrose Hartley glowered, just so Mrs. Van Cormandt could tell her husband that there was a *frisson* of drama going on underneath their noses, and wouldn't it make the house party a success after all? Columbine had briefed him well.

Tavish quickly made his way to Ned's private study. He felt strangely divided about his task. He knew something or someone had put fear into Ned's eyes, but he felt badly about trying to find out behind his back. He liked Ned—though not as much as Columbine, most certainly—and he told himself he was helping him, but even Tavish didn't believe that palaver wholeheartedly. He was still nosing through a man's private papers, no matter what justification he used.

With an approving eye, he noted the fine solid furniture, the Turner on the wall. Ned was one of the few millionaires these days who didn't decorate his rooms as though he expected to receive the Sun King in them. He was famous for his disdain for things French—excepting wines, of course. And Cora Van Cormandt set a good table, as well. Excellent wines and a perfectly done piece of turbot were hard to come by. If only, Tavish thought, stopping in his tracks in the middle of the room, if only he hadn't been too distracted to enjoy it. Just his luck. He finally got an excellent meal, and he spent all his time trying not to look at moonlit skin and a pair of dark gray eyes.

With a sigh, Tavish moved toward the desk. For the thousandth time, he wished he and Jamie had stayed in Solace where they belonged.

Darcy waited. Her room was in the front of the house, and she heard the crunch of the carriage wheels as they drove away. The house was quiet. Even Claude had been induced to go out.

Now that she was finally alone, she was restless. She turned the pages of the book. As much as she wanted to read, she couldn't concentrate. The print blurred in front of her eyes, then focused. Whitman wrote of love with a frankness that shocked her. But it was so exhilarating, all the same. The words sang with a rhythm that felt new. It seemed to capture the feeling of her skin, her heart, her limbs. Her body felt as electric as the poet described, altogether different, suffused and tingling, aching and full of energy all at once.

Suddenly, she couldn't bear to stay in her room. Perhaps a walk in the famous Van Cormandt gardens, now frozen and still, would calm her.

Solange had undressed her for her nap. Darcy laced her corset loosely, then quickly slipped into her white wool dress. She knew she needed every second of the two hours or so she'd be alone to compose herself for when she would next have to be in the same room with Claude and Tavish Finn.

She could hear the clatter of china and silver from the dining room as the servants set the table for dinner, but there was no other sound. Darcy slipped down the hall toward the conservatory in the rear. There was a small door to the gardens there, and no one would be about.

As she passed Ned's study, she heard the noise of shuffling papers. Surely Ned had gone out; she'd seen the top of his beaver hat as he'd climbed into the carriage and took the reins. Curious, Darcy pushed open the door a few inches. She nearly jumped back when she saw Tavish Finn at Ned's desk.

It took her a moment to realize that he was rifling it. Her heart thundered in her ears with the knowledge. He was an adventurer then, a swindler.

"Mr. Finn." She had to hand it to him; he didn't jump. He looked up composedly.

"Mrs. Statton."

Silence hummed between them while Darcy slowly became aware that he was not about to explain to her why he had his hand in Ned Van Cormandt's drawer. He was counting on the discretion bred in her bones to close the door and withdraw.

"Mr. Finn," she said at last, "you are going through Mr. Van Cormandt's desk."

"Yes. Ned graciously offered me the use of the room to write my letters. I'm searching for a pen."

Darcy walked into the room. "I see. But there are two on top of the desk, there."

"So there are," Tavish replied genially. "Perhaps if you lend your help, we'll find the ink."

He cocked his head and smiled at her, but Darcy responded with a frown. She was furious that he would think he could charm her out of this. And there was something else, a fury that felt so hot it must be personal. *She* felt betrayed; it wasn't just her anxiety for Ned. "I think not," she said icily. "I think I'd rather wait for Mr. Van Cormandt's return to inform him of what his guest was doing in his absence."

"Ah, Mrs. Statton, you leap to a conclusion which—"

"I did not leap, sir. And well you know it."

They stood, facing each other, Darcy obdurate, Tavish seemingly at ease. The slight smile on his face infuriated her even more.

"Mrs. Statton, perhaps we should talk." He skirted the desk and came toward her. He touched her arm.

Darcy hesitated. She felt his fingers move against her wrist, insistence in the hard, callused tips despite the unhurried tone in his voice. She felt unable to move. He was looking down at her now, and his green eyes were grave.

"I'm waiting," she said, the breath leaving her so that the words came out softer than she'd wanted. And he continued to look at her, catching her glance, not allowing her to look away.

Then, behind her, she heard the door open. Darcy turned, Tavish's fingers still around her wrist, and her eyes met her husband's. Claude stood in the doorway, tense and furious.

The shock was so great for all three of them that no one spoke for a moment. Then Darcy moved forward.

"Hello, Claude. Mr. Finn and I were just discussing how empty the Van Cormandt house is with this new emphasis of Cora's on outdoor sports. Why," Darcy said, "if Mr. Finn didn't run me down in here looking for a book, we wouldn't have spoken to a soul all afternoon, and that truly would have made us disagreeable company this evening."

"I was desperately in need of company," Tavish agreed lazily. "Poor Mrs. Statton was quite bewildered at my cries of joy upon finding her here."

"Perhaps you should have stuck to your original intention and slid down a slope with Miss Valentine," Claude said. "Cries of joy would be more appropriate there, I believe." His face was paler than Darcy had ever seen it, his full, pursed mouth now a line slashed across a forward-jutting chin. She'd so rarely seen Claude lose his temper, and never in public.

He turned to her. "I think it's time you retired to your room, Mrs. Statton," he bit out.

She almost did it—she almost bowed her head and retreated. But Darcy was filled with a new courage, and her chin lifted. With absolute, regal calmness, she said, "I've spent too much time in my room this afternoon. I believe I'll stay here with Mr. Finn, for just a little while."

"You will do as I say, madam!" The words were forced out of his mouth, tiny explosions of air.

"I will do as I choose, Mr. Statton," Darcy answered serenely, despite her trembling knees. "And I choose to remain."

Their gazes locked, her resolute gray one with his furious yellow one. Darcy willed herself not to surrender. She told herself to hold on from one second to the next. And Claude averted his eyes at last. He turned on his heel and walked out.

As swiftly as it had arrived, courage rushed out of her. Darcy walked on unsteady legs to the couch. She sank down into it.

Tavish was by her side in a moment. "Mrs. Statton? Can I help you? Or shall I go?"

Darcy found that she could not speak. She dropped her head in her hands and burst into tears. She was dimly conscious of him dropping to his knees in front of her, murmuring. And when she raised her head, ashamed and confused, all that rang in her ears was the sound of him saying "Darcy."

"I must apologize," she whispered.

"No," he said, pressing her hand briefly. He handed her his handkerchief, and she wiped her eyes. "You must not. I must thank you."

"Thank me?"

"You helped me, Mrs. Statton, very generously. I am in your debt."

Of course, Darcy thought. She had successfully diverted Claude from wondering why Tavish had been in Ned Van Cormandt's study. Why had her reaction been so swift, so instinctive?

"If I did so it was only so I could speak with you myself," she said slowly. "And if you are in my debt then you can tell me why you were searching the desk of your host."

He sat back on his heels. "I see you've recovered, Mrs. Statton."

"I've a duty to Mr. Van Cormandt," Darcy answered evenly. "If his guest is a swindler or a thief, I cannot conceal the information. And I have a duty to my father. I know you have dealings with him."

"So you think I'm a swindler?"

"I don't know what you are, Mr. Finn. That is why I have asked the question you've refused to answer."

Tavish wondered what to do. He couldn't tell her the truth, of course. But she had stood up to her husband, a formidable task—for God's sake, Claude Statton was enough to make anyone quail—so he could not refuse. He knew if he avoided her question again she would go straight to Ned Van Cormandt; her threat was not idle. Darcy Statton was a match for him.

He couldn't tell her the truth. But he would have to tell her part of it.

"I'm investigating railroad stock manipulation for the federal government, Mrs. Statton." Thank the Lord he was an Irishman and used to improvisation.

Darcy looked dubious. "A government agent?"

"Have you heard of the Interstate Commerce Commission?"

"I've heard my husband rail against it, yes. It was formed last year to enforce the Interstate Commerce Act."

"Authorized to investigate railroad management, including the examination of company books and papers."

Darcy smiled slightly. "But does this include the covert examination of such papers, Mr. Finn?"

"At times it does, Mrs. Statton. There's a secret consortium made up of men here in New York. I was sent here to discover who they are, and what they are doing." He held up his hands. "You can check me out, Mrs. Statton. I have an office in the Pinkney Building, near the main post office downtown. There are other federal offices in that building. You can come down and ask about me."

"I see. I didn't know Ned Van Cormandt was involved in railroads."

"That, Mrs. Statton, is what a blind pool is all about."

"And my husband? He *is* involved in railroads, as you know. So he is under investigation as well."

"I didn't say he was."

"But is he?"

"If he were, you would hardly expect me to admit it."

"No, I suppose you would not." Darcy looked at him. "But he is, I'm sure."

"Mrs. Statton, I hope you realize how important secrecy is in this case."

"Most assuredly. And my father?"

"Your father?"

"Mr. Finn," Darcy said impatiently, "if you have decided to trust me with so much information, you must not now be coy and retreat. You have approached my father with a business proposition. My father is counting on this proposition. Are you planning to take money from him, or just lead him on? Or are you planning to exploit his connections with men you are investigating? When you disappear without a trace one day, what will happen to my father?"

"I will not take money from your father."

"But you would lead him to . . . to take his money out of another interest that might be harmful to him in the long run."

He gave her an interested look. "He is planning to back out of another business interest?"

"I don't know," Darcy hedged quickly. "I am just imagining the consequences of what you're doing. As you should!"

"Mrs. Statton," Tavish said impatiently, "I am after bigger game than your father."

"But you would trample on him in the process. Mr. Finn, my father is not wise in the ways of business. He is innocent of wrongdoing, I'm sure. He is a gentleman."

Tavish looked grim. "As are they all, Mrs. Statton."

Her eyes flashed. "So his character is not a consideration for you. Mr. Finn, my father has known scandal and ruin. It almost destroyed him. He is a good man. Don't destroy him altogether.

73

Leave him out of this." The word was forced from her reluctantly. "Please."

Tavish shook his head. "You plead for your father and not your husband?"

"My husband," she said with difficulty, "in whatever he has done, has done it with full knowledge, with planning and cunning and premeditation. I cannot plead for a man like that. But I'm not pleading for my father, you see. I am only asking for what is right. I don't know if morality is part of your code, but I urge you to consider it."

"I cannot make any promises, Mrs. Statton," Tavish said reluctantly.

"Then neither can I, Mr. Finn."

The words sank in as he met her cool gaze. Tavish found himself speechless, a rare occasion for him.

"You see," she went on deliberately, "you forget that I'm holding the cards, Mr. Finn."

Darcy watched him carefully. He didn't move, but something in his eyes caused a shiver to slowly trace its way up her spine. For the first time, she saw that this man could be dangerous.

"Never threaten a poker player, Mrs. Statton."

She held her ground. "I merely state the obvious."

He stood up abruptly. "You're saying that you'll expose me?" His skin seemed bloodless, tightly stretched across the bones of his face. She watched him, fascinated—he was losing his temper, a bad tactical error. "Pledged to Claude Statton, you speak to me of morality? You married the most despicable man in New York, you sit at his table, you simper on his arm, you take his money for your gowns, and you talk to me of right and wrong?"

Fury coursed through her, and she shot to her feet. "How dare you! How dare you judge me! My marriage is none of your business, Mr. Finn, but your activities with my father *are* my business. Therefore, I will cheerfully and with all good conscience expose you if you do not accept my conditions."

"I don't accept forced conditions."

"Fine. Then accept the consequences." She started past him, but he grabbed her arm.

"You are being a fool, Mrs. Statton. This is a dangerous game.

It goes beyond stock manipulation or fraud. It could involve blackmail and . . . other crimes."

Her head jerked up. "Blackmail?" Blackmail such as her father's? Was Claude blackmailing others, too? Tavish Finn couldn't know about Edward, could he? "I must go," she murmured.

Furious, he kept his hand on her arm. "You're not going anywhere until we settle this."

Her eyes flashed at him. "Until I capitulate, you mean. You don't intimidate me, Mr. Finn. I don't care who you represent and who you are trying to capture—it could be the devil himself and I still would not be afraid."

They stood, toe to toe, eyes blazing. Darcy's hands had curled into fists that shook against her dress.

And then, as her hot words hung between them, something changed. She saw the hard, flat look leave his eyes. Something else entered them, something she knew in her limbs and her heart before her mind knew what it was. The moment had come. Despise him or fear him, it was here.

"And one more thing," she said weakly, needing to stall.

"Yes?" he asked, his eyes never leaving her lips.

"I don't simper."

"No," he said. "You do not simper."

Then he reached for her, grasping her hard by the arms, and pulled her to him. He said something; she didn't know what . His hands were impatient, almost rough, and his mouth was hot and greedy as it found hers.

Before, she had felt bloodless lust, cold fingers, shaking limbs, hands that despised what they touched, eyes closed from the fear of meeting her gaze. Never had she felt this.

Rushing desire flowed through her, almost lifted her off her feet. Barely aware of what she was doing, she rose up on her toes to encircle his neck, and her mouth opened against his. She felt hard lips and tongue and teeth, a confusion of senses, a roaring, tumbling rush in her ears.

When they broke the kiss and she stumbled backward, he reached for her. His hands grasped hers.

"Darcy—"

"I must go," she said numbly.

"Wait."

"No, I hear the guests returning. I hear them. I must go," she said urgently. She had to be alone. "Let me go!"

"As you wish," Tavish said, dropping her hands. "But only for now, Darcy."

She looked at him. He expected a mute appeal, a pleading glance, asking him to go no further. He expected fear in her eyes and a relinquishing of her will to his. But he saw none of that. Her eyes met his boldly. There was no fear; there was only honest acknowledgment of the importance of what had passed between them.

"Yes," she agreed quietly. "For now only."

Six

SHE KNEW OTHER women in her set had affairs. Unhappy as she'd been with Claude, she'd never understood it. It seemed so unnecessary, a sad attempt to inject some daring into a society life, replacing one pair of trousers and a tall silk hat with another. And then there was her mother, who had broken the rules altogether and taken her passion seriously. Darcy had always despised that worst of all.

Now, for the first time, Darcy pictured the cause, instead of the effect, of her mother's decision. She thought of Amelia posing for James Fitzchurch in her blue velvet gown. What did her mother feel as she looked across the room into his eyes? Did her heart beat wildly, did she think she had found something profound, something with a force so great it could detonate a life locked since birth in a careful, cast-iron plan?

As she sat across the long table from Tavish Finn for each splendid Van Cormandt meal that sat untouched on her plate, Darcy wondered. Could this be it, could this be the same, awful force? Her husband was at the same table, she knew the danger of that, and yet the effort it took for her to stop her eyes from seeking out Tavish's was painful. Was this why women risked so much? Was it for this, this man who was avoiding her eyes just as assiduously as she was avoiding his, for if they looked at each other, would not the whole world know?

As she went from room to room, as she participated in tablaux vivantes and smiled at Ambrose Hartley's sallies, as she ate and drank and talked, Darcy felt as though her old life was slipping away. It was carried away on a strange, hot wind that moved against her cheek, insistent and impossible to ignore. She could not stop it or control it. The earth had tilted on its axis just a few more degrees, and everything was new.

She was consumed with the physicality of her feeling. Her body seemed suddenly important, suddenly so much more *there* than it had ever been. She felt her fingers tremble and her heart beating and her skin heating up with his presence in a room. She always knew where he was standing, or sitting, who he was conversing with, how he moved his hands, but she didn't have to watch him, it seemed. The back of her neck could feel him behind her. Her thighs pressed together underneath her gown to prevent herself from squirming with the nearness of him. His presence was immediate and total, and it consumed her every moment.

Reading Whitman in her room late into the night, Darcy felt the charge of the poet's words fill her with courage. The verse made her physical longing suddenly natural, tied to the elemental forces of nature and earth and universe. No wonder Claude had forbidden her this book. It placed a knowing finger on her pulse and applauded its secret, racing rhythm. The words hummed inside her brain as she went through the prescribed rituals of the house party with a heart suddenly given voice.

Three stormy days had kept everyone trapped inside. But then there came a morning when Darcy opened her eyes and saw clear sky, and the knowledge entered her brain plainly: this was the day she would see Tavish alone. She didn't know how they'd manage it. But they would.

It was early; her breakfast tray wouldn't arrive for two hours. Darcy flung back the bedclothes and dressed hurriedly, praying that Solange would not appear. She slipped through the cold halls, shivering, and made her way downstairs.

He was there, as she'd known he'd be, standing in front of the fireplace in the drawing room. When she walked into the room, he smiled.

"I think a walk would be best," he said.

"Yes," she said.

It was dreadfully cold; no one in their right mind would walk in such weather. The sun hadn't had time to warm the frost on the lawn or melt the ice on the trees. Darcy and Tavish went quickly across the grass, their footsteps crunching through a thin skin of ice, until they were out of sight of the house. Hidden by the folds of Darcy's cloak, they held gloved hands, then stripped off their gloves to feel each other's palms. When their fingers turned to ice, they put their gloves on again. When they could no longer bear not to feel each other's skin, they removed them.

When their pace slowed and Darcy caught her breath, she felt the minutes already press against her. There was so little time for them! And there were so many questions she wanted to ask.

"What is it?" Tavish asked, squeezing her hand. "Is it Claude? Darcy, I didn't mean to imply the other day that your husband is involved. I simply don't know. But—maybe I have no right to say this—perhaps you should be careful. That's all."

Darcy moved restlessly. "Don't speak of it now. There are too many other things to say. I don't want to talk about Claude, or even about my father. We can do that later. I want to know you, Tavish Finn. I've been thinking for days of so many things I want to ask you. I don't know where to begin."

"I think we have about an hour before your reputation is ruined," he said. "So begin at the beginning, and we'll talk as rapidly as we can. I want to know all about you as well, Darcy Snow Statton."

She smiled. "But you have the advantage—you are in my world. My life holds few surprises—you can look around you and see how I was raised. You've been in the house I grew up in. You could probably tell me what kind of dress I wore at my coming out party. But I know nothing about you, where you came from, how you came to be here. Are you the scoundrel you appear?" she asked mischievously.

"Oh, undoubtedly. Ah, Darcy. My life is a long tale, I'm afraid."

She pressed his arm. "But I want to know it. Were you born in Ireland?"

"Yes. My mother had been living in England, but she returned to her folk when she was with child. But she had no husband, and Ireland is not easy for illegitimate children. When I was about two she'd had enough and returned to England to seek out my father and ask for help."

"And? Did she find him?"

Tavish gave a sardonic laugh. "Oh, yes, he was easy to find. That wasn't the problem."

"He was married," Darcy guessed.

"Married, and a lord, with a large estate and a son and daughter. They'd met when she'd been in service at an estate he was visiting. He wasn't very happy to see my mother at first. But he did give her a job." Tavish's eyes had a faraway expression. "My mother was hauntingly beautiful—she could have married many times, even considering her shame. This man, my father, he wanted her again, you see. And my mother loved him, so she stayed. She became a companion for his great-aunt, which gave her some free time. At least he didn't make her a maid. And later, when I was older, I was sent to the stables. I was great friends with the groom, and back then I had no higher ambition than to follow in his footsteps."

"Did you know about your father?" Darcy asked hesitantly.

"Soon enough. It doesn't take long, living on a country estate, to learn all its secrets. The other servants treated us differently; it didn't take a genius to see it. I knew by the time I was ten or so. My father took no notice of me, but I knew. And then . . ."

The pause was so long that Darcy wondered if he was planning to stop his tale. But she didn't prompt him. She waited.

"My father's legitimate son was kicked in the head by a horse one day. He died a week later without regaining consciousness. The family was destroyed. He was seventeen, the pride and joy of the family. Handsome, smart, high-spirited. We'd been friends, actually, though he was five years my senior. He made an effort to befriend me, and . . . well, no matter. I too was crushed when he died, though I couldn't mourn with the family, of course. A month passed, and my father's wife went abroad to recover, taking my half sister. My father took to riding long hours. He came, he mounted his horse, and he never said a word to me. Yet I saw him looking. Then, one day, he spoke to me. And my life changed."

"How did it change?"

"He trained me," Tavish said expressionlessly, "to be a gentleman. I don't know if he planned to make me his heir or not. But I do think he needed to replace Tony. He sent me away to school, though I didn't want to go. He took over the training on holidays and vacations. He pushed me and prodded me and humiliated me until I stood the right way and spoke the right way and could eat the right way. And on long vacations, he sent me away to some impoverished family relative and paid them to continue my education. I barely saw my mother for six years. He had to send me away, I suppose, because things would be difficult for his wife and daughter. How would they treat me? They couldn't very well ignore my existence, now in my tailored clothes and my new accent."

"It all sounds very awkward."

Tavish laughed. "You sound like an Englishwoman. Awkward. That's putting it mildly." He squeezed her hand again, so she'd know he was teasing. Then his voice grew serious once more. "I grew to be a gentleman, and I grew to wait for my father's love. I convinced myself that I had it, that it was something of which he could not speak. And I believed it. Slowly, I began to *feel* like my father's son. My mother and I moved to a small house on the grounds. One day I was unexpectedly befriended by my half sister. We found we had something in common: we both feared our father."

They stopped under a grove of trees. Without the faint rays of the sun, the wind invaded Darcy's furs and made her eyes tear. But Tavish didn't seem to notice.

"My father, in an act of sheer cruelty, forced my half sister into an advantageous marriage to a drunken brute that destroyed her spirit within a year. My father locked her in her room until she would agree—she was seventeen. I was furious with him, but it was 'inappropriate' for me to express it, as I wasn't a true son. Something shifted for me then. But it wasn't until my mother told me she was going to have a child that I broke. I was shocked; my father had made it plain that he had gone on to other mistresses. Yet, one night, he had visited my mother. I had no idea. My mother had been unhappy for so long, and then when she told me she was with child, she was radiant. I suppose she thought this would bring her back to him. I'm afraid I took the news badly. I was horrified. We became estranged."

Tavish laughed, and it was a bitter sound. "Estranged! I sound like a Englishman now. I was insufferable to her, awful, a prig. Our relations grew strained. And then one day she began to get pains. I ran to get my father. Her doctor was not available, and I begged him to send for the family doctor. He would not. He had made a promise to his wife, you see, not to use the family doctor for his mistress's pregnancy. His wife was afraid of exposure, I suppose. So I saddled a horse and rode to the next village, searching for any doctor at all. I brought one back, but it was too late. He was there for barely a half hour when she died. The child was stillborn. My mother was dead because of a gentleman's promise. And that was the day," Tavish said quietly, "I ceased being a gentleman."

"What happened then? What did you do?" Darcy whispered.

"I burst into the family dining room—they were all there, including my half sister and her husband—and I broke the news of my mother's death. It was a terrible scene. My father threw me out. I stayed in the area long enough for the funeral and long enough to see my half sister one more time. I was wild, I told her she should leave her husband, that my father did not deserve her obedience. I'm afraid I called her a coward and said she would be destroyed as my mother had been. She too threw me out. After a time in London I came to America. The East Coast seemed too much like England, so I went West. I got a job protecting railroad workers as they laid track across Indian country, but I soon switched allegiances when I understood the terrible greed of the railroad men. I was involved with the Grange for a while, I played poker in mining towns and lived by my wits for a spell, and I was a Pinkerton detective chasing outlaws until I quit—

well, I did after they fired me. And then I settled down in Solace, California, after I won a share in a lumber mill. And there I found a home."

"But when did you start working for the federal government?" Darcy asked, confused.

"Ah." Tavish cleared his throat. "But that's a story for another time. I'll tell you everything someday." His eyes glinted, and he turned her face to his. "Here I've told you my life story, and I'm knowing nothing about you," he said, putting on a soft brogue and a raffish grin that made her smile. "Sure, what kind of gentleman could I be, with all my boasting?"

"Sure, you are no gentleman, Tavish Finn," Darcy responded faintly, her lips already parting for his kiss. She had so many questions. But his mouth descended on hers, hard and hungry, and she forgot them in the pleasure of touching him again.

When they re-entered the house, they blundered onto Cora Van Cormandt and Maud Valentine. Significant looks were their reward. Darcy didn't care. It was just a walk. What married woman in New York society did not conduct a harmless flirtation? They would return to town, and it would be forgotten. No one but she and Tavish would know how profound their meeting was, how painful it was, even now, to trade pleasantries with the others and parry their drawling incredulity at an early-morning walk in such freezing temperatures. At least Claude had not been there to see.

But when he was there, did he notice? Claude seemed no different. He had always watched her carefully, he was always remote in public, he always left her to herself at house parties. He was still furious with her for dismissing him in the library, but he had not come to her to vent his anger. He was waiting, Darcy knew with a shivering certainty, for them to be at home. Three more days.

But that meant three more days with Tavish. What would happen when they returned to town, she could not begin to consider. Not yet. She was too busy feeling to think. She pushed aside everything—her father, Claude, blackmail and possible scandal, her own desperate unhappiness, her growing fear of her husband. She would take her three days, and be damned.

Darcy saw the letter, forwarded from town, on her morning tray and quickly snatched it up before Solange could see and report back to Claude. At home, he always opened her mail and passed it on to her. Here he could not enforce the custom. It was from Columbine Nash, and it merely said she was sorry their visit had been interrupted, and that she hoped to see Darcy again soon. Darcy marveled at Columbine's tact. She would not call at the Stattons, though she knew as well as Darcy that etiquette demanded that she do so. By sending this note to Darcy, she was letting her know that friendship could be on her terms, and Claude would never have to know of it.

Thoughtfully, Darcy tapped the letter against the tray. Truth to tell, she was disturbed by Columbine's note. She had simply forgotten her existence for a time, and the note reminded her of the easy familiarity between Columbine and Tavish. On what terms, exactly, were Tavish and Columbine? Believing in Tavish's integrity, she hardly thought now that they were lovers. But they must have been at one time.

Darcy frowned. Jealousy was a new emotion for her, and she didn't like the feeling. But it was difficult not to envy Columbine's ease, her lightness, her wit. That her honeyed-blond beauty should be joined to such keen intelligence! Columbine had done so many things in her life, had been so active, and knew so much. Why would Tavish be interested in Darcy, whose most strenuous exertion was planning a dinner or what to wear to a ball?

Reaching for pen and paper, Darcy resolved to write a friendly note back to Columbine, saying she would call as soon as she returned to town. She had to face this feeling head on. Remembering Columbine's honest friendliness, Darcy knew that despite her jealousy she looked forward to their next visit.

And perhaps, Darcy thought with a sudden twist of mind that surprised her, she would need friends such as Columbine. Friends not bound by convention. Friends with the courage to stand by her should everyone else turn their backs.

There was a soft knock at her door, and Solange, who had been setting out her dress for the day, opened it. Claude walked in.

"How are you today, my dear?" He touched his cold lips to her forehead. Silently, Solange left the room to give them privacy.

"I'm fine, Claude."

He tilted his head and looked at her. "Oh, but you look pale."

"I'm feeling very well," she repeated, trying not to let impatience creep into her voice.

"I think the combination of the weather and the energetic Mrs. Van Cormandt might have been too strenuous for you, dearest," Claude continued. His eyes moved over her correspondence. Casually, Darcy moved her arm so that her lacy sleeve fell over Columbine's note. But he was so quick. Had he seen the signature?

Abruptly, he turned his back and moved to the window. Still with his back to her, he clasped his hands behind him. "I've come to tell you that we're to leave today," he said.

Darcy sat up in bed. "Today? But we were to leave Thursday—"

"I have business in town."

"All right, Claude. If you think it's best to go back. But I think I shall stay on."

He turned. "I received an answer to my letter to Dr. Arbuthnot, Darcy. He's agreed to see you right away. Isn't that marvelous news? That's the other reason we must go back. He'll see you tomorrow, my dear. It was very difficult for him to schedule the appointment, and I would think you would be more gratified."

"But I'm in good health, Claude."

"Yes, you say that. But your behavior, Darcy, speaks otherwise. Your excitability the other day in the library, for example. At other times you've been very quiet—you've been barely eating, I've noticed, and that always means you've been indulging in that morbid sensitivity that troubles you so frequently. And I understand that you went for a walk in inclement weather yesterday morning. It must have been below freezing! My dear, I must confess I'm worried."

It was useless to argue. His face was set and cold; she knew that look. There was nothing for it but to agree.

Darcy sighed. Her fingers closed around Columbine's note for courage. "Yes, Claude. I'll tell Solange to pack my things."

To Darcy's relief, her foreboding about Dr. Arbuthnot's visit was ill-founded. He turned out to be a rosy-cheeked Santa Claus who chuckled and beamed and nodded sympathetically as he asked her questions about her childless state, her nerves, and her marital happiness. The physical examination was brief and hardly embarrassed her at all.

Finally, he smiled warmly. "Now, Mrs. Statton. You're quite right about your physical health. Your constitution is excellent. But I must admit, I am slightly concerned about your inability to conceive. I believe it must be related to your mental condition. Women's health, you see, is centered in the womb, and any disturbance there is reflected in the nerves. And, despite what you say, I *do* sense some agitation, some nervous excitability. Are you quite sure that your days are as calm as you say?"

"Well, perhaps things have been unsettled lately," Darcy admitted. This kindly man made her long to confide in him. But the knowledge that Claude had arranged for him to come held her back by a thread. It was thin as gossamer, but it was a thread. Both Tavish and her father had warned her to be careful. She felt that there was more behind their words than she knew.

"I see. Just as I thought. Excellent. So. I am going to give you a tonic, quite mild, that should help you. Just for a month or so, while this cold weather lasts. It can exacerbate the nerves, you know. Will you promise me to take it faithfully, or will you be naughty and forget?" His blue eyes twinkled at her.

Darcy couldn't help smiling back. "I shall follow your instructions to the letter, Dr. Arbuthnot."

"Then run away, Mrs. Statton, and rest in your room now. I will just reassure your husband. If you could tell him I wish to see him . . . He is very concerned about you, you know."

"Yes, Doctor. I know. I'll tell Mr. Statton you wish to see him."

Relieved that the experience was over, Darcy climbed the stairs swiftly in search of Claude. He wasn't in his room, where he said he'd be and, hesitating only a moment, she headed for the back stairs to his private offices.

As she approached he was already coming down, closing the door to the stairs behind him.

"Claude, Dr. Arbuthnot would like to speak with you."

"Good," he said absently. "I'll go down."

She walked with him to the top of the stairs. "He found nothing wrong," she couldn't resist saying. "He felt I was in excellent health."

"Good," said Claude. Not looking at her, he hurried down the stairs.

Darcy watched him for a moment. He'd seemed a bit distracted. And something nagged at her, something she couldn't place for a moment.

He'd not locked the door.

She could be in his private office in a moment. She could seize the chance.

It took barely a second for her to made the decision. She might not get another opportunity. Turning, she ran quickly back to the stairs. The door opened easily and made no sound at all. Her heart was beating wildly, and she felt her legs shake as she swiftly climbed the stairs.

It was strange, but she'd only been up here once before, when Claude had first showed her the house before they were married. She had been amused then, by the Eastern decor he'd chosen. It brought harems and seraglios to mind, with its thick Turkish rugs and brass ornaments and ruby curtains with bright gold tassels. She'd pictured Claude reclining on the low day bed, with a fez on his head and smoking a hookah, and a giggle had escaped her. When he'd asked her what was amusing and she'd shaken her head, not answering, she'd seen the first crack in his smooth facade. There had been a look in his eyes that day that had chilled her, given her a new glimpse into the future before her. She'd tried to forget it, and she had. Would that she had obeyed her instincts that day and broken the engagement!

Remembering, Darcy stepped into the dim apartments. They were just as she'd remembered. The long desk in one corner looked out of place amid the rich opulence reeking of sensuality. Now she was no longer amused by the incongruity of Claude's office. She only felt its strangeness. It disturbed her and made her wonder about the sweating, dismal nights he'd spent in her bed. What was her husband really like? she wondered, standing stock-still in the middle of the lavish room.

Then she gave herself a mental shake. For heaven's sake, she didn't have time for musing over her husband's oddities. She crossed to the desk but only gave the papers a cursory glance. It seemed routine correspondence, letters and balance sheets. But of course, Claude wouldn't keep any secret materials on his desk. Darcy spun around anxiously, her eyes darting around the room.

She tried the filing cabinet next. Flipping through the different files took long minutes. One drawer, then the next, then the next. Darcy wondered how long she'd been gone, and wished she'd remembered to note the time before she'd run upstairs. It couldn't have been more than ten minutes, she judged. Dr. Arbuthnot was loquacious. But how soon would Claude return?

One more drawer, and then she'd go. Hurriedly, she yanked open the bottom drawer. It seemed full of business items, like the others, at first. But Darcy's eyes suddenly widened in surprise when she recognized the handwriting on one letter. Keeping a finger to mark the place, she extracted it from the file.

It was a letter to her from her uncle Lemuel. It had been written from Boston on one of his trips and described the spring weather and the business he was doing. It mentioned a visit to her cousin Florence and her new husband. Innocuous, charming, inconsequential, like many letters. Why had Claude kept it from her?

Shaking her head, Darcy replaced the letter and saw that there were others from her uncle in the file. She looked through the rest and saw only more business letters from a man called Dargent, dating from last year to that January. They were sent from places like London, San Francisco, Chicago, and Boston.

And then she saw it—an envelope addressed to her. And it was in her mother's handwriting. Her fingers trembled as she plucked the envelope from the file and opened it.

Dearest Darcy,

I suppose it is strange to you that I am breaking this long silence at last. I will not say much, for fear that you do not wish to hear details of my life here in Paris. Know that I think of you daily, my darling child, and wish with all my heart that we could meet. I do not ask for your forgiveness, I only pray that one day you will feel ready to reopen relations of some kind with me. Despite what I have done, I love you. You are my only regret.

Amelia

Darcy sank to her knees. Amelia had written her directly. And Claude had concealed the letter! Surely this was even worse than concealing correspondence from her uncle. How many other of her letters had he held back from her? Darcy looked at the date. One year ago Amelia had written this. She doubted if she would have answered it then, but oh, how she would have wanted to receive it!

Darcy's legs trembled, and she sank down on the rug for a moment. She stared with unseeing eyes at the Eastern opulence of the room. Her mother had written her. Her mother thought of her every day. Her mother wanted to see her again. That had been plain in every line.

And as she stared across the room, her senses unfocused, stunned, she became aware that footsteps were climbing the stairs. Soft, light footsteps. Darcy raised her head. It was Claude.

Seven

IN HER PANIC, Darcy moved quicker than she could form a thought. She scuttled backward on her knees, then jumped up and ran. All she had time for was to slip behind a seventeenth-century embroidered damask screen. It was only after she was behind it that she wondered if she'd been wise. Perhaps she should have stood her ground, made an excuse for being there. She was his wife, after all; what could he do? Now she might be trapped here for hours, or worse, locked upstairs after he left!

Claude entered the room with rapid footsteps. Hardly daring to breathe, she peeked out through the tiny crack between the panels of the screen. His back to her, he moved to a small cabinet against one wall. She watched him fish inside his vest pocket and take out his watch. He snapped open the side and extracted a small key, then opened the cabinet. Darcy couldn't see what was inside, but he slid out a bundle wrapped in brown paper. He put it under his arm, closed and locked the cabinet, then left the room as quickly as he had come.

Darcy closed her eyes in concentration to catch the sound of a key in the downstairs lock. She had been so foolish, so reckless, to run up here. She must have been mad. Desperately praying

Claude wouldn't lock the door, she strained to catch the sound. But she heard nothing except the sound of his footsteps dying away.

Fear propelled her forward. She suddenly could not remain there a second longer. She ran across the room, almost slid down the stairs, and wrenched open the door to the upstairs hall.

The air tasted like freedom, and she realized how close the air upstairs was. She gulped it down as she ran to her room, glad there were no servants about. She closed the door behind her and leaned against it, trying to catch her breath.

At last her breathing slowed and she went to the mirror and straightened her collar, smoothed her hair, and tried to compose her features. Perhaps a drive in the Central Park would give her time to puzzle out what she'd found and what she should do.

The decision made, she rose to ring for Solange when there was a knock at her door and her servant appeared.

"You're wanted in the library, madam. Mr. Statton said to send for you."

"Thank you, Solange." Darcy cast one more look in the mirror and smoothed her hair again. She knew she did not look composed, but she would just have to do her best with Claude. Perhaps she could blame her agitation on her outraged modesty after the doctor's examination.

But she didn't get the chance. When she walked into the library, hanging onto her composure by her fingernails, she stopped dead. For there was a quiet triumph in Claude's eyes that he couldn't disguise. And, on the desk next to the kindly Dr. Arbuthnot, were her cloak and boots, a letter she recognized at once as the one Columbine had sent to her at Greenbriars, and the copy of *Leaves of Grass*.

"I've been talking to Dr. Arbuthnot about my concerns, my dear," Claude said in a voice as thick as honey.

Darcy had to bite her lip to prevent herself from crying out. *How dare you*, she wanted to say. She wanted to rail against him, against this invasion of her privacy, this injustice. But she did not. She knew that it was Claude's right as a husband to search her things, to read her mail. She dug her nails in her palms behind her back. She knew everything depended on her composure. Dr. Arbuthnot had seemed so kind, so fair. Surely he, too, must be outraged at Claude's conduct, bringing her private letters and her books to him.

"Now, Mrs. Statton," the doctor said, "please sit down."

"No, thank you," Darcy said. Her voice surprised her; it sounded strong. Perhaps that gave her courage, for she was able to turn to Claude. "I see you've been in my room, Mr. Statton."

"I felt that Dr. Arbuthnot should see the evidence of your instability, my dear. These cloak and boots were found hurled under the furniture in a room that is used only in summer. This letter reveals that there have been secret visits to a divorced woman who has scandalized every Christian in this nation with her views on free love. And this"—Claude picked up *Leaves of Grass* gingerly—"this depraved volume. I tell myself that you do not grasp what this man stands for, what he advocates. But the language, the sentiments—they are an abomination, which every right-thinking citizen knows to be as pernicious as—"

"Mr. Emerson did not think so."

"Mr. Emerson," Claude answered, his voice calm as he casually walked to the fire and threw the book on top of the burning logs, "was well known as a free-thinker himself and is not to be trusted as a guide for moral conduct. Where these ideas are leading you is obvious and a great pain to me, which I shall not speak of." Darcy watched, her throat full of tears, as the volume began to catch. "At the Van Cormandts' you disgraced yourself and me by your conduct—it was the talk of everyone there. It is obvious that you have fallen under a depraved influence, my dear, for how else could you have walked about with that Mr. Finn, an Irishman?" Claude picked up a poker and stirred the flames, and the book began to curl and burn merrily. "We do not know where he comes from, his family—"

Darcy couldn't resist. "But I do not know your family either, husband." It was a deft thrust, an allusion to the fact that Claude had always been touchy about his origins; it had always been obvious that the bare facts he'd told her had been invented, especially the existence of the blue-blooded mother who had died so young.

His face flushed purple, but he ignored her comment. "It is

clear to us that you need help, my dear, for I truly believe you do not realize the dangers your conduct will lead you to if your moral corruption is not rooted out now. Dr. Arbuthnot and I are quite concerned."

Darcy turned to the doctor. "Dr. Arbuthnot, surely you can see that my husband is exaggerating this case. If he does not approve of my reading materials or my friends, let him say it. But to suggest that this is leading me down the path to damnation is rather overzealous. I have done nothing wrong!"

Dr. Arbuthnot rose and put a hand on her arm. "Please sit down, Mrs. Statton."

This time, Darcy sat; her knees were shaking, and she was grateful for the suggestion. She looked up at him anxiously, searching for the kindness she'd seen in his eyes earlier. He smiled down at her, and she felt relief course through her. This man would help her, she knew. He would not listen to Claude's ravings.

"I am not accusing you of wrongdoing, Mrs. Statton. Of course I cannot judge your conduct; that is for your husband to do. Now, I don't want you to upset yourself. As I told you before, I did note some evidence of nervous instability, but I see no cause for alarm."

His manner was so matter-of-fact, so kindly, that she relaxed. "Thank you, Dr. Arbuthnot."

"My cure for ladies' ailments such as yours is simple, Mrs. Statton. To relax the nerves, I prescribe massage and rest, and perhaps, if need be, a simple medical treatment, done in a moment, to further aid the health of the womb. Now, I'll send a masseuse over, you will take this tonic, and I will see you next week. So. Is that so terrible?" He smiled.

"No. It is not so terrible."

He patted her arm. "Good. I'll see you next Wednesday. Now, Mr. Statton, I have a few more words for you. Mrs. Statton, I suggest you go for a drive in the park and let the fresh air revive your spirits."

"I was just about to, actually," Darcy said.

His eyes twinkled approvingly at her. "You see? We agree on your treatment. Good-bye, Mrs. Statton. It was a pleasure, I assure you, and I also assure you not to worry, and to relax."

"Yes, Dr. Arbuthnot. Thank you." Darcy rose, nodded at Claude without meeting his eyes, and fled the library. She had won. A tonic, a massage, a drive in the park. Claude had not been able to influence the doctor, after all his sordid accusations. Now she could turn her mind to other things, like how she was going to manage to see Tavish Finn again.

Thoughtfully, Tavish went down the marble stairs of the Van Cormandt mansion. Dusk was setting in, and he paused at the bottom to look around him. Across the street, the palace of Cornelius Vanderbilt II blazed, an impressive block of red brick with white trimmings that managed to simultaneously suggest Versailles and an English country house while dazzling the eye with its amazing size. Next to its magnificence, the Van Cormandt mansion in mellow light brownstone looked almost puny.

Tavish turned left, toward downtown. He walked down Fifth through the gathering darkness, past the Renaissance palaces, the medieval castles, the eighteenth-century chateaux of the new millionaires of New York. The styles elbowed each other with a hauteur that was undeniably vulgar, Gothic and baroque and Greek and Byzantine and rococo, and sometimes a horrifying melange of all of these. Call them shoddyites or swells or bouncers, the folk that inhabited these mansions were a force to be reckoned with, and they had succeeded in grinding the Golden Age of little old New York to dust. The genteel age was gone now, the quiet life that went on behind the brownstones of the Jones's and the Kings and the Roosevelts—it had been for a generation, perhaps two. The Golden Age had turned to the Gilded Age, as Mark Twain had said. Now the copper kings, the silver kings, the wire kings, the trolley kings ruled. They were who mattered.

And chief among them was the king of them all, Claude Statton, in the white marble palace built to rival them all. Leave it to Claude to build in marble when everyone else thought it unlucky—A. T. Stewart had died soon after completing his marble mansion, and then had the misfortune, it was said, to have his body snatched from his grave and held for ransom. And hadn't William Backhouse Astor died after his marble palace was built?

But Claude Statton flung the superstition in their faces—there could not exist a grander, more ostentatious marble edifice than this. Tavish stopped in front for a moment, staring at the lighted windows, wondering which room Darcy was passing through, wondering if she thought of him. A terrible vision was taking place in his mind, a vision of what really lay behind these palaces, these sumptuous dinners on gold plates, this careful talk that never once touched on anything more real than yesterday's weather. Would his terrible vision destroy Darcy Statton, a product of elegant Old New York trapped in the rushing, threshing machine of the new age?

He went on, down past Alva Vanderbilt's lovely replica of the Chateau de Blois, past the twin mansions her father-in-law, William Henry, had built on Fifty-first to Fifty-second. He saluted St. Pat's and stopped for a minute to gaze at Jay Gould's mansion at Forty-seventh, wondering if the infamous Gould, slowly wasting away from consumption now, it was rumored, would be interested to see how his cutthroat techniques had spawned a new kind of monster in a world that was changing fast. He passed the enormous Croton Reservoir at Forty-second and saluted Mrs. Astor at Thirty-fourth for gallantry under fire, trying to maintain a solid footing in a social world now suddenly turned to quicksand. Now the huge mansions gave way to the quieter mellow brownstones of the Old Guard. And he finally turned off Fifth when he reached the upper Twenties and found himself at Mrs. Fleur Ganay's door.

She, Tavish had been assured, ran the first-class sporting house of all New York, which was saying something. Only twenty years before, a Methodist bishop had made headlines by claiming that there were as many prostitutes in New York as there were Methodists in the city. Now the numbers had surpassed even Bishop Simpson's outrage. There were the whispered horrors of Water Street and the shame of the Greene Street houses, there were the waiter-girls in concert saloons, there were the Sixth Avenue streetwalkers, and there were places like this one, an elegant Greek revival mansion with scrubbed marble steps right off Fifth Avenue, frequented by the cream of New York society, for Fleur Ganay was as rigid in her exclusion as Mrs. Astor.

He rang the bell and was admitted by an elegant butler. He had a letter of introduction from Ned Van Cormandt, and he was expected.

The house surpassed even Ned's enthusiastic descriptions. It gleamed with slick marble, it cosseted with rich brocade and velvet, and it titillated with a mural one took for Boucher until a closer glance revealed scenes a Boucher would not dare to flaunt. The sound of a Mozart concerto tinkled from a room somewhere in the back of the house. Camelias bloomed in silver vases. There was a reflecting pool in the interior courtyard that gleamed with the light of candles that floated by on lilypads. It was extravagant and overdone, it teetered on the edge of the ridiculous, and Tavish admired it immensely for its knowing cheek.

And as Fleur Ganay rustled to meet him, gowned in green silk trimmed with black lace, with only a single spray of diamonds in her hair, he saw in a moment why she had been able to rise from a "flower girl" on Wall Street—those pretty young girls, some as young as fourteen, who sold flowers to the men in their offices and offered other favors, as well—to the madam of the finest house in the city. It wasn't just her beauty—her thick brown hair with a sheen of copper, her large liquid-brown eyes, or even the lush pale skin that brought thick English cream to Tavish's mind in a rare rush of homesickness; it was the mysterious conveyance of absolute elegance with the hint of absolute eroticism this woman projected, should a man be lucky enough to be allowed to explore it. It was said she took no clients anymore, though she could not be older than forty and looked ten years younger.

"I'm glad to meet you, Mr. Finn. Perhaps the private parlor is in order," Fleur Ganay said. "I have some very good Madeira."

Tavish bowed. "I would be delighted, Mrs. Ganay."

He followed her down the purple-carpeted hall past several sitting rooms, one of which was filled with gentlemen with glasses of brandy in their hands who were laughing uproariously at some joke. Beautifully gowned women laughed along with them, leaning over to relight cigars and refill brandy glasses. A tall golden-haired beauty said something quietly, and the men burst into loud laughter again. Mrs. Ganay's girls were known for their wit as well as their inventiveness upstairs.

Tavish was led to the rear to a small, exquisite room paneled in painted wood. The colors were shades of rose and soft blue, the cornices and wainscoting were gilded, and Tiffany-shaded lamps in red and pink cast a lovely glow. Fleur Ganay's perfect skin appeared even more ravishing in the light.

"Please sit down, Mr. Finn," she said as a butler appeared with a tray holding a crystal decanter and two glasses.

Tavish sat on the blue damask couch next to her. They exchanged pleasantries while she poured the sherry.

After a few sips, she put down her glass purposefully. "Mr. Van Cormandt feels that we may be able to help each other, Mr. Finn."

Tavish nodded. "He came to you when he was blackmailed, he said. And you suggested that you might know who was behind it."

"I don't know, Mr. Finn, but I do suspect. His letter, the method of payment, is remarkably similiar to . . . something I'm familiar with. But perhaps you can tell me what your interest is in this."

Tavish had already decided upon seeing her that he would resort to the practice he was most unfamiliar with: honesty. He knew that Fleur Ganay would not settle for less and just might throw him out on the street should he toy with her.

"I'm tracing the members of a blind trust that operates in California under the name of the Pacific Improvement Company. While trying to find the members, I keep running into something odd on the fringes—blackmail. And the reason for blackmail usually has its origin in a house such as yours—someone has informed on the victim, you see. I've found one too many coincidences for comfort. So, I've finally given in. Instead of conducting my investigation on Wall Street, I've finally realized I should do it in, shall we say, more pleasant surroundings."

Fleur Ganay inclined her head.

"When Ned Van Cormandt told me that you were willing to

speak to me, I was very glad. I've tried to talk to several girls around town, but I'm afraid they were uncooperative. You see, an acquaintance of mine is in a society that offers aid to such girls, and I went there first for information."

Fleur Ganay smiled. "You speak of Mrs. Nash?"

"Yes. I suppose she wouldn't be a friend of yours, Mrs. Ganay."

"I wouldn't say that, Mr. Finn. More sherry? No, I would say that in a strange way, Mrs. Nash and I are on the same side. I do not exploit my girls, Mr. Finn. Why should I, since I started just as they did? I give them a beautiful house and beautiful clothes, I bank their money, and if they choose to leave I let them go with their money—with interest—unless, of course, they go to another house. I've always taken great pride in that, Mr. Finn. Better they should find their way here than in some den on Greene Street. But lately things have changed." Her eyes glinted, and Tavish caught sight of something there. It reminded him of the look on Artemis Hinkle's face—the look of someone who has had enough, who has faced a wall and spun around to face his attacker and make a last stand.

"Yes, Mrs. Ganay?"

"I started this house with a loan from a friend, which I paid back with interest in three years. Since then I have been independent. But someone threatened me with ruin if I did not pay a percentage of the house's earnings. Fifty percent, Mr. Finn. I refused, of course, and within one week I had no customers. I found that rumors had been spread concerning the health of my girls—it was said that they were all diseased. And a prominent customer, a man I've known for years, was mentioned in Colonel Mann's paper as frequenting my establishment, though he was newly married."

Tavish nodded. He knew of the notorious Colonel Mann and his paper, *Town Topics*. He had a solid network all over town composed of servants and service people who gladly traded their intimate knowledge of society folk for cash. If the unfortunate refused to pay the colonel to suppress the information, he found himself featured in the next issue. Though Colonel Mann could not print scandalous news outright, he had devised an ingenious method—the delectable tidbit would use no names, yet one had only to look at the next paragraph or across the column to find the name in a harmless social mention. It was said he had received over twenty thousand dollars from a Vanderbilt alone.

Fleur Ganay sipped at her sherry. "Within another week I had capitulated. And now every week I put money in an envelope and hand it over to a messenger boy. Even though this person has forced me to steadily raise prices, my girls don't see the profits, nor do I. When Ned came to me with his problem and showed me his letter, I was very distressed, indeed. For this goes beyond intimidation—I am paying my percentage—and it means that my house is being used as some kind of conduit to blackmail. I have always been very scrupulous with regard to my girls. I demand integrity. A man must feel safe in a house. Now girls are sent to me, and I must take them. And I find that they inform on my customers. I've had enough. So I told Ned I would talk with you."

"Your clients, Mrs. Ganay—they're from the cream of society, the Old Guard primarily?"

"Oh, yes."

"So this man was able to spread his rumor through that society."

"I see what you mean, Mr. Finn. He would have to be one of them himself, wouldn't he?" Fleur Ganay's eyes widened. "He would have to be a gentleman."

"Exactly." Tavish frowned, thinking hard. Something had tickled at his brain, something he'd not thought important at the time. What had Columbine been telling him about the new problems of her girls? Something about paying more for sheets . . .

Could it be, he thought, horrified. He was almost tempted to laugh at the perverse audacity of it. *A brothel trust?*

"Mrs. Ganay," he started cautiously, "has by any chance this unknown person insisted that you charge more for board and linens? Or insisted on your dismissing girls should they get sick or in trouble?"

"Yes, it is abominable, a great trial to me." Fleur Ganay looked at him with new interest. "How did you know this?"

"Because those other girls I talked to—through Mrs. Nash—

have been complaining about the same thing. So that means that other houses have been blackmailed, just as you have. And they are all steadily raising their prices."

"So someone is making a great deal of money," Mrs. Ganay said grimly. "But I think I know his weakness, Mr. Finn. He is greedy. He is pushing us too far, and our girls. The latest demand is that I turn over the girls' incomes to him to bank. I have resisted for weeks, put him off. This is something I cannot do! What if those savings, small as they are now with these new charges, should disappear? I shouldn't be able to face my girls, or myself. Already things have gone too far. This house depends on laughter, on gaiety. Soon the girls will not be able to conceal their anxiety and worry. Even the price of abortions has risen through the roof! Oh, I'm so sorry, Mr. Finn, I forgot myself. I apologize for distressing you—"

Trying to hide his excitement, Tavish sat forward. He hadn't been offended; suddenly, a light had appeared. "Abortionists," he murmured. Mrs. Usenko. Claude's messenger boy had gone to her door. What if the money mentioned hadn't been to pay for services rendered? What if it wasn't a bill for Claude to pay but a percentage of the profits Mrs. Usenko would have to pay to Claude? Tavish put down his sherry glass, almost dashing it to the floor in his excitement.

"That's quite all right, Mrs. Ganay," he said quickly. "I'm not distressed at all. By the way, did you say whether your tormentor has a name?"

"Oh, I didn't mention it. A Mr. Dargent, he calls himself."

"And you've never met him."

"No. I've never seen him. Only one of my girls has."

Shock snapped Tavish's spine straight. "Someone here? Who? May I speak to her?"

Fleur Ganay fluttered a hand. "Oh, the girl disappeared long ago. She was recruited by Mr. Dargent. Apparently she was fired from her job and wound up on Wall Street as a flower girl. That's where he found her. He sent her to me. I found out later that she had agreed to give him part of her earnings under the table. That was his entree into my house. I don't know if he forced her, or if he was her lover, but she did tell him how the house was run. Eventually, she left—just disappeared one day—and Mr. Dargent offered me his 'proposition.' I suppose he missed her earnings and got a taste of what money he could make. You know the rest."

"You have no idea where this girl has gone?"

"None at all. She didn't stay in New York, that I know. I would have heard, somehow, were she at another house. She was very pretty," she mused. "Smart as a whip, but there was a kind of shining innocence in her eyes that she never lost. Some clients pay well for that."

"And her name? Do you remember?"

"I remember all my girls, Mr. Finn. Her name was Annie O'Day."

Tavish made a mental note of the name. "Tell me, Mrs. Ganay. Have you a client by the name of Claude Statton?"

She gave a sour smile. "I'm afraid my girls are too sophisticated for Mr. Statton. He was here once or twice, but not for years. I believe he frequents Irene Trimble's." She sniffed. "Her girls are young and depraved, an enticing combination."

"Young?"

"Well, young-looking, at least. There are some men, Mr. Finn, who enjoy girls who have not passed into womanhood. Is there something about Mr. Statton I should know, Mr. Finn?"

"No," Tavish said. *Darcy*, his heart cried. To be allied to such a man. "Nothing at all. May I have another glass of that excellent Madeira?"

Tavish waited underneath a large oak in the park. He tried not to look at his watch more than once every five minutes. She would come, he told himself. Somehow, she would manage. He had taken a risk by leaving a message at her house, but he had checked to make sure Claude was downtown first. Tavish looked at his watch again.

He was in a mess, that was certain. He wasn't sure enough that Claude was Dargent to tell Darcy. But he had to tell her he suspected him. If Claude wasn't the man himself, he was surely involved up to his neck. He could have committed the murder in San Francisco—Edward had told him that Claude was in Boston for three straight weeks in January. It would have been difficult, but it was possible. He knew it was foolish, he knew he was letting his heart lead him, but he had to warn Darcy.

He looked up and he saw her. She was heading down the snow-banked path, her hands hidden in her muff, her cheeks aglow with the exercise. Her coat was plum-colored trimmed with dark fur, and a dark green dress hung beneath it. She hadn't seen him yet, and then he moved out of the shadow of the tree and she recognized him. A slight scamper to her step was instantly corrected back to her ladylike pace, but then she gave in. With a grin, she grabbed her skirts and ran toward him.

Tavish's heart squeezed with something like pain and something close to joy. As he watched her run toward him, he looked truth in the face. He loved her. He knew the feeling for what it was, though he had never felt it. It was like the first taste of champagne his father had given him, festive and bubbling on his lips and in his throat, surprising him, then a cold draft that slid into his belly and changed, warmed and glowed and spread out through his body to his fingertips.

It shook him to the core. He had never been so shaken. It was inconvenient to say the least. It was mad. To fall in love with the wife of your enemy! Bad enough when he'd thought himself merely attracted. This would weaken him, it would tempt him toward mistakes. It could ruin him.

Closer now, she saw his expression and her steps slowed. A question rose in her gray eyes. He walked toward her. He took her gloved hand in his and remembered how he'd held it at the Van Cormandts'. The feeling had started then, though he hadn't been able to put a name to it. Now that he had, he knew he was lost. His heart beat furiously in fear, but he managed a smile.

"I'm glad you could come," he said.

"I had to come."

"We need to talk privately. May I take you somewhere where you won't be known? It's not far."

"Where?"

"It's a place where no one will see us and we'll have a room in which to be alone."

"I don't understand . . ." Understanding grew in her eyes, and her mouth opened in surprise. "Adelle has told me that such places exist, but I hardly believed her."

"They exist. And many women such as yourself use them. But that's not why I thought of it." He pressed her hand. "We need to talk, Darcy. Only talk. And it was the only place I could think of. We could be seen if we traveled down to Columbine's or went to a restaurant. I would not want to see you in Colonel Mann's paper, or to have Claude hear of our meeting. This will be safe, I assure you. I'm sorry that there is no better place, but—"

She put a gloved hand on his lips. "Let's go."

He hadn't expected to feel so awkward, but he did. He hadn't expected to feel so tender—but he did. Darcy seemed perfectly at ease, interested, really, in the fine furnishings, the privacy, of the house of assignation on the west side of Central Park. Tavish had heard of the house from Ned Van Cormandt, and he suspected that Ned had taken Columbine there. But he didn't want to know that.

He told her everything he'd learned. He left out only Jamie's death; he didn't want her to panic, and he had no way of linking Claude to the murder. Darcy listened, her face growing paler and paler. But she said nothing. After he'd finished, she went to the window and stared out for several minutes. He did not try to console her. He waited uncomfortably on the sofa, his hands dangling uselessly in front of him.

"If you feel," he said, "that your husband could not possibly be involved, I will listen."

Darcy didn't turn. "Oh, he is involved," she said softly. "I saw copies of Dargent's letters in his files."

Tavish looked up. "Letters addressed to Claude? Or copies of letters to others?"

"I don't know. I only noted the name in passing."

Staring at her straight back, he let out a long breath. "Darcy," he said gently, "it looks bad. But there is still a chance that Claude isn't—"

She halted him by lifting one hand aimlessly, then dropping it again. Again, she said nothing for long minutes. Then she turned to face him. "Yes, we don't know if he's Dargent. But we both know he's involved if he knows the man. Tavish, I've been reflecting on the fact that this information does not surprise me. I feel no need to rush to my husband's defense, I'm afraid. And I am trying to understand how I could live with a man who I could learn such things about and *not* be surprised. I feel implicated in his crimes."

"That's absurd. You did your duty as a wife. Once you married, you had to carry on."

She looked beyond him, her gaze far away. "Did I?" She hugged herself and shivered. "That's what I've been thinking, Tavish—Did I? I've lived my life with Claude in a certain accepting fashion, an inexorable obedience to the way things are. I never acted. I was only acted upon. And I put my trust in the things that I was told to put my trust in—my position, my husband, society. The great Snow name. Who to call on, and who to snub. You might be surprised to hear that I was not always this way."

"No, love," Tavish said. "I would not."

It was as though she didn't hear him. One corner of her mouth lifted in a grim smile. "I was a rebellious child, an impossible adolescent. And then my mother ran away. Perhaps if she hadn't I would have become a different woman. But instead I changed. I changed because I *had* to, because my father collapsed into himself. He became a stranger with dead eyes, staring, mute. I was so frightened! And so I told myself that I loved the world I knew growing up, that it was deserving of my sacrifice. I forgot that every step of the way I had chafed against it. But my father took to his bed and I opened my arms and embraced every convention I had scorned. I had to keep things going, and to do that I had to forget the way I had been. I had to keep believing in that world to keep everything from flying apart."

She seemed to be pleading with him to understand. And of course he did. "Yes," he said. "Certainly you did."

"I never examined the trust I invested in my world. I never wondered, I never deviated from the path. Marrying Claude kept my feet on it. I've been such a fool."

"No—"

"A silly, blind fool," she said bitterly. "I've been a dray horse, pulling my cart, following my same route, day after day after day, never altering, never faltering, never even looking down an unfamiliar street. And now I see the depths and heights of my blindness. Of what I've missed," she whispered.

He looked at his hands, at the bed, at the window, for he could not bear to look at her and see unhappiness. "I'm sorry I've caused you such pain."

Then, surprising him, she ran to him. She knelt in front of him, and when he looked in her face she was smiling through her tears. "No, no, Tavish, don't you see that you've saved me? I'm glad to see it all crumble to dust. I'm glad to wake up—at least I have at last! I can look down that unfamiliar street, I can take my chances and walk down it. And the intoxicating thing, the amazing thing, Tavish, is that *I am not afraid*."

"I love you." He hadn't meant to say it. He blurted it out, and the sound of the words pleased him. He touched her face and said them more gently. "I love you."

"And I you. And Tavish, oh, my love, isn't it a miracle that we should find each other?"

He kissed her then, and before long his arms were around her, insistent and urgent. He felt desire flood him, and he had to break away. He stood and put out a hand to bring her to her feet. "I'll walk you to the park. You'll be all right walking home from there?"

She took his hand but made no move to rise. "But I don't want to go," she said softly, still kneeling in front of him. "Don't you understand what I'm trying to say, Tavish?" In a gesture so tender it broke his heart, she kissed his fingertips.

"Stay with me," she whispered. "Show me, help me, don't leave me. I'm ready to leave it all behind, I'm ready. Oh, Tavish, let's stay and love one another."

He had to pull away, for her words inflamed him so that he wasn't capable of thinking. He crouched beside her and put his hands on her shoulders. "Darcy. Do you know what you're saying?"

She nodded, her eyes huge in a face ecstatic with emotion. She put her hands on his face. "Don't you see, my love? Now I have something to believe in."

Eight

VIRTUE. MODESTY. DUTY. They were bonds she'd accepted without question. She'd never asked what they meant; she'd swallowed the explanations whole and washed them down with fine champagne to aid her forgetting that she had a mind with which to draw her own conclusions. Duty had meant marrying Claude. Virtue had meant coming to that marriage without knowing one single detail of what awaited her—what else could she do, then, but accept her husband's perversions as natural? And then when she slowly realized that other women did not have to suffer this way, modesty had meant not confiding her anguish to anyone.

Now, some force within was unshackling those bonds she'd believed necessary to hold her together. When she reached for Tavish she reached for her own duty, her own virtue, and she left modesty behind forever.

He brought her up to stand next to him. He looked for a long time in her eyes, and then he put his arms around her and drew her to him, his face grave. He kissed her. It was a slow, gentle kiss, and she felt herself warming, fluttering underneath him like the wings of a bird. Her mouth opened, she leaned into him, and he groaned suddenly and drew her closer. She came up against the hardness of him.

Unexpectedly, she laughed.

Tavish pulled away and frowned down at her through hooded lids, half-amused. "Am I so ridiculous, my love?"

"No," she said, shaking her head, smiling. "It's me. It's just that—I didn't know. I didn't know about this."

Awareness, then surprise, crossed his face. Then he grinned. "Good," he growled, satisfied, and bent his head to kiss her again. "Good."

"Good," she murmured, her mouth opening for the warm taste of him again.

They kissed, standing, close up against each other, murmuring and laughing and running their hands over each other with a freedom she had never dreamed possible between a man and a woman. She was afraid, but she forced herself to go on, and soon, before she was aware, she was in bed and her clothes were on the floor next to her.

The air was warm and sultry from the fire blazing in the hearth. The bed was wide and warm, the sheets soft against her nakedness. She had a brief flash of contentment as she stretched luxuriously, but then he slid in beside her and she saw him naked. He seemed too big, his masculinity arching toward her insistently. Seeing her fear, Tavish touched her face gently.

"I love you," he said.

"Good," she said. "Because I'm rather frightened at the moment."

He laughed and took her in his arms, and he was patient. He curbed his urgency. His touch was delicate, sure, as he roamed her body, and he brought her forward again and again to meet him with a slow deliberateness. His love held no room for shame, and he would not let her hide or retreat. Time and again he pushed the sheet back to uncover her or forced her to look in his eyes. She felt his love overtake her like a wave and spin her forward into the unknown, and then he was there, with her, in her, around her, and as suddenly as it had come, her fear went away.

"You can't go back," he said.

"I must."

He lay behind her, cradling her against him. Her luminous skin was tinged pink from the light of the setting sun. He traced the ridges of her spine with his fingertip. Steel, her spine was.

Too stubborn by half, she was. He hugged her tight, closing his eyes and burying his face in her scented ebony hair. "I won't let you go."

"But I must go back. You need me to go back, Tavish Finn, though you will not admit it. I got into Claude's private office once. I can do it again. And I know where he keeps the key to his cabinet now."

Horrified, he sat up, dislodging her from his arms. "No. Darcy, promise me you won't attempt such a thing. Let me handle this. I can't let you put yourself in danger—"

"Danger?" She sat up next to him, holding the sheet against her. "But I'm in no danger. Claude is my husband. What can he do? I can find evidence for you of Claude's crimes. I can look at those Dargent letters again. If it's true what he's done, how can I not?"

He was already shaking his head. "Darcy, please leave it to me, love. Promise me. I'm very close. If I can find the woman who Dargent recruited, she can identify the man."

"But she disappeared, you said."

"Nobody can disappear completely. Believe me, I know. The past has a way of following you."

Darcy shivered. "I suppose you're right. But, oh, I don't want that to be true." She put her hand on his arm. "I don't want my past to follow me. That's why I must go back. I must be free of him, my family must be free of him, once and for all."

"Your family?" Tavish twisted around to look her full in the face. "What haven't you told me?"

"I only meant that—"

He pinned her down with his keen glance. "Something about Edward."

Darcy pressed back against the pillows. "No, I—"

"Here I've told you everything, and you're holding back something from me."

She raised an eyebrow. "You've told me everything?"

Tavish frowned. "There are things you shouldn't know, don't need to know. I'm trying to protect you, my love. But you cannot hold something back from me—it could be important. Has Claude actually threatened Edward?"

"Yes," Darcy said reluctantly. "He is blackmailing him. I over-heard them talking."

"So at last he does the job himself," Tavish murmured. When he saw Darcy looking at him quizzically, he said, "I suspected Claude had a hold over Edward. There was something in your father's eyes . . . What hold does Claude have over him? Saints above, does every man in New York have a sordid past?"

"Edward doesn't have a sordid past! It's something . . . I can-not tell you what it is, it isn't right for me to tell you, and it doesn't affect your investigation."

Tavish hesitated, then sighed. "All right. But do you know how your—how Claude found out about whatever it is?"

"A parlormaid saw something she shouldn't, that's all."

"No brothel involved?"

"Brothel?" Darcy looked at him curiously. "No. Why?"

"No reason, darlin'."

"Mmmmm." Darcy reached for her clothes. "I should be going. The sun is almost down."

Tavish watched her for a moment as she untangled piles of underclothing. He enjoyed her feminine frown as she shook out her lace and grimaced at a tiny button he had torn off. He rev-eled in the intimacy of watching her in such a private ritual. Then he thought about where she was going, to whom she was going, and he felt as though he'd suffered a blow.

He stood up and strode across the room toward his trousers. He stepped into them, then sat on the end of the bed and ran his fingers through his hair.

Darcy held her clothes against her. "What is it, Tavish?"

"Don't you see," he said woodenly. "Don't you see why I can't let you go back there? I can't think of it."

Slowly, his meaning sank in, and she let out a long breath. Darcy knew she must be careful. To her, Claude had shrunk to nothing, he was no longer important. He had given up all rights to her loyalty through his cruelty to her and her father. But Tavish didn't—couldn't—see her husband as unimportant in that way. Not when she was returning to live with him.

She moved toward him. She pressed against his bare back and slipped her arms around him. "I have never been touched before

110

today, Tavish," she whispered. "I have never touched. I have never been kissed before today. I have never kissed. I have never been loved before today. And I have never loved. You have changed my life utterly, and nothing has meaning right now but you."

With a groan, he turned to her and pressed her against the rumpled bed. He found her mouth again, and this time he took her with desperation. There was little of the tenderness of discovery that had existed before. Darcy understood the need, and matched it, for she wanted to possess him, too, and be possessed. And together as they moved and sighed and wound strong fingers around each other, not letting go, never letting go, they forgot the white marble mansion ten blocks south, splashed crimson in the rays of the setting sun.

Darcy was relieved to find that Claude had sent a message home that he'd be delayed, for she walked in the house a brazen woman. She even smiled at dour Tolliver, the butler, as she whirled past him toward her room. If Claude had been there, he would have known. He would have known she'd been with a man, for she knew how it showed.

Walking back down Fifth Avenue, she had looked at the houses and the streetcars and carriages, and she had marveled at the change. Now she knew that there had always been an undercurrent going on beneath the placid, sunlit surface of her world. It was sex; after today she could think of no euphemism. The undercurrent ran, steady and sure, tossing some, pulling others out of the main stream, drowning still more who tried to fight. The trick was, Darcy thought as she entered her room and removed her hat with trembling fingers, to swim with it. To keep your head above the waves.

She'd thought she'd known about marital relations, but she'd known nothing. Now she knew a strong pull of yearning that was no ladylike melancholy but a swift tide in her blood that ran with the moon. All those vague, puzzling feelings at the Van Cormandts' had coalesced into this. They were concrete, after all: they had an object. They had a home.

Tavish. Darcy stared at her glowing face in the mirror and touched her lips with her fingers. She saw the blush on her cheeks as she remembered the things she had allowed him to do, the things she had done herself, wanting to do them. To hold that masculinity inside her, to feel it arch against her, to arch against it and curl around it and welcome it with wetness and warmth. To gaze with eyes that were not veiled with false modesty but naked, hot with truth.

If this went on, if other people did these things—and Tavish had assured her, laughing, that they did—how did the world go on? How did people move, and speak, and work, when there was this to be explored?

Oh, now she understood husbands and wives, the satisfaction on some faces, the bitterness on others, the wide eyes of a newly married bride following her husband around the room, the pressed lips of the older settled women who watched her, some with jealousy in their hearts, others with recognition. She understood the women who went astray, and she understood her mother. She would never think of her as poor or sad again.

Something ticked inside her now. As she dressed for dinner that night, she looked at a new face, so rosy with hope she had to keep turning away from Solange to hide it. She went to a dinner at the Cornelius Vanderbilts', she sat through the nine courses—the oysters, the soup, the mousse de jambon, the terrapin, the asparagus, the canvasback, the sorbet, the salad, the cheese and fruit—in a dream. She went to the opera, she rode home in the carriage with Claude. She did it all, she followed every rule of her former life, but inside she knew that her heart had broken every rule, and she didn't care. Claude was silent, but that was usual; he didn't care for talk at the end of an evening. When they reached the house, she climbed out of the carriage and tilted her head back to look at the dark sky. Tomorrow, she would see Tavish again. They would meet at Columbine's.

Claude surprised her the next day by appearing in the downstairs salon where she sat in the mornings. Darcy put down the menu plan she was working on.

"Claude, I thought you'd left."

"I decided to stay home today, my dear," he said, walking over and pressing his lips against her forehead. "I went early to the office, as is my custom, but I brought work back with me."

"I see. Are you feeling poorly?"

"No, of course not. Dr. Arbuthnot thought it would be better if I stayed close to home for a few days."

Darcy sighed. Once this would have frightened her. Now she merely felt irritated, tired of the constant allusion to her delicate nerves. Before, there had been a nagging doubt in her mind that Claude was somehow right, that her melancholy arose from some defect in herself. But that doubt was gone forever. Tavish Finn had blown through her life like a sharp, fresh wind. She knew now that she wasn't delicate in the least.

"I suppose you will, despite any assurances I might make," she said, picking up the menu plan again.

"Have you been taking the tonic?"

She'd completely forgotten about the tonic. "I've felt so much better since the doctor came that I—"

Claude was already ringing the bell. He directed the servant to fetch Solange. Then he began to pace. "You see why I need to stay close to you. You cannot follow the simplest of directions. I will surely inform Dr. Arbuthnot of this. And I think it would be best if you rested at home until he comes on Friday."

"Claude, that's ridiculous. I will take the tonic, but I have calls to make, social obligations to meet. I cannot remain at home. The season is in full swing. Mrs. Astor called two days ago, and I must leave my card. And we dined at the Rhinelanders' last week. You know I must call on them as well." She knew how important their social position was to Claude; reminders of duty would most likely change his mind.

"You can send round your cards, Darcy. That is enough." He stood by her chair, his hand a steel claw on her shoulder. "I must insist, my dear."

Solange entered, and Claude directed her for Darcy's tonic. It was her duty to remind her mistress from now on, he said, to bring her the tonic at the times indicated by Dr. Arbuthnot. They sat in silence, waiting for the maid's return, and Darcy dutifully swallowed the double dose Claude insisted upon as he stood over her. It tasted sweet, and it burned all the way down her throat. But it left a pleasant warmth behind.

Claude sat back down to frown over the correspondence he'd brought with him. After long minutes had passed, Darcy began to feel more cheerful, more relaxed. Surely he couldn't lock her up in the house. She'd find a way somehow to get out. He couldn't forbid her a drive in the park. Wasn't that what Dr. Arbuthnot himself had prescribed?

And then salvation came in the form of Adelle's card on a silver tray. She was there in person, waiting to be received.

Claude frowned. "This is not the day you're at home."

"I know." Darcy stood up. "But I must receive my cousin. Show her into the drawing room, Tolliver."

"No. Show her in here," Claude ordered.

So he would not even let her see Adelle alone. Darcy sat back down. Adelle rustled in a few minutes later. She greeted Claude, and then her eyes swept Darcy's morning gown.

"But you're not dressed to go out."

"Go out? But where am I going, Adelle?"

"Sakes alive, Darcy Statton, don't you remember you're to pay a call with me today? You promised—and not only that, you *must*. I know William Archer isn't a blood relative, but I am related by marriage, and I have to call on his fiancé. She's sitting there in that huge house, all alone—no relatives on *that* side, so she'll be depending on William's. I know it's tiresome, but you *did* promise."

"Oh, Adelle, of course I did." Darcy made an effort to concentrate. Like the tonic, the engagement had completely flown out of her mind, but she remembered now that she had promised Adelle last week. How fortuitous this was. "I'm so sorry I'm not ready, but it will take me only a moment. Have a cup of tea with Claude, and I'll be right back down."

"Now, Darcy, I don't know," Claude said. "You said you would stay home today, my dear."

"Don't be silly, Claude. She's not staying home, she's going with me. It's a family obligation." The green feathers on her gay little hat quivering, Adelle sat down with the air of a person in the right. "And she promised," she said to Claude, as though that settled it.

"Well, if you take our carriage and come right back here with her. No shopping at A. T. Stewarts or tea at Sherry's. Will you give me your promise, Adelle? Darcy hasn't been well."

"I promise faithfully, Claude, I will deliver your wife back to your doorstep immediately after the call," Adelle said solemnly. "But I came in my carriage, and we will take it."

Claude wasn't satisfied, but he nodded; he wouldn't risk offending Adelle by suggesting Darcy should travel in something more stately than Adelle's bright canary carriage with the maroon upholstery.

Smiling to herself, Darcy left the room quickly. Solange helped her into her new ruby velvet dress with an underskirt of the palest pink. It had a matching coat with a fur cape and muff, and she turned in front of the mirror for a last look. Her cheeks were a bit pale, and she pinched them for color.

Adelle rose as soon as Darcy entered the room. "Darcy certainly looks very well to me," she said, rising and holding out a hand to Claude. "Come along, Darcy."

The sun outside was very bright. Darcy faltered for a moment and pressed her hand to her forehead.

"Are you all right, dear?" Adelle said by her elbow. "Don't tell me that Claude had reason for concern. I thought he was just being fussy."

The momentary dizziness cleared. "It was just the sun. It's very bright today." Darcy climbed into the carriage and sank gratefully into the leather seat. It was warm and comfortable inside from sitting in a pool of sunlight.

Perhaps it was the sleepless night spent thinking of Tavish. Perhaps it was the result of dressing so hurriedly. Perhaps it was the effort of trying to figure out how, after they paid the call, she'd be able to get away from Adelle without too many questions. But she suddenly felt rather drowsy. Darcy leaned back and closed her eyes.

Adelle wasn't at all put out when Darcy fell asleep, but she did poke her rather sharply in the ribs when they were ushered into Julia Hinkle's parlor. She shot Darcy a warning look that told her to wake up and join the conversation. They had fifteen minutes to talk about the weather and social happenings around town—excluding any gossip, of course—and perhaps a word or two about the wedding plans.

"I was so glad to hear about you and William," Darcy said.

"Are you enjoying New York, Miss Hinkle?" Adelle asked.

"If I were not, you could hardly expect me to own up to it," Julia Hinkle said. Her hazel eyes had a gleam of sharp intelligence in them, and her thick coiled hair gleamed. She had an hourglass figure, fashionably plump, and was beautifully dressed in dove-gray peau de soie with pink roses embroidered on the bodice and along the scalloped skirt. Valenciennes lace trimmed the sleeves and neckline. "I know how New Yorkers are about their city. Still, I can honestly say that I *am* enjoying the bustle of New York. My father is homesick for San Francisco, though, I fear."

"I hear it's a lovely city," Darcy said. "I'd like to see it someday."

"It is so very beautiful. I think you would enjoy it, Mrs. Statton, for I cannot imagine anyone not admiring its beauty—the blue bay and the golden hills. That is to say, if you survive the train trip there," Julia said, her lips quirking upward with a hint of mischief. "We had a private car, but it was still quite grim. We were stuck for a day and a half in a snowstorm on the way. I did not know what would have been worse—to take my chances in the elements, or be cooped up with my father. Ladies, there were wild bears outside, but inside was no safer when my father began to run low on cigars."

Darcy laughed, an uncommon occurrence at a morning call. She thought Willie Archer was doing well for himself, despite the talk about his "Wild West girl."

"I hope the snow is behind us this year," she said. "Spring feels just around the corner."

"Yes, tomorrow is the first of March," Adelle said. "Your stepmother was unable to make the trip, I understand, Miss Hinkle."

The good humor on Julia Hinkle's face flickered for an instant. "She has been ill, and we thought it better that she not make the trip," she said. "I miss her, especially at such a time."

"I expect that you do," Adelle murmured. The admittance of an emotion was also an unusual occurrence at a morning call. Perhaps to change the subject, Adelle pointed to a painting over the fireplace. "Is that her likeness?"

"Yes. It's quite a good one, actually."

Darcy looked at the portrait. It was an unusual one; all the society portraits Darcy had seen—such as the one of Mrs. Astor that she received under—relied on the richness of dress and the magnificence of jewels to convey the importance of their subject. But the woman in this painting was not wearing a single jewel— only a plain gold wedding band. She was dressed in a simple and rather shocking Oriental robe of butter-yellow satin. She was slim, and her vivid flaming hair was piled high, making her seem very tall. She held a closed-up scarlet fan negligently in one drooping hand. Serene blue eyes stared out into the middle distance with a kind of innocence belied by the sophisticated trappings.

"She's very beautiful." Darcy looked closer at the portrait. It was strange, but the woman seemed familiar somehow. "What is your stepmother's maiden name, Miss Hinkle?"

An odd request, almost rude. Julia looked surprised. "Anne Madison."

"When the weather is nicer, you must walk over the Brooklyn Bridge," Adelle said. "I assure you . . ."

Darcy didn't hear the rest of Adelle's chatter, for her attention was riveted on the portrait. She blinked and swayed, suddenly realizing that the room was uncomfortably warm. She found it difficult to concentrate. She'd never met an Anne Hinkle or an Anne Madison, but the elegant woman teased her memory. Perhaps she had called on her mother. It was on the tip of her tongue to ask if Anne Hinkle had ever visited New York, but then Adelle was rising, giving Julia her hand, and Darcy had to rise, too. The visit was over. Darcy's head felt a bit woozy, and she hoped the chill air would clear it.

She took deep breaths of it unobtrusively as they passed through the porte cochere into the carriage. "Well," Adelle said, "I must say I don't know what to make of her. Willie is crazy about her, his mother says. I wonder what John would have thought, if he'd been alive; he was always so fond of his cousin. Now I must take you back home to your husband, Darcy. Perhaps you should lie down and rest when you get there. I suppose my company isn't very stimulating, but I would think you'd manage not to yawn."

The carriage began to jounce down Fifth Avenue. "You always wake me up, Adelle," Darcy said, making an effort to sound brisk. "As a matter of fact, I feel so much better that I'd like to walk home."

Adelle shook her head. "Oh, no. I promised Claude I would bring you home directly."

"But we're so close—I have only five blocks to walk, Adelle. And it's such a fine day. Don't concern yourself, I'll explain to Claude."

Adelle shook her head more firmly. "I would not for the world bring the wrath of your husband down upon my head."

"Adelle, really, I—"

Darcy faltered as Adelle turned to her, her small dark eyes suddenly shrewd. She gave Darcy a sweeping glance that caused color to stain her cheeks. Then she turned front again.

"Honestly, Darcy, you must think I don't have two eyes in my head."

"I don't know what you mean—"

"I would think you would feel free to confide in me. You saw me through the worst of it when John died, and I would do anything for you. Don't think I haven't heard the rumors Cora Van Cormandt is spreading."

"Cora? What kind of rumors?"

Fussily, Adelle began to adjust her gloves, finger by finger. "Now, I don't want to cast stones, understand me. Nobody knows better than I do what you've had to endure. And don't I know that Cora Van Cormandt was using your little indiscretion to cover her glaring one with Ambrose Hartley. It was the only way she could divert the rest of the house party, let alone her best friend Maud Valentine, from what was going on."

"What are you saying?" Darcy whispered.

"You and that Mr. Finn, of course. He is *very* handsome, I

admit. But really, Darcy, if half of what Cora Van Cormandt says is true—the looks, the walks, the interrupted kiss—"

"Interrupted kiss!"

"Oh, that was fabricated, was it? Well. It doesn't matter."

Darcy found herself speechless. She realized that her overriding emotion wasn't shame. It was anger. She stared ahead stonily.

Adelle looked at her uneasily. Then she patted her knee. "Don't fret, dear. Everything will be forgotten next week. Now, where would you like me to drop you right now?"

Darcy felt emotion flood her. Adelle was so kind; she'd had a friend here all along. "Twenty-third Street," she whispered.

Adelle informed the driver, then turned to her. "I'll drop you, and then take the carriage back to my house and wait for you. I must insist, Darcy. I must bring you home. I'll give you two hours, no more. It will not do to inflame Claude, especially now."

"Yes. I'll be there in two hours."

"I'll say Aunt Catherine asked to see you. Surely he won't object to that," Adelle said decidedly. Then she pressed her mouth firmly shut until they reached Twenty-third Street. Never before had she stayed silent for so long in Darcy's presence.

Darcy pressed Adelle's hand and thanked her with her eyes as the carriage pulled over. Holding her skirt with one hand, she got out.

Adelle leaned out of the window. "And Darcy? Everything *will* be forgotten next week. But do be careful."

Darcy found Columbine reading *Looking Backward*, a new book by Edward Bellamy, by an indifferent fire. Her feet were up and her hair was a bit disheveled, but she rose with a warm smile.

"Hello, Mrs. Statton. I've been reading the most marvelous book. You just missed Mr. Finn. He'd been here an hour but had to leave. He'll be disappointed to have missed you."

Exhausted, disappointed herself, Darcy felt like bursting into tears. "I do wish," she blurted, "you would call me Darcy."

"Please sit down, Darcy, and please call me Columbine. You need tea. How lucky I have some here and don't have to ring for it. We would have to wait until spring for it." Columbine poured her a cup of tea and gave her a concerned look. "Are you quite all right, Mrs.—Darcy?"

"Just a bit tired. Thank you for the tea."

"It is such a pleasure to have company. Perhaps you could call on me tomorrow, Darcy, at this time. We should make a habit of it. Sometimes Mr. Finn will come by at this time, I hope you wouldn't mind that."

Darcy had wondered how much Tavish had told Columbine. Now she realized that Columbine must know something of what had happened, at least. "No, Columbine, I wouldn't mind that." She sipped her tea, then put it down. If Columbine had been taken into Tavish's confidence, then Columbine would not think it odd if she left, she reasoned. "I hope you won't think me rude, but I should be leaving. I only came to—I stopped by to thank you for your kind note. And I will come tomorrow, when I have more time." She stood up, and immediately sank down into the chair again. Her legs felt so weak!

"Mrs. Statton—Darcy, are you all right?"

"I'm fine," she murmured. "I'm so tired today, I don't know why."

"Perhaps you should consult a physician."

Darcy stood again. "Oh, I have. A Dr. Arbuthnot, he's quite well known. He's given me a clean bill of health and a tonic and told me to get plenty of fresh air. So perhaps I should."

"Yes. Yes, that will bring the color back to your face."

Columbine watched Darcy go, her brows knit. Darcy Statton did not seem like herself. It was almost as though she was in pain, though why Columbine thought that she couldn't say. Perhaps she'd been disappointed that Tavish had left. Perhaps she'd heard—or her husband had—the rumors that Ned had told her about. But why should a woman in love look so pale? Thoughtfully, she took a pencil and looked around for paper. Bell had tidied up in her usual annoyingly fastidious way, so there was none to be found. Exasperated, Columbine scrawled a name in the margin of her new book: *Arbuthnot*.

Darcy pushed on. She had enough time to get farther downtown and still make it back to Adelle's by her deadline. Why she needed to see Tavish so badly, she didn't know. It was a numbing feeling now, pushing her tired feet, anchoring her mind to the one idea that she must see him. She must tell him that it would be difficult for her to leave the house, perhaps impossible, for a few days. She headed for the Sixth Avenue El.

A train came almost immediately, and she made it downtown easily. The streets were unfamiliar, but she found the Pinkney Building near the post office easily; it was enormous. She found everything in fact, except Tavish Finn. A stone-faced federal employee told her that yes, there were some federal offices in the building, but no, there was no Interstate Commerce Commission office, and yes, he was quite sure of that. Try Washington, he said.

"The street?" Darcy asked.

"The capital, ma'am," he answered laconically, and tipped his cap and headed back up the stairs.

Darcy found herself back on the street. The information slowly filtered through her brain. He had lied to her. It seemed silly that it was all it could take, a lie. But the world she had constructed over the past few days cracked and smashed in an instant with the infusion of doubt. She kicked through the debris of her hopes and headed back toward the El. She was so tired. There was nothing to do but go home.

Nine

CLAUDE WAS UNEXPECTEDLY so kind. He interpreted her mood as exhaustion and sent her immediately to bed. He spoke to poor Adelle sharply and came close to forbidding her the house completely. Adelle left in a huff, but Darcy was too tired to care. She swallowed Dr. Arbuthnot's tonic and fell asleep, wonderfully warm, wonderfully oblivious.

The next day, Claude came to her bedside. "I'd like to cancel our engagements for the rest of the week. If you agree."

When had Claude ever asked for her agreement? He seemed uncertain, almost shy. "Yes, Claude. I think it would be best."

"The doctor is coming tomorrow to see you again." He paused. "I'll leave you alone now, Darcy." He started toward the door, then turned back. "I *am* concerned about you, my dear. I know you think me harsh at times. But it's the way I've learned to be, had to be."

"I know, Claude."

"I never wanted you to be unhappy."

Tears began to roll down her face. She nodded.

Without another word, he went out. Darcy turned her face against the pillows. Claude's stiff words seemed to have been torn from him with reluctance and made her remember his courtship. At first she had refused to consider him, despite Edward's steady pressure. She had suffered his calls with the minimum of politeness, just to keep her father happy. But one day he had come in the rain, a hard, driving January rain that had kept all other callers inside.

She had been feeling so melancholy. Edward had recovered from his breakdown enough to entertain new fears. They were close to ruin, and he knew it. Darcy had kept things going as long as she could. She'd slowly learned about finances and taken over completely, giving orders under Edward's name so that no one would suspect he was in his bed, his face to the wall. But she could hold out no longer. There was a note coming due that she could not pay.

And then Claude had arrived. But this time he did not sit, haughty and proper. He had seemed suddenly shy and yet angered at his own shyness. It was customary for him to take a great deal of care with his appearance every time he called, but that day even his care had been defeated by the wind and rain. His thinning hair was plastered to his skull, and he did not look his best.

Something that day had made them talk like never before. Claude had told her a story of his childhood in California, of when his beautiful mother, highly born, had succumbed to an illness. His father, a drunkard, had sold him. And in that story, Darcy had seen the fear of her own ruin, sitting in her comfortable house, as nothing next to the privations others could suffer. She'd known that before, of course, but never had it struck her as it had that day, looking at the damp man sitting across from her who had endured a past she could not begin to fathom for its cruelty and brutality. That day she had begun to respect Claude. That had been her undoing. Respect had led her to some small understanding, and that was enough to tip the balance in his favor. A week later, she had accepted him.

And after she married him she never saw Claude Statton vulnerable or ill at ease again.

Why today? Darcy thought, turning in bed. Had he heard the rumors, did he know that he was close to losing her? Or did he just sense her misery, and did it spark some small humanity still left in him?

She wondered where her brazen confidence had gone. Yesterday morning she had felt so sure of Tavish. It had taken so little for her faith to be shaken, but she had to be honest and admit that it was. It made her wonder how strong her faith had been in the first place, and it made her wonder if Claude was perhaps right about her strength in general.

If she weren't so dreadfully tired, she would demand an explanation, she supposed, and guard herself against that quicksilver Irish tongue. But perhaps it was better this way. Hazily, she shifted position. Everything she believed in told her that redemption was possible. Was it right for her to turn her back on Claude if he sincerely wished to change? She couldn't seem to concentrate on the question, though she knew it was important. She would think of it later. As soon as she had rested, just a bit more.

Columbine had started pacing long ago. Every now and again she would attempt to sit, do some work, pick up her book. But agitation would send her fingers tapping and her mind racing, and up she would pop again.

Where was Darcy? She should have been here an hour ago. She was beginning to suspect that she would not turn up at all. And Tavish was late as well. Could they have met somewhere else? She had to talk to Darcy. And where was Tavish?

It hadn't taken her very long to find out about the illustrious Dr. Arbuthnot. Darcy could be in great danger if she continued under that man's treatment. If she couldn't tell Darcy, she would have to tell Tavish what she'd discovered.

This failure of both of them to come seemed ominous. She had to talk to Darcy. Columbine twisted her hands together. She peered out from behind the faded velvet curtains. Where was Tavish?

Tavish smiled pleasantly and sipped his tea. He nibbled at a cake. He wanted to throw the whole mess on the floor and stamp his feet like a child, but he didn't. He was late. He only hoped Darcy could wait. He'd give Mrs. Irene Trimble's establishment five more minutes, and if something didn't happen, he'd leave. He'd been waiting for a messenger boy to pick up an envelope of money, and then he could follow the boy back downtown. Simple. except the delivery boy, who Fleur Ganay told him came every Wednesday at one, didn't come. Tavish had figured that the boy would stop by Irene Trimble's as well, since the two houses were three blocks from each other, Trimble's on Sixth Avenue. But he was wrong, obviously.

Irene Trimble's house was very different from Fleur Ganay's. The lighthearted sophistication, the cosmopolitan atmosphere, the overdone lushness of the decor of Fleur's house that winked at the visitor with a knowing good humor was here exaggerated into what Tavish thought of as the worst excesses of the times. Every square inch of the parlor was awash in crimson hangings and little gold tassels. Everything that could be gilded was gilt. There were bronze statuary and cupids galore. And Mrs. Irene Trimble herself presided over it with mountainous vulgarity.

She was a large woman, double-chinned, with skin that looked so white and baby soft that Tavish wondered when the last time was she'd been outdoors. He'd been told that she always dressed in white. Perhaps as a young girl she'd been told that she looked well in it, for the day had long gone where it had flattered. Now her elaborate white satin dress, inappropriate for midday, billowed around her short little legs and strained across her expanse of bosom. She resembled a large, tiered cake slowly melting in a heatwave. For the house was impossibly hot; if the business failed, Jay Gould could raise his famous orchids here in the parlor.

Her "little girls," as she called them, must have ranged in age from fifteen to thirty, though they all appeared to hover in that age when the hair is not yet up and the skirts are not yet down. Their manner leaned heavily on giggles and wide-eyed stares. They sat in laps and squirmed; they wore bright satin bows. They played childish pieces on the piano. Here was one brothel where a woman did not have to be accomplished in order to charm. Tavish found them sad. How could their customers miss the hard knowledge in their eyes? He also noted that, though in Fleur's house she chatted and laughed with the girls, here not one girl looked at Irene Trimble.

Here, there was only one public sitting room, where Irene

Trimble presided. This was not a house where men came to socialize, to be entertained, like Fleur Ganay's. Here, men did not use their names, only their initials. They drank their brandies quickly and eyed the girls, making their choices and disappearing. Tavish was beginning to be noticeable by lingering with Mrs. Trimble, although at least that lady seemed flattered by the attention. He had already been able to discern, by rising to walk to the mantel in order to see the hall stairs, that there were other entrances to the house. He'd heard that many men had private keys, Claude Statton among them.

Irene Trimble remained unmovable as ever on her red damask sofa. Whenever he tried to steer the conversation toward her business, she stolidly returned to the topic of weather and fashions. He would get nothing here. Tavish was bored, he was desperate to see Darcy again, and he decided it was time to shake the trees here.

He stood.

"Leaving so soon, sir?" Irene Trimble asked. "My other little girls will be down directly. They take their lessons at this time, you see."

Tavish smiled to cover his involuntary grimace. He reached in his pocket for his card case. "I've enjoyed your excellent hospitality, Mrs. Trimble. And I shall return. My card."

"Oh." This was obviously not a custom at Irene Trimble's, but she recovered quickly. Her tiny fat fingers reached out to grasp the square of white pasteboard.

Tavish bowed. "Good day, Mrs. Trimble."

"Good day, Mr.—" She squinted at the lettering. Tavish was almost to the door before she got it out. "Mr. Dargent?"

Columbine took him by the wrist and almost dragged him into the sitting room.

"You're late."

"Darcy isn't here?"

"Where *were* you?"

Tavish eyed her warily. "I don't think I'd better tell you, Columbine. I'm sorry I'm late, it was unavoidable. Did Darcy come at all?"

"No, she did not." Columbine moved across the carpet and sat down purposefully in her favorite armchair. "Tavish, I need to tell you something."

"All right." Tavish sat across from her. "Did she send a note?"

"No. Tavish, are you aware that Darcy has been seeing a doctor?"

His distracted attention immediately focused on Columbine. She knew that look in the green eyes, precise, alert, watchful.

"No," he said.

"Yesterday she seemed fatigued and pale, and somewhat—unfocused, I suppose is the only word I can come up with. There was something about her voice, her movements—I thought she might be in pain. Then last night I realized why I'd thought so. I remembered when my mother was in so much pain during her illness—"

His face was frozen, a mask. "You think she's in pain?"

"No! No, I think that there's something that's making her seem that way—"

"You think Darcy was drugged? My God, Columbine, that's impossible!"

"She said this doctor gave her a tonic. I don't think she knows, Tavish. Anyway, I—"

He got up and went to the fireplace. "It's Claude Statton, I'm sure. I'll have to warn her. She'll just have to stop taking it, that's all. You think it contains laudanum, Columbine?"

"I don't know. Tavish, listen—"

"For God's sake!" Tavish exploded. "What will that man not resort to!"

She rose swiftly and took him by the arm. "Will you listen to me! I'm not finished. This is important."

"What more?" he asked impatiently.

"She told me the name of the doctor. I wrote it down so I would remember. And this morning I paid a call on Dr. Meredith Dana, you remember my friend who just began her practice?"

"Yes, yes."

"I thought the name sounded familiar, and it was. Dr. Francis Arbuthnot is well-known for his treatment of neuranthenics. Women, primarily. And his treatment for extreme cases is . . ." Columbine hesitated.

"Columbine, for God's sake, what is it?"

"Removal of the womb."

The color drained from Tavish's face. He gripped her arm. "Columbine, you don't think . . ."

Columbine went on rapidly; she had to get it out, he had to know. "And sometimes, Meredith told me, sometimes, he does an additional procedure, for women who have shown what is thought of as unnatural passions. Tavish, I don't know how to say this, it's quite dreadfully embarrassing, but—"

Now he gripped both her elbows, forcing her to look at him. "You can tell me, Columbine. Tell me. *I must know.*"

"Meredith called it female castration," she whispered. "It is thought to have a calming effect. He calls it a cure."

Now he actually reeled. He felt the walnut mantel hit his back, and he threw out a hand to steady himself. Columbine's bowl in robin's-egg blue crashed to the floor. Neither took note of it.

Then he was moving across the floor, grabbing his hat on his way. He didn't say a word; he didn't have to.

Columbine ran after him. She grabbed his arm and pulled hard, jerking him to a stop.

His voice was expressionless. "Let me go, Columbine. I don't want to hurt you."

"Listen to me, Tavish," Columbine said rapidly. "We have to do this intelligently. You cannot run up there and expect Claude Statton to receive you."

"I'll break down his door, by God—"

"And he will send his servants and his strongmen at you, as many as it takes, and you will be vanquished. They will take you to Five Points or Hell's Kitchen and beat you senseless and leave you for dead with no one the wiser," Columbine said quietly. "But if we are smart, if we think, if we act wisely, we can reach her. I will go."

"What makes you think Claude will receive you?"

"If he is there, he may not. But no one has been instructed to keep me out, I'm sure. Claude doesn't know that Darcy came here to see me. To pay a return call is a natural thing. Once, I didn't go deliberately because I knew she had come here in secret. But if I can see her alone it will be worth his discovering that she came. Do you see? At the very least," Columbine said grimly, "no one will attack me physically." She shook his arm a bit. "It's worth a try, Tavish. Then, if I fail, you can do your best."

Tavish looked down at Columbine's fingers on his sleeve. Her hands were strong and capable. Columbine had traveled across two countries, had visited slums and brothels and shanty towns, had spoken and shouted and railed against kings and queens and presidents. She would not be afraid of Claude Statton.

"All right," he said. "Try."

"But I am expected," Columbine said to the poker-faced servant.

"Mrs. Statton is not at home," he repeated again.

Columbine thought furiously, but she knew she was beaten. She could not get past the largest footman in New York, and to go where? To run down the marble halls hollering "Darcy" up stairwells and down galleries?

Sighing, she extracted her card. She turned without another word and went through the door another servant held open. She supposed that at Claude Statton's, you needed more than one servant to answer the door.

But she wasn't beaten yet. Columbine headed down Fifth, but she turned at the corner and went to the side of the house. She knocked at the door to the kitchens.

A petite maid opened the door. She was so tiny and pretty that Columbine wondered how she handled the hard work the job entailed. She looked startled at the fineness of Columbine's appearance and unsure whether to direct her elsewhere.

"Good day," Columbine said. "I realize you must be very busy here in the kitchens, but if you'd allow me just a moment of your time. I represent the New Women Society, and we are specifically campaigning for enrollment of women like yourself." As Columbine talked, she moved. The young maid was easier to get by than the footman, that was certain. In a moment, she was almost in the kitchen.

The maid recovered quickly, however. "I'm sorry, I can't help you, ma'am."

"Oh, but I think you can, uh—" Columbine raised her eyebrows to ask for the maid's name.

"Daisy."

"Daisy," Columbine said warmly. "My name is Columbine Nash."

"Columbine Nash! Oh, of course, I've heard of you, ma'am. My mother saw you speak. She was inspired, she was."

"How kind of you to tell me. I wonder if I could trouble you for a glass of water, Daisy. I've been walking for some time, and . . ." Columbine put a hand to her forehead. "Oh, dear me, I feel a bit faint."

A surprisingly strong hand gripped her forearm. "Let me help you to the table, ma'am. You can sit a spell, and I'll get you your water."

Columbine allowed herself to be led to the kitchen table. The kitchen was busy, with cooks and assistants and scullions and maids scurrying about. Daisy gave a quick introduction to the chef, who seemed to be in charge. He nodded at her and went about his tasks busily.

A tall, dark woman in a navy-blue silk dress with white lace at the throat and wrists walked in. Her face was thin, her mouth severe. "Madame's tea," she said in a strong French accent. "I rang ten minutes ago, Mary, and—" She stopped when she saw Columbine.

The kitchen maid looked uneasy. "Yes, yes, Mademoiselle Foucard, I'm getting it. This here is a young lady who felt faint. She'll be gone in a minute."

Daisy appeared and handed Columbine a glass of water. Mademoiselle Foucard turned without a word and left the kitchen.

"Oh, dear," Daisy said, her pretty face creased with anxiety.

"Perhaps you'd better be going now, ma'am," Mary said kindly. But she looked quickly at the closed kitchen door.

"Of course," Columbine said, sipping her water slowly. She

looked from Mary to Daisy. Daisy was better dressed and seemed less nervous. She might have access to the upper floor of the house. "Daisy," she said, "I wonder if you'd do me a favor." She folded a bill around a small envelope. "I wonder if you'd give this to your mistress."

Daisy's blue eyes rounded. "Oh, I couldn't do that, ma'am."

"I would so appreciate it," Columbine said, pushing the card closer so that Daisy could see the dollar amount on the bill. "It would help your mistress, Daisy. I promise. She's acquainted with me, you see, but I'm afraid they won't let me see her upstairs."

"Well, then, I couldn't—"

The masculine voice boomed behind her. "What is this?" Columbine didn't have to turn; she knew by the scurry and flutter in the kitchen that the master had entered. Daisy placed a dishtowel on top of Columbine's note.

Columbine stood and turned, blocking the dishtowel on the bare table and praying he had not seen the envelope underneath it. Claude Statton stood in the doorway to the kitchen. His yellow eyes gleamed at her, and his mouth was pursed.

"I left my card at your door, Mr. Statton, but on my way I'm afraid I had a dizzy spell. So I found myself here. Your servants have been very kind."

"I see." His manner told her clearly that she was not welcome in the least.

"I'll be going." Columbine turned and reached for her purse and shawl. She walked out of the kitchen under Claude Statton's cold glance. She pitied Daisy and Mary and every servant in the kitchen. But most of all she pitied Darcy Statton.

But perhaps Daisy would take her courage in her hands and deliver the note. It depended on how much she hated Claude Statton—or how much she feared him, Columbine admitted. She walked back to Fifth Avenue, digging into her purse for change for a hansom cab. Her fingers closed around the small envelope she'd tried to pass to Daisy. The banknote was still wrapped around it.

"Damn," said Columbine, though she never swore. It gave suffragists such a bad name. She looked up at the fortress of a house that Claude Statton had built. Her eyes roamed the second-floor windows, pausing at a pair of French doors at a small balcony. A lace curtain flickered, and then she made out the face.

"Darcy," Columbine breathed. She raised a gloved hand to get her attention. But she stopped in the middle of the wave. Darcy had seen her, all right. But she gave no sign. She stared out, her expression inscrutable. Then she moved away and was swallowed up by the shadows of the house.

Claude stood in the doorway to her room. "You know I don't like you to stand at the window, my dear. They'd be lining up outside and charging a nickel for the privilege of watching Claude Statton's house."

"Yes, Claude."

"Get back in bed, dearest. Solange is getting your tea."

"Yes, Claude. I'm so tired."

"I know, dear. I know. But the doctor is coming tomorrow. He'll fix everything—tomorrow."

Ten

DARCY AWOKE FROM her nap slowly. It felt as though dense, heavy earth lay on top of her body, and she had to fight her way through it to consciousness. Perhaps she had dreamed she'd been buried alive, but she did not remember her dream. She licked her lips; her mouth was so dry. She opened her heavy lids and the room slowly came into focus. She was alone.

What is happening to me? she wondered groggily. No matter how she slept, she only seemed to grow more fatigued and sluggish. Was Claude right, was she really ill? Suddenly frightened, Darcy tried to rise.

"Father . . ." she murmured.

"It is only me, Madame," Solange said. Darcy hadn't even heard the door open or close. Solange approached the bed, her skirts whispering across the carpet. Her cold white hands darted out and adjusted the pillows behind Darcy's head.

"You can sleep again, Madame. But first, your dose."

Darcy tried to organize the blur of Solange's features into a face. "Solange . . ."

"Yes, Madame, it is Solange." The maid smiled. Her bared teeth were wet. They seemed to glow in the darkened room. Darcy shrank back against the pillows.

"Yes, relax, Madame." Solange drew back. The sibilant sound

of her skirts seemed loud to Darcy's ears as she moved away. She headed toward the dressing table where the tonic was kept along with the porcelain cup Darcy drank it from. Solange's thin hands curled around the bottle. She approached the bed again. Her dark green dress rustled as though she were gliding through dry weeds.

Darcy watched Solange pour the tonic into the cup. Her head felt so heavy, lolling on the pillow when she tried to hold it up. The honey color of the tonic was so beautiful in the soft light. Solange moved so slowly, so gracefully, her hands an arc of undulating movement. Darcy felt her eyes begin to close. Soon, she would sleep again.

Solange held out the cup. Darcy had to force her fingers to grasp it. The porcelain felt cold against her skin. The tonic would be warm. It would warm her so pleasantly.

The tonic. How she had begun to look forward to it. And yet . . . She had existed in this strange twilight for some time now, she thought. A day, two days? When was the last time she'd felt strong? Darcy struggled to think.

She closed her eyes, and an image floated into her mind. Tavish Finn was standing, dark and tall, under a bare oak in the park. His eyes were fixed on her. She saw him; her heart lifted and she began to run. She ran toward his strength, she smiled at his handsome face, but as she drew closer she saw something more: pain.

He loves me, she thought with sudden force. He loved me that day, and he loves me still.

Why had she turned her back on him? Was it that one afternoon that had changed it all for her? It had been a little lie, really, and perhaps he could have explained it. Why had she decided to suddenly retreat, when she had gone forward so boldly? Darcy twisted in the sheets, trying to remember, trying to understand.

"Come, Madame. Drink. Then you can sleep again."

Darcy's eyes flew open. Solange bobbed her thin, long head encouragingly. Her tiny tongue flicked out and licked her lips.

"Drink," she said soothingly.

Darcy nodded. But this time when her lips touched the cup

something revolted. She mimed a swallow. "I'm cold," she said, shivering. "My shawl . . ."

"Yes, Madame. If you would drink this first, I will fetch the shawl."

Darcy forced sharpness into her tone. "I'm cold, Solange. Fetch it now."

"Of course, Madame." Solange turned and went toward the shawl at the end of the bed. Concentrating hard, Darcy reached over to pour the tonic into the Sèvres jardiniere on her bedside table. But her arm was so weak. It trembled, and the cup clinked against the porcelain. The tonic spilled down the vase and pooled on the table.

Solange twisted around. Her eyes glittered. "Madame," she said, "I cannot allow this."

"I don't want to take the tonic, Solange," Darcy said, settling back against the pillows. She remembered that Solange was her servant, and summoned up the appropriate attitude, folding her hands to disguise their trembling. "You may go."

"But I'm afraid I cannot, Madame. I take my orders from Monsieur, you see." Solange wound the shawl around Darcy's shoulders. The soft cashmere felt like a vise. "So. I shall get you another dose of tonic. The doctor has just arrived. He is dining with your husband. They will wish to see you afterward. But first, you may take a little nap."

So Solange was her master, after all, and the doctor was downstairs. Darcy closed her eyes again with impotent fury. She listened to the rustle of Solange crossing the room. She heard the chink of glass against the cup, the liquid pouring. Her brief rebellion had exhausted her.

Tavish, help me. I need you.

She heard Solange rustle toward the bed again. Her maid had won; Darcy would have to take the tonic. She would sleep. And then, perhaps, she would have the strength to try again.

Tavish saw the failure in the set of Columbine's weary shoulders as she stepped down from the hansom cab. Her footsteps faltered on the front stairs. He could tell she was wondering how to tell him that she'd not succeeded.

He went toward the front door, brushing by Bell in the hallway. "I'll see to Columbine, Bell."

Bell curtsied and turned back toward the kitchen, where she was undoubtedly gossiping with Mrs. Hudson over a cup of tea while the older woman prepared dinner. Tavish felt a sudden longing to sit in a warm, fragrant kitchen and listen to Bell's sharp-tongued assessment of the neighbors. Sure, he was a base, cowardly fool, he was. It didn't matter how present and important the danger. It never failed that across his mind would flicker a longing for a good hot meal and some peace.

Cursing himself, he opened the front door. "You didn't see her," he said to Columbine.

She shook her head as she came in. "I tried the servants' entrance, too, Tavish." Wearily, she began to remove her hat. "I did my best. And then I saw her, up at the window. She didn't even nod at me." Columbine shivered. "Something's not right. We'll have to come up with another plan. At least I saw no sign of a doctor."

"Yet."

She nodded. "Yet. Perhaps tomorrow we can—"

"Tomorrow . . ." The word was a question. Tavish felt suddenly confused, as though his brain was having trouble catching up with the rest of him.

"Surely nothing will happen tonight, Tavish. It's nearly seven o'clock."

Tavish didn't answer. He stood still in the dark hall, Columbine a shadow beside him. He heard her breathing, waiting. Something gripped him, a force, a premonition, a feeling that had suddenly invaded him and settled into his superstitious Irish bones. He shouldn't wait until tomorrow. Darcy needed him tonight.

He turned to Columbine. "Tonight it will be, Columbine, mark my words. I have to go tonight."

"But how will you get in?" Columbine asked as he swept his coat and hat off the hook and slid his cane from the rack like a sword from its scabbard. "You'll never get past the front door,

Tavish. You have to think this through!"

He stood at the door, elegant, trim, for all she knew a gentleman on the way to the theater and to dine at Delmonico's afterward. But then his eyes glinted at her, and she saw the renegade in him that always lay in wait.

"Oh, I'll get in," Tavish said. "I'll be ushered in like a guest of honor, Columbine." With a swirl of coat and cane, he was gone.

Solange dressed her in a black velvet mantua robe. The white satin lining was cold against her bare arms, and she felt odd without a corset. The robe was heavy, encrusted with seed pearls, and the long train seemed to pull her backward with every step.

"Monsieur and the doctor are waiting for you in the library, Madame," Solange said.

"Yes."

"I will walk down with you."

"Yes."

It seemed an interminable journey. Darcy concentrated on her white satin slippers descending the stairs, one after the other. So slowly. "I'm tired," she whispered.

"Of course, Madame. And when you have finished with the doctor, you will sleep again. And when you wake up, you will be so much better."

"Better."

"Yes, Madame. One last step. Good."

Solange seemed to undulate next to her. Her hand snaked out and grabbed the heavy bronze knob of the library door. The door lunged inward.

"Darcy." Claude came toward her, his hands outstretched to take hers. His head looked impossibly big, his red mouth a long scar. Darcy stepped backward and bumped into Solange. She curled her hands up so that the folds of the long sleeves of her robe fell over them.

Claude dropped his hands. "Here is Dr. Arbuthnot to see you."

She turned and fixed her eyes on the doctor. He seemed so far away, a small, expensively dressed dot by the fireplace.

"I'm so happy to see you again, Mrs. Statton." His warm voice flowed toward her. She wanted to sink into it like a featherbed.

"Hello."

She felt a hand at her elbow, urging her toward the armchair by the fire. "Come, dearest." A clipped tone was thrown over the shoulder. "That will be all, Solange. I'll call you afterward."

"Yes, Monsieur."

"Sit here, my dear. In the armchair."

She was steered into the blue satin Sené chair. "*Fauteuil*," she said.

But Claude was ignoring her, moving toward the doctor. She heard him whisper. "She seems . . . very sluggish."

"She is in a perfect state, Mr. Statton. Perfect. She is prepared for the procedure. She will feel no anxiety, no nervousness. She will be led to the room upstairs, she will want to sleep. I am very pleased."

"All right."

Darcy forced the word out through lips suddenly thick. "Procedure?"

Dr. Arbuthnot came rapidly to her side. She was surprised his tiny feet could move his bulk so quickly. She stifled a giggle.

"I told you of the procedure before, Mrs. Statton. I told you that your womb is the center of your health and that it has led you to your condition. Remember, Mrs. Statton?"

Dizzy, she looked into his kind blue eyes. She nodded.

"Of course you do. So, it becomes simple, does it not? Remove the offending organ, and your problems will be over. You will be peaceful, happy, cured. Do you agree?"

Peace. How she wanted that. She nodded slowly.

"Of course you do." He patted her hand.

"I'm thirsty," she said.

Claude loomed behind him. "Doctor, perhaps you should see to your nurse's arrangements in the room upstairs?"

"Yes. I'll see to Nurse Bellows." He patted her hand again in a lingering way. "I'll see you upstairs, Mrs. Statton. I'll call for you shortly."

"Yes," Darcy said. "I'll be up directly, Dr. Arbuthnot." She felt pleased when the doctor beamed at her. But then he went away.

Claude's shadow fell over her, and she was afraid. She started to rise. "I want to go," she said.

He pressed down on her with his shadow, with his hands. "No, Darcy. No."

"I want to go!"

"No." There was sweat beading on his forehead. She saw fear in his eyes. Why would Claude be afraid? Claude was never afraid.

"Claude," she said, trying to keep her words clear and precise. "What are you doing to me?"

"I'm watching out for you," he said. He tried to pat her hand as Dr. Arbuthnot had done.

"Don't touch me," Darcy said wearily. She closed her eyes. "Just don't touch me."

"All right, dearest."

"I'm thirsty," she whispered.

She heard a knock, footsteps. She struggled to open her eyes again. The footman was bringing in the silver tray with a card on it. That was odd; even in this state, Darcy thought, smiling at her cleverness, she knew it was too early for after-dinner calls. She couldn't be completely insane, knowing that.

"I'm not at home," Claude snapped. "To anyone."

The footman bowed and began to retreat.

"Wait." Claude strode across the room and snatched the card from the tray. He blanched, his face losing color rapidly while the tips of his ears seemed to be burning red. He stood stock-still in the middle of the room, holding the small, stiff card.

"It must be one of my relatives," Darcy said dreamily.

"Show Mr. Dargent into the salon," Claude said. "I'll meet him there. But first, take Mrs. Statton upstairs right now. To the east bedroom. The doctor is up there. Now!" he barked, as the footman hesitated. It was not his job to escort the mistress of the house upstairs. But he obeyed. Darcy rose under the pressure of his fingers. The name Dargent buzzed in her head. Where had she heard it before? Whoever the man was, he'd had a devastating effect on Claude.

She smiled at the young servant, whose eyes were strangely uneasy. "I'm very thirsty," she confided.

* * *

Tavish kept his face calm, but relief rushed through him like a hot spring when he was ushered into the house. He was deposited in a small salon that held a small, exquisite Vermeer, a large Delacroix, and an abundance of Louis XVI furniture. Tavish was wary of the spindly appearance of the small gilt chairs. Even the satin sofa looked questionable. He wasn't staying, anyway.

He waited until the footsteps of the servant died away, then he opened the door and peered down both ends of the hall. No one was in sight. Claude would make him wait, he knew. But his curiosity would be too strong to make him wait long.

Thank God he was near the stairway. As Tavish strode to it and began to climb, he wondered how many servants Claude employed. Rich men such as Claude Statton often had as many as fifty or more minions running about making the master and mistress's life easy. Not counting kitchen help and stable help, there could be as many as ten or fifteen servants roaming about the house at this time. Less than those would be upstairs. Perhaps a personal secretary or two. A few maids. He had to worry most about Darcy's personal maid, who seemed a dragon in his few glimpses of her at Greenbriars. And, God help him, the doctor. Tavish just might tear the man apart if he was here.

Swiftly he climbed the wide staircase. When he reached the upstairs hall, he was almost past caring if he ran into anyone. He knew Darcy was near; he could feel it. His boots sounded too loud, though the floor was carpeted. A maid came out of a room ahead, closing the door softly, and without looking in his direction headed down the hall in the opposite direction. He wondered what to say when he overtook her, for he was steps away from her scurrying back. But to his surprise, as he came closer, she suddenly turned and faced the wall. Tavish walked by, wondering what kind of bizarre house he'd forced his way into.

He blundered on, pretending he knew where he was going. He could feel her behind him; with his senses so sharp, he could even feel her hesitancy.

"Excuse me, sir."

Damn. He turned. He tried to look haughty. "Yes?"

"You would be the doctor, sir?"

He nodded.

"You'd be looking for the east bedroom, then. The red one. It's around that corner and two doors to the left."

"Thank you." Tavish marveled at his luck. With her a few paces behind, he reached the door she indicated and, while she nodded shyly at him, pushed it open. There was nothing like getting unexpected assistance when it came to a kidnapping.

At first he saw nothing. The room was so dark. There were lamps everywhere, perching on tables and shelves, especially near the bed, but they were unlit. He saw a form on the bed, and then a small, rotund man came toward him out of the gloom of a far corner, where he'd been conferring with a white-swathed figure.

"Can I help you?"

"I'm Mr. Statton's secretary," Tavish said. He bowed slightly. "He sent me to bring Mrs. Statton downstairs."

"Downstairs? But we're almost ready to begin the procedure."

"Those are Mr. Statton's orders, sir." Tavish spoke quickly. The form on the bed moved. He looked over, and his heart broke. She looked so pale. And there was no spark in her eyes. They were filmed over, dull. And then her vision cleared, she seemed to recognize him, and she smiled. Briefly, secretly, and then the mask rolled down again. He took courage from the smile. Perhaps she was not as drugged as she appeared. Tavish moved toward the bed.

"I must protest," the doctor sputtered.

"Protest to Mr. Statton," Tavish said.

"I will. Yes, I will. Stay here. Don't move her. This is absurd. Nurse Bellows, watch the patient." The doctor scurried from the room.

Tavish bent over Darcy. "Can you put your arms around my neck?"

She nodded. Her arms slipped around his neck, then fell back.

"Sir, I must protest. The doctor asked you to wait—"

"Get away!" He spoke so fiercely she scuttled backward with fear in her eyes. "I do not take orders from the doctor."

He bent over Darcy, murmuring to her so soft the nurse couldn't hear. "My love, my own, I'm taking you out of here. My poor, poor love, my acushla, heart of my heart. My wild rose."

He poured out his endearments, words from the land he came from, desperate and tender, wanting his love to fill her with strength. He slid his arms underneath her slight body and lifted her. Her hands came up and locked around his neck.

"I'm sorry," she whispered into his neck. "I tried to—expel some of it, but I'm so weak. "Don't let me go. Don't let them—"

"I won't, my love." He went toward the door. The nurse moved forward, stolid and determined. Tavish ignored her. Moving fast now, he left the room and started down the hall.

"Back stairs," she whispered.

"Where, love?"

"Turn right, there," she whispered. "I'll show you."

His stride lengthened. He had her now, and he would die before he let her go. That was something. But he knew that Claude would be fully within his rights to kill him—or have someone else do it. So he tightened his grip and he stepped briskly and listened to her weak voice directing him. He alternately swore under his breath and prayed.

He heard footsteps heading up the main stairs as he hurried down the hall. He heard Claude's voice sharply questioning the doctor. He heard how rapid the footsteps were. But a moment later the back stairs were there, looming before him. Darcy tightened her grip, and he was clattering down them, fast.

He hit the bottom. "Kitchen," Darcy whispered. "Straight ahead."

He burst into the kitchen, not caring for deception now. A maid backed into a corner, fear in her face. A male servant, probably a footman, looked up, startled, from his dish of tea. A scullion gaped at him over a steaming sink of dishes, her rosy arms dripping suds. The French chef looked up, irritated, from straining a sauce.

Tavish ignored them. He gazed around quickly. There were three doors leading out of the kitchen. He could be trapped in a pantry or a passageway to the back of the house if he chose the wrong one. The footman looked large and capable. He pushed back his chair as the knowledge sank in that this was not the regular thing, a crazy Irishman carrying out the mistress through the kitchens.

"Darcy, love," he murmured. "Would you mind telling me the way?"

"I don't know," she said.

Then a petite maid he hadn't noticed before stepped forward. Her pretty face suddenly blazed with determination. "That one," she said, pointing.

"Bless you," Tavish said simply, and moved. As he passed the footman, he shoved out one foot with such force that the chair toppled over backward. The man hit the floor with a thump and a cry. He probably had riled the man's temper, but at least he'd gained a moment or two.

He reached the street with a feeling of vast relief. The stars overhead twinkled benignly at him, and he almost smiled. But the carriage he'd paid a fortune to hire was around the corner on Fifth Avenue. He still had half a block to cover.

"Halt, sir."

He'd have been less nervous if the voice wasn't so calm. Tavish turned slowly. As he'd expected, Claude had a small gun tucked into a very steady hand. And he was alone.

"Hang on, darlin'," he said to Darcy quietly.

"Put me down," she said. Her eyes were on her husband. "I can walk now, I think. The air helps. I'll talk to him."

"I'm not letting you go now," he said. "Not now."

"Mr. Finn," Claude said, "I suggest you turn my wife over to me."

"No, sir. I'm not leaving her here to be butchered."

"Put her down, sir!"

Tavish considered his options and found them wanting. He did still have his cane—somehow he'd had the presence of mind to hang on to it. It was in his left hand, hidden under the material of Darcy's long robe. But a cane wasn't much defense against a gun, no matter how small and prettily pearl-handled the gun was. And he'd have to put Darcy down to use it.

"Keep moving toward Fifth," Darcy said in his ear. "Tell him—scandal."

Of course. Tavish took a step backward. "Millionaire's Row, this stretch of Fifth Avenue is called," he said softly to Claude. "The twin Vanderbilt mansions start at Fifty-first. William

Kissam and Alva are just a a block away on Fifty-third, aren't they? And Cornelius is a few blocks north of us. Not to mention the Goelets, Darius Mills, Huntington, Hinkle—they're all around us, aren't they?" He took another step.

"Are you giving me a lesson in New York geography, Finn? If you take another step, you're a dead man."

Tavish stopped. He was in a dilemma, to be sure. He didn't want to let go of Darcy, but as it was, she was shielding him from a bullet. "Times may be changing, but scandal is scandal. Divorce is less offensive than murder, Mr. Statton. Especially when the wife involved is more than willing to be carried away. Especially when servants have eyes and ears and access to Colonel Mann."

Claude laughed. "Colonel Mann is in my pocket."

"But is Mrs. Astor in your pocket, Mr. Statton? And are the Rhinelanders, the Roosevelts, the Joneses, the Cuttings, the Van Rensselaers, the—"

Claude's lips bared back from his teeth. "Shut your mouth, sir!"

"Do you really think," Tavish said in a low, steady voice, backing away again toward Fifth, "that the blessed four hundred you craved acceptance from would accept the word of a Statton, even with all his money, and not a Snow? You know the Old Guard would not. And they are what matters to you, aren't they? Times are changing, but not that rapidly. Money cannot win out over blood. Not yet."

"Claude, please." Darcy twisted to look at her husband. "Please let me go. There will be no scandal, I will say nothing about tonight. Just please—"

"You don't understand, do you?" Claude said, and he took several strides forward, eliminating the distance Tavish had managed to gain. "I *own* you, Darcy. I *bought* you! I saved your pathetic father, and I saved you. This is my reward! Tonight. This when you pay. Were you such an innocent? Were your eyes not open five years ago when you accepted me? Did you not live with me for five years and eat my food and wear the diamonds I placed around your neck? Did you think I would let you get away when you are just as guilty as I?"

Tavish could feel her shrinking against him, wetness against his neck. She was crying. "No," he whispered fiercely. "Don't listen to him."

Claude reached out then, before Tavish could move, and fingered her black velvet gown. "This is mine." He ripped off a satin slipper from her foot and crumpled it in his hand. "This is mine." And then he slid his hand up her bare leg, even as Tavish, horrified, struggled to back away as Darcy shook and sobbed against him. "And this," Claude said in a voice thick with insinuation, "this white, perfect limb is mine, has been mine. Many, many times." His yellow eyes gleamed, and he smiled.

Tavish cracked. He wrenched backward from Claude, and without planning it, Darcy was sliding down the length of his side and his cane was flashing out from beneath her skirts. He transferred it to his free hand, and it whistled through the air, coming down on Claude's thin white wrist.

Claude howled and stepped backward. He raised the gun. Tavish struck out again, this time at Claude's temple. Claude's slight body crumpled, and he fell to the pavement.

Tavish grabbed her hand, and they started to run.

Then behind them he could hear the footmen, the bodyguards coming, spilling out of the kitchen door. Perhaps Claude had told them to wait, had wanted to take Darcy back himself. Whatever the reason, they were there, and Tavish knew he couldn't fight them. He pulled Darcy's wrist, urging her on, faster. She was running unsteadily from missing one slipper, but she kicked the other one off, and she was able to keep up.

They made it to the cab seconds ahead of the largest pursuer. Tavish pushed Darcy into the cab ahead of him, then lashed out with his cane at the man with fists like hams who was too damn close. The cane was nothing more than an intrusive fly, and the man ignored it and kept coming. Still a bit off-balance from his attempt with the cane, Tavish saw one huge fist heading for him. And then a whip appeared from nowhere and slashed in the giant's face. The fist glanced Tavish's shoulder with enough power to send him sprawling back against the cab. Blood was in his attacker's eyes, and it gave Tavish time to haul himself upright. He leaped into the cab, screaming at the driver to hurry.

The driver flashed the helpful whip again, this time over the horse's head, and they were off, streaming down Fifth Avenue with Darcy sobbing helplessly against his chest. Free.

Eleven

DARCY SPENT ALMOST all the next day sleeping. She woke occasionally to find Columbine at her bedside, and once she swallowed some broth, and once some tea and toast. She asked for Tavish, and Columbine said she had sent him away until Darcy was better. Darcy slept again—she seemed to have a voracious appetite for sleep—and it wasn't until she woke the following morning that she felt anything like herself.

Columbine had left a soft blue merino dress for her. The underclothes and stockings looked brand-new. Darcy woke early and dressed herself, though she occasionally had to sit and rest. She hoped her weakness was due only to the lack of solid food over the last few days and would dissipate.

She peeked out into the unfamiliar hall and made her way down the stairs. The house was so small that she had no difficulty finding Columbine's front parlor. She'd thought she'd be alone this early in the morning, but she was surprised to see Columbine already up, reading a book with a tea tray in front of her.

"I'm sorry," Darcy said, hesitating at the door. "I don't want to disturb you—"

"Whatever are you doing up and dressed?" Columbine rose and hurried toward her. "You're as weak as a kitten. Why didn't you stay in bed, you silly? I had everything planned. I was to bring you your breakfast in bed, and Bell would help you dress. You've spoiled it." She led Darcy to the armchair across from her. "Now, sit here for just a moment, and I'll fetch some fresh tea. I don't like to disturb Bell so early." Columbine ran out and Darcy sat, feeling her usual warm rush of confusion in Columbine's presence.

She also felt out of place. Why had Tavish brought her here instead of her father's? She barely knew Columbine, for all that she liked her. But the lamps were lit on this chill morning, there was a fire in the grate, and Columbine had tucked a soft quilt around her knees. Tea was on its way, and Darcy decided to revel in her contentedness for the moment.

Columbine came back quickly and poured a cup of steaming tea for Darcy. She sipped it gratefully; it was good and strong. They drank their cups in a companionable silence.

When she'd eaten a biscuit and Columbine had poured her a second cup, Darcy felt stronger. "Thank you," she said. "I didn't know food could taste so good."

"Mrs. Hudson will fix a proper breakfast for you later," Columbine said. "But until then, have another biscuit. Mrs. Hudson is from New Orleans, and there's nothing like Southern biscuits, I always say." She held the plate out to Darcy.

Darcy took a biscuit and put it on her plate. "You mentioned to me that Tavish had called yesterday," she said. "I think—it's difficult to remember what I dreamed and what—"

"Yes. He called, and I sent him away. Lord knows I'm not one to follow the proprieties, Darcy, but I feel I should point out to you that there will be less talk if you don't see Tavish for a little while. Your husband can make things . . . very difficult."

Darcy spooned some jam on her biscuit, but she put it down before taking a bite. "Has Mr. Statton called?" she asked hesitantly.

"No, he has not. I wouldn't think he'd have the gall, would you?"

"I would think he had the gall," Darcy said softly.

Columbine gave her a long, steady look. "Heaven only knows what you suffered. Do you know what he was to do to you, Darcy?"

"Tavish told me a bit in the cab. I—"

"I am sure he left the worse of it for me, Darcy, for I can be blunt. Your husband wanted to render you childless and sexless. Once Dr. Arbuthnot did his work, not only would you be unable to bear children, but you would not be able to receive pleasure from the sexual act again."

Darcy set her teacup down. "I see."

"It was an abomination. It was not enough for him to keep you there, locked away, to monitor your movements and read your mail—oh, Tavish told me. That wicked, evil man—"

"Don't!" Darcy cried. She rose, knocking over her teacup on the table in front of her. "Don't speak of him that way. Can't you see what it means when you say such things?" she said wildly, clasping and unclasping her hands. "It means that I, too, am evil. I, too, am guilty—"

"No! Darcy, you—"

"I stayed!" Darcy fell to her knees in front of Columbine. Tears streaked down her face. "He told me that night that I allowed myself to be bought and paid for. That I closed my eyes to his character and allowed him to place jewels around my neck and drink champagne at his table. And what he knows and the rest of the world does not is that I also allowed him rights that . . . that perhaps no one, not even a husband, has a right to inflict . . . I allowed him to degrade me," she said with difficulty. She raised her brimming eyes to Columbine. "Was I not as guilty as he of crimes, perhaps even more so?"

Columbine wrenched Darcy's hands apart and took them in her own. "What did you know of Claude Statton when you married him?" she asked urgently.

"I knew that he was rich. And I knew that I did not like him," Darcy said bitterly.

"If such a thing were a sin, women everywhere would be damned for eternity," Columbine said dryly, "and I among them. Darcy, if this was the best of all possible worlds, such things would not happen. If the world was as I would wish it, women would not be forced to do such things. What were your alternatives? To watch your father be ruined? It wasn't as though you could use your brain and go to work, Darcy. You had been bred for your destiny of idleness since the day you were born. And even if you had wished to, what doors would be open for you, with no education, no skills? Why, you couldn't even have been a decent prostitute, I'll wager! No, you did what you had to do. And you were a child!"

"Hardly. I was twenty-two."

"A child," Columbine repeated, "not a woman, for you were shielded from reality, cosseted, not talked to as a person, not encouraged intellectually. What decision *could* you have made?"

"So I have no responsibility for my life?" Darcy asked her.

"Of course you do," Columbine said impatiently. "You made a bad choice with Claude Statton, and in a better world you would have made a different one. In a better world you would not have felt compelled to wifely loyalty to a man who did not deserve one *second* of such fealty. You made your choices, and you did your duty for as long as you could, but you *woke up*. Are you guilty?" Columbine shook her head so violently that her silver earrings danced. "No. I will not allow you to say such a thing. I will not allow you to feel it!"

Darcy smiled at Columbine's vehemence. "So what am I to feel, then?" she asked, gently teasing.

Columbine smiled, then stood and gently raised her to her feet. She gripped her hands. "You are to feel proud of your bravery, and lucky. Sad for a time, but not for long. And you will begin your life today, your life as a woman. You will escape the rules of the four hundred, and you will find your own rules. You will take one step forward, and then another, and one day you will look behind you and see that you left the horror behind long ago but had been too busy to notice."

"But what shall I do?" Darcy asked. Panic shot through her at Columbine's vision of that strong, resolute figure. She felt rather helpless in the face of it.

Columbine laughed her loud, exuberant laugh. She placed her hands on Darcy's shoulders. "Oh, Darcy. Whatever you choose! That is the best thing of all."

Darcy and Columbine were reading by the fire when Adelle was announced. Columbine looked over her spectacles at Darcy, whose face was flushed with surprise and pleasure.

"Do you wish to see her?"

"Of course," Darcy said. "She's come here, imagine. Adelle has always been a good friend to me, Columbine. I want to introduce you."

Columbine nodded shortly and removed her spectacles. "Of course. Show her in, Bell."

Adelle seemed cool at the introduction Darcy gave with such pleasure. Perhaps she felt uncomfortable, Darcy reasoned. In the comfortable, shabby parlor, she looked even more overdressed in her bright yellow coat with beaded passementerie and a matching hat with stiff black feathers that seemed to lunge at the world aggressively.

"If you will excuse me," Columbine said, "I have some business to attend to."

"Of course, Columbine," Darcy said, and Adelle nodded stiffly.

Darcy turned to Adelle. "I'm so glad you came," she said. "I—"

"Darcy, really," Adelle burst out. "You didn't have to introduce me."

"May I remind you," Darcy said in a stilted tone, "that you are sitting in Mrs. Nash's front parlor at the moment. And she is my friend." Relenting, Darcy patted Adelle's gloved hand. "I know that a woman like Columbine is not found in your usual circle, Adelle. But I have grown to care for her. She has been so kind, and I honestly think you would like her."

Adelle stared at her. "Perhaps you *are* mad," she said.

Darcy drew her hand back as though it had been burned. "Excuse me?"

"Of course I didn't believe the rumors, not for a moment. And they're so contradictory, how could one know what to believe? One minute you're quite mad, and the next you're off with an Irishman at a house of assignation on the Central Park."

Darcy felt faint. "Is this what has been said?"

"Yes, of course. Darcy, I must say I'm shocked. If the second is true, the first must be, as well."

Darcy tried to remember what order her transgressions had come in and gave up. "But that day," she protested. "That day we went to see Julia Hinkle, and you drove me to Twenty-third

Street. You knew I was meeting Tavish Finn. Not only did you condone it, you seemed almost to approve."

"I didn't know you were planning to leave Claude for him," Adelle said matter-of-factly. "There is a difference, Darcy, between an indiscretion and a scandal. Don't you understand? Your husband has turned you out. You're no longer received."

"Claude didn't turn me out. I left."

"All the worse, then. And you compound the problem by seeking refuge in the home of a woman like Columbine Nash. You don't even take yourself off to Europe, like our mother had the decency to do, at least. Darcy, Columbine Nash was one of those Fabian socialists in England during her so-called rest cure! I heard it on good authority."

Darcy smiled. "Oh, in that case I shall leave today." Adelle bristled, and Darcy said in a conciliatory tone, "Adelle, truly, I don't understand. I could see your objection if it was based on the fact that Columbine is a single woman and isn't family, but you see, that night, everything was very confusing. Perhaps I should have gone to Father's. But he is away just now, and besides, I wasn't able to think properly. Claude had—"

Adelle rose. "Darcy, I'm sorry. But I must go. I cannot see you while you are under this roof. I thought it right to come and tell you that. I'm . . . I'm sorry. Be well, dear."

"You're saying good-bye to me?" Darcy asked, incredulous. "You don't want to hear my side?"

Adelle settled her veil back over her face. "Oh, Darcy. If I were married . . . perhaps I could help you. But I'm a single woman. Aunt Catherine quite agrees. I cannot support you in this. I cannot risk my reputation as long as you continue to associate with such people as this Mrs. Nash and her confederate Mr. Finn. Are you certain you know what their relations truly are?" Adelle shuddered. "An Irishman and a freethinker! Who knows what relations they enjoy."

Icily calm, Darcy stood. "You're quite right, Adelle. It is better that you go."

Adelle hesitated. "I wish I could have that day over again," she burst out. "I wish I had not driven you to Twenty-third Street, or indeed had spirited you from your husband's house at all. Perhaps none of this would have happened."

Darcy felt a wave of fury shake her. Only Adelle could dare to turn her back on her, and then see Darcy's troubles as so trifling that Adelle herself could have prevented them.

"Do you really believe that we were such intimates that you had a hand in events, Adelle? You who would turn the subject if I dared to hint at my unhappiness? Is that what you want to believe? If it gives you some small sense of importance, if it gives you something to gossip about to those ladies you think so much finer than Mrs. Nash, then I hereby give you permission to believe it. It may give you pleasure on one of your many idle afternoons."

"There's no need to be cruel," Adelle said, turning toward the door.

"You're quite right, Adelle. There was no need to be cruel. No need at all." She watched her cousin, whom she'd known all her life, walk out the door. So this was what Columbine had meant when she told her to escape the four hundred. But the four hundred was more than a generalized block of society: it was individuals, it was people she'd grown up with. People she had loved, people who could break her heart.

Adelle brushed by Columbine without a word. The front door closed. Columbine took one look at Darcy and came to her side.

"I'm so sorry," she said.

"Tell me again of my courage," Darcy said woodenly.

"I must say I was quite surprised to hear the hammering at the kitchen door and discover, not a tradesman, but a pretty little face glaring at me defiantly," Columbine said, laughing. She poured a glass of wine for Darcy. They were having no guests for dinner, but they both had changed, Darcy into a lovely gold velvet dress of Columbine's. "I must confess I didn't recognize her for a moment. Then it hit me: Daisy! The maid I met in the kitchen at your house, Darcy."

"Daisy! She helped us to escape. I'm afraid I didn't know the way out of my own kitchens," Darcy said with a sheepish laugh.

"Oh, dear, of course not. So Daisy informed me that your husband promptly fired her for giving you directions. Apparently the chef informed Mr. Statton of this. So she said, 'Do you remember me, Mrs. Nash?' and I said, 'Of course, Daisy,' and she said rather fiercely, 'My name is Marguerite, ma'am.'"

"Marguerite? That's pretty."

"Apparently Mr. Statton, upon hearing her name, said it was a ridiculous one for a maid, and told her she'd be Daisy from that time on."

"Isn't it just like him," Darcy mused. "So what did Daisy—uh, Marguerite—want?"

"Help. A job. She's going to be a secretary at the New Women Society. I think she'll make a good one. She hated being a maid."

"Oh, Columbine." Darcy sank back against the pillows, almost upsetting her wine. "As long as I live, I'll never be as useful and good as you."

She'd only been half-serious, but Columbine frowned. "Darcy, I am not terribly useful and good, not all of the time, and not nearly enough. I have a shocking penchant for idleness and luxury, which I still do indulge, I'm afraid to say."

"Oh, yes, but—"

"Perhaps it's time I told you about my origins," Columbine mused.

"I wish that you would. You seem to know things about me, about my marriage, without my having to say them."

Columbine stared at the carpet. "That is because I was in a marriage such as yours. I don't like to think about it, talk about it. Oh, I was once a useless creature with barely a thought in my head. My father arranged a marriage with an ignorant lout with a large fortune, and when I protested, he locked me in my room for weeks. I married the man, and I was desperately unhappy. He beat me occasionally, and I did nothing. I did not tell my father, who surely would have done something if he'd known. Or perhaps not, I've never been able to decide, and I suppose it doesn't matter. In any case, when something happened that showed me that my father was mortal, that he was capable of a wickedness I hadn't dreamed of—that I had obeyed him out of blindness and continued to obey him, and my husband, out of weakness—I *still* did not leave. And I turned my brother out of my life because he dared to tell me the truth."

Darcy slowly sat erect. "Tavish. You and Tavish are brother and sister."

Columbine nodded. "Half brother and sister."

"Why is it a secret?"

"Several reasons. One, because my mother is still alive and wishes it. It is her great humiliation. But also because Tavish does not wish to acknowledge the connection to my father, and I cannot blame him. He told you the story?"

"Yes. How did you find each other again?"

Columbine smiled. "I was on a lecture tour out West. He came to the hall. It was . . . oh, a bad time in his life. He had seen terrible things, injustices, with the railroad fight against the Grange laws. And then he was involved in the flight of the Cheyenne— are you familiar with that tragedy?"

"No, I'm sorry to say I am not."

"He told me the story fairly recently—he couldn't speak of it for years. Tavish had several friends among the Cheyenne, and he was called in as a go-between when a group left the southern Indian Territory marked for them and traveled north. They'd been starving due to the sorry record of the Indian Bureau in sending supplies, and they'd been wracked with malaria because of the climate they were unaccustomed to. They were heading for their former hunting grounds. All they asked for was to be allowed to go to the Pine Ridge agency in the Dakota territory. It was a long, sad story, like so many others. The government refused, the Indians would not return south—they would rather die up north than in a strange land, they said—the army threw them in a fort, Camp Robinson, I think it was called, in Nebraska. Tavish was in the area, Lord only knows what he was doing then, and they called him in to 'reason with' the Indians."

"Did he have any success?"

Columbine shook her head. "No. Because, of course, he agreed with them. And they were determined. It was cold that winter—anywhere from ten to forty below. The captain ordered that no more firewood be sent to the rooms where the Cheyenne were held. Then no food. And finally, no water. Tavish said they scraped frost from the windows to give their thirsty children."

Darcy was horrified. "There were children?"

She nodded. "Tavish went to the captain—he would do nothing. He went back and forth between them. And then the captain called a council. Tavish had hopes. He convinced two of the chiefs to go. And they went, and the captain put them in irons and would not let them return to their people. That was the final blow for the Cheyenne, who wanted to die like free people. They broke out of the fort and began their flight through the snow. The army pursued them. Out of one hundred and fifty that broke out, only half survived, and those wounded and crippled. They were sent to the Pine Ridge Agency, where they'd wanted to go all along. Tavish saw it all. He helped collect the bodies of the children. Of the women. Of the men he had known." Columbine shook her head. "When he first went out West, he had seen many things, things he wouldn't tell me about. But this broke him. When I saw him in the audience, I barely recognized him."

She'd always known, Darcy thought, that he was a man who had seen too much. There was that hard, flat look in his eyes at times, a look no woman could reach, no man. She opened her mouth to urge Columbine on, but Bell came in. "Mr. Lemuel Grace is here to see you, Mrs. Statton."

Darcy rose nervously. "Oh, I see. Show him in, Bell."

"Do you want me to stay?" Columbine asked her.

"No, it's all right, I should see him alone, I suppose." She smiled unsteadily at Columbine. "I'll be all right."

Lemuel entered and took Columbine's hand. He bent over it in the continental manner favored by August Belmont. "I am so grateful, Mrs. Nash. I owe you a great debt for your kindness to my niece."

"I was happy to be of service, Mr. Grace. If you'll excuse me."

He bowed. "Of course." As soon as Columbine had left, he came to Darcy. He kissed her on the cheek and took her hand. "How are you, my dear?"

"I'm fine, Uncle." Darcy wanted to believe in his kind tone, but she was wary after Adelle's visit.

"Please, let us sit down. First, I want to tell you that your father is in Boston but will return tomorrow."

"I know. I sent a message to him this morning."

"Good. Secondly, I want you to tell me everything that happened."

"Adelle was here. She told me that apparently there are rumors questioning both my sanity and my virtue. That I am no longer welcome in many houses in New York. I must admit, I am surprised at such societal dispatch. It's only been a day."

Lemuel's eyes were kind, and he pressed her hand. "I am on your side, Darcy. I know the manner of man you married."

"If only I had heeded your warning about him before my marriage," Darcy said.

He put a finger to her lips. "Don't waste time on 'if onlys' now, Darcy. It is fruitless and will give you nothing but heartache."

"You sound like Columbine."

He grinned. "Ah. That must be good, for I've heard she is very wise. Now. If you'll be so kind as to pour me a glass of wine and start from the beginning."

Lemuel's face went from shock to horror to gravity. When she finally finished her story, his face was almost expressionless, except for the cold, hard fury in his iron-gray eyes. He didn't say anything for long minutes.

"I blame myself," he said finally, quietly.

"No, Uncle Lemuel. How could you know?"

"I should have done something. Edward was obviously not prepared to protect you. I know how you feel about your father, Darcy. Your loyalty is admirable, but he can be damned ineffectual, and that was dangerous in this case."

"Please don't say that. There's something I didn't tell you."

"Yes?"

"Claude was blackmailing Edward. I can't tell you why, but you should know that my father was trapped. He could do nothing."

Lemuel's face paled. He stood up and paced quickly for several moments. Darcy's hand went to her throat. Lemuel was not young anymore. Was all this too much of a shock to him? She shouldn't have said anything, she should have kept that to herself. It should have been enough to hint to Lemuel about Claude's treatment of her. He didn't need to know that she suspected him of being a criminal as well.

"How do you know this?" he demanded, stopping and turning to her.

"I overheard them talking. Uncle Lemuel, it was just a way to control my father so that he wouldn't encourage me to leave."

"I cannot fathom such a mind, such a . . ." He came back to the sofa and sat down. He took her hands. "I will protect you. I want you to pack your things and come to my house."

"But, Uncle Lemuel, I am disgraced. You can't take me in."

He shook his head, disregarding her interruption. "I've spoken to your aunt Marie, and she urges me to press you to come. Your father won't be able to stand against Claude, that is painfully obvious. But I have no financial dealings with your husband, and he knows I despise him. He will not come to my house. You'll be safe. Isn't that what you need, Darcy?"

"Yes," she said hesitantly.

"And as much as I admire your friend Mrs. Nash, I do think it would be better for you to remain with family, at least for a little while. We need to make legal arrangements, and they can be troublesome."

"I suppose you're right. But wouldn't Father be hurt if I didn't go to him?"

Lemuel sighed. He patted her hand and let it go. "Ah, Darcy, how can I say this? I think Edward just might be relieved."

Darcy thought about this. She saw that Lemuel looked anxious, afraid of offending her. He and Edward had never been close. But Lemuel wouldn't lie about Edward's capabilities. "Yes, Uncle. Perhaps you're right. There is just one thing . . ."

"Yes, my dear?"

"Would you forbid the house to Columbine Nash?"

Lemuel looked shocked. "Of course I would not. I wouldn't dream of restricting your callers. You may receive anyone you want, Darcy."

She swallowed. "And Mr. Finn?"

"Ah. Mr. Finn." Lemuel frowned. "You may receive him if you wish, of course. But I would strongly advise you to wait, Darcy. It would be better for you in the long run."

"Columbine says that as well. Uncle Lemuel, I would be happy to come. Thank you."

"Splendid. The preparations have all been made. I'll send another carriage for your things—"

"But I have no things. I left in something of a hurry, remember?"

Lemuel laughed. "Of course, how stupid of me. You can come with me tonight, then. And tomorrow I will have Claude send your things."

"I don't think he will agree . . ."

"He will agree," her uncle said darkly. Darcy sipped her wine, feeling relieved. Her uncle, that model of courtliness, had an unexpectedly tough strain that surfaced in times of trouble. She'd forgotten how stubborn the Graces could be. Her mother hadn't been the only strong one in the family. Oh, there were plenty of Adelles in the list of the four hundred. But thank God for the Lemuels.

It wasn't that Darcy disliked Lemuel's wife, her aunt Marie— she just didn't think of her. As a debutante, Marie had possessed a pallid, blond prettiness, and that coupled with her good Dutch name and her fortune had gained her many suitors. But now, at middle age, she was faded and pale, and one had to search for the marks of her former beauty. Her nose was fine, her eyes were blue, her teeth good. But she was so dour, and her slimness had turned to a skeletal thinness.

She saw kindly to Darcy's comfort, and she did not utter one word of censure. Darcy was quiet and withdrawn, for truth to tell she was melancholy at parting from Columbine and not being able to see Tavish. Her aunt naturally interpreted it as the reaction to the dissolution of her marriage—not to be mention her blacklisting from society. Marie stole looks at her as she bustled around the bedroom, straightening a curtain here and a knickknack there.

"I hope you'll be quite comfortable," Marie said.

"I'm sure I shall, Aunt. Everything is lovely."

Marie nodded and began to withdraw. But then she said suddenly, fiercely, "I'm glad you left him. It was good you left him. Don't waste your tears on *him*."

Darcy was still staring, open-mouthed, when her aunt Marie retreated and shut the door.

It was the first and last outburst from Marie. Life at the Graces' was quiet and serene. Columbine called both Friday and Saturday, Darcy and Marie had silent but companionable lunches, and Lemuel canceled their guests in order to have quiet family dinners.

Saturday afternoon, Darcy sat down to do the thing she'd been thinking of for two days. She went to Lemuel's study, took pen and paper, and went back to her room to compose a letter to her mother. She opened her window halfway, for spring was in the air, and she wanted to feel the softness of the breeze while she wrote.

She had torn up a half-dozen attempts when Marie knocked and entered her room, wringing her hands. Darcy stared, transfixed, at Marie's bony, accentuated knuckles appearing and disappearing underneath her curling thin fingers.

"He's here, Darcy. I could not keep him out. I said I would not receive him, but he walked in, brazen. Such cheek, such insolence—if only Mr. Grace were here!"

Darcy stood. "Do you mean Claude?"

"You don't have to see him. Don't worry, I do not think the man will come to your bedroom. But I wanted to warn you that he is sitting in the parlor. And, Darcy, he said he will not leave until he talks to you!"

"I see."

"I'll telegraph to Mr. Grace downtown, and he can be here within the hour, if we're lucky. Oh, I wish we had a telephone. Mr. Grace keeps threatening to put one in—"

Darcy patted her aunt's shoulder. "Don't worry, Aunt. I'll see Mr. Statton. You don't have to bother Uncle Lemuel. Claude

just wants to talk to me. I'm sure he won't be disagreeable."
Darcy spoke with an assurance she didn't feel in the least.

She walked slowly to the parlor. Claude was standing by the window, his back to her, his hands clasped behind him.

He turned. "Thank you for seeing me."

She nodded. She did not offer her hand.

"Your uncle has informed me that I am to send your things here. Do you wish this, Darcy?"

She nodded again.

He didn't move; his face was rigid, tightly controlled. But she saw that he had been ravaged by what had happened. His eyes were sad, so sad that she found it difficult to believe that she was looking at her husband.

"I want you back," he said.

Twelve

"YOU CANNOT BE serious," Darcy said.

"But I am. Will you sit, Darcy?"

She shook her head, and he sighed. He looked down at his hat on the floor, with his pearl-gray gloves tucked inside, the cane beside them—the signs of a gentlemanly afternoon call, always placed on the floor or a windowsill, not on the furniture. He was dressed impeccably as manners dictated. But she could see now, from the sun streaming through the embroidered net curtains, the bruise on his temple, yellowish-green and nasty-looking, and she remembered Tavish's cane lashing out, and the small, mean gun in Claude's hand.

"How could you have the gall to come here?" she asked slowly. "After what you tried to do to me—"

He rushed in so quickly, it was as though he was only waiting for her to bring up the subject. "Dr. Arbuthnot is a highly respected surgeon. I was following his advice, medical advice that was put to me in the strongest possible terms, Darcy. I was worried about you, I felt I needed to do something. If I picked the wrong advisor—"

"The wrong advisor? You speak of this as a business deal! This is my *life*, Claude! My health, my ability to bear children—"

"But it seemed you could not bear children. Dr. Arbuthnot felt this was clear, that the womb was diseased. You can see why I felt his treatment would cure you."

"Cure me of what? Unhappiness?" Darcy shook her head. "It does no good to talk," she said wearily. "I am sure you knew exactly what you were doing, Claude. You are not such an innocent, nor do you blindly follow the advice of anyone."

"Perhaps that is true in business. But not in medicine, Darcy. I am ignorant in such matters. I was lost. But you're right. Let's not speak of it. In a way I am glad of Mr. Finn's interference. I see that now. What is more important to me is the continuation of our union."

Now Darcy did sit down. "I do not believe this," she murmured.

He sat opposite her, his hands on his knees, leaning toward her. "We would start again—I would start again. I was too possessive, I know that now. You would have your freedom, Darcy, the freedom to come and go as you please, make the friends you please. And if you wished it, I would not trouble you at night."

She gave him a dry look.

"I would not. You would be free, and I would be free. But we would be married. Forgive me for being so blunt, Darcy, but I believe it is time we were honest with each other."

"You speak of honesty?" she said, almost bemused. "And freedom? This from a man who censored my letters, who kept my correspondence from me—oh, yes, Claude, I know that you did!"

He stood and turned his back to her. She knew he was struggling to tame his rage, to compose his face. "You went into my private office," he said icily, his back to her. "You went through my files."

She stood and went around to stand in front of him. "Yes, I did, Claude. Tell me it was wrong. Tell me from the vantage point of a man who went through my letters and censored them. Innocent letters from my uncle, and worst of all, a letter from my mother who I have not seen in more than ten years."

"I am your husband!" he shouted, his face mottled. "I have such rights!"

She shrugged lightly, though her limbs were trembling from the violence of his words. "And you speak to me of freedom," she said contemptuously. "You speak to me of change."

He controlled himself; she could see the effort. He was breathing hard now. "It is this man, this Finn. This shanty Irishman who is in your bed."

"As you have seen fit to inform all New York."

"I have said nothing, madam," he said quietly. "Nothing, though your lover invaded my house and attacked me, for which I could have called the chief of police that evening and had him thrown in jail. But I did not, for I still wished for you to return. But you have made it very clear to me that you are past rehabilitation, that you are sunk in the lowest levels of depravity." He bent and picked up his hat, gloves, and cane. "And I shall leave you there, madam."

"I'm so pleased we are able to part on good terms, Claude," Darcy said sardonically. She didn't know how she managed it; perhaps it was because she knew it was the only tone that would disturb him. He would want to see her upset. He would want to see her cry. He had always derived such pleasure from her tears. God help her, she would not give him that.

He went toward the door. Then he turned, as though for an afterthought, something that had just lightly occurred to him. "By the way, Mrs. Statton—I think you should know that I will destroy Tavish Finn."

She said nothing. Now, she was truly afraid, for his face was too calm.

"This man who talks of his work with the Grange, who belly-aches about the rapacious railroads—how interesting it would be for people to know that he is working secretly for them. That he is a traitor. That he was the one who sold out his ragged home-town in California."

"It isn't true," she said scornfully.

Claude laughed and put on his hat. "What does it matter?" he said. "Truth is so irrelevant, isn't it? Good day, Darcy." He touched his cane to the brim of his hat and departed.

Edward Snow arrived sheepishly later in the afternoon. He embraced her for a long time.

"Lemuel told me everything. Awful business. Dreadful. I was in Boston to see your cousin Florence and that new husband of hers. Even though it's the Grace side, I felt I should pay the wedding visit—she was Amelia's favorite cousin. She was dressed in the most unfortunate shade of green . . . Oh, Darcy. I had no idea, I should have been here—"

"It's all right, Father," Darcy said, guiding him to a chair. "I'm all right."

Edward looked around at the parlor. "I haven't been here in so long. It is always so quiet in this house. Do you want to come home with me, Darcy? I would love to have you—I'll play Bach in the evenings on the piano, you know how you love that. It doesn't seem right, your being here."

"I think it better for the present, Father. It's not that I don't want to be with you. But if you still have dealings with Claude, I—"

"He hasn't said anything, yet. I haven't heard a word." Edward smiled grimly. "He wants me to suffer, waiting and wondering. And I suppose that I am."

"But surely he can't ruin you. You told me that you'd removed much of your income from his control."

Edward nodded. "Yes, yes. That's true. He cannot ruin me." But he didn't meet her eyes.

She had to tell him. It might change their relationship forever, but she had to tell him. "Father, I know that Claude is blackmailing you. I overheard part of your conversation that night. I came back for my gloves, and . . . I heard. So I understand why you can't take me in, not yet. But, Father, we can find some way to threaten him as well, so that he will never speak such horrors against you, such unspeakable lies. I promise you."

Edward's face seemed to crumple. His head slowly sank into his hands.

165

"Father, please. Don't. We can fight him. We can fight the lies."

"Not lies."

The words were muffled, but they were quite clear. "Not . . ." Darcy put a hand over her mouth. "Not lies," she said, then rubbed her hand against her lips to remove the taste of the words. She looked at her father's soft white hands and felt revolted. She stood up, but she couldn't move a step.

"Darcy," he said. He was crying. She could hear the tears in his thick voice, the plea. "Please."

"Please what, Father?" Her voice was calm. Cruel.

His fingers plucked at her skirt like a baby's, like a child's. "Please."

She stood over his chair, waiting. She could make no move to comfort him. She concentrated on standing still, on waiting. Finally, his head still in his hands, he spoke.

"It was so long ago. Nobody knew, nobody."

"Apparently someone did."

"The maid—Annie—she was in love with him, too."

In love with him, too. Darcy felt sick.

"I'm so horribly ashamed," he said.

"Is that why mother left?" Her voice was cool. How could it be so cool?

"No." He looked up, his face tear-stained. "I swear to you. She didn't know."

"How did Claude find Annie? I don't understand. She was dismissed years before."

"I don't know. Perhaps he met her somewhere else. What does it matter?" He dropped his head again.

"Father, calm yourself. Listen to me. What exactly does Claude have as proof? Do you know? Just Annie's word that she saw—something?" Darcy shuddered.

"There was a letter. From me to Andre."

"You wrote to him?" How insufferably stupid, she thought, looking at her father's head, the hair carefully styled to conceal the thinning at the crown. Lemuel was right. Edward was so weak, so foolish.

"Yes. When he was leaving."

"Dear God." Darcy moved back to her chair and sat down. "But how could Claude have gotten the letter?"

"Perhaps Annie found it. That's the only thing I can think of. She could have been in Andre's room, perhaps it was lying about." Edward gave a strange, twisted smile. "He was a careless man."

"Dear God." Claude had the letter, she was sure of it. And he would have no difficulty revealing it, Darcy knew.

As if he'd read her mind, Edward said, "He'll do it, I have no doubt. That is what I'm waiting for. Every day, I expect the word to get out."

"But, even if it is true, Father," Darcy said, swallowing hard against the disgust that constricted her throat, "I still believe we can fight him. We can expose his activities. If you only knew how he makes his money now—"

He was shaking his head. "But I do know. It is how I make my money, as well."

Horrified, she stared at him. "You knew all along . . ."

"No!" he said quickly. "No, it was recently that he told me—and he took such pleasure in it. You see, years ago I very obligingly brought other gentlemen into the pool. Friends. Men I've known since I was a boy, men who would not forgive me."

"Do you mean to tell me," Darcy said, "that the Old Guard is making their money off brothels and abortionists?"

"They don't know it. But I do." Edward's face constricted, as though he was in pain. "I've made a mess of it, Darcy."

"Yes," she said absently, thinking hard. Layer upon layer, the surfaces of her old life were peeling back. The bright green paper money that paved Fifth Avenue in such springlike profusion was a grassy carpet for secrets and depravities. The Old Guard had to keep up with the swells they scorned, and the blind pool was the way to do it. What did it matter how the money was made, as long as they didn't know the details? It was as clean as the stock market. It had nothing to do with people's lives.

It was the first time she'd seen Columbine angry.

"How can you be so unforgiving, so childish?" Columbine paced in front of Darcy, her silver-willow skirt swishing furiously. "You surely can't turn your back on your father this way. Disgusted, you say you are. Well, I am disgusted with you."

"He's my father!" Darcy almost shouted. Her throat felt tight with tears at her friend's attack.

Columbine turned and spread out her hands. "Precisely," she said gently. Relenting, she went and sat beside Darcy. "Perhaps I've seen too much of the world. Perhaps you haven't seen enough. Your father's . . . inclination is not uncommon. I do not believe it is sinful, either. But whatever you might think, should you not leave such punishment, if there is to be one, to God? You are his daughter, not his confessor."

"But I cannot think of what he did!"

"Then don't think of it—why should you? Think of the consequences now. Could Edward stand to have such a rumor bruited about?"

Darcy shook her head. Tears began to slip down her cheeks.

"He stands beside you for infidelity—no matter how justified you were, Darcy, it *was* infidelity, we can call it by no other name—"

"Love," she whispered.

Columbine patted her hand. "And your father?" she murmured. "His love may be strange to you, but it is also love, nonetheless, no matter what the world might call it."

Darcy burst into tears. She felt Columbine press a handkerchief into her hand, and she cried into it, sobbing so violently she was afraid she would not be able to catch her breath. Columbine waited beside her, occasionally murmuring a word or two of comfort.

"What should I do?" Darcy whispered.

"Help your father, or you shall regret it the rest of your life."

"I shall help him. But I'm not sure how. How I wish I could see Tavish!" Darcy sat up suddenly. "But why shouldn't I see him? Columbine, you could arrange a meeting. If I am to dispense forever with convention, I might as well start now, today."

Columbine nodded decisively. "Good. I shall arrange it, then. This very evening, if you can get away. I've been waiting for you to ask."

Darcy dried her cheeks. "But I thought you felt I shouldn't see Tavish."

"I never said that. I felt that you should know that such a decision could hurt you. But, Darcy, I only wanted you to make the decision with your eyes open."

"How splendid it is," Darcy said seriously, "not to care what people say. However did you learn it?"

Columbine grinned at her. "I was lucky enough to be an outcast, my dear."

Darcy shuddered. "Once I thought it the severest punishment."

"It does take awhile to see it as a bit of a blessing," Columbine said composedly. "But you shall."

The beautiful day mellowed into an evening that smelled of promise. Darcy headed for Madison Square at dusk to meet Tavish. She felt impossibly hopeful as she started out, despite her worry over Claude's threats and her unsettling meeting with Edward. She would see her father for Sunday dinner the next day and make peace with him then.

She walked over to Fifth Avenue for the horsecar, enjoying her freedom. How marvelous not to have to call for a carriage, to have the household know where she had been and who she had seen!

She left in plenty of time, so she wasn't too worried when traffic inexplicably snarled a few blocks from Twenty-third Street. Darcy decided to walk the rest of the way. It was such a fine evening, and Madison Square was so pleasant, the very heart of fashionable New York.

The sidewalks were crowded with men, women, and children. Perhaps there was some kind of rally at Madison Square, for they were all in high spirits, the children trying to control their skipping steps, the adults indulgently watching them, almost as excited as they. Darcy was tempted to ask what the crowds had come for, but her training still held true; she couldn't ask questions of strangers on the street. She supposed she would find out eventually, and she was too intent on seeing Tavish again to care very much.

She was dismayed when she finally reached the northern corner of Madison Square. The crowds were so thick; how could she ever find Tavish in this throng? Darcy felt ridiculous, personally affronted by the laughing faces pushing close to her, the excited voices, the sparkling eyes. She felt like an uninvited guest at a dinner party, standing in her silks and laces watching everyone else at table eating lobster and drinking champagne.

All because she couldn't ask a question of a stranger. Whatever had happened to that courageous woman, struggling to be born? Darcy shook herself and purposefully turned to the gentleman on her left.

"Excuse me, sir. What is going on?" she ask him. "What is going to happen?"

She need not have worried about strange gentlemen; this man was young, gay, his innocent eyes alight, caught up in his pleasure. "It's old P. T. Barnum himself! It's the circus parade, ma'am—they're opening on Monday!"

"Thank you, sir." Darcy pushed ahead through the crowd, heading for the southern end of the square, where she was to meet Tavish. As she grew closer, she could see torches in the street, held by men who would undoubtedly be lighting the parade. The crowds were even thicker here, gaily laughing at the gaudily dressed acrobats who tumbled over one another on Broadway, keeping the crowd amused while they waited for the parade to begin. A chariot full of clowns rolled by, pulled by stolid-looking baby elephants. The clowns' faces were chalk-white, their painted mouths gaping. A cage on wheels rolled behind them, with scrawny monkeys grinning and screeching at her horribly. Following it rolled a cage with one lone wolf, who paced back and forth with menacing grace and eyed her through the bars.

Darcy shivered. She felt bodies pressing against her from

behind, and she was suddenly afraid that they would push her into the street, that she would end up sprawled underneath the wheels of the cages. She fought her way back to safety, holding on to her hat. She struggled to breathe slowly and normally, now truly hating the cries of the crowd, the still air, the smell of the animals.

And then he was at her elbow, supporting her, his familiar low lilt of a voice in her ear. "It seems I need to rescue you again, Mrs. Statton."

She looked up at him and a wave of relief washed over her. It was so very good to see him. "Please, don't call me that. Not anymore."

"Darcy."

"Tavish." They stood staring at each other, smiling faintly.

"Ah, it's good to see that little face of yours again, it is," he said. "Come. Let's get away from this madhouse. What a place to pick—leave it to Columbine."

He took her arm and somehow got them through the crowds, walking quickly down Fifth and then left on Twenty-first Street toward Gramercy Park. It was quieter there, the noise of the parade fading as they walked eastward, and they slowed their steps gratefully.

Under the shelter of trees and gathering darkness, he raised her hand to his lips and kissed it. "How are you?"

"I am well. Rested and well fed, completely recovered, in fact. But I've missed you."

"And I you."

"Have you discovered anything further about—"

"Must we speak of it?" He pressed her arm against his side. "I want to hear about you first."

They walked through the darkness, Darcy's skirt swishing against the sidewalk, and she told him of Edward's confession, her reaction, and Columbine's anger. Tavish listened, not offering a word.

"I suppose I am ashamed of myself," she said when she'd finished. "But there is a part of me that is still disgusted, Tavish. I can't seem to help it."

"Of course there is. It is bred in you. But the thing is, Darcy my love, is to look at things the way they are, not through a mirror held up by other people. If you don't, then the world becomes a reflection, a shadow, and you see only what they want you to see. It takes something like this to shatter that. I've known men like your father—I went to public school in England, you know. Read your Whitman—he speaks of it. Oh, it doesn't disgust me. Men like Claude disgust me."

"Yes," she said. "Nothing is as it seems. Even you."

"Me? And here I thought you could see right through me."

She did not match his teasing tone. "You aren't working for the government, are you?"

His step faltered, but only a bit. "No."

"Then who are you, Tavish Finn, and why are you investigating Claude?"

"I'm glad to have a chance to tell you, Darcy," he said. He tucked her arm more securely into his, and he told her everything he knew and suspected in one circuit of the park.

"Now you know everything I know," he said at the end.

"You think Claude is the man who killed your friend?" Darcy asked, shivering at the thought.

"I think he might have. But I don't know. I can't place him in San Francisco, though I know he was gone in January."

"Yes, he was in Boston. I even got letters from him."

"Ah. Well, then. But letters can be mailed by confederates, too."

"I see. I cannot see him cold-bloodedly murdering someone, though. Claude is very fastidious, Tavish, even squeamish."

"You never know what deeds a man can be driven to do," Tavish said grimly. She didn't like the look in his eye when he said it.

She let a moment pass. "He came to see me this morning."

"Claude?" Tavish's muscles tightened. "I don't understand. Didn't your uncle forbid him the house?"

"Still, he came. Uncle Lemuel was downtown. I saw Claude. He said that he would prove that you were in league with the railroads, Tavish. That you had sold out your town—he said he would ruin you."

"A bluff. What kind of evidence could he have for such lies?"

"Forged evidence. I'm afraid of what he will do, Tavish."

"Love, don't be." He paused and tilted her head so that she could see his eyes. "I'm very close to figuring out his game. I tipped my hand, you see, when I arrived that night and gave the name of Dargent. I'd already done it before at a—an establishment he frequents. So he's been running about town trying to cover up his tracks. The only difference now is that he knows I'm the one chasing him, and he knows that I'm trying to link him to Dargent. But he'll make mistakes now."

Darcy started to walk again, this time with a quicker step. "I know him, Tavish, I know him too well. I wouldn't take his threat lightly. And he doesn't make mistakes."

"Everyone makes mistakes, Darcy. And I've been up against worse men than Claude Statton."

He did not take the threat seriously. But he had not lived with Claude for five years. He had not seen the look in his dead yellow eyes. "You don't understand, Tavish. He has more power than you know—judges, and police—"

He patted her hand. "Now, don't worry about it, love."

She stopped so abruptly his hand was jerked from her. "Don't do that. I've had enough of that to last a lifetime, Tavish Finn." Darcy felt exasperated and angry. She didn't think it would be possible to be so angry with him. And he was still smiling at her! He took her arm again, but she shook it off. "If you don't stop smiling at me," she said deliberately, "I am leaving."

Her eyes were blazing, and Tavish stopped smiling. "All right," he said quietly. "I'm sorry. I didn't meant to smile at you that way. I suppose I feel too much pleasure in simply being with you again. I was taken up with watching your face. I'm not discounting your concern about Claude's threat. I take it very seriously indeed. It's only that I don't want you to worry, Darcy. You've been through so much."

"Exactly. I've been through so much, more than you could possibly imagine. And I've lived with coddling for too long. I will not stand for it, ever again," she said grimly. "And if we are to—to be together, you must stand with me, shoulder to shoulder."

"You've been talking to Columbine."

Darcy looked at him. "Perhaps some of your sister's good sense should rub off on you."

"Perhaps I . . . my sister? She told you?"

"I guessed. Perhaps you won't underestimate me again, then."

"I will most surely attempt not to." He held out his arm again. "May I?" She nodded stiffly, and they resumed their walk. "You're absolutely right, Darcy. There are times when I try to protect too much. You shall have to watch me, and I shall have to try to be better."

"Good," Darcy said grudgingly. "Just make sure you succeed."

He laughed. "Agreed."

She looked at him carefully. "Are you still playing with me, Tavish Finn?"

He seemed genuinely surprised. "Absolutely not."

"Oh. Do you mean that you truly listened to me?"

"Of course I did. You were right."

"Oh." Darcy's breath caught. So this was the way things could be. He would listen to her, and he would try. And she would listen, and she would try. And they would be together.

"I wish I had longer, Darcy," Tavish said as they rounded the northeastern corner of the park again. "But I have an appointment."

"And I should get back to my uncle's. What is your appointment?"

"It's just a man who has helped me with information in the past." At Darcy's arch look, he grinned and elaborated. "A man who worked for the pool through a dummy company and then was blackmailed to keep him in line. Artemis Hinkle."

"Mr. Hinkle—I haven't met him, but I have met his daughter, Julia. She is marrying a cousin of Adelle's by marriage. I liked her."

"Yes, I like her, too. Hinkle is worried that the marriage will not come off."

"But I've heard that it is a love match. I quite envied her at the time."

"But he is being blackmailed, you see."

"Ah. And it could come out and ruin Julia's chances. Oh, Tavish! We must do something. I liked Julia so. Even though that day is hazy in my memory, I do remember that. And I remember her stepmother," Darcy said thoughtfully. "I mean, I remember the portrait."

"I've seen it. A Sargent, over the mantelpiece? A titian-haired woman in a yellow robe?"

"Yes." Remembering that day and her confusion, her whirling brain, Darcy shook her head. She had been so struck by the portrait. What had she been thinking? She'd been trying to remember something . . . Her steps slowed. "It couldn't be," she murmured.

"What couldn't be?"

She shook her head. "No. And yet—"

He joggled her arm. "Darcy!"

"Extraordinary." She turned to him. "Tavish, the woman in the portrait looked familiar to me at the time, and just now I realized why. She could be the twin of a maid we had once—the very maid that Claude is using to blackmail Edward."

"But Artemis met his second wife in California."

"I'm not saying it's the same woman, but it *could* be. The likeness is so exact! And my father had fired Annie—she could have gone anywhere."

Tavish frowned. "Annie?"

"Annie O'Day."

He gripped her hand so hard her bones hurt. "You're sure?"

"Of course I'm sure. She was with us for several years. What is it? Have you met her?"

He relaxed his grip, but only so that he could pull her into a hug and kiss her soundly. "You've solved the case, and don't I love you for it, woman."

"Solved the case! Kiss me again, please. That's better. Now tell me. Do you know Annie?"

"No," Tavish said, taking her hand and pulling her down Twenty-first Street. "But I've heard of her. She *is* Hinkle's wife, I'm sure of it. And she's met Dargent. That means that we can tie Claude to this whole thing, if in fact he's Dargent. We can blow the pool wide open, Darcy! We have to see Hinkle. We have to get him to send for Annie—I mean Anne."

"But what is it that ties her to this business, Tavish? How do you know she's met Dargent? I'm confused." Darcy struggled to keep up with him. She wondered if she'd ever feel free enough to go without a corset, for with all the running and laughing and crying she'd been doing in this new life, she often found it difficult to breathe. "It's a coincidence, yes, but—"

"I can't tell you." Tavish slowed his pace a bit when he heard her labored breathing.

"Tavish, you cannot mean to tell me that after all I said you will conceal this from me."

"You don't understand. I have to. It has to do with the blackmailing threat against Artemis Hinkle. He swore me to secrecy, Darcy. And if he were to know that I told you—especially you, a Snow, related to Adelle Archer—I would lose his trust."

She pulled him to a stop. "You think I could not keep it secret?"

"Of course I know that you could," Tavish said impatiently. "But it should be Artemis Hinkle's decision to tell you."

"Then take me to him."

"I am trying to, love. If you would move those lovely limbs of yours."

Darcy laughed, and they walked on quickly through the dark streets. They blundered onto the parade again when they reached Broadway. Tavish cursed under his breath and held her hand tightly as he darted through the crowd, pulling her along.

Darcy kept pace with him, uneasy once more by the moonless night, by the strange shadows of the torches, the animals prowling in their cages, the high, excited voices of the children, all of it a background to their desperate haste.

They passed by the parade, by the monkeys, the hyena, the magnificent, stately lion, the chariot with Cinderella and Mother Goose, Tavish half laughing in exasperation at the whole impossible assemblage. But as they moved away, seeking the quieter streets and a hack, she once again saw the rolling cage of the wolf. He stalked across the tiny space, his yellow eyes gleaming in the orange wavering glow. Watching her. She gazed back at him, not able to tear her eyes away, as Tavish gripped her hand tighter and they plunged into the blackness beyond.

Hinkle could not help them. It was a broken man who received them, who shuffled in front of them toward his study. With only one quick, questioning glance at Tavish, he willingly told Darcy his story. But it was too late for all of them. Anne Hinkle had written him that morning to tell them that she'd left him. She could not bear disgracing him, she could not bear chaining him to a job that sickened him, and said it would be easier for him if she was gone from his life. He did not know where she had gone. She did not say.

There was nothing for Tavish and Darcy to do but go home. He took her arm and led her outside. But before the door closed behind them, he touched her arm.

"Wait one moment."

Darcy nodded.

He stopped the door from closing and explained to the butler that he'd forgotten something. The butler gave his usual sneer to Tavish, but he went past him and hurried back to Hinkle's study.

Hinkle was sitting at the desk, staring into space.

"Where did your wife say she came from—before you knew the truth about her. Where did she say she had lived?"

Hinkle's eyes flickered. "Denver, Colorado. She received letters from there. She had a friend there, a woman."

"Do you think she'd go back there now?"

Hinkle shook his head slowly, expressionlessly. "No. I do not."

"Why not?" Tavish demanded impatiently.

"Because she does not look back, Mr. Finn. No, I discounted Denver from the start."

Tavish said good night again and returned to Darcy. Anne Hinkle couldn't have disappeared. There had to be a way to track her down. Hinkle could be wrong. Perhaps she would return to a place where she'd been happy or had a friend.

"Anything?" Darcy asked?

He shook his head. "Nothing."

Darcy stared at Tavish's compressed lips. She knew what she had to do. She had to get back into Claude's study. There would be evidence there. She had to gather her courage in her two hands and walk into the house again. Perhaps offer herself to her husband again. For Tavish, yes. For Julia Hinkle, of course. But most of all, for Edward. For her father. Sometime tonight, somehow, she had found her love for him again. She slipped her hand inside of Tavish's pocket and prayed that the man she loved would never find out what she might be forced to do to free them all.

Thirteen

IT WAS AN overcast Sunday, gloomy and threatening a hard rain that never arrived. Incredibly, Claude had sent over three trunks of Darcy's dresses the night before, and she'd had her sapphire-blue velvet dress, Edward's favorite, pressed by Marie's maid in preparation for her visit. But Edward sent a message that he had caught a terrible cold and could not receive her for Sunday dinner. Disappointed, Darcy spent a quiet day with Lemuel and Marie. She skipped church, unwilling to face everyone there; there was no sense pushing her new-found courage.

Strangely, she did not think of how she would fare the next day with Claude. She had made her decision: she would go to the house in midmorning, after he'd left for his office. If she could not gain access to his private office or his files, she would wait for him to return. And then she would see. If she could get the key from his watch, she could perhaps slip upstairs in the early-morning hours. Anything was possible, anything could be attempted. She would find a way, she told herself as she fell asleep to the sound of the pattering rain, which had finally arrived in full force.

She slept badly, awakened several times by the sound of a high wind. When she woke, she could hear the difference before her senses were fully alert. Her room faced the front of the house at Thirty-eighth Street, but she heard no sound. It couldn't be, she thought, rising and pushing back the lace curtain. It couldn't be snow. Not now, not after such lush, springlike days.

But it was. And it was deep, wind-swept, and still falling. It was an odd sight, for the south side of Thirty-eighth Street, where Lemuel's house was situated, was almost clear of snow. But the opposite side was piled high with drifts, all the way up to the front doors. A few showed signs of shoveling, but the snow had almost filled the paths up again. She wondered if the Fifth Avenue horsecars would be able to get through the snow.

As she stood at the window, she saw a woman coming down Thirty-eighth Street, holding her black coat collar up near her face. Probably a maid heading for work. She was on the south sidewalk, but she was walking carefully, taking small steps, and Darcy realized that the sidewalk must be a sheet of ice. Suddenly, a great gust of wind came—Darcy saw the telegraph wires fly overhead and the bare tree limbs rattle—and the woman's feet flew out from underneath her. Darcy watched, horrified, as the woman slid into the gutter. Luckily, there was a pile of soft snow to cushion her. She saw the woman shake her head, then begin to crawl back to the sidewalk again.

Darcy would have to wrap herself well, that was certain. She hoped that Claude had sent her fur-trimmed coat and fur-lined boots, her warmest items of clothing. If she couldn't find a hansom cab on Fifth, she'd have to walk the fifteen blocks to Claude's. She'd walked in snowstorms before; it could be exhilarating.

But when she came down, dressed and ready to face the storm, her usually mild aunt put up a fuss.

"No, Darcy, I cannot let you go. You don't realize how bad the storm is. Why, the second chambermaid barely made it here this morning. She turned up half-frozen, poor dear. She had to climb down a ladder from the El tracks, can you imagine such a thing!"

"I am not taking the El, aunt. I'll find a hack on Fifth Avenue and be snug as can be."

"Darcy, I must insist. I don't know why you feel this need to see Claude—will he even be there?—Lemuel would be horrified. And I would worry so dreadfully. I am half out of my mind about Lemuel already. I don't know why he went to work at all this morning!"

"I'm sure he'll be fine."

"What will I do if he can't make it home!" Marie twisted her hands. "And now with your leaving I'll be alone."

"Only for a few hours, I promise. I'll be back for lunch, Aunt. We'll have a nice lunch together."

And she left, with Marie protesting behind her. Her aunt shrieked when Darcy opened the door and a gust of wind sent fine snowflakes swirling into the front hall. It took Darcy, Marie, and the maid to close the door behind her.

"I *must* be a madwoman," Darcy said as she stood on the stoop. Then she put one foot on the top step and went flying. She landed on the third step unhurt and slid down the rest of the way. As she sat, befuddled, on the sidewalk, something plopped on her hat. She plucked it off with difficulty, her gloved fingers moving clumsily through the fur of her hat. She nearly screamed when she brought her hand back to examine the object. A tiny frozen sparrow lay in her palm.

"I *am* a madwoman," she said.

It was not the last time she fell. She'd been right; the sidewalk was solid ice. Time after time she would have to grab onto a tree or a fence to keep herself upright during the terrible gusts of wind. She almost turned back, but Darcy was determined. She was sure things would be better on Fifth Avenue; at least she could catch a cab or a horsecar.

But when she finally reached Fifth, the funnel of wind that bore down upon her made her gasp, and she saw with tearing eyes that it would be impossible to find a cab or squeeze onto one of the horsecars, which were not only crowded but few and far between. Looking down the avenue, she saw one abandoned near Thirty-seventh Street, the horse probably led off to the stable. She saw other abandoned vehicles, left at odd angles in the street, the horses gone. But there was some traffic on the avenue, hacks and carts still trying to make headway. They appeared and disappeared through the whirling snow.

The force of the storm was unlike anything she had ever felt. Surely it could not continue with this frenzy. Surely the winds would abate, the snow would slacken. It was March, too late for such weather. This must be a fierce, short squall, she told herself. She turned right, toward uptown, and immediately staggered back from the force of the screaming wind.

Her veil had frozen with sticky flakes on the short block there, and she had pushed it over her hat in order to see. Now, fully into the northwest wind, her eyelashes iced over within minutes, and she had to stop and cup her hands over her face every few steps and breathe in sharp puffs to thaw them. Darcy tried turning backward and walking, as she saw a couple of other women doing, and that seemed to help. At least here on Fifth there were no telegraph wires down to trip over, for they weren't allowed on this fashionable street.

When she did face the snow, it was no soft delight against her cheek. It felt like sharp needles hitting her skin, and she noticed that some of the men and women hurrying past had blood on their faces. Ash and dirt mixed with the snow as it was flung into their faces, and she saw one woman, her eyes streaming tears, wander blindly into a drift over her head near a basement entrance of a house. Darcy started to struggle toward her but a policeman was already moving, dragging the woman out of the drift and rubbing her bright red ears with snow to thaw them.

Navigating over the cross streets was bad work. Often Darcy allowed whatever male was handy to help her. She envied their flat boots, so much better than the delicately curved heel on her smart boots. She dreaded the point where she would have to cross the icy blasting corridor of Fifth Avenue. She had seen one woman try, go over in a flurry of skirts and petticoats, and slide into the path of an oncoming cart. She would have been trampled underneath the wheels if a passing gentleman hadn't rescued her, falling down himself in the process.

Darcy picked a spot to cross where two gentlemen were standing, waiting until a horsecar went by. It was packed with people, but they might as well have been walking, for the two poor horses were making scant headway against the wind. They stamped and slid on the icy pavement, and finally the conductor and the male passengers got out and pushed. The car slowly and inevitably slid into a snowbank, and the passengers got out, straightening their scarves and ducking their heads against the wind. Some undoubtedly headed home, but Darcy imagined many did not; she knew that if they didn't show up for their jobs, Claude and men of his ilk would fire them.

The two gentlemen next to her eyed each other and the avenue. Darcy tugged on one man's sleeve.

"May I cross with you, sir?" she screamed, and pantomimed her object, for the wind snatched her words and sent them down Fifth Avenue. Whether he had heard or not, he nodded and tried to smile, though his beard and mustache were almost completely iced over.

The two men, with Darcy sandwiched in between, inched their way across Fifth. The three of them were almost knocked flat in the middle of the avenue, but they managed to slide their way to the opposite side. Relieved, Darcy clung to a hitching post and nodded her thanks. The men bowed and the younger one shouted an offer to escort her to her door. Darcy refused with thanks and went on her way again. She had only three more blocks to go.

There were less people on this part of Fifth, Darcy noticed as she struggled against the wind. She cupped her hands over her ears to warm them, for though she'd forsaken high style to tie a woolen scarf around her head to keep her hat on, the scarf was encrusted with snow and ice and was now most likely freezing her ears faster than the wind would have done.

But she was so close now. She had to discipline herself not to hurry, for she'd never be able to keep her footing. She would have found it amusing that she was looking so forward to reaching Claude's house if she didn't feel like a solid column of teetering ice. Any shelter would be welcome. Especially since Claude wouldn't be there. Like Lemuel, he would have struggled downtown to his office early this morning. And for that, Darcy was relieved. She would need time to thaw, change into dry clothes, and take a shot of Claude's best cognac before she plunged back into the storm again.

Perhaps it was the thought of comfort that distracted her. But most likely the ice was just too slick, and the wind cooperated at that moment by gusting with such force that it actually lifted her off her feet. Darcy felt herself propelled toward the bank of snow that lay against the fences to the houses on her left—except that the fences had been long covered, and the snow in some places was over her head. She landed in one of the drifts, and the wind tore her scream from her mouth.

Angrily, Darcy pushed at the snow and only succeeded in driving herself deeper into it. She discovered that, hampered with her wet skirts, now like iron, it was difficult to move at all. Any struggle seemed only to bury her farther into the drift. Irritation changed abruptly to fear. She knew that she could freeze to death in here, not found for hours. There was no friendly policeman in sight to help her out.

Panic shot through her, and she moved her arms furiously. Her fingers hit something to her left—something hard and smooth, curved. A railing? But the thing moved in her hand, and she tugged, feeling sweat bead up on her face with effort and panic, incredible in this cold.

An umbrella. It came loose, and she eased it across her body until it was free of the snow. Then she hoisted it upward like a flag, and moved it back and forth. Holding on for dear life with both hands, terrified the wind would snatch it away, she kept it aloft.

Presently, two round blue eyes underneath a solid horizontal line of crystallized eyebrow peered over the mound of snow. "Good Lord! Begging your pardon, miss. Let me give you a hand if I may, miss."

"If you would be so kind," Darcy screamed, and a meaty hand grabbed hers and hauled her forward. She almost pitched to the sidewalk, but the hands grabbed her waist and steadied her.

"Begging your pardon, miss."

It was a driver whose cart could go no farther. He'd been in the middle of unharnessing his horse in order to walk him back to the stables when he saw the waving umbrella. "Awfully clever, that," he shouted admiringly, and would brook no argument but saw her safely to the door of Claude's mansion. With shaking fingers, Darcy removed her glove to fish in her bag. She pressed a silver piece into his hand and thanked him.

She rang the bell. The door was eased open by Tolliver, the butler.

"Mrs. Statton," he said, surprised. But he did not move out of the way.

She'd been afraid of that, that Claude had ordered the servants not to admit her. Darcy summoned up her dignity, the imperial manner Claude had pressured her to adopt. Raising her chin and ignoring the wet and tattered feather that hung over one eye, she swept past him without a word.

"I'll need hot tea and towels, Tolliver. In my room, directly. Mr. Statton is at his office?"

"Yes, madam, left early this morning."

She handed him her ice-crusted coat and scarf, her bedraggled hat. "He is to be home for tea. Please inform the chef. I'd like something special, if he can manage it." She didn't know what she was saying, but she kept talking, giving orders, smoothing her wet hair, desperately hoping that Tolliver would believe that she and Claude had reconciled and Claude had neglected to tell him. And what could he do? No messages could get downtown today.

So the blizzard turned out to be a blessing, in a way, for the servants didn't dare question her arrival and could not get confirmation from the master. Darcy went up the stairs, the hem of her skirt trailing snow on the Persian carpet runner. She would bathe—it would look odd if she did not, and besides, she was chilled to the bone—and leave orders that she was not to be disturbed. Then she would try to get upstairs to Claude's office.

The first step was Claude's bedroom. The key had to be there. She'd given much thought to that. Closing her eyes, she had remembered nights she'd returned to her room in her ball gown, Claude having said he would be working late. He always went to his room first—she remembered hearing the click of the door shutting as he came out again. Claude could have gone to his bedroom for many reasons, but somehow she felt he would keep the key there. He hated superfluous items on his person; he hated to carry things, to have things in his pockets. He was a neat, fastidious man without ornamentation of any kind. That, he reserved for his wife.

It was the slimmest of chances, but what else did she have? Darcy sat in her bedroom until she was sure Solange had gone back to her room in the servant's quarters. Her hair was still damp, spreading out over her shoulders to dry. Her fawn-colored dress, put away because it was from last season even though hardly worn, was thick velvet lined with cashmere. She was finally warm and relatively dry, and she was ready.

The corridor was dark, as though it were night. Darcy slipped down it, making no noise. She eased open the door to Claude's room and hurried inside, her velvet skirt rustling in the silence. It was cold and dark, the heavy curtains drawn against the storm, the fire long out. Darcy surveyed the room, standing against the closed door. She thought quickly. The top drawer of the bureau, of course. It was meticulously arranged, she knew, sections for handkerchiefs, collar stays and shirt studs, and the dress watch that he used in the evenings—thinner and more elegant than the everyday watch, the top delicately chased.

She carefully went through the handkerchiefs, the studs, and the second drawer of French socks before she thought of it. Claude's other watch! Of course! Yanking open the first drawer again, she took it out. She opened one side, and the face was revealed. Then her fingers followed the delicate seam around the other side, feeling for another catch. There was none. So he only kept the key in his daytime watch.

Disappointed, Darcy replaced the watch and resumed her search. But there were no keys in the bureau. No keys in the small satinwood desk, no keys in any pockets in the huge wardrobe. No keys in the nighttable. No keys.

Time was running out. It had taken her an hour and a half to walk to Claude's. Thirty minutes to bathe and change and give Solange enough mending to keep her busy for several hours. And the storm hadn't abated; she could hear the wind, still howling outside the windows. She would have to leave shortly; she'd missed lunch, of course, but she should be back at Lemuel's in time for tea. Unless she had to stay. But somehow Darcy could not face being trapped in the house with Claude during a snowstorm. Difficult as it was, she would have to wait more long days before attempting this again. But by that time, the servants would know that there was no reconciliation.

What should she do? Darcy thought frantically. Stay or go? Try to force the lock on the door? Why not? she realized. Claude would not be in a position to protest if she found evidence linking him to Dargent, or evidence that he was Dargent himself. She picked up the ivory and gold paper knife on Claude's desk.

The hallway was dark and deserted. Darcy crossed swiftly to the small door around the corner that led upstairs. She tried the knob and it turned. The door was unlocked.

She almost laughed aloud in relief. Why hadn't she checked the door first? Then she frowned with her next thought: why would the door be unlocked? Claude had left it unlocked that day she'd slipped upstairs only because he knew he was returning within minutes. Could a man who forgot nothing have neglected something so important as locking his private office before he left for the day?

Darcy pondered the question, but really there was nothing for it but to go on up. She slipped inside, shut the door behind her, and climbed the dark, narrow stairs. It could be midnight, not midday, by the look of things. Or rather, the way things would look, if she could see past the nose on her face. She wished she had brought a lamp, for her heart was beating fearfully. Suddenly panicked in the enclosed space, she hurried her steps and felt the wood of the door at the top with relief. She pushed it open.

She still could see nothing. The curtains were drawn here, too. She could smell the ashy burnt aroma of a recently lit fire. The space was wide and open, and even with no lamps lit she was sure that Claude wasn't there. She'd been afraid that he had returned without the servants knowing and come up here. But the place was empty; she could feel no human presence here.

She inched her way across the carpet. There was a lamp on Claude's desk, she knew. It should be just ahead, a few feet ahead and slightly to the left . . .

Her foot hit something. Something soft, yielding. Looking down, she could see it now, gathering form in the grayness. A human form. Someone was lying on the floor, face down. Someone who was very still, still as death . . .

Darcy shoved her fist against her mouth so that she would not let loose the scream that had formed in her belly and was now filling her throat. Her chest felt too tight, too small for her thundering heart. Panting with her panic, she inched down. Her fingers searched for the wrist. It was Claude, of course it was Claude, she'd known that it was her husband from the moment she saw the still, black form.

No pulse on the thin wrist. The skin felt cold. Darcy dropped it and braced herself against the floor so that she could sit. Her right hand slid in something sticky and wet.

"Dear Lord." She began to sob with terror. She could not move. She was afraid she would go mad, that she would scream and never stop screaming.

Claude was dead. Suicide, accident? It took several long moments for her to gather her nerve to crawl to the desk to light the lamp. Not too high, she only needed to turn the gas up a bit . . .

The room seemed to spring forward at her. Darcy shrank against the desk, swallowing her involuntary cry. One hand of Claude's was outstretched, the fingers splayed open. He was lying on his belly, but now she could see his face half-turned toward her. One yellow eye stared at her in mild surprise.

Sobbing under her breath now, she crawled back toward him. Blood was on his white shirtfront and pooled underneath his hip. But there was no gun near the outstretched hand or near the body, so how could he have . . .

She sat back abruptly, almost falling. Murder?

If they were indeed bullet wounds, or stab wounds, it would be murder. With a deep shudder, Darcy realized that she would have to turn over the body.

Inching forward on her hands and knees, she told herself over and over not to look at his face. She concentrated on his shoulder, his upper thigh. If she could grasp both of these, she could turn him. Claude was a small man.

She was making odd noises, small but high-pitched, as she tugged. And then suddenly he spun over and came to rest on his back. Both hands were now outstretched in a grotesque parody of the Crucifixion. His mouth was open. His skin looked like wax.

188

And then her eyes traveled downward and she saw his wound. She crawled to the brass cuspidor by the damask screen and emptied the contents of her belly into it.

Edward watched the storm from his comfortable armchair, a rug over his knees. Although he had exaggerated the extent of his ailment to escape facing his daughter's eyes over the dinner table on Sunday, he was coming down with a cold, and he knew it would be a bad one. Edward hated colds. His great-uncle on his mother's side had died of pneumonia not so long ago. He sneezed, remembering.

The last thing in the world he wanted to do was to go out in that storm. It was a blizzard, a raging, furious, savage tempest of howling winds and bitter cold and blowing icy pellets of snow. But he had to see Darcy. Edward told himself strongly that it was only ten short blocks uptown to Lemuel's. There would be hot tea, maybe even whiskey if the teetotaling Marie wasn't about, for him when he got there.

He had to see his child. He had to tell her he'd been weak, he'd been a coward. But he was no longer afraid. He had gotten courage from a strange source: from Claude.

His son-in-law had called briefly on Sunday not only to repeat his threats of exposure of Edward's secret, but also to hint, ever so delicately, that it was perfectly possible for him to get Darcy committed as insane. He would have no trouble receiving the necessary papers from Dr. Arbuthnot, as well as the sworn statements of the servants who had seen Darcy's condition the week before.

Strangely, Edward had felt relief. His enemy had revealed himself. His enemy had gone too far. And Edward was ready.

For Claude did not know the most important thing: Darcy knew the truth about Edward now. He did not have that to fear, at least. He could run off to Europe as Amelia had done, taking Darcy with him. He'd heard Amelia was happy there. Perhaps he could call on her one last time to settle things between them, to tell her that finally he was able to wish her well.

So things, Edward decided, looking out at the snow, were not so very bad as they appeared. At least he would have the satisfaction of redeeming himself in his daughter's eyes. And at least he could bring Claude down with him.

He knew enough of Claude's operation—the brothels, the houses of assignation, the society abortionist, Mrs. Usenko—to bring him down. There was a new mayor in office now, a mayor Claude did not control. Abram Hewitt had been elected on a platform of reform. Edward would go straight to him if he had to.

He got out his fur cap, his heavy overcoat trimmed in lamb's wool. He wrapped a scarf around his face, then unwrapped it and went into the library. He poured himself a large glass of whiskey and drank it standing up. That should help warm him. He drank another half glass, just to be sure.

Edward felt better when he walked out on his stoop. The snow was rather deeper than he'd thought; he couldn't even see the outline of the stairs. He considered them dubiously. A piece of cardboard, blown by the wind, skittered onto the porch, distracting him. Edward pushed at it irritably with his foot, then reconsidered. He picked it up, positioned it on the top step, and sat down on it. He pushed off and went flying down the stairs, holding onto the cardboard and laughing in delight. He rolled off at the bottom, still laughing.

But now that he was out from the partial shelter of the overhang over the front stoop, he felt the full force of the wind, and the laughter was torn from his throat. Edward picked himself up, adjusted his scarf over his face, and told himself he was a strong man who got plenty of exercise. He walked everywhere, he rode his horse in the park twice a week, and last fall he had even purchased a bicycle and rode it in the park on Sundays. He had taken Darcy one Sunday. What fun they had had! But then Claude had forbidden her to go again . . .

He could manage a ten-block walk, gale or no. He headed toward Madison, staggering in the face of the wind.

It was hard going, but he managed it. His thigh muscles ached from pushing through the snow on his street, but Madison was a bit better, the foot traffic having packed down the snow a bit. And it was cheering to see a few other souls about, even if they were barely discernible through the blowing snow. One woman passed him, her face streaked with a horrible gray-green color. Edward began to go after her to see if she was hurt, then realized that the dye was running on her fashionable but soaking-wet hat and veil. It had probably once been emerald velvet, but now looked a sodden bird's nest on top of her head. He continued on.

It was at the corner of Thirty-eighth that it happened. The wind had picked up a sign—Edward was able to see it as it flew toward him; MR. WINTHROP MILES, DANCING CLASSES, it read—and as he watched in amazement, the wooden sign flew like a feather through the air and clouted him on the forehead.

Edward fell awkwardly. He pitched backward, his arms windmilling furiously, and landed in the stairwell leading to the basement of a brownstone. His leg twisted underneath him and caused him sharp pain when he went down. He was grateful at first that there was a soft pile of snow to receive him. But that was before the snow gave way before his pushing hands and he was unable to lift himself out.

Dazed, he watched the snow keep falling. He struggled again, then fell back. His leg ached horribly; what if it were broken? There would be a devil of a time getting to Lemuel's, once someone pulled him out. And damn and blast, he would have to be put up at his former brother-in-law's, and that would be deuced awkward. There was no love lost between him and Lemuel. Lemuel had never liked him, no, not from the very beginning, when Edward had first called on beautiful Amelia and stolen her away from that dour household of Graces. Lemuel with his old French books, his French this and his French that, everything so classical, everything perfect. Amelia had been so eager, so hungry for mess, for life spilling over the edges, for jokes, for laughter, for wine and food enjoyed, not in delicate sips, but heartily.

But at least Darcy would be there to smooth things along. That scarecrow of a wife Lemuel had wouldn't be much help.

And so Edward mused about the problems he would have adjusting to the Grace household for a few days, as soon as some nice hearty fellow came along and hauled him out. He began to feel drowsy, and his eyelids began to close. Perhaps they would freeze shut, Edward thought with sudden alarm, for his eyelashes were caked with ice. He struggled to keep them open, but they began to close again.

It was then that it occurred to him that there might not come along a nice hearty fellow to haul him out. Perhaps he would die here, Edward thought. How absurd, to die in a storm a few doors from safety. From his daughter. The lovely, passionate, fierce daughter he had failed time and again. She would never know how he'd found his courage in the end.

Darcy let the curtain fall back again. It was impossible, but the storm seemed even more ferocious. She could not see the street. Only a white, swirling mass.

She turned back again to the desk. It had taken her a long time to compose herself enough to begin her search, but she had, with the help of a strong draft of Claude's whiskey.

However, her efforts had proved futile. Everything suspicious was gone. The extra accounting books were missing. The letters from Dargent were gone, the whole file taken so that her letters from Lemuel and Amelia were gone, too. And there was no letter from Edward to Andre Maubert. Even the cabinet was empty, left open. The only thing left were Claude's records of legitimate stock transactions. Perhaps everything had been burned in the fireplace. Perhaps that had been the smell she'd noted when she'd walked in.

Tavish had told her, his eyes avoiding hers, that his friend had not only been shot, but mutilated. Mutilated, she was sure, in the same way that Claude had been. So whoever had killed Jamie Alden had killed Claude, as well. Dargent. The only person who knew what Dargent looked like was Annie O'Day, and there was no evidence here of her. No record of money passed on, no address. And no letter from Edward to Andre Maubert.

Darcy went to the window again and leaned against the cold glass. Every nerve in her skin screamed escape. She could not bear to remain in the room with Claude's body any longer. But she knew she would not be able to survive the walk back to Lemuel's. Could she spend the night in her room here, knowing Claude's lifeless body was upstairs?

She glanced at the clock on the mantelpiece. It was almost tea-time. She would have to go downstairs, give some explanation to the servants. Of course they would assume Claude would sleep downtown tonight in a hotel. She was safe for tonight, at least. It would be a sleepless night, to be sure. But tomorrow she would get to Tavish somehow.

Darcy was so absorbed in her thoughts that the rustling noise on the stairs escaped her attention. But she jumped when the door banged open. She whirled around. Solange stood in the doorway. In one swift glance her black eyes took in the scene, then ticked over Darcy's dress. Darcy looked down and realized that her dress was blood-stained, her hem dark with the stuff, as well as her right sleeve. The lace was brown with dried blood. Then Solange's gaze returned to Claude's body. Darcy had covered his face and torso with a blanket, but his thin legs stuck out, his expensive boots shining in the lamplight.

Solange took a step toward Darcy, hate blazing on her thin, white face. "You killed him," she said.

Fourteen

"No," Darcy breathed. "Solange—"

Solange walked over to stand by Claude's body. She lifted the blanket with a tenderness that gave Darcy an eerie chill.

"Claude," Solange murmured. *"Bon compagnon."*

"What did you say?"

Solange replaced the blanket. "We were friends, your husband and I."

"Friends."

"We talked, often, he sought me out. He consulted me about you—"

This had to be a dream, a nightmare. "About me?"

"Of course," Solange said contemptuously. "Who knew you better than I? Your trifling moods and petty concerns. You never helped him! You only set him back."

"You don't know anything," Darcy said.

"I know everything," Solange answered calmly. "Everything. He told me everything. Your inability to bear children—how he wanted them, *le pauvre!* Every man needs a son. But you locked your door to him—where was he to turn?"

Darcy was fascinated by this glimpse into the soul of the gloomy, taciturn Solange. "To you?"

Solange gave her a scornful look. Her thin face looked very

white, very still. "No. He respected me, Madame. And he loved me in his way, I think, because I saw his unhappiness—"

"*His* unhappiness!"

"And I saw the cause of it. He married a child, not a woman—"

Darcy began to shake. "Stop this, Solange."

"A child who did not know how to please him, who locked her door against him."

"I never locked my door." Darcy laughed, a high sound. "I was unable to lock my door! He had the key!"

Her words didn't register. Solange went on steadily. "You knew that he could put you in a madhouse for it. And why shouldn't he? Weren't you mad? Didn't you refuse your husband—yet take a lover? Didn't you attack your husband with a cane?"

"He said that?"

"You were violent, deranged. It was the only course for him. And wasn't it true, for didn't you kill him in the end?" Solange let out a huge, shuddering sob, but her tense face stayed strangely still. Only her lips twisted in agony. "Yes, you killed him! You killed him!" Solange grabbed Darcy's bloodied sleeve. *"And you will pay, Madame!"*

Darcy tried to shake off Solange, but the fingers were like talons on her arm. "Solange, listen to me. I did not kill my husband! Tell me, if I killed him, where is the gun?"

She shook her head violently. "You have concealed it. But the police will find it. What does it matter, what does it matter now?"

"This is absurd! I discovered his body, just as you did."

Solange's face was calm now. It was as though a curtain came down on her grief. The narrow face loomed closer to Darcy, the tiny birdlike eyes opaque. "Then why were you up here so long, Madame? Were you prostrate with grief over his body? Pardon me, but I do not think so, Madame."

"I don't care what you believe," Darcy said firmly, finally succeeding in shaking Solange's bony hand off her arm. "Now, we'll go downstairs. I've had enough of your hysteria. You will fetch Mrs. Amboy and the extra set of keys. We'll lock the door until tomorrow, when the police can get here."

"No, I will give the orders now. Mrs. Amboy does not have a key, there is no spare key. Surely you knew that. I will tell Tolliver to post a guard. We will need ice from the kitchens . . ."

Darcy shuddered involuntarily, realizing what the ice would be for.

"Yes, guilt makes you shiver. And I will also tell Tolliver to send the strongest man to the police. Now."

Darcy felt the first beginnings of fear. "Now? But the man won't be able to get through—"

"He will get through," Solange said. "I suggest you remain in your room, Madame Statton, until the police arrive. If you try to leave, I will stop you. Why should you leave, anyway? The police will look everywhere for you. You won't be able to leave the city."

Darcy saw the wild gleam of fanaticism in the Frenchwoman's eyes. Solange would do what she wanted. Darcy's denials and claims would be ignored. Solange would tell the servants that Darcy had killed Claude, and they would listen and obey her. Everyone would believe Solange's story: that Darcy had attacked Claude with a cane, that she was mad. Darcy saw it all in front of her, the whole stately progression of events. She looked so guilty! Why hadn't she screamed and run downstairs when she found the body? Why was there so much blood on her dress, on her hands? And didn't they all know how she hated him?

"Come, Madame." Solange took her arm again.

With apparent calm, Darcy pried the long, thin fingers off her arm. She walked ahead of Solange, skirting Claude's body, and went down the stairs and directly to her room.

She heard Solange go down the main staircase. Darcy laced herself into her walking boots, still slightly damp from this morning. She picked up her coat, scarf, muff, and gloves. She wished there was time to change her dress, but she was certain Solange would post a guard on her door, as well.

Moving quickly, she slipped out of her room and went down the back stairs. Without a word, she faced the servants in the kitchen, who were too surprised to see her to say much of anything. Giving an imperious nod to one and all who gaped at her over their cups of tea, she very calmly walked out into the raging storm.

Tavish was having a hell of a day. He had been set upon outside his door late Sunday night, kicked and beaten with weighted gloves, then bound and gagged and bundled into the back of a cart with a tarpaulin that smelled of manure tight over his head, and jounced over miles of New York streets. It was a freezing, painful journey, and Tavish entertained himself by running his tongue over his front tooth, which felt as though it had been snapped in half, and imagining what his new smile would look like. He was comforted only by the thought that his captors were having a rather rough time of it, as the cart slid precariously over the ice from one side of the street to the other, bucking like one of Colonel Cody's broncos in his Wild West show. Tavish had heard some imaginative cursing in his day, but these fellows would take any prize hands down.

It must have taken hours. Tavish wasn't sure. Incredibly, he had fallen asleep for part of the journey. He'd always had a knack for catching sleep when he could. His captors woke him up with a distinct absence of tender concern. A small but very powerful man slung him over his shoulder like a cat and carried him into a ramshackle, filthy, smelly, horrible house on Eleventh Avenue. Terrific. He was in Hell's Kitchen, that most notorious area of Manhattan ruled by Irish gangs who'd sooner gouge out your eye than hear the reasons why not.

While the storm rattled the windows and the snow seeped in through the cracks of a small, bare kitchen, the men argued in thick Irish brogues and drank whiskey. The problem seemed to be that after they killed him, nobody wanted to venture out in the storm and dump him in the usual place, wherever that was. There were some for dumping him right outside the door, but apparently the policemen from the nearby 20th Precinct, who only ventured forth in groups of three, had been unusually zealous lately in breaking up the infamous gangs. Another murder victim dumped on the avenue just might invite a severe crackdown. And nobody wanted that, with spring coming on and summer around the corner, when they'd all want to be outside.

Tavish listened and dozed. He considered the fact that the beating and the clubbing might be a moot point, since he would probably freeze to death on the floor. He thought about Darcy a vast amount. Would she still love him without a front tooth?

He awoke to the sound of singing. He recognized it as an Irish air his mother used to sing. "Mairi's Wedding." Tavish had a fine tenor voice, and he loved the song. The men were murdering it. He'd been trying to work the gag loose between naps, and now he wiggled his chin and used his teeth, trying not to think of his truncated one, and the gag came loose enough to slip down his chin. Tavish began to sing. His voice came out croaked at first. Then it improved a bit. He sang louder.

Chairs scraped. "What the hell—"

He braced himself for the blow but kept on singing. There was no blow, but the tarp was ripped off and a circle of dirty faces stared at him. Clouds of foul whiskey-breath drifted toward him. Tavish stopped singing and blinked up at them.

"Holy Jesus, it's an Irishman," one of them said.

Another one spit. "Can't see it makin' a difference."

"Aye," the small one with the impressive muscles said. One of his eyes was gone, but he wore no patch. Perhaps he was proud of it. "But he can sing. Where're you from, paddy?"

"Galway," Tavish said, thickening his accent slightly.

"Terry here is from Galway."

Tavish nodded. "I sure could use a sip o' that whiskey," he said.

"Might as well," the man called Terry said.

"We aren't getting to be friendly, now. I don't want to be knowing what you done to get yourself here," the one-eyed man warned him as he put the bottle to Tavish's lips.

After taking a quick gulp, Tavish answered, "Sure, I tried to help a lady in distress is all." The whiskey burned all the way down to his belly, feeling fine.

"I said—"

"He seemed like a rotter, that one who hired us," one man broke in, taking the whiskey bottle and slugging from it. "All his bags of money won't make him a gentleman."

"No worse than you, Seamus," Terry said, taking a long sip and passing it to the one-eyed man again.

Tavish took another sip as the one-eyed man held the bottle to his lips again. He noted that the man had given him a sip before taking his own. It was a good sign, despite the man's tough words, not to mention the disconcerting absence of eye. "Well," Tavish said, "I won't be telling you what I've done, then, since you're asking me not to. But let me tell you what the bastard tried to do to his wife. It makes a good story, anyway."

"What the hell," Terry said. "We've got all night. But do you know 'Nell Flaherty's Drake,' now?"

Within three blocks Darcy knew that if she didn't get shelter she would die. She was exhausted, every step an effort, and she kept staggering and falling to her knees. She got up as quickly as she could, but she was growing slower and slower at pushing herself up again. The last time she fell, she'd been tempted to lie down and rest for a minute. She knew if she did she might never be able to get up again.

She wasn't sure of the time; the day had been so dark that the coming of night was imperceptible. The wind seemed more ferocious than it had been that morning. She kept to Fifth Avenue to avoid the tangled wires on the side streets. In places the snow was up to her thighs. Darcy began to sob. She would never be able to make it to Lemuel's house. She would never make it out of this unending landscape of ghostly shapes covered with frozen snow.

She had almost passed her only salvation before she recognized it: Hinkle's brownstone mansion. Darcy stopped. Pushing her way through the snow, she grasped the wrought-iron gate and looked up at the house. He would help her. But would she put him in danger by coming here for shelter? Surely he was in enough trouble with the blackmail threat. Claude was dead, yes, but his death had proved that there was another man for Hinkle to fear. Perhaps more than he knew.

As she hesitated, she saw the front door open. Julia Hinkle

stood clutching a shawl, her hand shielding her eyes. "Is that you, Father?" she shouted. "I can't see—who's there?"

Darcy stepped forward. "It's Mrs. Statton, Miss Hinkle." But the wind took her words away. Julia peered out into the storm. Darcy was in the light from the hall now, but Julia didn't seem to recognize her. Floundering in the snow, Darcy struggled to move up the steps. Julia pulled her out of the last drift with a soft but strong hand.

"Mrs. Statton! Why, you look a sight! I didn't recognize you. Come in, come in."

She did indeed look a sight, Darcy discovered when she took off her wraps in the hall and saw her face in the mirror. Her hair was encrusted with ice and snow—even her eyebrows were frosted. Her face was bright red from the wind, and her eyes were streaming tears. She could not feel her ears at all.

"Not a word, not a sound," Julia said. "Come upstairs and I'll have my maid attend to you. You need a warm bath and dry clothes, a hot drink . . . Follow me, please, Mrs. Statton."

Julia's maid was French, of course, but totally unlike Solange. She clucked and cooed and treated Darcy like a naughty child. It was just what she needed. Darcy slowly began to warm as she drank an entire pot of hot tea and Annamarie sponged her off with warm water. When Darcy's ears began to hurt terribly, Annamarie moaned along with her in sympathy. She wrapped her up in shawls and blankets. Then, when the pain had subsided, Darcy was slipped into a hot, scented tub. She was dried lovingly with heated towels. Annamarie bundled her into a nightdress and a ruby cashmere robe with white satin trim. She added a cashmere shawl in soft rose for her shoulders.

Finally, Darcy sat gratefully in a gold armchair by the guest room fire. In a few moments there was a knock on the door and Julia came in. She had changed into a lilac robe like Darcy's ruby-colored one, and Darcy was touched by her effort to make her feel at ease.

Julia smiled and went to sit in the matching armchair across from Darcy. "Well, I finally recognize you now. You look so much better."

"Thanks to you. I don't know what possessed me to think I

could walk home from my uncle's. It was terribly foolish, I know."

"It sounds very much like something I would do. I get an idea in my head, and nothing can shake me. But I daresay fifty-mile-an-hour winds would shake me a bit," Julia said, laughing. "I had the good sense to stay inside, even though I was to have tea with Willie today. Oh, your husband will be worried. Should I send someone—"

Darcy broke in quickly, perhaps too quickly, for Julia's hazel eyes widened a bit in surprise. "No! No, I would not want to be responsible for sending someone out in this storm. It is too fierce, Miss Hinkle. Tomorrow will do. I would be surprised if Mr. Statton was there, anyway. He most likely stayed downtown in a hotel."

"I hope that is what Father has done. I'm dreadfully worried. He left this morning very early for Wall Street."

"I'm sure he is enjoying his dinner in comfort at the Astor House at this moment," Darcy said reassuringly.

Julia smiled. "I'm sure you are right. Now, I ordered trays for both of us. We can eat here in front of the fire. I thought it would be nicer than going downstairs. Is that all right?"

"It sounds marvelous. Exactly what I would like. You've been so kind, Miss Hinkle. I don't know how to thank you."

"You've saved me a solitary night of desperate anxiety," Julia said, "so not another word on that score. Here we are, tête-à-tête for the whole evening. Thrown together by this terrible storm. I'm sure we'll tell our grandchildren about this night."

"I'm sure we will," Darcy said faintly, looking away, anywhere but Julia Hinkle's frank intelligent gaze.

Julia eyed her for a moment. "Perhaps you should tell me the true reason you were out in the storm, Mrs. Statton. We have a long night ahead of us, and I assure you I am quite a good listener."

For some reason, Darcy thought of Columbine. The two women looked nothing alike, but Julia somehow reminded Darcy of her friend. She felt the same attraction, and the same trust, with Julia Hinkle. Darcy would need help tomorrow. Julia could give her that help. She had spent so many years being too proud to ask, to confide. Where had it gotten her?

She took a sip of tea. "I'm afraid I might have brought more trouble onto your house," she confessed.

When they rose at dawn, Julia and Darcy were cheered to see the weak appearance of the sun. "The storm is over, thank the Lord," Julia said, turning away from Darcy's window.

"And I should be leaving," Darcy said dubiously, still staring outside. The sun might have been out, but the snow looked as impossibly deep as ever. And she had the feeling the storm was not over, not yet.

"Wait until afternoon," Julia urged. "The walks will be cleared by then, perhaps. And the horsecars might be running, and the Els."

"But Fifth will be cleared late this morning, I'd wager," Darcy said. "I might be able to find a hack." She pressed Julia's hand. "I can't stay any longer, you know that." She had told Julia about finding Claude's body, though she hadn't told her the rest. Julia had no idea how her father had been involved, let alone her stepmother. And Darcy had asked several questions about Anne Hinkle. At last, she had a place to head for—Denver, Colorado. Julia hadn't told anyone—not even her father—but she'd had a message from her stepmother from there. Just a telegram telling her not to worry, that she would be in Denver for a time.

So Darcy now had a way to clear her name, and Edward's, and even Artemis Hinkle's. She would bring Anne Hinkle back with her to New York, and they would threaten exposure of Dargent, whoever he was, in exchange for silence. They could do it, she felt sure of it.

She had only one obstacle in her way: Tavish. He had sworn to avenge his friend's death. But if Dargent went to prison, all of their secrets would be revealed at the trial. Tavish had to understand that stripping Dargent of his power would have to be punishment enough. How could they hurt so many to put him behind bars? Perhaps it was womanly logic, but it made sense to Darcy. At least it had last night.

She had an uneasy feeling that Tavish would not agree at all. So she would have to move behind his back.

Julia sighed. "At least let me get a good breakfast into you. And I'll have Annamarie pack my warmest things. Are you still determined to leave the city?"

"Yes. I must. Until my friends here are able to help me."

"Tell me, Darcy, how do you think you will go? The ferries could be watched."

Darcy slowly walked back to the armchair and sank down in it. "I hadn't thought of that. Do you think that's true, even in this weather? How could the police pass the information along downtown, Julia? All the telegraph and telephone lines must be down, surely, all over the city. I've seen them all on the streets."

"That's true. But they could go from precinct to precinct . . ." Seeing Darcy's stricken face, Julia added quickly, "Perhaps it will be safe. But keep a careful eye out, Darcy. Claude Statton is an important personage. You would be a great prize to the New York City Police Department."

Darcy felt the color drain from her face. "I suppose so," she said.

"Oh, my dear. I didn't mean to frighten you. I just want you to be careful, that's all. I'm sure the storm has disorganized everything. Come to breakfast."

Julia took her arm and led her downstairs, where Darcy was served potatoes and eggs and corned beef and coffee. After breakfast Julia gave her a thick wool dress, black, good for traveling, and added a black coat with a lambswool collar. Darcy would be warmly dressed, but she would not look too rich, too noticeable. She would blend in with the rest of the women in their black traveling dresses. Julia also gave her a small grip with toilet articles, another warm dress, an extra pair of boots, a nightgown, and fresh underthings.

They went downstairs together, arm in arm.

"Godspeed," Julia said, impulsively drawing her into a hug. "And don't worry about things here. I never saw you. The servants will be discreet as well. My father," she said wryly, "has always insisted on that."

"I shall never be able to repay you for this," Darcy said. She opened the front door and turned to look at Julia one last time. She looked like a Rubens painting, all pink and lush feminine curves. But she stood in the icy draft from the door, the wind blowing her hair slightly, and she didn't flinch or shiver from the cold.

"You will always be in my heart," Darcy said. Then she shut the door on Julia's quiet smile.

Luck was with her. She found a sleigh. An enterprising young man had borrowed an old one of his uncle's and was searching for passengers when she hailed him on Forty-ninth Street.

"Joe Heron at your service. Excuse me if I don't tip my hat, ma'am, but I just might lose it if I did."

"I wouldn't dream of asking you to, Mr. Heron."

"Where will you be going, ma'am? Home?"

"Yes. I'm leaving the city."

"Leaving the city!" he said, astonished. "There's no trains going out of Grand Central, ma'am, if that's what you're thinking."

"I was thinking of the ferries. The one to Jersey City. I'm heading for Pennsylvania Station."

Joe considered this. "That might be running. I heard the Hudson ferries were running." She thought he frowned, though it was hard to tell, since his drooping mustache had iced over. "But I don't think the trains would be running from Pennsylvania Station. No trains running for a hundred miles, maybe. Hard to tell, with all the telegraph lines down. And I wouldn't want to go on a ferry ride today, no sir. Not in this wind. Where are you headed, ma'am?"

"I'm heading for . . . Philadelphia."

"I'd stay put if I were you, ma'am. If you don't have friends or money for a hotel, I could . . . maybe my sister could help . . . she has an extra room."

Darcy hung onto the sleigh, thinking. She had to get off Manhattan Island, she knew that. Another day of waiting would be too late for her. But if Joe Heron was right, she could be trapped in Jersey City just as well. The days were gone when one could escape the law in Jersey City, as Jim Fisk and Jay Gould had done in the Erie scandal, living in splendor in a hotel room away from Manhattan justice.

"Too bad you don't live in Brooklyn," Joe said good-naturedly. "I hear the East River is frozen over, right by the Brooklyn Bridge. A chap I just picked up told me so. He spent the night in the ferry building there. You could walk right across it, pretty as you please."

Brooklyn. At least she'd be off Manhattan Island. And maybe she could find someone to take her to the Long Island Sound ferries.

"The East River it is, then," she decided. "I'll try for the Sound ferry, and then get to the railroad from there."

"Are you daft?" Joe exploded. Then recollecting himself, he shook his head. "Excuse me, ma'am. I don't know if you'll get a ferry across the Sound, and even so, how would you get to a railroad station, and what would you do when you got there? I've heard trains are stranded all over . . . All right, all right—to the East River it is. Thirty dollars, then."

"Thirty dollars! I don't want to buy your rig, Mr. Heron!"

"Weeeellll now, perhaps you should catch a horsecar then, ma'am. I'm sure they'll be one coming along in a day or so."

The young man was a rogue, no doubt about it. Darcy almost smiled. "Ten dollars," she said firmly. "Not a penny more."

"Twenty."

"Sold. Can you give me a hand up, Mr. Heron?"

Darcy watched the ten dollars—the balance would be due when he dropped her at the ferry building—pass from her gloved hand to his with misgivings. She didn't have much money, just what she'd taken from Claude's desk, about fifty dollars. She had adamantly refused Julia's offer of money. What she had might not last too long. But it had to get her to Denver.

The snow held off on the journey downtown, but the wind was fierce and it felt even more bitterly cold than yesterday. The temperature must have been near zero. The wind picked up the snow on the ground and flung it in their faces, pelting their cheeks like tiny nails. Darcy ducked under the fur robe in the back. She couldn't believe she was out in this weather again. But Joe Heron was cheerful.

"I'll get you there, never fear!" he shouted over the roar of the wind and the sharp ringing of the bells on his reins.

He got her there, all right. But they got stuck in drifts six times, and it took them an hour and a half. Joe pulled over at Madison Square and went over to the Fifth Avenue Hotel to fill a flask with hot tea for her. Darcy sipped it, noticing that the abandoned horsecar next to her had been taken over by a group of jolly passengers who passed a whiskey bottle up and down the line. They were burning scraps of cardboard in the coal stove in the rear to keep warm. They toasted her silently across the white polar expanse of Fifth Avenue, and she raised her mug to them.

Joe remained impossibly good-natured through it all. Perhaps it was the money he was making. Whatever the reason, he kept her spirits up. Darcy wanted to knight him, but she settled on a small tip when he pulled up in front of the East River ferry terminal at nine-forty with a great cry and a ringing call for a passenger back uptown.

Darcy climbed out of the sleigh, thanked Joe one more time, and pushed her way to the pier. It was crowded with would-be ferry passengers thwarted by the ice, but a holiday mood prevailed. Some intrepid souls were already on the ice, taking a stroll to Brooklyn. They looked like tiny black dots near the Brooklyn side. Dogs cavorted and skidded. Crowds on the Brooklyn Bridge cheered them on.

"Why, it's frozen over," Darcy said aloud.

"Not really ma'am," a man standing next to her replied. "It can't freeze over completely because of the tides. It's just a big ice floe you're seeing, a harbor master. Very dangerous to be crossing, I'd say. Them folks could get swept out to sea if they're not careful. And I'd hate to see what happens when the tide changes, whenever that will be."

"I see," Darcy gulped. She looked down the river and saw that the man was right; she could see now that the ice only appeared to be an even expanse over the river. Actually, it was one giant floe and some smaller ones.

Darcy looked out at the great expanse of ice and her heart

sank. She fervently hoped that the rest of her would not follow suit.

She went toward the ladder at the end of the pier. A man in a cap was standing at the head of it, helping someone climb up. "Fifty cents to go down, miss," he said.

"Don't let her, man, can't you see the tide is changing?" a man in a fur overcoat said. He put a hand on her arm, but the man in the cap disengaged it with such a look in his eye that the other man turned away.

"Come on, miss, just fifty cents it is, and you can tell your grandchildren about it. You can just go down, have a look around, come right back up again. Don't listen to that gentleman there. It's perfectly safe, other ladies have been up and down all morning."

Darcy hesitated. She glanced back toward the ferry building—perhaps the ferries would be running later this morning. And then she saw the policeman, standing, bored, by the shuttered ticket window. Waiting to see if it opened.

Quickly, she took fifty cents from her purse and paid the man. He steadied the ladder, and she climbed down carefully, hampered by her skirts. Her foot hit the ice. It felt firm as a rock. She'd be just fine. She'd be in Brooklyn in a matter of minutes, and they'd never find her. All she needed was a bit of courage and nerve.

She felt almost gay, starting across the ice. This was historic. Wasn't it true the British soldiers had crossed like this during the Revolution? And they'd made it to a man, hadn't they?

She was a little over halfway across the ice when the tenor of the noise on the bridge changed. The shouts of glee were now high-pitched, insistent, anxious. She looked up and saw what looked like a hundred people on the bridge—surely there couldn't be so many—all waving their arms and shouting to those still on the ice. They were pointing . . .

Darcy looked out to sea. The tugboats were beginning to move. So was the ice. She saw a huge floe break away and move toward open sea. A group of men and boys were on it. One fell to his knees, praying. She saw one tall man put his hand on the shoulder of a boy, probably his son.

Now she could hear the cracking noise, and it was horrible. Darcy picked up her skirts with both hands—thinking crazily that this was totally against any rule of etiquette; skirts were to be picked up by one hand only—and moved faster, afraid to run for fear of falling. It was hard to hold her small suitcase against her skirts, but she couldn't dare leave all her clothes and money behind. As she moved, she felt the ice move.

She thought she had felt fear yesterday, standing over Claude's dead body. But that was tame compared to this. She tried not to think of the cold water closing over her head. She couldn't swim, of course, not that she'd be able to. She'd be crushed by the shifting floes of ice first . . .

Darcy concentrated fiercely on moving, one step after the other. She could hear the people screaming from the piers on the Brooklyn side, and now she could hear the ice groaning against the piers as it moved.

The wind was behind her back, thank God, and it pushed her along. Then she saw the first crack in the ice ahead of her, saw the open sea, gray and cold as a gravestone, and she didn't hesitate, she jumped across it to the next floe with a tremendous burst of energy fueled by fear.

Her feet hit the ice and she didn't slip; she kept moving. The people on the pier were urging her on, waving and calling for her to hurry. And then she was at the end of the drifting floe. The ladder was ahead of her. But so was two feet of cold gray water. Darcy stopped. The ice moved even farther away from the ladder. She was paralyzed. She stared at the iron rung. It seemed impossibly far away.

Someone was scrambling down the ladder then, a young seaman by the looks of him, with a beard and a dark blue short coat and cap.

"You're going to have to jump miss. Leave the bag."

She shook her head. She couldn't leave the bag. Her money was in it.

"Throw it to me, then. Throw it now."

She threw it. He caught it with one hand, scooping it against his body. Then, bracing himself against the ladder, he tossed it up to the pier in one sweeping motion.

"Jump," he said. His voice was calm. "Now. I'll catch you, don't fear. Jump, miss."

She jumped. Her boot hit the bottom rung and slipped. Panic shot up from her belly. The crowd up above was screaming, but she didn't hear. Her fingers were scrabbling for the top rung. One hand hit it, the other missed, but her wrist was grabbed by the young seaman and pulled with such strength and power that she found herself, cheek against the iron ladder, secure, safe, and sobbing.

"Come on, now. Come on. You don't want the floe to crush you." His voice was still calm though urgent. Darcy began to climb. She was helped up the last step by a group of arms and hands thrust at her, and she landed on her hands and knees on the wooden slats of the pier, congratulated and patted, a flask up to her lips and some voice urging her to drink. She drank the burning liquid and coughed and looked across the ice. She could see more water than ice now, most of the ice moving out to sea, quicker than before. A tugboat was rescuing a group of men on one floe. One fell in the water but was fished out again. She saw the group of men and boys on another tug, heading for the Manhattan shore.

She was lucky. Damned lucky, Darcy thought, cursing mentally for the first time in her life.

Across the river was Manhattan. She was safe, but only for the moment. Darcy took another slug of whiskey and wiped her mouth. Right now, a moment was enough.

Fifteen

SEAMUS, TERRY, AND Billy Doyle fell dead asleep sometime Tuesday morning. They considerately untied Tavish's bonds somewhere after the second bottle of whiskey; he supposed some unspoken signal between them had decided this. They were horror struck at the story of a man sterilizing his wife, and though they didn't quite believe it, they roared at the story of the rescue and demanded a detailed but gentlemanly description of Darcy.

He left at nine o'clock to the rhythmic snorts of their breathing. Outside, he couldn't believe the snow. For a block he struggled against the wind, feeling awed by the thirty-foot drifts against the windows on the opposite side of the street. But his awe changed to concern by Tenth Avenue. He began to wonder if he'd be able to make it to Columbine's. His ribs ached and his face ached and the weather was frigid. Tavish decided to make it home like an Irishman—from bar to bar.

They were open this early, some crowded with folks who had spent the night. But it was a friendly atmosphere, and some places still had free sandwiches left from yesterday. He was careful not to drink too much—he didn't want to get drunk—but he'd order a small whiskey in each tavern, sip it, and warm himself before struggling on. Lucky for him the boys hadn't gotten the dollar he kept in an inside pocket in his trousers. It came in handy for cases such as this.

It took him five hours to get to Columbine's. The last stretch down Twenty-third Street was the hardest. He staggered through the front door and promptly fell at her feet. He stared at the buttons on her shoes and wondered curiously why he was unable to rise.

Columbine yelled for Bell with a voice that shook with fright but still had power. They managed between them to get him to bed. He told her what happened, his eyes closed so he wouldn't have to see her face. Then Columbine put on her warmest cloak and struggled down the icy sidewalk to Dr. Meredith Dana two doors down.

He saw the faces of the women blur and recede around his bedside. He tried to talk but failed. He heard it pronounced by Dr. Dana that he would in fact live.

He slept until Wednesday afternoon. When he woke, Columbine was by his bedside. She was asleep, sitting in a chair, a book open in her lap.

Hearing him stir, she opened her eyes. "You're awake."

"What time is it?"

"It's Wednesday afternoon."

"It can't be. I have to—"

"Don't you dare get out of that bed. The city is still paralyzed, so you can't do anything, Tavish. You gave me quite a scare, so you must listen to me now. You looked like bloody hell when you walked in the door."

He raised his eyebrows. "Such language."

"It fits," she grumbled, and he saw that she was pale, and there were dark purplish smudges under her eyes. This wasn't like Columbine, this quiet woman sitting so composed by his bedside. He'd expect her to be blasting him out of bed, spitting fire at his stupidity for letting a band of Eleventh Avenue toughs get the better of him.

"I'm sorry I worried you so," he said.

"How are you feeling now? Your ribs are cracked, Meredith said, but they'll heal. Does your head hurt?"

"A bit. I'm fine. Just a wee bit ravenous is all."

She began to rise. "I'll tell Bell—"

He stopped her. "Wait for a spell. Let me wake up properly. Sit and talk to me a moment. How are you, Columbine? Have I been such a trial to you? You don't look well."

"I'm just fine, Tavish, don't be silly." She smiled at him, but her lips were trembling. "I've just been a bit worried."

"No, it is something more than that. Tell me."

Columbine sighed. Her hands twisted in her lap. "Oh, I'm embarrassed to tell you. It's Ned Van Cormandt—it's over. Cora dropped Ambrose Hartley into Maud Valentine's lap and decided she was in love with her husband again. I have a notion this sudden transformation occurred because of the rumors that Claude Statton threw his wife out because of you. Perhaps it suddenly dawned on Cora that Ned could get fed up with her one day. No matter. She cast her line and started reeling him back in. Ned told me it was over on Sunday evening." Columbine looked away. A pulse was jumping in her throat. "I rather thought I was in love with him, Tavish."

"I didn't know."

"I didn't know, either. I pushed him away, I pushed thoughts of him away. But he made me laugh so. I know he seems your typical New York gentleman of good family, years of money and breeding and boredom. But he isn't, not at all. Oh, Lord. So I told myself I couldn't possibly be in love with him, and then he called Sunday evening and said good-bye, and I thought . . . I thought I might die."

"Maybe you weren't in love with him at all. I mean, seeing you discovered it just because he was saying good-bye."

"Maybe so." Columbine's eyes were tragic.

"I'll kill the bastard."

"Oh, there's the answer, right there. That will be just fine," Columbine said with her old spirit. "Bring more problems on my head, thank you very much. Men!"

Tavish laughed, and she laughed, too, reluctantly.

"Well," she said, "I suppose I'll get over it soon. I'm too old to waste away on account of a lost love. Next time I fall for a man, I'm going to make sure he doesn't have a silly wife."

"Columbine, not that I'd be giving you advice, now. But what if you found a man without any wife at all?"

Columbine looked at him, aghast. "But then he might ask me to marry him!"

"Heaven forbid! Saints alive, Columbine, you are the most difficult woman—"

"I daresay I am, I can't help it," Columbine said sorrowfully, and they laughed together again.

There was a knock at the bedroom door, and Bell hurried in without waiting for Tavish to answer. Tavish opened his mouth to tease her, but the look on her face stopped him. A newspaper was clutched in her hand, and her eyes went from Tavish to Columbine and back again.

"What is it, Bell?" Columbine asked composedly.

"It's the *World*," Bell said faintly. Her enormous dark eyes were worried. "A special afternoon edition on account of the storm . . ."

"And?"

"And it's about Mrs. Statton, Mrs. Nash."

"Darcy," Columbine and Tavish said together, exchanging one quick, anxious glance.

"She's all right," Bell said quickly, "I mean . . . oh, dear. Here." She put the newspaper down on the bed where Tavish and Columbine could see it. Her finger pointed to a prominent headline.

DOUBLE TRAGEDY

Prominent Financier Murdered

Father-in-Law Found Frozen in Drift

Society Wife Disappeared in Storm, Sought for Questioning

They scanned the story quickly. Claude Statton and Edward Snow were dead.

"Sweet Jesus," Tavish murmured, reading on.

And Darcy was being sought for Claude's murder. Authorities believed she was still on Manhattan Island. All exits from the city were being watched.

"Sweet Jesus!" Tavish roared. "Bell, where the devil are my pants?"

He was dressed and pulling on his boots when Columbine hurried in to tell him that Lemuel Grace was waiting for him in the parlor. "He looks rather dreadful," Columbine said.

Tavish strode into the room impatiently, shook Lemuel's hand, and said immediately, "Have you heard from Darcy?"

Lemuel's eyebrows went up only a fraction. "I have not heard from my niece," he said.

There was nobody like a gentleman for pointing out when you were being rude, Tavish thought. Just a slight inflection in the voice would do it; Tavish knew the tone well. But he deserved it. He mentally kicked himself. Lemuel Grace had suffered a loss as well. Tavish bowed. "Allow me to offer my condolences to your family. I am truly sorry about Mr. Snow. I liked him very much. Where was he found?"

"He was found four doors away from my house," Lemuel said. "He was trying to get there, apparently. There was a rather large bump on his forehead, they believe he was hit by a flying object of some kind. And his ankle was broken."

Tavish nodded. He pictured Edward, who loved comfort with such gleeful joy, dying in a snowdrift with a broken bone and a bump on his head. The disturbing image hurt his heart so much, he had to push it away. Darcy should be spared as much of that picture as possible. "And Mr. Statton?"

"He was found with two gunshot wounds to his body."

"Where?"

"In his office at home."

"I meant, where on his body?"

"One near the heart," Lemuel said stiffly. "That was the one that killed him."

"And the other?"

Lemuel looked annoyed at Tavish's persistence. "Surely there is no need—"

"But there is a need, Mr. Grace. Please tell me."

214

Lemuel didn't hesitate. "The thigh," he said. "Now may we sit down, Mr. Finn?"

The old stuffed shirt wouldn't tell him if it had been in the crotch. Tavish sat down. If the wound hadn't been in the thigh—and Tavish would bet it was not—then whoever had killed Claude had probably also killed Jamie. Their deaths were too similarly grisly to be a coincidence. That meant Claude Statton had not killed Jamie Alden. Tavish would bet on it. And Claude was not Dargent after all. Tavish was fresh out of suspects, and there was someone else involved, someone dangerous and on the loose.

"I want you to find Darcy," Lemuel said. "I'll pay you to find her. I think . . . I think you're the only man who could."

Tavish nodded slowly. "Why do the police think she killed her husband?"

"That maid of hers. Solange Foucard. She found Darcy with the body. She said that Darcy was unstable, under a doctor's care, and that Claude was considering whether she needed to be confined. She said that Darcy attacked Claude with a cane."

"That's a lie!"

Lemuel gave him a keen look. "You know this?"

"Yes," Tavish said impatiently. "Because I was there. It was I who attacked him with a cane."

"I see. Well. That's something, anyway. Will you try to find her, Mr. Finn? I am sure she must be frightened, alone . . . I am terribly worried. I need your help." Lemuel bowed his head.

Tavish looked at Lemuel Grace's crown of thick yellowish-white hair. The man was frantic; Tavish could sense the panic beyond the measured words, the careful control. He loved Darcy, too.

"Of course I'll help you, of course I'll find her," he said. "Do you have any thoughts on where you think she is?"

"I think she's still in Manhattan," Lemuel said. "Probably at a boarding house somewhere. No trains have left the city, and the police have been watching all the ferries. Besides, I don't think she would leave the city. Where would she go?"

"I can't imagine."

"Do you agree that it would be better for her to face down this

215

absurd charge?" Lemuel rose and began to pace back and forth over Columbine's shabby rug. "It merely looks worse for her now. The *World* has just about come out and said that she's guilty. Of course Claude had had a feud with them, and they were licking their chops at this opportunity to slander his wife. I don't know what to do, where to turn. I'm all she has, you know."

No, you're not all she has. She has me, and you know it, Lemuel Grace. But I suppose that fact is unacceptable to you. Tavish thought all this, but he did not blame Lemuel. In his position, he would probably feel the same.

"Does Darcy know that Edward is dead?" he asked.

Lemuel shook his head. "No. She left for Claude's that morning. My wife attempted to dissuade her, she said, but she failed. As always," Lemuel added fiercely, then recovered. "It is a miracle Darcy made it to Claude's at all Monday morning. Then she left again—she couldn't have gotten far, not in that storm. It can't be too difficult to find her."

"I sincerely hope it is not, Mr. Grace." Tavish rose. "If there's nothing else, I think I should begin. Every minute counts."

Lemuel picked up his hat, stick, and gloves. "Yes. I'll leave you now." He twisted the hat in his hands. "There's one more thing, Mr. Finn."

The old fellow looked decidedly ill at ease. He had the look of a gentleman who was about to say something ungentlemanly.

"Yes?" Tavish asked neutrally.

"My niece has been frank with me about her relations with you, Mr. Finn. At least, she has made it clear that you and she have a deep friendship."

"That is true, Mr. Grace."

"Forgive me for prying, but I must know. Do you care for my niece?"

Lemuel Grace had found his courage now, for his gray gaze was steady. Tavish didn't flinch. "Very much."

"I see. Forgive me again, but I must say this—you tell me this, and yet I come to Mrs. Nash's house and find you here. You must admit I have some cause for concern . . ."

Anger flared up in Tavish but just as swiftly was tamped down.

216

What was the man to think? He didn't know about Tavish's relationship to Columbine. He was merely trying to protect Darcy—of course he would have to bring up the subject.

"Mr. Grace, Mrs. Nash and I have known each other for more than twenty years," Tavish said evenly. "We were childhood friends, no more than friends as adults. Perhaps you noticed that I'm a bit bruised. I was set upon by some toughs the other day. I barely made it to Mrs. Nash's door. She very kindly took me in during the storm and fetched a doctor for me. I have been loyal to Darcy. I will be loyal to Darcy for the rest of my life."

Lemuel was silent for a moment, keeping his eyes on Tavish's face. "All right, Mr. Finn. I hope you are sincere, for all of our sakes."

Lemuel nodded shortly and went out. Columbine must have been waiting, for she came back with a quick step, closing the door behind her. Tavish stood at the window, watching Lemuel walk through the towering piles of snow on either side of the sidewalk, looking small and almost frail.

"What did he want?" Columbine asked anxiously. "Is Darcy all right?"

"I must leave, Columbine," Tavish said, still gazing out the window. He turned and went to her side. He took her cold hands in his. "I don't want to leave you now. But I have to find her."

Columbine's face was strained. "Of course you do," she said softly. "Go, dear brother. Be careful. Find her and bring her back to us."

"I will find her," Tavish said darkly. "But only to take her away again. We can't stay in New York."

She touched his face tenderly. "Sooner or later, Tavish, you will have to make a stand."

"I tried. I tried in Solace. It was a place without memories. I can do it again, with Darcy. I can find a place. The West is full of places . . ."

"Yes. Full of places without memory. Perhaps that is what is wrong with us, Tavish. We never stop and turn to face our memories. We turn our backs. We don't make a stand."

Tavish grimaced. "I can't think of this now. I must go. I'll find her. She couldn't have gotten far. I have one stop to make first."

"Oh, do be careful." She kissed him on the cheek, and they embraced. Tears were in her eyes when they moved apart. "Godspeed," she whispered as he moved to the door.

"My father cannot see anyone," Julia Hinkle repeated. "He is ill. He walked far in the blizzard and had to sleep sitting up on an armchair in the Fifth Avenue Hotel."

"Miss Hinkle, I would not dream of endangering your father's health. But this is a matter of life and death. I do not exaggerate!"

Julia Hinkle looked doubtful. Tavish almost expected that delicate eyebrow to arch sardonically at him. But she frowned in genuine distress. "Perhaps if you could tell me what this concerns, Mr. Finn. I could go up and see if he will receive you."

"Thank you, Miss Hinkle. Tell him it concerns Darcy Statton. She needs our help."

She started. "Darcy Statton?"

"Yes. Please tell him."

She nodded shortly. "Please wait here, Mr. Finn." And then she hurried out, her russet silk dress billowing out behind her.

He hardly had time to become impatient before she was back. There was heightened color in her cheeks, and her hand was not quite steady when she briefly touched his sleeve. "Please, promise me you will not stay long, Mr. Finn. He really is quite ill. I, too, do not exaggerate."

Tavish nodded brusquely, anxious to follow her upstairs. Then he was moved by the look in her eyes. He took her hand in his and spoke to her gravely. "I promise, Miss Hinkle."

She nodded and without another word led him to Hinkle's bedchamber upstairs. She went before him into the darkened room, led him to a chair by Hinkle's bedside, then retreated, softly closing the door behind her.

Hinkle looked terrible, grayer and older. Julia had not exaggerated one whit. His jowls sagged and his usually ruddy face appeared as white as the pillow it rested on. His meaty, purposeful hands looked odd plucking listlessly at the sheet.

"I'm sorry to disturb you, Mr. Hinkle," Tavish began. "Please believe I would not do so were there any other choice."

Hinkle coughed. He nodded.

Tavish felt decidedly uncomfortable. He had come to extract the truth from Artemis Hinkle, perhaps bully him a bit. But what could he say to this coughing man who appeared to be at death's door? And he had promised Julia not to upset him.

He sighed.

"Tell me," Hinkle whispered. "Mrs. Statton?"

Tavish leaned forward, clasping his hands in front of him. "Artemis," he said, using Hinkle's Christian name for the first time, "I believe you lied to me the last time I was here. I've been turning it over in my mind, and there it is. I believe that you wouldn't have done so if someone near to you hadn't been threatened, for if you yourself had been threatened you would have told them to go to hell and be damned. So I am here to ask you for the truth. I realize I may be putting your wife in danger. But I think that she is in danger already, and this might be the way to get both of you out from under this cloud of blackmail forever. We need to end this, Artemis. Darcy has risked so much to help us, and now she has had to run, accused of murdering her husband. She is to me what Anne is to you, most dear to my heart. And I cannot threaten you, or browbeat you, or shake the truth out of you." He spread his hands. "I can only ask."

The beefy hands grabbed the sheet, then relaxed again. Hinkle turned his face away. "He sent me a message. He threatened Julia as well as Anne. He said they would never be safe. Never. That if I didn't tell you Anne had run away, Julia would be ruined. That he would first destroy her beauty and then her name."

"So Anne did not run away?"

"That was the strange thing. She had, but he did not know it then. We thought it was best that she go into hiding, so she left one night secretly, telling the servants to inform everyone she was ill. Now Dargent thinks I don't know where she is. But I do."

"She is not in Denver, then?"

He shook his head bleakly. "He wanted you to think that. If you hadn't asked me I was to let it slip, just enough information to convince you."

"But you didn't, Artemis. How could you know I would come back that night?"

"I couldn't do it. But don't get me wrong—perhaps I would have done it the next day, or the next. I was worried about Julia, I'm still worried about her. He wants you to go to Denver, looking for Anne, and I suppose he will be waiting for you there. If you had decided to go, Tavish, I would have had to warn you. But until you decided that, I thought it best to do nothing."

"I see. So where is Anne?"

Hinkle coughed again. His chest sounded bad. Tavish held a glass of water to his lips and he sipped it. When he leaned back against the pillow, he looked even more exhausted.

"Where?" Tavish repeated softly.

"I don't know at the moment; we thought it best. But she's to meet me in Colorado Springs. I had planned to leave next week." Hinkle covered his face with his hands. "She will wait for me, she will wait forever. She is ready to have the exposure break on her head, as am I. And now I am tied to this bed. She won't believe me if I wire that I'm sick. She'll think it's a graceful way to bow out, she'll think that I changed my mind . . ."

"I'll go," Tavish said. "Where and when were you to meet her?"

"At the Cold Springs Hotel, the last week of March. Tavish, I've failed my daughter and my wife, I could not protect them . . ."

The door burst open, and Julia ran in. Her step was purposeful, her eyes alert and angry. Tavish opened his mouth to apologize for staying so long. She cut him off with an impatient gesture.

"How could you not tell me this?" she demanded of her father. "Do you think me such a child? Do you think I have not noticed that something is terribly awry? Could you not trust me with this, whatever it is? What is it Anne has done? Did you think I would turn my back on her?"

"Julia, Julia." Artemis shook his head, back and forth. A bit of saliva trailed down from his mouth.

Julia bent over him and gently wiped his mouth with a lace handkerchief. "Dear father. You should have trusted me. You must tell me all now."

Tavish stood. "Miss Hinkle, I have no time to lose. Your father can tell you, but I must remind you of how you cautioned me earlier."

She rose, her hazel eyes furious. "I am well aware of his condition, Mr. Finn. It is impertinent of you to remind me of it. You have upset him terribly—"

"It was unavoidable, and I'm sorry."

"Yes. Then allow me to help him now."

Tavish bowed. He started toward the door.

"Mr. Finn, a moment, please." She came up behind him and followed him into the hall. "I think you should know that Darcy came here the night Claude Statton was killed."

"Here?"

"Yes. She spent the night here. I sent her off the next morning with a traveling case."

Tavish felt his color rise. "You sent her out into the storm—"

"Be careful, sir!" Julia snapped. "Perhaps you exaggerated your intimacy with Mrs. Statton, for you could not know her very well if you did not know how difficult it is to dissuade her from a course she is bent on."

"Of course. Forgive me. Did she say where she was going?"

The anger left Julia's face and reluctance stole over it. "I'm afraid I may have done something I shouldn't, Mr. Finn. I didn't know . . . how was I to know? She asked questions, I answered them. I told her that my stepmother had lived in Denver. That her happiest days had been spent there. And that I had received a telegram from Anne only three days ago from there, saying that she is well and will stop for a while. At least, I thought it was from Anne. Now I am not sure."

"Oh my God," Tavish said. He felt his whole body shake. "Darcy is on her way to Denver."

"I'm afraid I agree with you, Mr. Finn."

His eyes met Julia Hinkle's. He saw fear in them, and he knew it mirrored his own. "She's walking into a trap," he said.

"I'm afraid so, Mr. Finn."

"I was a fool," Ned said.

"Yes," Columbine agreed. "You were."

He put his arms around her. "But will you forgive me?"

Columbine was surprised to find herself twisting out of his

arms. Hadn't she dreamed about this moment? Hadn't she imagined Ned coming to call to tell her he'd been a fool? What she hadn't imagined was that she would have trouble believing in him again.

"I'm sorry, Ned," she said, sitting down on the sofa and folding her hands in her lap. "Things have been so unsettled here, I cannot even begin to think of what to do about you. Tavish is off searching for Darcy Statton—I'm worried about both of them. And now you come to me asking for forgiveness. It isn't as though I expected very much of you—of us. But I did expect consistency, at least. I expected that our . . . friendship would end when one of us tired of the other. I never dreamed that you would fall for a ridiculous appeal by your wife. It isn't as though she truly loved you. *That* I could understand."

He sat beside her. "I know. I was unsure of your feelings, and then when Cora said that she would devote herself to our marriage, I of course had to agree. I was cowardly, it was the easiest way."

"And it is that cowardice," Columbine said steadily, "that gives me pause now." The effect of her words was like a slap; he actually flinched. "I don't mean to hurt you," she whispered.

"Why not, when I deserve it?" he said bitterly.

They sat side by side, not talking. What was there to say? Columbine wondered at herself. She was thirty-three. Of all the lovers she'd taken since her divorce, Ned was the first man to touch her heart. Had he been destined to fail her? Had she prepared the way for him by her lightness, her mockery, her laughter, her refusal to take his avowals of love seriously? If the only man she trusted was her brother, how could any other man help but fail her? It was all very confusing.

"I wish I could trust you." Unthinkingly, she spoke the words aloud; they came from her heart.

He slipped his hand into hers. "But you can trust me," he said. He kissed her neck near her ear, where the soft tendrils escaped. "You can trust me," he murmured.

Columbine disagreed. But his lips were so very soft. "Stop this at once, Ned," she said sternly.

But her neck arched back. And Ned did not stop.

* * *

On Thursday morning, Darcy found the small purse Julia had tucked into the grip. She nearly fainted with relief. She had spent thirty dollars already, what with the amounts she had to pay the driver in Brooklyn to get her to the Sound and the tugboat captain to get her across the water. Thank God Julia had not listened to her when she'd said she did not need money.

She spent the night in a railroad station and then sat on a train for two days in freezing temperatures waiting for the tracks to be cleared. It was then she realized the full extent of the storm, and how foolish she'd been to imagine her troubles would be over as soon as she crossed the Sound and bought a ticket to Chicago with connections to the Kansas Pacific and on to Denver. There was nothing to do but wait, cold and hungry, for the train to move.

By the time the snow began to be cleared and the mess untangled and the locomotives able to push through, she felt lightheaded and warm. Her right ear hurt terribly. She felt feverish and dizzy, but she told herself she would get better. She couldn't fall ill now. Not now.

She sat up, half-awake and dreaming, for two days and nights. She slipped in and out of sleep, her head aching, her ear giving her pain so intense at times she thought she'd scream with the effort of not screaming. Faces blurred in front of her. The porter was kind and brought her tea when he could. But somewhere outside of Chicago, she was carried off the train, unconscious.

Sixteen

DARCY HAD THE immense good fortune to land at the home of a kind woman. Harriet May Watkins was busy, her small boarding house by the depot continually full of travelers, but she somehow found the time to prepare beef tea and chicken broth and run up and down the stairs to see to Darcy's comfort. She called in a doctor and paid his fee herself until her boarder was able to. And she managed to do all this with a brusque cheerfulness that made Darcy feel safe. After Darcy's fever broke and she lay weak as a kitten in her bed, she grew to look forward to the sound of Mrs. Watkins climbing the stairs, scolding her hired girl over her shoulder as she trudged up with a tray for Darcy.

Then one day Darcy realized that when she sat in the armchair by the window, she did not hear Mrs. Watkins approach. Only if she was in bed, propped up on pillows, could she hear the heavy tread. Sometimes, when lying down on her right side, she didn't even hear Mrs. Watkins knock.

Harriet May Watkins sent for the doctor once more. He pronounced Darcy on the road to recovery, but said that she had sustained a hearing loss in her right ear. She would never hear very well out of it again.

"Well, dearie," Mrs. Watkins said philosophically after the doctor had gone, "considering the state you were in when they carried you here, I'd say you were lucky."

Darcy cupped a hand around her right ear. "What was that, Mrs. Watkins?" she asked in a loud tone.

Mrs. Watkins blanched. Darcy grinned to show she'd been joking, and they laughed heartily together. "Yes, Mrs. Watkins," Darcy agreed, "I would say that I'm very lucky indeed."

The next day Darcy decided she was ready to leave. True, she weaved a bit when she was dressing, and she was still weak, but she had no time to lose. With every passing day, Anne Hinkle could move on and disappear forever.

Mrs. Watkins came upstairs with the morning tray and shook her head when she saw Darcy dressed and half-packed.

"It's pure folly, Miss Snow. The doctor told you to rest up the whole week. Do you want to get sick again?"

"Mrs. Watkins, I can sit up on a train just as easily as I can sit up in the armchair."

"That's a fool thing to say. As if a foul, filthy train is as pleasant as a seat by the window watching the birds. And weren't you sitting on a train when you took ill before?"

"Yes, but I had come through a blizzard."

"And now you've come through nearly dying." Mrs. Watkins crashed the tray down on the table. "I never heard such a fool thing in my life."

She stalked out. Darcy sighed, finished packing, and then went over to her breakfast. A bit lightheaded, she had to sit down on the armchair to rest. She reached over and plucked a piece of ham off her plate and ate it with her fingers.

The door banged open, and she dropped the ham. Mrs. Watkins poked her head in, smirking at her triumphantly. "Now we'll see if you'll be leaving," she said.

Darcy stood up, wiping her fingers on her napkin. "Whatever do you mean, Mrs. Watkins?"

"Your husband is here, *Miss* Snow. Now, we'll see if he—" Mrs. Watkins stopped abruptly, stricken. For her favorite guest has just keeled over in a dead faint.

* * *

225

Darcy opened her eyes and looked into a pair of green nes.

"My Lord," she murmured.

"Yes, that's right, it's your husband, my dear. I've come to say I'm sorry, and to take you back home."

"Sorry?" Darcy murmured. "Home?"

"Yes, dearest." Tavish turned to Mrs. Watkins. "It was such a silly quarrel, really. But I'll make it up, I swear, or my name's not Egbert Snow."

Darcy's head whirled. "Egbert?"

"Oh, it's all my fault she went down like that, Mr. Snow," Mrs. Watkins said. "I let the information out, quick as you please. I feel a fool."

"Nonsense, Mrs. Watkins. How were you to know?" Gently, Tavish eased his arm around Darcy's shoulders. "Can you sit up, dear?"

"I think so." The miasma in her head was clearing. How could Tavish have found her? Why had he said he was her husband? And why Egbert?

"Let me help you to the bed." He supported her as she crossed the room, then helped ease her down. Perching on the edge of the bed, he fussed with her pillow.

"You devil," she said softly. "How did you find me?"

"I was a Pinkerton once, remember?" he said in a low tone, his eyes twinkling. Then in a louder voice for Mrs. Watkins's benefit, he said, "I couldn't rest until I did."

Darcy noticed that something was different. Tavish's front tooth had a substantial chip in it. "Your tooth . . ."

Tavish patted her shoulder. "Now, my dearest, there's no need to bring that up. I forgive you. You just didn't realize how good your aim is. I should send you to the New York Metropolitans! Excepting the fact that they'd have to give you a kerosene lamp to pitch instead of a ball they'd welcome you, I'm sure."

Mrs. Watkins stifled a laugh, enjoying this new insight into the mild Mrs. Snow's temper.

Darcy narrowed her eyes at Tavish. He smiled at her innocently, and she sniffed and reached for her handkerchief. "You were very cruel," she said. "I don't know if I can forgive you. Really, Egbert—a dancer!"

Tavish gulped, but recovered. He put a hand on his heart. "I was never untrue to you, my darling."

"And does that go for that petite member of the Lilly Lamour Blondes, as well?" Hidden from Mrs. Watkins's view, Darcy grinned at Tavish.

Mrs. Watkins cleared her throat. "Well, I can see you two have a great deal to talk about," she said. "So I'll be going downstairs."

Mrs. Watkins closed the door behind her. She heard a shriek, a thump, and a tinkle, as though a pillow had sailed through the air and knocked over her glass bottle of water from Lake Windermere on the way to the floor. She paused long enough to hear the sounds of muffled laughter. Apparently, the handsome couple, so obviously in love, was making up after all. Smiling broadly, she continued down the stairs.

After the initial rush of elation, Darcy found herself exceedingly annoyed. Tavish refused to budge from Mrs. Watkins's boarding house. No amount of threats or stubborn refusals could move him. They would stay, Tavish insisted, for two days. They could manage that. He would nurse her for that time, and if she wasn't stronger, they would stay another day. After he heard more details of her illness from Mrs. Watkins, he would brook no argument on the subject.

Darcy resisted stubbornly. But when she asked about her father and he told her, reluctantly, what had happened, she succumbed. She collapsed in bed and cried steadily for hours. Tavish didn't leave the room. He held her and rocked her, and when she turned away in her anguish he let her grieve, but sat nearby. He held Mrs. Watkins at bay by slipping downstairs for a tea tray. He sat up and watched Darcy drop off into exhausted sleep, and he was up early the next day to get a breakfast tray from Mrs. Watkins. He brought it upstairs himself and urged her to eat something.

Darcy stirred her coffee. Her face felt taut, her eyelids puffy. "I was so cruel to him that last day," she said. "I can't stop thinking of that."

"Hearing the truth about him was a great shock. Of course he understood that."

She raised her bleak eyes to his. Her lips trembled. "How can I know that?"

"He was coming to see you that last day," Tavish said. "Of course he understood."

"They say that freezing to death is like falling asleep. They say you feel wonderfully warm at the end, content and drowsy."

"Yes. I'm sure it was like that for Edward." He hadn't told her about the broken ankle, the bump on the head. He didn't want her to think of him suffering.

A painful sob was torn from her. "I failed him!" she cried. "I failed him, Tavish, and he's dead. My father is dead!" The hurt was so deep and wide that it filled her belly and choked her throat.

"Darcy, my own love," he said, coming to sit on the edge of the bed and taking her hand, "it seems to me that your history with your father is one of struggle and forgiveness. Your mother's departure, Edward's financial ruin, your marriage, Claude's treatment of you—all of those things caused you and your father pain. Perhaps Edward let you down when he allowed you to marry Claude, or when he asked you to stay in the marriage after you had decided to escape. Perhaps you let him down when he told you the truth about Andre Maubert. What does it matter, dear? You both loved. You both came to each other in times of trouble. You both struggled for each other, you both continued to fight for each other and forgive each other." He touched her cheek. "He knew that."

"Do you really think so?" she whispered.

"Yes, I do."

Tears began to slip down her face again. "I don't know how to go on."

"You'll go on with me."

For the first time in days she smiled. "Yes. I'll go on with you."

They spent the day in Mrs. Watkins's comfortable front parlor, Darcy well-wrapped and not permitted to fetch so much as extra

228

milk for her tea. "The first rule of adventure," Tavish instructed her, smiling over his copy of *The Adventures of Huckleberry Finn*, "is to take comfort when you can. I never thought I'd find such excellent cooking in a depot boarding house."

Darcy smiled wanly at him. "Voluptuary."

"Precisely. Will you pass me another turnover, please? Thank you."

They ate supper with the rest of the guests. A red-faced lawyer dominated the conversation with his tales of what he'd seen and done out West. As a representative of various railroad companies, he claimed he had been instrumental in challenging many of the Grange laws back in the seventies.

Tavish was hard put to keep his tongue. After working as a guard for different railroads laying tracks, and later as a Pinkerton guarding shipments, he'd seen the way the railroads were squeezing out the farmers and turning thriving towns into empty storefronts and rolling tumbleweed. He'd worked hard for the passage of laws to end practices such as charging more for a short haul than a long one, or giving rate breaks to large monopolies. He hated the kind of lawyer that would search for loopholes in a law designed to help the common man; he despised the kind of railroad company that would penalize a region known for Grange activity by bypassing its towns, leaving passengers and freight high and dry.

By dessert, the lawyer was ponderously informing the table that the Supreme Court had made an excellent decision the year previous when it declared no state could regulate the railroads, since the railroad crossed state lines. Thus, the Interstate Commerce Commission was formed, and the railroads relaxed, for it satisfied the country and was ineffectual in controlling the rapaciousness of the railroad magnates. Someday, Tavish thought gloomily, the United States would pay for not regarding its railroads as a public service as well as a profit-making industry to be plundered.

"I knew them all, all the Granger leaders," the lawyer was saying expansively as he sipped his coffee. "Communistic anarchists, the lot of them."

Tavish couldn't stop himself. "I don't quite see the two philosophies as compatible," he said, his dry tone barely concealing his irritation.

"Mr. Huntington himself called them communists, sir," the lawyer replied huffily. "And I've seen them, I know it. There was one Granger, he made a legend of himself when he left the railroad and joined up. He'd been a hired gun, like Bat Masterson or such, protecting the railroads, made a name for himself there. But he up and quits one day, joins the Grange. He wasn't a farmer, either, so he must have been an anarchist. He was a foreigner, too. Name of Finn. Some folks, they think him a hero, a legend of some kind, trying to save the towns and the farmers. But I heard he was involved in Haymarket, even. He—"

"May I have just a bit more of your delicious rice pudding, Mrs. Watkins?" Tavish asked smoothly. Darcy shot him a look, which he ignored.

Darcy smiled to herself. So Tavish Finn was a folk hero. Were there more surprises in store for her from this enigmatic man with the quicksilver tongue?

She sought him out in the parlor after supper. Reaching for a book on a shelf, she faced him and raised her eyebrows.

"Haymarket?" she asked softly. Despite his fiery nature and populist sympathies, she found it difficult to believe that Tavish would be involved in that notorious anarchist bombing in Chicago.

He shook his head. "Can't take credit for that one. I was in Solace by that time—so I'm most likely about as guilty as those they sentenced to hang. I wasn't an anarchist, anyway. I leave that kind of politics to my sister. Columbine was the one who marched to free those poor souls at that travesty of a trial."

"But you were known around the West?"

He smiled sourly. "Inflated rumors and tall tales made me popular for a time. Most of the stories weren't true. I had a notion the Grange itself created the legend to further their cause. Can't prove it, though."

"So," she murmured, "I'm in love with a legend."

Smiling, he leaned against the wall. "As am I, Darcy Snow," he said softly. "Do you think your departure from New York didn't make you a public figure?"

"Perhaps a scandalous one," she admitted. "I was the talk of the town, then?"

"Lemuel tried to keep the talk down," he said. "But he couldn't. To hear the newspapers tell it, you are a cross between Belle Starr and Helen of Troy. They haven't had a scandal like that since . . . well, since James Gordon Bennett, Jr., came to call on Caroline May on New Year's Day."

Darcy laughed softly. All of New York knew the story, though of course no polite person would allude to it. Naturally, Tavish would. The notorious Mr. Bennett, who inherited the *New York Herald* from his father, was rumored to be rather fond of the bottle—indeed, it was said he liked to ride a bicycle around and around his house in the middle of the night, pausing only for a nip at a brandy bottle held by his butler. He'd called on his sweetheart Miss May during the formal New Year's visits, an old Dutch custom practiced in New York. Darcy had heard the story in whispers from Adelle, how he'd arrived in the May parlor rather the worse for wear and then answered a call of nature in the May family piano—or the fireplace, Adelle wasn't quite sure which one. Her brother horsewhipped him on the steps of the Union Club, then fought him in a duel in Delaware. New York society was horrified and made it quite plain that Mr. Bennett was welcome no longer. He could ride up the steps of the Newport Reading Room on his horse, he could torment the young ladies from a nearby finishing school walking two by two past the Union Club, just for sport. But he had gone just a bit too far this time.

"Well, I'm glad I gave them something amusing to talk about," she said lightly. "Now that Mr. Bennett has retired to Europe, New York has been rather free of scandal."

"Good of you to divert them." Tavish spoke in the same tone, but the newspaper stories had worried him. If Darcy ever had to go to trial, the whole town would turn against her. He wished she was more aware of her danger. But as he looked back at her, catching her unawares, he saw the worry in her gray eyes that she'd tried to hide from him. He pressed her hand silently. There was still a long road ahead.

The guests began to head off to bed. Tavish told Darcy to go on up; he would have a last cigar. Darcy nodded, relieved. He'd done it last night as well, somehow guessing her shyness. Their encounter in the house of assignation seemed to have occurred in another life, and Darcy still felt bashful about sharing her bed. She slipped under the covers and wondered how long he would be, if he would expect to make love to her. Last night she'd been crying, upset about Edward, and he'd merely held her. She felt thin and weak from her illness, and her heart was beating in nervous anticipation as she imagined his reaction should she refuse him that night. Still worrying, convinced she would be awake the night through with nerves, Darcy fell asleep.

She woke sometime near dawn. He was sleeping next to her, his back to her. Her heart felt full as she studied him. She placed her palm against his bare back and felt the warmth of his skin, the living presence of him, the miracle of him beside her in the hush before morning begins.

He stirred, then turned over and opened his eyes. They looked at each other for what seemed like ages in the dim shadows of the dawn. They kissed. She felt so slight underneath his hands, so tremulous. The birds were beginning their morning noises outside the window, but the house was not yet stirring. The gray light was gentle, and they made barely a sound. She felt something move in her chest, some last heavy hurt that dislodged and was gone. The cool air moved against her skin. She was free now, she belonged to him. No longer wife, no longer daughter, she had only herself to give. His face was above hers, intent and serious, and she kept it between her hands. Pink light stole around the edges of the curtains, and she was crying silently, kissing him now, holding the kiss, and sighing. She had come home.

When they were finally packed and ready to set off, Darcy was shocked to discover that Tavish expected her to return to New York while he went off in search of Anne Hinkle.

"I thought we were partners," she said angrily. "I thought that we would stand together—"

"Yes, we will stand together," he said grimly. "Symbolically, not in fact. You will return to your uncle. I will go on. I will not have you in danger. Not again."

"I won't be in dan—"

"I will not lose you!" he broke in fiercely. "Of course you'll be in danger. Dargent knows exactly what you're about to do."

"How can he? Julia told no one that Anne telegraphed her from Denver."

Tavish shook his head. "Anne did not telegraph Julia."

"She did, Julia told me she did. If you're trying to get me to retreat, Tavish, I must tell you that—"

"Anne couldn't have written to Julia. She's not in Denver. And the only people that know that are Artemis Hinkle and me. Dargent must have telegraphed Julia. He wants me to go to Denver—he expects me there. And if you had gone," he said gently, "you would have walked into a trap."

Darcy took this in. "I see. Well, then. Where are you going to look for her?"

"I don't have to look. I know where she is. And I will go and find her, and you will return to New York."

"Tavish, I have a right to go with you. My father's life was ruined because of Dargent, and we know that man was behind Claude's machinations. Perhaps I can succeed with Anne Hinkle; I knew her as Annie O'Day, remember? I was fond of her, and she of me. I can talk her into coming back with us, uncovering Dargent's identity, and forcing his silence."

"His silence? But we must have him arrested."

Darcy fell silent. Before her eyes, a gulf opened up between them. She nodded slowly. "Of course he deserves to be in jail, but do we have the right to ask Annie to destroy the happiness of her new family for his punishment? What of Julia and Willie Archer, and Artemis Hinkle? What of Ned Van Cormandt, who is being blackmailed as well for a dalliance that occurred five years ago? If it were just a question of the Old Guard exposed for their part in the blind pool, I would accept it. But this would destroy a good man and his daughter, Tavish. And it would destroy a friend."

"But Dargent committed murder. Two murders, maybe more. He killed my friend in a horrific way. Not to mention Claude, no matter if he deserved it. I will never forget it. And I will not rest," Tavish said grimly, "until he pays for Jamie."

"Revenge," she said dully.

"Yes, revenge," he said, taking her hand, "but not only that. He needs to be put where he will harm no one else. Do you think if we silence him that he will reform? I don't think so. This is a criminal mind, Darcy, and a cruel one, an amoral one. I'm sorry, but I cannot agree with you. I will try with all my power not to let Anne Hinkle's secret past come out. But I will not shirk my duty. It is too clear to me. Artemis will stand by Anne. He will deny the rumor. And Willie, if he is the man Julia thinks he is, will stand by her, too. And Ned—well, Ned will just have to fend for himself. His marriage is unhappy anyway, and Cora is not in a position to throw stones."

She looked at his face, and she was swayed by his argument. He was right. She had wanted to pretend that no one would be hurt, that they could sweep the past away with nothing on their consciences. That they could go on with no regrets, no pain. But of course they could not.

She held his gaze steadily. "All right. But I want to share that duty. I want to help. Tavish, I *need* to help. Let us free ourselves of this together. Let me stand by you, not sit and wait in Lemuel's parlor in New York with my embroidery in my hands. How can you possibly ask me to leave you now? How can you bear it?"

His face was full of pain. He hated to do it; he'd die before he'd put her in danger again. But he loved her courage, and he knew she was right. He could not bear for her to leave him now. "Yes. We'll go together," he said. His fingers linked through hers. "We'll stay together, from now on."

At St. Louis, they both rushed off the train, Darcy to telegraph Lemuel, and Tavish to find some food. They had both been horrified at the fare served in railroad hotel dining rooms, Tavish calling them "a slow downward journey to the ninth circle of hell." The steaks were gray meat dredged in flour and fried in an abundance of lard; the taste bore no resemblance to meat, but suggested the metallic tin flavor of the pan it had been cooked in. At one stop Tavish could have sworn they dined on prairie dog. He decided to keep this information from Darcy. Until they reached the Atchison, Topeka and Santa Fe railroad, which was famed for its excellent food at Harvey Houses along the route, they would have to make the best of it.

Darcy rushed back onto the train with minutes to spare. Tavish passed her the sandwiches and pie he'd managed to buy for them. "Did you succeed as well in your mission?" he asked.

"Yes," she said, settling into her seat and unwrapping her sandwich. She peered between the two thick slices of bread. "What is this?"

"Don't ask," Tavish answered cheerfully.

"I told Lemuel not to worry, we were on our way to Colorado Springs."

Tavish swallowed with difficulty. "Oh."

She eyed him over her sandwich. "Was that all right?"

"Well, I should have asked you not to tell him. It's better not to let people know our business. It's a habit of mine. What if someone asks him and he lets it slip? Or if he tells your aunt."

"Don't worry, Tavish. Uncle Lemuel can keep a secret."

"I hope so." Tavish chewed energetically. "I don't know what this is, but it's terrible. I just hope I finish chewing by the time we reach Kansas."

It was a slow journey, even after they had transferred onto the Atchison, Topeka and Santa Fe, the line Tavish knew well since he'd worked along it. There were numerous delays due to the snow that was still piled high along the tracks, and the train was often cold, though at various points there would be an inexplicable burst of heat, and passengers would groan and remove their scarves and gloves. At least they both had a Pullman berth; Tavish had insisted on that. Darcy had been prepared to sit up for the journey, not having enough money for a sleeper after her doctor bills. But Tavish had pointed out that they both needed plenty of sleep for whatever might lay ahead, and he paid for both of them. Perhaps he'd borrowed some money from Columbine, for he told her he'd refused Lemuel's offer to pay his way.

Plenty of sleep was an optimistic view, Darcy had thought the first night she'd struggled in her berth. Perhaps the impossible effort of undressing and dressing lying down would exhaust her enough to be able to sleep in the narrow space. She'd been spoiled, of course, by her luxurious, large bed in New York. But it wasn't just a longing for space and comfort; she was terrified she would roll out through the curtains and land on some poor unsuspecting passenger's head. But she found that after the first few nights, she slept well, perhaps better that she had in her soft bed. She loved the clacking sound of the train wheels against the tracks. Closing her eyes, she imagined the astonishingly wide prairie outside, with its never-ending sea of softly waving grass.

Soon she was used to the dust that was engrained in every crease in her clothing. She was used to the smell of cattle, grass, and open air. She was even used to the scrambling with the other passengers to line up for the morning trip to the washroom, everyone blinking sleepily with towels in hand.

But she never got used to the land. After the berths were converted into plush seats for day traveling, Darcy settled next to Tavish for the best part of the trip: the scenery. She had never imagined such space and such beauty existed as on the long trip across the prairie. She could see for miles and miles across the grass, only glimpsing an occasional cowboy or a herd of cattle. She had never seen such skies. She had never felt so free.

They passed Dodge City and the Kansas border, and were now well into Colorado. Tavish was glowering and telling her about the massacre of the buffalo and the cruel effect on the Indians when it happened. Suddenly there was a loud explosion, and the brakes of the train squealed painfully in the straining effort to reach a quick stop. Realizing what was to come, Tavish tried to throw his arm across Darcy, but he couldn't prevent her from flying out into the aisle as the train jolted and swung crazily. She landed on top of someone else and hung onto the side of her seat for dear life. Screaming and shouting mingled with the shrieking of metal, and after a series of heart-stopping jerks, the train bumped to a halt.

A train wreck. But Darcy could see, even as she pulled herself up to a sitting position, that everyone in this car appeared relatively unhurt. There were bumps and cuts and crying children and bellowing men, but it hadn't been as bad as it could have been.

"We might have jumped the track. I can't tell whether the explosion was on the train or on the track," Tavish said, peering out the window.

People were beginning to move now, some still panicked. Some people worried aloud about the train blowing up, others muttered about train robbers. Passengers were pushing one another to get near the exits.

"Just keep your heads," Tavish shouted. "We're all fine."

But they all continued to push, and soon all the passengers were spilling from the train to walk alongside the tracks. Some stumbled onto the grass and sat, holding their heads. A doctor moved along the wounded, binding their scrapes. Tavish and Darcy jumped off and moved down the track with the rest. There was no sign of robbers, at least. Just the wide-open prairie and an empty sky.

And then the murmur was passed down the line. Sabotage. The train workers had confirmed it; there was an explosion in the engine room. Someone had deliberately sabotaged the train.

Tavish frowned. He wasn't sure he liked this.

More rumors, more questions, more wondering. The air was full of it, people milling and grouping and re-forming, asking questions, speculating, expostulating on the delay. If they could get their hands on the person who did it . . .

A tall, lanky man leaning against the train with a handlebar mustache and a thin cheroot in his mouth was watching him. Tavish could feel his eyes. Danger prickled the hairs on the back of his neck.

No, he didn't like this at all.

When the speculations reached a fever pitch, the man pushed casually off the train. He eased into the largest group with the most vociferous men, their hats pushed back on their heads with exasperation.

"Isn't that Tavish Finn?" the lanky man asked softly.

Softly, but Tavish heard it. He spoke quietly to Darcy. "Get back in the train. Now."

She looked up at him, confused. "Why?"

"Don't ask why, there's no time. You must help me. You must be free to help me. Get back in the train, mingle with the crowd. You don't know me." His one fear was that, if what was in danger of happening actually transpired, Darcy would be taken as his accomplice.

Without another word, another glance, she picked up her skirts with one hand and walked away from him. He breathed a sigh of relief. But behind him he could hear the mutters. The voices.

"He hates the railroads like poison. It was him that did it, I'm bound."

"I heard he was at Haymarket," the lanky man drawled. "They know how to make bombs, you know."

"Look at him there, pleased as punch. Not a scratch on *him*."

Tavish began to stroll away. He hoped they'd be too disorganized, too unsure, to follow or raise a cry. But he could see the lanky man's lips moving, urging a round, beefy fellow on, and the man raised a cry. A trainman heard, another came over, quick words were exchanged, he was ordered to stop.

He saw Darcy watching from a window, her eyes wide, her fingers clenched into fists as his hands were roughly bound. An enemy of the railroads, an anarchist, they said. To the nearest jail, they said. He was marched there, pushed along, by an angry mob.

And that was how he found himself alone in a jail cell in Redemption, Colorado.

Seventeen

No one in town seemed to care that there was no evidence against Tavish. Not the easygoing deputy, not the train conductor, not the townspeople. They all enjoyed the sight of a fine man dragged through town and locked up. It made for a rousing day in tiny Redemption, and the three saloons did a brisk business.

Darcy soon discovered that the circuit judge who would hear the case wouldn't be through town for another two weeks. There were no lawyers in Redemption. She had to travel to either Pueblo or Colorado Springs, and there was no one to take her. She'd already missed the train, which had left six hours later, once the track had been fixed. The owner of the tiny livery stable was dead drunk, and so, it seemed, was every other able-bodied man in Redemption. Darcy checked into the town's only hotel and decided to wait till morning to take action.

She returned to the jail. She and Tavish kissed through the bars. "I'll get you out," she said. "I'll wire for a lawyer from back East if I have to: My cousin Florence in Boston just married a lawyer. I understand he's quite well known—"

"You have to be careful, love. Remember," Tavish said delicately, "you're, uh, wanted, as they say. What's the use of getting me out if you get in?"

Darcy looked crestfallen. "Oh. I hadn't thought of that."

"So you see, we'll just have to wait. I'm hoping the railroad will see the light. For heaven's sake, they know I haven't been involved with the Grange for years. And the Grange never blew up trains."

"Well," Darcy decided, "then you'll just have to wait while I go to Colorado Springs and bring Annie here."

"What?"

"It's the only way. Oh, Tavish, I hate to leave you, I truly do, but what can I do here? I might as well go to Colorado Springs, find a lawyer and Annie, and bring them both back to Redemption. Lord knows no one will look for us here."

He frowned. "I don't like it. I don't want you going by yourself."

"But I have to. We can't wait two weeks. And I have to find you a lawyer anyway. If I can't wire back East I'll have to go to Colorado Springs."

"No. Wait, Darcy—"

She kissed the tips of her fingers and laid them against his cheek. "I'll be back to say good-bye before I go."

"Darcy, no—"

Waving over her shoulder, she went out. As she passed the deputy's desk, he looked up. Young, impossibly young for such a job, he was redheaded, freckled, and had a wiry beard. "Have a nice visit?"

"Yes, very nice," she said, smiling back. There was no sense getting on the wrong side of Tavish's captor. "Thank you so much for letting me see him," she said. Briefly, she laid a gloved hand on his sleeve. "You're very kind."

"Anytime, ma'am," the young man replied, blushing furiously. "Anything I can do, you just let me know."

"I just might take you up on that, deputy," she sweetly replied.

She started back toward the hotel. Strange how beautiful the country was and how ugly the towns could be. Redemption was a mining town with nothing more to mine. It had hung on because of its railroad depot and trade, she supposed. The town consisted of a ramshackle group of buildings on one main street. There was one very obvious brothel, one general store, one tiny square building with a whitewashed cross that she assumed was a church, an assay office, a livery stable, one dubious-looking boarding house, and her hotel. Darcy had no idea what the other buildings housed. The only businesses that seemed to be booming were the saloons and, of course, the brothel. Time must lay heavy on the hands of the miners around here.

As she approached the Bonanza Saloon, surely an example of wishful thinking if she ever saw one, she quickened her steps. It seemed to be the most disreputable building of the lot, and she paused while a drunken man reeled out through the swinging doors and began an unsteady trek down the alley. She averted her eyes, not interested in the least in what he planned to accomplish down there, and she found herself looking in the long mirror over the bar inside the saloon. Darcy gave a start. A lanky man with a long, handlebar mustache was threading through the crowd. It was the man who had fingered Tavish as the saboteur. He had disappeared from sight after reaching the town.

She stood on her tiptoes to watch him. There were too many bodies in her way, and she strained even higher to see. She saw the lanky man stop at the bar. She couldn't see the man next to him, but she saw a gloved hand signal for a drink. A glass was placed before the lanky man. Then the gloved hand pushed a fat envelope toward him. And she would bet there was money in it.

Darcy's calves were beginning to shake from the effort of staying on her toes. No matter how she moved, she could not see the face of the man with the gloves. Then the door swung open in her face, and she stumbled backward. Two men came out, taking no notice of her. But when she had a chance to peer inside again, both the lanky man and the gloved man were gone. Two empty glasses stood at their places. It was then that she noticed that the saloon also had a side door. She dashed to the alley, but there was no sign of anyone except the drunken man relieving himself against the side of the livery stable and occasionally on his boots. She'd come a long way from the four hundred, that was certain.

Darcy started again toward her hotel. Something was wrong with what she'd seen. The lanky man had been paid to finger Tavish, of course. But what was it that was bothering her?

The gloves. She'd seen the men in this town. Miners, mostly, cowboys, drifters. She'd seen their clothes, their hands. Their gloves were made from animal hide of one sort or another, creased, dirty, designed for work. But this man's gloves would have been at home in a drawing room on Fifth Avenue. They were spotless. They were the fine kid leather of that pale lavender shade that denoted a gentleman.

Darcy stopped in her tracks. Dargent wasn't in Denver, she realized with a sudden, sharp shiver. He was here.

They made their plans. Tavish instructed her to return at eleven. Rory, the deputy, had already been on him like a June bug, asking about his sweetheart. Darcy had impressed him. The genial son of a Kansas farmer, he was no friend to the railroad, and he knew Tavish had a bum rap. If Tavish could soften him up enough, or Darcy could distract him enough, perhaps one of them would be able to get the key. It was worth a try. Better than sitting in the jail like a dead duck, just waiting.

Darcy hurried back to the hotel again to rest for the night ahead. She managed to nap, as Tavish had suggested, and she arranged for a meal to be brought to her room. They looked at her strangely, but they delivered it.

After she'd eaten, she sat down in a chair by the window to wait. Strangely, her thoughts turned to her father. He'd always claimed he was a coward. But how she would love his enthusiasm, his jokes, right now. Edward, the way he used to be. She remembered the day he came to see her, when in the midst of their troubles he couldn't help but comment on her cousin's dress.

And then Darcy sat up. Edward had made a wedding visit to her cousin Florence. She'd married that fall, had gone to Europe for her wedding trip. But the letter she'd read in Claude's files, the letter from her uncle, spoke of his making the wedding visit last spring. Florence hadn't been married last spring.

What could it mean? The letter had been dated April 7. She remembered it clearly. Could she have confused Florence with someone else, another Florence? No, he'd mentioned her husband Charles, as well. There could be no mistake. But what could it mean? Darcy wondered again.

She nearly jumped a foot when there was a knock at her door. Then she recovered. It must be the gangly youth who'd brought her dinner tray returning for it. Good—it was almost time to head for the jail. This way none of the staff would know she had gone.

She went to the door and opened it. Ned Van Cormandt looked anxiously at her.

"Thank God I found you," he said.

"Mr. Van Cormandt." She backed up a step. "What—what are you doing here?"

"Forgive me, Mrs. Statton," he said, closing the door behind him. "But I must be frank. Mrs. Nash sent me. She is terribly worried. She thinks something is awry. She sent me here to help, if I could. Tavish told her where he was heading when he left New York."

"I see." Darcy backed into the room even farther. Her heart was beating, and she was trying to think.

"But how did you know I was in Redemption?"

"I was in Colorado Springs. Waiting for you. I heard about the train wreck. I came down to investigate and found that Tavish Finn was in jail. I'm a lawyer, Mrs. Statton. I can help you."

"Mr. Van Cormandt—"

"Don't you think it's about time you called me Ned? Seeing that—"

"Ned, I have to think. I don't know what to do, I—I'm so tired. It's so late. And with the wreck and Tavish in jail—" She sank into a chair. She summoned all her strength to throw him a wan look.

"Of course. How inconsiderate of me. Perhaps we could break-fast together? There is time to talk of what we should do. And I should wire Columbine now. She's frantic with worry. She sent me with a message for Tavish. I'll see him tomorrow," he said, retreating toward the door.

"Tomorrow."

He nodded. "Tomorrow. Don't worry, Darcy. I can help."

Rigid, she watched him shut the door behind him. Then she

collapsed with relief. Thank God he had left. She could think. Could it be Ned? Could it be someone she knew, someone she'd gone to dancing class with, for heaven's sake? Someone whose family knew her family?

She shook her head. She couldn't believe it. Could it be that he had only been pretending to be blackmailed to divert Tavish? She couldn't imagine Columbine revealing to anyone where Tavish was going. Unless she trusted him with her life. But she could be mistaken.

She had to tell Tavish. She could go early to the jail and tell him. She waited only until Ned's footsteps had died away. Then she quickly reached for her cloak. Throwing it over her shoulders, she eased open the door.

She nearly screamed when she saw a tall figure with his back to her. She pressed a hand to her mouth, and the man turned. It was her uncle Lemuel.

"Darcy!"

"Uncle Lemuel!" She pulled him inside quickly, dropping the cloak to the floor. "How glad I am to see you! What are you doing here? How did you find me? Oh, Uncle Lemuel, I am so very glad to see you." She was swept into his arms, and she felt tears well in her eyes. It was almost like having her father there. Family. Everything would be all right now.

"I've been traveling for days," Lemuel said as he held her. "I heard about the wreck in Colorado Springs. Marie had forwarded your wire, I'd been chasing you and Tavish since I knew he'd left the city. I came here immediately. Don't worry now." He patted her back. "I know the governor of Colorado. Nothing will happen to Finn. And I won't let anything happen to you, Darcy. When one has money, everything is possible, *n'est-ce-pas?*"

It was as though a sonorous bell slowly tolled in her brain. *Money*, she thought. *D'argent*. The name was an effete joke, a slap in the face from a Francophile. Foreboding snaked through her. Ned hated everything French. He was one of the few people she knew who couldn't speak a word of it. But maybe the translation had no significance at all.

"Don't cry, now. Here, let me get you my handkerchief."

Darcy drew away, still thinking, while her uncle stripped off his glove to get his handkerchief from his pocket.

His fine glove in the softest kid. His fine, lavender glove.

Tavish had plenty of time to think, that was certain. And for the first time he looked at the problem from a new angle. Rory, the deputy, obligingly gave him a pencil and paper. He scratched out clues and suppositions, he crossed them out and started again. He made a timetable. He made lists.

It was when he was eating the indifferent supper Rory had pushed underneath the bars that it all started to come together. Then, like slow dawn over the Rockies, tiny fingers of light began to sneak into his mind. Then illumination flooded in.

Tavish put down his tin fork. If he was right, eleven o'clock could be too late.

"Hey, Rory," he called through the bars, forcing his voice to sound light. "Come and eat your dinner back here. No sense both of us eating alone, is there?"

"Sure enough, Tavish. I'll just put the chair right here against the wall."

"Sure. I just thought we could both use a bit of company is all," Tavish answered cheerfully. "Now, tell me, was your father in the National Grange?"

"H-he was, yes," Rory sputtered. "How did you guess?"

"Oh, I can tell a Granger," Tavish said. "And I can tell a Granger's son."

She had lived with Claude for what seemed like an eternity, concealing her feelings, her thoughts. It was the only thing that saved her now, for she felt close to collapse.

She barely heard her uncle speak of what they should do—he would send her to Denver on the late train, he would explain everything to Tavish tomorrow, then he would follow her after doing what could be done here, and finally he would petition the governor personally. Through a pounding in her temples, the facts thudded into her mind with sickening logic. Even while she nodded and thanked him, she remembered.

She remembered everything. Lemuel had been away in January when Tavish's friend was killed. In St. Augustine, he'd said. But he'd been away for two months, time to get to California and back, and do business in between. Oh, she'd had letters. Letters that spoke of the warm weather, the business he was doing. Letters that had arrived, like many of her letters, on her tray already opened by Claude. And they were letters, Darcy was sure now, that Lemuel had written before he'd even gone away. He'd given them to Claude, and Claude had passed them along.

The letters in Claude's file that had been written from Boston were not from last year. Lemuel hadn't made a mistake about Florence's marriage. He'd been planning a trip somewhere—back to California, most likely—and had already given the letters to Claude so that he would have an alibi in Boston.

Had they both come up with the scheme then, to open her letters so that they wouldn't have to mail them to cover their tracks? Or had Lemuel seen that he could use Claude's practice to create an alibi whenever he wanted one?

Everyone thought that Lemuel and Claude had hated each other. They hardly spoke. But what better cover for their business activities could there be? They would never slip in public, never betray by their eyes that there was more between them. For they rarely saw each other in public. And when they did, they did not speak.

And then Darcy remembered her mother's letter. The only letter with an envelope, an envelope with no canceled stamp, no postmark, because Lemuel had received it in Paris himself on one of his trips. Why it had never been given to her, she didn't know. Perhaps it was because despite the dutiful annual visit, Lemuel hated Amelia. Darcy knew that. He blamed Amelia for so much. Just as Darcy had, once. And who had led her to hate her own mother? Not Edward. Lemuel.

When she'd told him that she'd seen the letters in Claude's study, he'd been furious. Not because of what Claude had done. But because now there was a danger that she would find all this out if she had gone back and read the letters through.

So he'd killed Claude and taken the letters himself.

And Annie O'Day! Who better than Lemuel would recognize her on Wall Street? Claude hadn't known her by sight, but Lemuel had.

She'd been so blind! Claude should have taught her that no surface, no matter how glittering, how safe, could hide a depraved soul, could hide anger, could hide greed. She had blinded herself to Lemuel's nature for the most egotistical of reasons: because he had praised her, he had made much of her. Even while he had disdained her father, turned his back on her mother, been cruel to his wife—no wonder poor Marie was so silent, so cowed!—he had made a pet of her. And so she had trusted him, she had loved him. Because her husband had hated her, she had yearned for love. And because someone had loved her, she had loved him back, turning a blind eye to his selfishness, his cruelty to others. He was not cruel, she had said stoutly. For wasn't he kind to her?

A sob broke from her, and Lemuel looked up sharply. "Darcy, dearest, what is it?"

"It's all been too much," she said, using the same excuse she'd given to Ned. Ned! If Lemuel would leave, she could go to him. Of course if Columbine trusted him he must be trustworthy; Columbine was no fool.

But what if Columbine had been blinded by love as well? What if Ned was in league with Lemuel? Darcy moved restlessly; she felt she would go mad. She hadn't the knack for deciding who to trust; she didn't know how it was done. She'd never known.

She had to get to Tavish. He was in danger, she knew that now. Would Lemuel be content to wait for the judge? Or would he send her to Denver and exact his own brand of justice?

She leaned her head in her hands to disguise the fear in her eyes. "I'm so afraid," she murmured. It was the truth.

"I know. But you must be strong. I'll leave you now to pack. I'll send up a brandy for you. Come downstairs when you're ready. We have only a half hour. I'll be waiting." He pressed his lips against her hands. They felt thin and cold. She shuddered.

"I'm cold."

"Dress warmly. I'll telegraph ahead to Denver, you'll have a fine suite to rest in. And I will join you as soon as I can. Now, hurry, Darcy. I'll be downstairs."

She forced herself to look at him. "Thank you so much, Uncle Lemuel. You don't know what you've done for me tonight."

"You know that I would do anything for you, Darcy."

His eyes were as kind as ever. He bowed, picked up his lavender gloves, and he left.

She forced herself to wait. She counted off the minutes. In five, a large brandy arrived. She ignored it; after her experience with Claude, she would not risk even a swallow of it to steady her nerves.

She thought carefully. He could be having a nightcap himself in the bar downstairs. He could be waiting in the lobby or in the street. She would have to go through the kitchens; there must be a back door for deliveries. She had to warn Tavish, she had to try.

Once again, she put on her cloak. She turned down the kerosene lamp and went to the window. Waiting until her eyes had adjusted to the darkness, she stared out into the black night, trying to discern shadow from substance.

She was squinting so hard at the shadows on the porch of the hotel that she almost missed it. A man was coming slowly down the street. He was keeping close to the buildings, and his hat shadowed his face even further. But she knew him. Tavish.

She started to turn away, hurry downstairs to meet him, but something made her stop, turn back, and look again. Another shadow. Her heart stopped. Under the porch, there, near the corner of the building. And then the shadow that was Tavish moved past, stopped, went back. And the two shadows merged into one. They stood, then moved off together. One long black shadow that passed into the alley between the buildings and disappeared.

She didn't wait another instant. Lemuel had found him. Waiting for her, he had caught a bigger prize. Her heart in her throat, Darcy ran.

• • •

"Much better that you do not try to walk into that hotel," Tavish's companion said. Swinging his cane, he walked as though he were strolling down Broadway. "Everyone in town knows your face. They're drunk and, like everyone out here in the savage West, trigger happy. However did you manage to break out of jail, anyway?"

"The deputy's father was in the Grange," Tavish said.

"Ah. Of course. A subversive group, rather like the Masons—or the Union Club. So he would not hesitate to let you go, accused saboteur or no.'"

"Only for an hour," Tavish replied. "A gentleman's promise."

"Which you will break, undoubtedly."

"Not if I can help it. I only wanted to speak to Darcy."

"And so you shall. She should be at the depot in just a few minutes. I made sure she was all right before I left her."

In his pocket, Tavish clenched his fist and unclenched it again. What the hell did that mean? he wondered. Did the devil want him to think that he had Darcy under his control? Was she truly all right? Tavish's mind roared with questions. He wasn't sure how far the man would go. Surely he wouldn't harm his own niece.

"And I don't think you have to worry about jail," Lemuel said. "I had dinner with the governor two nights ago in Denver, and—"

"You were in Denver, Mr. Grace?" Tavish's question was light.

Lemuel faltered for the first time. "Yes, I'd been following you and Darcy for some time—"

"But why did you think we would go to Denver?"

"I didn't. I received a wire from my wife—"

"Darcy sent that wire from St. Louis—that would be rather too late for you to catch up with us. You were already in Denver, then?"

"I was wandering—hoping to catch news of the two of you."

"I see." They were at the deserted depot now. It was a dark night, the moon obscured by long streaks of clouds. No one from Redemption was taking the eleven-thirty train. The tiny station was deserted.

"Shall we be frank, Mr. Grace?" Tavish said, turning casually to face him. "I, sir, am unarmed. Rory's sympathies did not include handing over his gun to me. And I must tell you that I'm tired of lies, and you must be, too. Why should we hide from each other? So, tell me—how could you stomach having Claude Statton as a partner?"

Lemuel's eyes caught a shaft of moonlight. They glittered, ice against steel. Dead eyes.

I've seen warmer gazes on salmon I caught.

Suddenly grief nearly knocked Tavish down. Jamie Alden, dead. For this man's greed. Perhaps this man's pleasure.

"I discovered rather quickly," Lemuel said, smoothly taking a gun from his pocket, "that you can stomach anything if considerable sums of money are involved."

"You sound like a shoddyite," Tavish said. "Like Claude Statton, one of the vulgar new rich you abhor."

Lemuel shrugged. "A man has a private life, and a public life— one learns that rather quickly in my class. I met Claude Statton when I was investigating opportunities for investment out West. I knew he could make me money. He was so hungry, so unscrupulous. And I had already found Annie O'Day, brought her to Fleur's. I saw how much money passed through there. Claude seemed to be the perfect one to handle it. So I brought him to New York."

"You brought him—"

"I backed him. He did well. He took over the day-to-day handling of the business, plus the expansion and the blackmail. I handled the out-of-town business—the railroads in California, the lumber, the mines. Even a little business in Europe. Then when we needed more capital, we got Edward to approach the Old Guard. But first we had Claude court Darcy. It was wise to be allied to a good name. That was Claude's idea. It was good for Darcy, too. At least I believed so in the beginning."

Tavish felt his blood pound. Good for Darcy to marry such a man. "Why?" he asked. "Why did you risk everything for this, your name, your position, your *niece*? You had money."

"Yes, I had money," Lemuel spat out. "Money by any standards but today's. I saw the men who moved up Fifth Avenue, how much they had, how much they spent. I knew it would only be a matter of time before they'd taken over society completely. And I was proved right! The Vanderbilts and their ilk *run* society now! I knew that names like the Graces and the Snows and the Archers would be destroyed if I didn't do something. I *had* to do it."

"But why kill Jamie Alden?" Tavish whispered.

"Because he got too close," Lemuel said dispassionately. He motioned Tavish closer to the tracks with his gun. "He was hanging around the brothels in San Francisco—he could have put the pieces together. There were quite a few hostile madams there—tough women. They weren't afraid of me like Fleur Ganay was, but we were starting to make inroads there. We'd taken over some of the Chinese crib houses—your friend found that out. I just wanted to scare him. But it was so easy to dispense with him completely." A dreamy expression came over Lemuel's face. "So surprisingly easy to kill a man."

Tavish heard the whistle of the train. Still not very close, but coming. He realized why Lemuel was keeping him here, talking. This time, he wanted it to look like an accident. Would he knock Tavish out first, or simply force him onto the tracks? Would he risk shooting him first? And if he *did* shoot, where would he aim?

Cold sweat snaked down his sides. Lemuel still looked a bit unfocused. Tavish kept talking. "So you killed another man. Claude."

"He was stupid. Careless. Letting Darcy get into his private files, using Annie to blackmail Edward. That was foolish. Annie was a girl of integrity, she would never follow through. I tried to tell him that. And Edward was family, no matter what I thought of him, I could not let Claude blackmail family. But that isn't why I killed him. I killed him for what he tried to do to Darcy. He went too far. He thought we were equals, he thought I would not dare question what he did with his wife. But he was wrong. Don't you think he deserved to die?"

Tavish shrugged. "It's not for me to say." He eyed the gun. It might be worth getting shot to get it away from Lemuel. He'd been shot before. Lemuel didn't look very strong; perhaps Tavish could manage it. "Why all this concern for Darcy?" he asked. "Aren't you going to kill her, too?"

"Of course not. I'm going to take her back to New York, where she belongs. That murder charge won't stick, it's absurd. That maid of hers is mad. I was going to get the engineer in town to flag down the train, but I think I'll let Darcy stay at the hotel now. There's no need to rush her out of town if you're gone."

"Ah. Am I getting on the train, then?"

"No, Mr. Finn." His teeth gleamed. "You're getting under it."

"I see. That's what I thought," Tavish said. He could hear the noise of the wheels on the track now. Close.

"You shouldn't have bedded her." Lemuel lowered the gun a bit until it was dead level with Tavish's crotch. He smiled. "This is my favorite part," he said.

She must have kept along the shadows of the depot building, for they hadn't noticed her. Now she was running toward them, shouting his name, stumbling a bit on the uneven ground, but coming fast, his courageous, glorious woman, with no regard for danger. "Tavish!" she was screaming. Then the train hooted, drowning her out.

Tavish could see the anguish in Lemuel's eyes. So he truly cared for Darcy. He could not harm her. But as Darcy came up, Tavish was already moving, grabbing Lemuel's wrist and forcing it down. Lemuel twisted away with surprising force; Tavish heard a pop, perhaps Lemuel's wrist was broken. The gun dropped. Tavish kicked it. Lemuel went after it and his foot twisted on the uneven ground. The train was on them now, and as he stumbled, arms flailing, he fell against it. He was knocked into the air like a rag doll and landed in the dirt.

Darcy rushed forward and dropped to her knees by Lemuel's side. She touched his bloodied face, and he looked at her.

"Do you forgive me?" he asked.

Darcy looked up at Tavish. He saw the old Darcy in her face, the fine bones that spoke so eloquently of breeding, of the code she'd lived by. But something flashed out of her eyes as well, and he saw a hawk, an eagle, a cougar. The wildness, the courage in her that he'd loved, that he'd seen from the beginning. The woman who gave no quarter.

He knew that months ago she would have eased the dying man's pain by forgiving him for what he'd done and tried to do, for the loyalty she owed him. But that woman didn't exist any-more.

"No, uncle," she said. "I cannot forgive you. Perhaps God will."

Epilogue

It was a quiet wedding. Afterward, they all sat around the table in their private dining room in the Palace Hotel in San Francisco and toasted their good fortune.

"Here's to your marriage," Columbine said. "Now the adventure really begins. And thank you for waiting for me to begin it."

"We couldn't do it without you," Darcy said.

"Or you, Ned," Tavish said. "If it weren't for you, I'd still be in jail in Redemption and Darcy would still be facing charges in New York."

"I just wish I could have saved you from considerable anxiety that night," Ned said. He threw a teasing glance at Darcy. "If only I hadn't been a suspect."

"I'm not used to this adventure business," Darcy defended herself. "I didn't know who to trust." She took a sip of champagne. She felt wondrously lightheaded. "Now, of course, I am a professional adventuress. I have no idea what lies ahead of me. Here I am in San Francisco with my rogue of a husband, not a penny in our pockets. This is our last splurge, I'll warrant—"

Columbine looked baffled. "But surely—"

"Oh, Columbine," Darcy broke in, "how can I keep any of my inheritance—from Claude, Lemuel, or even Edward? No. I'm signing all of it away to my cousin Adelle. Tavish told me that they have a custom in Ireland—when they catch an informer, they throw his body off a cliff and all the money he took as well, no matter how poor they are. There is such a thing as tainted money," she said softly, "a lesson my father and my uncle never learned."

"But I didn't mean that," Columbine said, still puzzled. Her eyes questioned Tavish. "Didn't you—"

Tavish put down his glass. "I have something to tell you, my bride," he said. "I'm afraid I'm a bit rich."

"A bit rich? What does that mean?"

"About seven years ago, when I was kicking around Montana, I played poker with a gentleman who'd bought a large share in a played-out silver mine. He put up some of his share, and I won it. Shortly afterward, before I had a chance to lose it myself, they discovered that indeed the mine was played out in silver, but they found quite a bit of copper. The name of the mine was the Anaconda."

Darcy fell back against the cushions. "You have a share in the Anaconda?"

"A little one. But it's, well, quite profitable. It allowed me to retire to Solace, and now we can do whatever we want, I'm afraid."

"I don't know what to say."

"We could toast your good fortune again," Columbine said helpfully.

Ned gave a shout of laughter. "I would say so! Here's to Mr. and Mrs. Finn! And," he said with a meaningful glance at Columbine, "may you be toasting us someday."

Columbine's smile felt a bit stiff. She had confided to Darcy that now that Cora was suing Ned for divorce, she was nervously awaiting his proposal of marriage—and her response. She had no idea what she would say. She imagined it would be no. Marriage and her work were not compatible. If only he would let things stay as lovely as they were. If only he wouldn't ask her. But he would.

She toasted, not wanting to spoil the moment. Darcy smiled at her; she knew what Columbine was thinking, no doubt, and despite her happiness with Tavish, she sympathized. What a treasure, to have such a sister now. Columbine's face clouded and she put down her glass. "I do wish you would change your minds about living here. I will miss you."

Darcy touched her hand. "I don't think I could return to New York," she said. "I want to live my life in the open air. At least for a while."

"You'll just have to make long visits, Columbine," Tavish said. "There's plenty of reforming that needs to be done here, too. Artemis Hinkle and I are talking about buying a newspaper together. Perhaps I'll give the Big Four a piece of my mind. Time to make a stand, you know."

Columbine laughed. "It's about time."

Darcy watched the two of them over her glass. Tavish didn't know it, but she had brought up the idea to Artemis Hinkle. Little did she know then that Tavish would have money to invest. But what Tavish didn't know was that she had every intention of working on the paper herself.

For an instant, tears swam in her eyes from pure happiness. This was her new family, she thought. Her new life. Columbine, struggling with love and work. And Tavish—could such a man settle down? He had a fortune, but she wouldn't be surprised if he lost it and made another. Life would not be what it had been for Mrs. Claude Statton, a serene, sunlit surface that dazzled the eye with false brilliance while it concealed a tainted, churning sea beneath. For Darcy Finn, life would flow clear and sweet. There would be no murky undercurrents, no parallel life running underneath, half-glimpsed and turned away from, hidden, depraved. Life would be what it seemed to be—regrets and sorrows, pain, laughter, happiness. That was the real adventure.

Tavish directed a private smile at her, and she smiled back.

"Here's to the future," he said, reading her mind.

A future that had no roads to follow, no signposts, no fences, no maps. She and Tavish would make their own.

She raised her glass. "To the future," she said. "Lord only knows what it will bring with you, Tavish Finn."

"Oh, indeed," he replied. "But I have plans, Mrs. Finn."

She drained her glass and licked the tiny cold drops of champagne from her lips. It tasted marvelous.

"As do I, Mr. Finn," she said.